The raiders' wags rolled through the smoking ruin of the convoy.

Intermittent machine-gun fire sounded, blasting out in full-throated roar over the occasional small-arms chatter. The raiders left no one alive. Almost no one, Brigid amended when she saw one of the wag groups unload and pull out a man dressed in Magistrate black.

She focused on the man, barely able to discern his features at the distance even with the high-power magnification available. "Do you know him?" she asked.

"Kearney," Grant answered. "Bastard must have rated a promotion."

A warwag stopped in front of Kearney. His guards forced him into a kneeling position, their weapons trained on him.

The warwag's side door opened and Brigid focused the binoculars again as the raiders' leader stepped out. She wasn't prepared for what she saw....

of the bond between them.

Other titles in this series:

JAMES AXLER

OUTLANDERS™

WREATH OF FIRE

A GOLD EAGLE BOOK FROM
WORLDWIDE.

TORONTO • NEW YORK • LONDON
AMSTERDAM • PARIS • SYDNEY • HAMBURG
STOCKHOLM • ATHENS • TOKYO • MILAN
MADRID • WARSAW • BUDAPEST • AUCKLAND

First edition February 2000

ISBN 0-373-63825-6

WREATH OF FIRE

Thanks to Mel Odom for his contribution to this work.
Special thanks to Mark Ellis for his contribution to the
Outlanders concept, developed for Gold Eagle.

WREATH OF FIRE

The Road to Outlands—
From Secret Government Files to the Future

Almost two hundred years after the global holocaust, Kane, a former Magistrate of Cobaltville, often thought the world had been lucky to survive at all after a nuclear device detonated in the Russian embassy in Washington, D.C. The aftermath—forever known as skydark—reshaped continents and turned civilization into ashes.

Nearly depopulated, America became the Deathlands—poisoned by radiation, home to chaos and mutated life forms. Feudal rule reappeared in the form of baronies, while remote outposts clung to a brutish existence.

What eventually helped shape this wasteland were the redoubts, the secret preholocaust military installations with stores of weapons, and the home of gateways, the locational matter-transfer facilities. Some of the redoubts hid clues that had once fed wild theories of government cover-ups and alien visitations.

Rearmed from redoubt stockpiles, the barons consolidated their power and reclaimed technology for the villes. Their power, supported by some invisible authority, extended beyond their fortified walls to what was now called the Outlands. It was here that the rootstock of humanity survived, living with hellzones and chemical storms, hounded by Magistrates.

In the villes, rigid laws were enforced—to atone for the sins of the past and prepare the way for a better future. That was the barons' public credo and their right-to-rule.

Kane, along with friend and fellow Magistrate Grant, had upheld that claim until a fateful Outlands expedition. A displaced piece of technology…a question to a keeper of the archives…a vague clue about alien masters—and their world shifted radically. Suddenly, Brigid Baptiste, the archivist, faced summary execution, and

Grant a quick termination. For Kane there was forgiveness if he pledged his unquestioning allegiance to Baron Cobalt and his unknown masters and abandoned his friends.

But that allegiance would make him support a mysterious and alien power and deny loyalty and friends. Then what else was there?

Kane had been brought up solely to serve the ville. Brigid's only link with her family was her mother's redgold hair, green eyes and supple form. Grant's clues to his lineage were his ebony skin and powerful physique. But Domi, she of the white hair, was an Outlander pressed into sexual servitude in Cobaltville. She at least knew her roots and was a reminder to the exiles that the outcasts belonged in the human family.

Parents, friends, community—the very rootedness of humanity was denied. With no continuity, there was no forward momentum to the future. And that was the crux—when Kane began to wonder if there was a future.

For Kane, it wouldn't do. So the only way was out—way, way out.

After their escape, they found shelter at the forgotten Cerberus redoubt headed by Lakesh, a scientist, Cobaltville's head archivist, and secret opponent of the barons.

With their past turned into a lie, their future threatened, only one thing was left to give meaning to the outcasts. The hunger for freedom, the will to resist the hostile influences. And perhaps, by opposing, end them.

Chapter 1

"Hold it right there, outlanders. Come any closer and we're gonna let some daylight through you."

Kane reluctantly stopped, struggling to curb the initial surge of anger. Domi halted beside him and began to raise the Winchester .30-30 lever-action rifle she held.

"No," Kane whispered. "Let them think they've got the upper hand."

"Fuckers do have upper hand," Domi complained in a low voice. "Double stupe walking in like this." An albino, Domi's skin was pale as milk and had pinked from exposure to the sun for the past few days. Despite the genetic defect that so visually marked her, she hadn't developed a weakness to the sun; she just didn't tan.

She was a lot shorter than Kane, looking childlike next to him. A survivor of the Outlands, she was the most dangerous child Kane figured anyone would ever meet. Her bone-white hair was cropped close to her head. She wore boots, khaki trousers and a pink tank top that brought a little femininity to her appearance. A gray-and-green plaid shirt with long sleeves was tied around her waist.

Kane didn't waste time arguing. In a way, Domi was right. There just hadn't been any options given the terrain. His back and shoulders ached from pushing the ancient motorcycle for the past three miles. He'd known his advance into the territory would be spotted, but he hadn't been exactly sure when.

He was sweltering from the blistering heat that was finally abating as the sun dropped in the west. An easterly wind had picked up less than an hour ago, but it made only a halfhearted attempt to drag cooling fingers across the sun-scorched hills of what used to be the Uinta Mountains in northeastern Utah.

He peered across the pale earth. Not much existed in the way of vegetation. Hardscrabble bushes stubbornly fought the harsh conditions, lack of water and volcanic winds that sometimes overran the area. The landscape before him went steadily upward, and the trail he followed twisted like a spine-broken snake to climb the grade.

"What do you want?" Kane asked in a loud voice. He gazed at the irregular stand of rocks above him, knowing from experience that the prickling sensation brushing the back of his neck meant gun sights were on him. He'd walked into the trap, but not blindly. His friend and former Mag partner, Grant, was covering their backs.

"We'll have your business first," the voice called out from behind the rocks.

Kane thought he saw movement behind one of the triangular stones to the trail's left. He filed it away, relying on senses honed by his Mag training. As a Magistrate for Cobaltville, he'd encountered situations like this before.

The speaker was female. Her voice was soured with hard whiskey or jolt, or maybe it was deep and scratchy from an old wound. Though, if she was leading the group of men he believed to be on the other side of the rocks, Kane had no doubts that she'd be trouble.

"Trading," Kane lied. It was an answer he knew they'd be expecting, since trading routes from west and east, and north and south, converged in this part of Utah.

"If you're trading," the woman yelled back, "looks like you done fell on hard times."

"Mebbe," Kane said. "Heard there was a roadhouse at the end of this river. Unless I've been lied to."

"You been lied to before?"

Kane offered a feral grin. "A time or two. Had a woman told me she loved me once."

"Probably told you that you were handsome, too."

In truth, Kane was handsome in a rough-hewn way. He was tall and rangy, carrying most of his weight in his shoulders and arms above a slim waist, like a wolf. His dark hair held sun-kissed highlights, and his skin was bronze from exposure to the sun and the elements. His blue-gray eyes burned from the high planes of his face.

He'd dressed in patched-over denim jeans, the same kind a man living by scavenging would have. The green chambray work shirt he wore had the sleeves hacked off, and it sported patches of contrasting colors and materials. He hadn't stinted on the tough steel-toed boots, though, because a true scavenger knew that good footwear often meant the difference between living and dying.

A fourteen-inch combat knife rode in a handmade scabbard in his right boot. He also carried a double-barreled Remington 12-gauge shotgun on a sling across his back. A single bandolier strapped his broad chest, and nearly every loop was filled with ammo. A military-style flap holster that kept the dust out of the long-barreled Model 1911A .45-caliber pistol inside rode his right hip. He missed the Sin Eater that he normally carried. The 9 mm handblaster was the chief sign of office of the Magistrates, and he'd trained with it since he was sixteen. It was normally secured to his right forearm, where it could be brought into play by tensing his wrist tendons.

"Worst lie of all," Kane went on, "was when she told me I was good enough at it she didn't have to go nowhere else to get it.'' He kept his hands on the motorcycle's handlebars, using it to partially shield him.

"Fucking around," Domi said irritably. "Gonna get us chilled."

"Shut up," Kane growled low enough that he wouldn't be heard up the hill. "We'll do this the way we planned it. You get a count of how many we're facing?"

"Six. Mebbe seven."

Kane had counted four definite shadows flitting around the rocky escarpment. He'd run pointman for Mag forces, since his senses were far and away better than those of his peers. But Domi had an animal cunning. He knew she probably hadn't seen any more of their opponents than he had, but her primitive instincts might have picked up on the way they'd ranged around the rocks above.

Taking another look at how tightly the four he'd seen were grouped, he upped his own estimate by one more man. There would be at least one more adversary to the left to better cover that side.

"What do you want at the roadhouse?" the woman asked.

"It'd make me feel better," Kane said, "knowing who I was talking to."

There was a hesitation before the answer. "Call me Nell."

"Okay, Nell." In the periphery of his vision, Kane noticed a puff of dust to the right. He knew the woman had people surrounding their position now, entrenching their defenses. "First thing I want is some fuel. I was told the roadhouse had some. I'm tired of pushing this piece of shit."

"They got some," Nell replied. "Rotgut puke you gotta filter again yourself to get all the water out of it. Wouldn't advise putting it in your tank till after you've done that. And it don't come cheap."

"I'll keep that in mind," Kane said.

"You don't look like you've got much to trade."

"I've got some jack. I think it'll spend fast enough."

"Might not. Peabody down at the roadhouse, he don't just take any jack, not even baron's notes. And it don't look like you people are from around here."

"We're not," Kane admitted. "We're from up in the Darks." And that was true enough because the Cerberus redoubt was located in what used to be called the Bitterroot Range up in Montana. Before fleeing to Cerberus, he'd spent his life over in Cobaltville, a barony farther east in more civilized territory.

"What're you doing down here?"

Kane gave her a mirthless wolf's grin. "Got invited to leave the Darks."

"Must have been invited pretty fierce to chase you down into this," Nell said.

"It would have taken a lot of chilling to stay there," Kane told her. "We thought mebbe it'd be easier just moving on."

"Mebbe you won't find anybody so sociable here, either."

"These are the Outlands," Kane said. "Nobody's sociable here. At least a man knows where he stands." His pointman's senses were registering a silent warning. "If you're going to claim this trail to the roadhouse so hard, mebbe we'll just find another way around."

The woman laughed, a good-natured sound in spite of the tension of the situation. "You'd go miles out of your way to find another way to the roadhouse."

"You're not leaving a man much room to work in here. Are you planning on letting us through?"

"This here's a tollgate, outlander," Nell said. "Anybody going through here has to pay for passage."

"The ore prospector I talked to a few miles back didn't mention anything about a tollgate," Kane said. "Man told me the roads through here were free to traders and travelers." He spotted a puff of dust to the left now, as well.

"Boxing us in," Domi muttered. "You move or I move. Soon."

"It's kind of a seasonal thing," Nell admitted. "We move around."

"Who're you sanctioned by?" Kane asked. "The closest baron around here is Baron Cobalt over in Colorado."

"Shit," Nell said, "we're sanctioned by Smith & Wesson, outlander, and backed up by Colt and Heckler & Koch. I don't think we need any more bona fides than that." Evidently feeling safe, the woman stepped into view less than a hundred paces away.

Nell was in her mid-twenties, Kane guessed, with her white-blond hair pulled back in a flowing mane. She had a good figure, tall and kind of leaned out. Her midriff shirt revealed her narrow waist and a lot of brown skin under her small breasts. Leather pants covered her generous hips. She held a Mini-14 Ranch Rifle in her hands.

A man moved into position beside her. He was a little taller and twice as broad. Scars from burns tracked his ugly face, leaving the skin dead and white. Suppurating sores the size of predark dimes stood out on his cheeks and forehead, but they looked old, disease worn into the flesh that he'd take to the grave with him. He held a bolt-action Winchester .308 hunting rifle with telescopic sights.

"What have you got for trading, outlander?" Nell repeated. Her voice held an edge.

Watching her, Kane knew the time to make the play was now. He readied himself, sliding his thumb over the motorcycle's electronic ignition. It was an old Enduro that had been outfitted by the military back in the twentieth century, before the rain of nukes had descended upon the world on January 20, 2001, and forever changed its landscape. The chassis was set well clear of the ground, with twin pipes curling back on the right side.

He'd found the bike in the transportation stores in the Cerberus redoubt, then repaired and refurbished it. When the recent mission had come up, he'd decided to take it, knowing it would fit the character he would be trying to play, and it would be a potent weapon.

Scavengers in Utah used wags and motorcycles instead of horses in the harsh desert lands. A man had to water and feed a horse, and the scent of a horse sometimes brought predators down out of the mountains. Since skydark, Utah had become a virtual no-man's-land. It was too hard to find good water. No wells could be dug in the alkaline dust, and even the rivers and creeks spilling through the surrounding mountain ranges were often poisoned, carrying the taint of radioactive dust.

Lately, though, the area had slowly become inhabited, as the Utah territory again became an active mining area. Copper and gold were the chief targets of the prospectors, but they also brought in ore with molybdenum, silver, lead, nickel and zinc. The nine baronies of the Program of Unification and other nearby villes with smelting capabilities used much of the ore. Cobaltville had even started shipping some ore to the other eight baronies when there was a surplus.

But it wasn't the threat of a mining empire that had brought Kane and his team to Utah.

They were investigating a series of raids on the ore caravans, and of particular interest was a caravan leader named Chapman. Kane focused on Nell and her companion, knowing the chilling time had come before the trap closed completely. He depressed the electronic ignition. The Enduro's engine caught smoothly, protesting in a short, stuttering cough when the fuel fired through the carburetors. Nell had been right about the quality of the local fuel.

The Enduro's engine blatted strongly, chugging out a throat-burning, noxious cloud of gray-white smoke. Kane twisted the throttle and threw a leg over the motorcycle's seat, his mind whirling with what had to be done.

Domi went to ground to the right, digging in behind a rock large enough to completely hide her. She snaked the Winchester's barrel forward. The albino wasn't the best shot Kane had ever seen, but she'd be cause enough for concern to the coldhearts confronting them.

Nell was already in motion, bringing her Mini-14 to her shoulder.

Kane settled onto the Enduro's seat and jammed his left foot on the gearshift. When he popped the clutch and twisted the throttle, the motorcycle reared into the air for a moment. The back wheel spun out a rooster tail of sand and gravel.

Bullets cut the air where Kane had been as he roared up the incline straight into the gun barrels of the coldhearts that had been lying in ambush along the trail. Everything was on the line now, and he hoped Grant was in place to cover his back the way the man had done for years.

HIGH ATOP A HILL to the east of the trail, Grant gazed through the telescopic sights of the big Barrett sniper rifle he'd brought from Cerberus. He moved his field of vision, keeping both eyes open so he wouldn't lose his frame of reference. He took shallow breaths, concentrating on the action as Kane shoved the coldhearts' trap down their collective throats.

The sheer brass of the situation made Grant grin even though his friend could be speeding to his death. His response derived from the Mag training he and Kane had

shared back in Cobaltville, back when they'd believed in
the barons. Or, at least, had believed nothing else better
existed.

"What the hell is Kane doing?"

Grant didn't glance over at his companion.

Brigid Baptiste was from Cobaltville, too. She'd been an
archivist, responsible for filing papers and rewriting history
according to the wishes of Baron Cobalt. Though she often
accompanied Kane and Grant on field missions proposed by
Lakesh, she hadn't developed a warrior's mentality. She had
no problem fighting, though.

The Enduro was in motion before the sound of the engine
ever reached Grant's ears. Light traveled faster than sound
waves, and a bullet was only slightly faster than sound. It
was a sobering thought as he placed his forefinger on the
Barrett's trigger and hunted for a target. He estimated he'd
get at least two shots off before the coldhearts below heard
the sounds of the shots and knew he was there. He intended
to make both shots count.

"Kane's just getting acquainted," Grant answered. He
stood six feet four inches tall, a thick, broad man carrying
scars from past battles. Gray sprinkled his short-cropped
curly hair. His drooping black mustache stood out in sharp
relief against his coffee-brown skin. His faded road leathers
were nearly the same sandy-red color as the land around
them.

In contrast, Brigid Baptiste's tall frame was dwarfed by
Grant's as she lay on the flat rock they'd chosen nearly a
thousand yards from the trail where Kane was. Slender and
full breasted, she had her reddish-gold hair pulled back in
a ponytail to keep it from her beautiful face. She studied
the scene before them through powerful binoculars. She carried a Copperhead close-assault weapon, one of the subguns
Grant had carried as a Cobaltville Magistrate.

Grant knew there wasn't time for any more conversation. He shifted the Barrett in front of him, scooting it forward on the built-in bipod. He pulled the buttstock in to his shoulder, preparing to handle the massive recoil the sniper rifle offered. Chambered in .50-caliber ammo, the Barrett had originally been introduced to take down lightly armored targets and materiel, and for shooting through concrete walls.

Grant counted seven men, including the two who'd taken up positions on either side of the trail Kane had followed. Grant was pleased to see that Domi had found shelter, and appeared to be using it. He'd never quite figured out what his feelings were for the little albino, though Domi hadn't been reticent about announcing her own intentions about him.

Letting out half a breath, Grant centered the telescopic sights over the two-man crew operating the portable .30-caliber Browning machine gun. It shook and stuttered as the triggerman fired a short stream of rounds while the beltman kept the ammo feeding through.

Grant knew the short burst was supposed to make Kane aware of what he was up against. Most men would likely have turned and run or surrendered on the spot. Kane wouldn't, Grant knew, and part of it was because his friend was counting on him.

Brigid shifted beside him, careful to avoid disturbing his aim. "Grant." She pointed down to the right where the trader caravan they'd targeted was advancing up the trail.

The sounds of the first shots had rolled over the caravan's scouts. The men turned their motorcycles around and waved to the wags in warning. Almost immediately, they put together a skirmish line that roared toward Kane's position little more than a mile away.

"Easy," Grant replied softly, shifting his attention back to the Barrett. Time was running out all the way around. If the trader sec men caught up with Kane in the middle of the firefight, there was no doubt they'd kill them all—including Kane and Domi.

Grant put the crosshairs over the machine gunner. With both eyes open, he saw that Kane had not stopped in his advance despite the carnage wrought by the machine-gun burst.

The woman who led the coldhearts turned to shout at the machine-gun crew as Grant centered the crosshairs on the gunner's head, then raised them an inch to allow for the distance.

Grant didn't try to hurry the shot. Given the distance, if his aim was off even a fraction of an inch, he'd miss by several yards. He slid his finger over the Barrett's trigger, then squeezed. The big sniper rifle slammed against his shoulder with an explosion of movement. The breech snapped back and forward, stripping another bullet from the 10-round clip. He centered and fired again in less than a second.

His first bullet hadn't reached the target yet, and the line of machine-gun fire ripped across the ground toward Kane.

Chapter 2

Kane roared up the incline, leaving the trail as the machine-gun bullets chopped into the ground ahead of him, chipping shards from the flat rocks that jutted up from the alkaline earth.

At least two rounds tore through his shirt at the back, letting him know Nell's other gunners were getting the range and almost leading him the proper amount. Dodging and ducking across the treacherous ground wasn't an option. Even the Enduro's knobbed tires would mire up, slide out from under him and leave him easy prey for the hammering machine gun.

Without warning, the roar of the machine gun died away. Kane stayed low over the handlebars, squinting against the blowing grit, his mouth closed. A bullet ricocheted off the handlebars with a screech that was lost immediately in the rumble of the high-performance engine.

Nell was scrambling up over the ridgeline, but the big man with the scarred face stood his ground, calmly working the bolt action on the rifle.

Kane cursed, his pointman's senses alive with the movement around him. Without turning to look, he knew Domi had engaged one of the men who'd crept down toward their position. He leaned hard on the motorcycle, dragging his knee for just a moment along the ground. The front end came around, bearing down on the big man.

Shifting up again, Kane popped the clutch and hoped the

rear tire would find enough purchase and not merely slide out from under him. For the moment, the Enduro would have to serve as transport and weapon.

The rear tire spun and slipped for a heartbeat, then dug through the alkaline grit to the sandstone beneath. The front wheel came up as the tall man pointed the hunting rifle at Kane's head.

DOMI ABANDONED the sheltering rock, shoving the lever-action Winchester ahead of her. She knew Grant would give her hell over the way she was treating the .30-30 rifle, but she didn't care. She'd learned as a child of the Outlands that the only thing that mattered was survival. A clean weapon was a good tool, but not to a corpse.

She slithered like a snake through the dust, hooking a forefinger into the bandanna around her neck up to cover her lower face. The dust seeped into a person's sinuses and lungs, filling them with grit that inspired days of coughing and sneezing to get them clear again.

Less than ten yards away, the coldheart to her right rose confidently, expecting to catch her behind the rock she'd just left. He carried a .357 magnum handblaster and had put two rounds into the dirt before he realized the albino wasn't where he'd thought she'd be.

Calmly, Domi rose on her elbows, the .30-30 in her hands. She pointed the rifle at the man's stomach and squeezed the trigger. The Winchester bucked, driving hard against her hundred-pound frame, and she had no doubt her shoulder would be sore. It hadn't been that long since she'd had to have the ball-and-socket joint replaced after a gun-shot wound.

The bullet caught the man in the stomach, doubling him over at once.

Domi cranked the lever, ejecting the spent casing from

the side and feeding another round under the firing pin. She fired, aiming for the man's center mass again. Blood leaped from the man's rib cage as the bullet cored through.

He fell, whimpering and holding his stomach. His weapon lay at his side, totally forgotten.

A round thudded into the alkaline sand between Domi's legs.

"Got you now, you white-assed bitch!" a woman yelled.

Domi lunged forward on her elbows, pulling her lithe body over her head, tucking into a roll. Grant had once told her she was the most limber, most acrobatic woman he'd ever seen. Domi had offered to show him interesting variations on how it could be used to mutual benefit. Grant had wordlessly declined.

Rolling forward, Domi pulled the Winchester rifle under her as she went. She stayed low, knowing if she stood up she'd become an easy target. Two bullets pursued her, spaced far enough apart that she knew the coldheart's weapon wasn't a semiautomatic.

As soon as her feet touched the ground, the albino shoved with her right leg, flipping herself to the side and back onto her stomach. She landed with her elbows extended, the .30-30 resting in her hands and pointed back in the direction the shots came from.

Another round stabbed into the ground in front of her, kicking sand into her left eye. Her vision blurred instantly as the alkaline grit burned. She steeled herself, reminding herself it wasn't nearly as painful as some of the things Boss Teague had done to her back in Cobaltville before she'd slit his throat and thrown in with Kane and Grant.

She levered the action, putting the open sights over the profile of the woman shooting at her, then squeezed the trigger. The .30-30 round slammed into the coldheart's left breast, just missing the chest cavity.

The woman's breast stained red when the heavy round hit. Spinning around, she crumpled to her knees and had time to start a keening cry of surprised agony before Domi levered the rifle's action again and put a bullet through her heart.

Without another sound, the twitching corpse collapsed face forward onto the ground.

Domi swiveled her attention back to the ridgeline, watching as Kane's motorcycle rushed headlong at the tall man with the scarred face. No one seemed to be interested in her. She pushed herself up and sprinted up the hill, her shoulder throbbing as if it were filled with angry bees, and hoping she'd get to Kane's aid in time.

"CHILL THE SON of a bitch!" Nell yelled over the motorcycle engine's yammering. "Kill him, Joad!"

Joad was either incredibly brave or stupe, Kane decided. Even with the Enduro bearing down on him, the big man didn't flinch. And he still wasn't flinching when his finger pulled the hunting rifle's trigger.

Kane felt the heat from the bullet whip by his face as he turned away. Joad had been completely on target; only Kane's incredibly fast reflexes had saved him from having his brainpan emptied. The Enduro smashed into Joad, not giving the man any room to sidestep.

Kicking away, Kane scrambled to avoid being caught up in the tangle of man and machine. He saw the two dead men near the Browning machine gun. The head of one of them had split open and emptied its contents across his companion. Evidently the second man had tried to get up, maybe to avoid the blood and brain matter, or maybe to attempt to use the Browning. Grant's sniping skills hadn't allowed it, and the second shot, the echoes of which Kane could still hear, had slammed through the man's chest.

Still on the move, Kane rolled across the ground as the motorcycle bore Joad back and down. The man screamed shrilly, fighting to push the Enduro off him.

Bullets cut the air around Kane as he shoved himself to his left, pushing hard to get his feet under him. One of the coldhearts, a short man with a shaved head and a fresh human bite mark on his cheek, fired the .44 magnum handblaster he carried again.

Kane fisted the double-barreled shotgun at the end of the arm sling and brought it up. He eased the hammers of both barrels back with his thumb and grabbed the barrel from the top with his free hand. Aiming it in the general direction of the coldheart, he squeezed off the first barrel.

The blast of double-aught buckshot caught the man in the groin and across both thighs, blowing him off his feet. He hadn't even come to a stop when Kane touched off the second barrel point-blank at the man's head. The skull crumpled, shredding flesh and blood.

Kane pushed himself to his feet and flipped the lever to open the 12-gauge's breech. Both empty shotgun shell casings erupted, shoved out of the barrels by the spring mechanism. He pulled two shells from the bandolier and seated them with practiced ease as his eyes swept the battlezone. He snapped the breech closed and rolled the hammers back.

"Damn outlander mutie!" Nell shouted as she scrambled farther uphill. She disappeared between two tall stone columns that framed a barren trail.

Kane went after her, intent on his quarry. It wasn't necessary for the coldhearts to die for the plan to work, but his old Mag training kicked in, pushing him to destroy anybody who dared confront him.

He ran easily, his body a machine that he was thoroughly familiar with. His throat was dry from the arid desert heat and dust. Sweat made his clothes stick to him and the dust cake on his skin.

As he turned a narrow corner along the crevice he was following, a slug from Nell's Mini-14 chipped stone splinters from the rock beside him. He ducked down, levering the shotgun up.

"Should have shot you when I had the bastard chance," the woman snarled.

"I wouldn't have been that easy to chill," Kane replied. He raked his eyes through the crevice. It was scarcely four feet wide where he was, and grew to nearly ten feet farther on. The sides climbed to twelve and fifteen feet, sloped steeply and were scaled in broken rock barely defying gravity. The blue sky showed above. Loose sand inches deep filled the crevice, sucking Kane's boots down into it.

"Everybody can be chilled," Nell replied. In the narrow confines of the crevice, it was hard to tell exactly where her voice was coming from.

Loose rock skittered against stone ahead of Kane, letting him know the woman was still in motion. He pushed around the stone he'd taken cover behind and kept going, aware of the stillness trapped in the crevice.

"How familiar are you with the area, outlander?"

Kane gazed ahead of him, following the bend of the canyon. The sides were irregular enough that he thought Nell would have been able to climb up, but when he pulled at an outcropping sticking out from one of them, it broke off in his hand and triggered a brief avalanche. He felt confident that she was trapped in the crevice but he had no idea why she'd come that way.

"I don't have to be too familiar," he told her. "Not with the way you're leaving tracks in the sand."

"You've got a problem here if you don't know your way

around, outlander. Death has a way about reaching out for you,'' Nell said.

"You're in a hell of a situation to be warning others," Kane told her. Another turn brought him to a pile of bleached ivory bones bound up in wisps of rotting clothing. In the desert, there was no way of knowing if the bones had lain there months or years.

Kane's trained eye studied the bones, finding none of them scored by blade or broken by bullet that would suggest they died by violence. It was possible the bones belonged to travelers who'd journeyed with too little water and succumbed to dehydration. Except one of the skeletal hands was wrapped around a knife, suggesting the person had gone down fighting.

"If you'd surrendered your motorcycle and blasters, I might have let you live," Nell said.

"I'm living okay now," Kane replied. He couldn't tell for certain, but her voice sounded closer. He turned another corner where rocks overhead had collapsed against each other and created a shadow that drifted down to the sandy floor of the crevice.

"Out here," Nell said, "that can change in between heartbeats."

Her voice was definitely closer. Kane slowed, eyes forward, gazing out of the periphery of his vision for motion. He continued following the corner, spotting small islands of rock among the loose white-yellow sand. A fallen tree, the bark bleached ash-gray by the unforgiving sun, canted across the crevice ahead.

Kane halted for a moment, spotting the dim shadows at the other end of the crevice that suggested it plunged beneath the earth there. Or it might end. He checked the ridgeline above the crevice, expecting that the coldheart leader might have used the fallen tree to climb up.

Nothing occupied the ridgeline on either side except an irregular scattering of scraggly brush.

Kane's pointman senses flared as he gazed into the bowl-shaped portion of the canyon ahead of him. It was nearly ten feet deep, dropping in a controlled slope around the corner another five feet from his present position. The bowl was twenty-five feet across, with a kidney shape that narrowed back into the shadowed crevice across the sand-covered expanse.

Footsteps ahead led to the fallen tree to the left. The naked, splintered branches shoved out in all directions, but the ones on the underside stabbed into the sand, mute testimony to how deep the sand was.

Kane raked the area with his gaze, settling on the shadowed end of the canyon. He didn't think Nell had run into a dead end on purpose, nor did he think she'd accidentally chosen the wrong path. She'd come that way on purpose.

A flash of light illuminated the darkness at the end of the crevice.

Kane yanked his head back as a bullet whined from the woman's Mini-14 and gouged the wall only inches from his face. Loose rock flew free of the wall, rattling against both sides of the crevice and plopping down in the loose sand.

Wheeling, Kane shoved the shotgun forward and pulled the first trigger. The shotgun's detonation sounded incredibly loud trapped in the crevice. The double-aught buckshot smacked into the shadowed crevice, tore a lot of rock from the walls and sent dusty smoke curling toward the crevice.

Nell's curse told him she was still whole but that the buckshot had come close. The sound of movement rustled from the end of the crevice.

Kane fired the second barrel into the shadows, hoping the pattern would spread enough to catch her. Another slug hammered into the wall near him, driving him back. He broke open the shotgun's breech and popped the empty shell casings free, then rammed home two fresh ones.

Time was running out. He knew the trader caravan they'd targeted had been only minutes behind them. The sounds of gunfire had to have carried back to them. Chapman, the trader leader, was by all accounts a cautious man. And he was vicious. If there was a chance he was walking into an ambush, Chapman had the reputation of killing everyone to make sure nothing happened to him or his freight.

Kane only briefly considered letting Nell go. If they hadn't spotted her waiting for Chapman's wags at the ambush point, she'd have shot the trader caravan to pieces. She might have known about the freight Chapman was carrying in his wags back to Cobaltville, which made her too dangerous to live.

"Back the fuck off, outlander," Nell called, "and I won't chill you."

"That's generous," Kane said. "But the way I see it, I'd be walking away from a certain chilling."

"The chilling would be your own," Nell replied.

"I don't think so."

"A stupe man never does."

Pressured by time constraints, Kane broke cover. He drove his legs hard through the sand, keeping the shotgun lifted in both hands. He headed for the fallen tree, figuring the sand in the center of the bowl-shaped depression was too deep to get through easily.

Metal flashed at the center of the bowl. He got a brief glimpse of a rectangular piece of steel that quivered on top of the loose sand. He leaped onto the tree trunk, only noticing then that a path had been chopped through the branches. The uneven stubs of the cleared branches were gray with age, indicating they'd been cut with a heavy knife a long time ago.

He had only an instant to recognize the work, then Nell ducked around a corner of the darkness ahead.

"Die, you stupe bastard!" The woman lifted her rifle, her finger locked down on the trigger. Another slug ripped into the wall and tree branches in front of Kane, splitting rock and splintering a branch.

Having no choice, Kane leaped from the fallen tree toward the center of the crevice. He fell, landing in a prone position to stay low. He tried to raise the shotgun to get the coldheart leader in his sights.

Before he could, the thin layer of alkaline crust exploded upward to his right in a shower of grit and a dusty yellow fog. He had a brief impression of a scaled creature nine or ten feet in length shoving upward through the sand.

Tentacles sprouted from the ugly wedge-shaped head that was at least two ax handles wide. A rectangular chunk of stainless steel dangled from one of the center tentacles as they waved madly. Eyes occupied space on either side of the huge curved mouth, but they were milky white with blindness. The scales were a mottled bluish brown, some of them black with disease or age.

Kane tried to push himself up and away. Before he cleared the ground, the tentacles flared out and wrapped around his legs, yanking them from under him. He went down hard, but held on to the shotgun.

Nell's maniacal laugh filled the small canyon as she stepped out of hiding. "You're going to die now, outlander," she promised. She leveled the rifle.

Even before she could pull the trigger or Kane could bring up the shotgun, the mutie creature disappeared under the dust, pulling Kane with the tentacles. The two of them sank through the loose sand as if it were water.

Chapter 3

Brigid Baptiste trained her binoculars on the advancing line of four scouts on motorcycles from Chapman's caravan. She identified the trader leader from the bright purple birthmark on the left side of his face, visible despite the goggles and bandanna he wore as protection from the dust.

"Stay down," Grant whispered to her. "Get your profile up too high, they're going to spot you and there'll be hell to pay. Not just for us, but mebbe for Domi and Kane, as well. Four people in a group are going to look more threatening than two."

Chastised, Brigid flattened back against the ridge where they'd set up a support position. She adjusted the focus of the binoculars, trying to bring the figures of the four scouts into sharper relief. Aches filled her body from the past few days of hard overland journey from the Darks. Even traveling by Sandcat, one of the two-tracked fast-attack vehicles kept in Cerberus redoubt, they'd had a difficult trip. And the coldheart scavenger bands that crossed the area slowed them even further.

Since they'd been in Utah, she hadn't seen another fast-attack vehicle like the Sandcat. The trader caravans were usually made up of older wags that had been pieced and jury-rigged back together.

The two wags making up the caravan stopped immediately when the gunfire reached their position. The drivers staggered them in a loose diagonal formation with all guns facing the outside.

"That coldheart band must have been foolish to think they could have taken that caravan," Brigid commented.

"They had the machine gun," Grant reminded her. "And the high ground. If they'd wanted, they probably could have knocked the motorcycles flat with a few bursts, chopped the tires out from under the wags with the next few. I could have made it work."

"They could have done that to Kane, as well." Brigid clamped down on the fear she felt inside. She'd seen Kane chase after the coldheart leader, but she'd lost sight of him when he disappeared into the small canyon. She'd since caught only fleeting glimpses of him when the zigzag pattern allowed her to see in.

"No," Grant replied. "Kane knew they were trying to keep the ambush quiet. He knew they'd try to bluff him out of whatever they could but that they didn't want to fire unless they had to. Those shots warned the caravan. Chapman's people would have overrun the coldheart position. Surprise was everything, and Kane took that away."

"I know," Brigid replied, raking the binoculars over the ambush area. She spotted Domi walking through the dead men littering the ridgeline. "But he was taking a risk."

"A risk he had to take if we're going to make this work," Grant pointed out. "Chapman's not a man to trust anybody."

Brigid knew. She hadn't agreed with all aspects of the plan, but she understood what Kane was trying to do.

Below, Domi crossed over to the two men whom Grant had killed with the Barrett sniper rifle. She fired additional shots into them with methodical precision.

"Good girl," Grant said, peering through his scope.

Brigid was confused. The men were already clearly dead. "Why did she do that?"

"Chapman's not some nuke-blasted fool," Grant replied. "Man would have taken one look at those bodies and mebbe realized nothing Kane or Domi's got would make holes as big as a .50-cal rifle. Shooting into those wounds is going to confuse things, mask how it really happened."

Brigid nodded, understanding, but she still felt cold inside. Despite the things she'd seen and done with Kane, Grant and Domi, she knew violence would never be something she got completely used to. Violence had been part of the life in Cobaltville, but as an archivist she'd been insulated from most of it.

At the foothills of the ridge, Chapman split the four motorcycles into two groups of two, fanning them out to either side in their approach. The motorcycles went slowly, their engines popping and snorting, the sound echoing over the immediate area.

Brigid glanced at Domi's position behind a rock, then brushed away a stinging trickle of sweat that had crept down into her eye. "There's a chance they'll blast Domi before they even talk to her."

"A small chance," Grant agreed. "But we knew that going in. Like Kane, I'm betting Chapman and his people are going to be more curious when they see that ambush has gotten chilled. Mebbe not thankful, but curious all the same."

"And if they're not?"

"Then this plan is fucked," Grant said casually, "and we find out how good I really am with this Barrett."

For the first time, Brigid noticed Grant had never removed himself from behind the long sniper rifle. The big barrel floated over the four motorcycles. Chapman and his scouts closed on the ridge cautiously, blasters at the ready.

The trader leader stood up on the motorcycle pegs and leaned into the incline as his machine roared up the ridgeline.

Beyond him, Brigid spotted Kane in the canyon again. He darted across a wide, bowl-shaped depression to a fallen tree, then hurled himself off. It took a second or two for Brigid to realize he'd been shot at, that the jumping rock and broken branch fragments showed the path the bullets had taken.

Then the ground around Kane spewed upward, and one of the ugliest creatures Brigid had ever seen in the Outlands jerked up from it. Her breath caught in her throat as her mind spun. She watched helplessly as the tentacles wrapped around Kane's legs.

A scream died on Brigid's lips and she started to get to her feet.

In the bowl-shaped area of the canyon, the tentacled monstrosity yanked Kane below the surface of the sand. Only a slight depression remained in the yellow-gold alkaline dust to mark his passage.

Grant roughly grabbed the loose material of Brigid's blouse and yanked her back down.

"Something's got Kane!" Brigid told him. The horror of the moment wrapped cold fingers around her spine.

She knew the creature for what it was—the monster named in folklore as Ourboros Obscura, the giant worm of the deserts. Anyone born in postskydark America had heard rumors of its existence drifting in from hellzones. Outlanders had sworn to the stories of the predatory beast, mutated and adapted to life underground.

The thought of Kane trapped in its tentacles, dragged down to its lair, sent panic surging through her—not so much panic at the concept of his death but at the breaking of the bond between them.

Grant didn't release her blouse.

She struggled against him, drawing a foot back to kick him. The urge to do something, *anything*, threatened to explode inside her.

Pulling on her blouse and pushing himself up on one hand, Grant rolled over on her and covered her body with his. His fierce brown eyes held her emerald ones. "It's too late," he told her. "Whatever got Kane, you're too far to do a goddamn thing about it."

Brigid pushed at him, her palms flat against his chest.

Grant didn't move. "Listen to me, Brigid." His brown eyes looked liquid. "Kane and I have spilled blood for each other, shared it between us at other times. But I know I can't get to him. Whatever's got him, he has to fend for himself. Our job is to stay here—and not get chilled."

Brigid let her breath out through her nose. She calmed herself, pushing the fear away. But the image of Kane disappearing beneath the sand stayed in her mind. She made herself go limp. "I know."

Gazing at her for just a moment, Grant nodded. He released her uniform and pushed off her, sliding back in behind the Barrett again.

He was a little surprised by Brigid's reaction to Kane's danger. He knew something had happened in the past few weeks which drove a wedge between her and Kane. Grant wasn't sure of the details, but he guessed it revolved around an old point of contention between them—Kane's tendency to plunge into reckless action without taking the consequences into full consideration.

Although the two people weren't exactly estranged, their relationship had definitely turned cold and stiff. When they did speak, it was to quarrel. Kane and Brigid often argued, but now there was an unmistakably bitter edge to it and, in her case, a tone full of unspoken accusations. The bond of trust between the man and woman wasn't broken, but it was apparently strained.

Numbly, forcing herself to function, Brigid took up her binoculars once more. She caught a brief glimpse of the motorcycles roaring to the top of the ridgeline. She didn't look at Domi, though; she trained her gaze on the bowl-shaped depression where Kane had disappeared.

She tried to figure out how long he'd been under, tried to guess at how long he could survive—if the mutie creature hadn't killed him outright.

Chapter 4

Kearney steeled himself as the pneumatic-powered elevator disk came to a stop on A level. In the past two months, since he'd been promoted in the Magistrate Division at Cobaltville, he'd been to the top level of the Administrative Monolith only three times. On each occasion, his stomach had twisted and turned on itself worse than during any of his sorties into the Tartarus Pits with a grudge force scouring unauthorized Dregs. Killing people who'd slipped through the ville's sec systems was a necessary job, and he did it well.

Part of the queasy feeling he was experiencing was due to the vertigo induced by the elevator. It was shaped like a pancake, large enough for only two men to stand on, and it climbed all the way up to A Level like a bullet.

But his uneasiness also derived from the knowledge he was about to see Baron Cobalt, and very few men were granted an audience with the baron. Kearney would have been content never to see him. A baron held a man's life in his hand, chose life or death by cool calculation or idle whim. There was no telling how a baron would act, and some of it was to keep themselves mysterious. Or maybe they really were that mysterious.

Kearney didn't know. He was grateful for the promotion, though. All his life he'd felt born to command, yet destined to be overlooked as other men, even younger ones, had been given the promotion he'd felt entitled to.

Not all Mags felt that way. He knew most of them were satisfied with enforcing rigid baronial regulations. It was a simple life, with clearly defined rules.

Kearney hadn't known becoming a senior officer would involve so much thinking. He'd expected the baron to tell him what to tell others to do. That hadn't been the case. Baron Cobalt had expected him to come up with a solution to the raiders taking down the trade caravans west of the Great Salt Lake.

At present, he'd constructed a trap that he hoped to spring the next day. He wondered if Baron Cobalt was calling him to the baronial hall to give him further information on the operation. Or if the baron was going to have his head, then replace him for failing to end the raids.

The elevator hissed to a stop. A heartbeat later, Kearney opened the door and stepped across the ramp into the baron's suite. Chandeliers hung from the high ceiling overhead, showering the foyer with harsh bright light that reflected from the huge ivory-and-gold-inlaid double doors at the other end.

Kearney forced himself never to break stride and never to look around. He kept his eyes focused forward, every inch a trained Mag in his black Kevlar-weave overcoat and dark glasses.

At six feet eight inches tall, Kearney knew he looked like a death machine and took pride in that appearance. His jaw was hard and square, setting the tone for the flat planes of his face. He was thirty-nine, his broad body kept fit and hard by the conditioning the Magistrate Division was expected to adhere to. He combed his wheat-blond hair straight back, hacked off at the collar. The Sin Eater on his right forearm was a comfortable weight that brought with it a feeling of security. His boots clacked hollowly across the tiled floor.

Two members of the baronial guard stood on either side of the inlaid double doors. They wore white uniform jackets, red trousers and high boots colored coal-black.

Rumor had it that the baronial guards were a product of genetic manipulation, something more and less than human. Normally they were taller and bigger than most men, positioned to intimidate any who were called into an audience with Baron Cobalt.

Kearney, though, was a genetic anomaly, too, although a normal one. He got his height from his father, who'd been a Magistrate before him.

The guards glared at him, knowing from experience that he wasn't intimidated as easily as others before him. Even Kearney couldn't ignore the threat they offered. Their positions afforded a superiority that couldn't be found elsewhere in the ville.

They opened the double doors without a word, and Kearney stepped from the brightly lighted foyer into the waiting darkness. When the doors closed behind him, he could barely see at all. While the hallway outside was kept blazing, the inner sanctum of the baron's suite was kept in deep twilight. A Level had no windows, whether for sec reasons or personal preference on the part of the baron Kearney didn't know.

He kept walking forward, crossing room after room until he reached the gray light that filled the last room under the high arched ceiling. He stopped at the edge of the enormous Persian rug that covered the center of the floor and automatically dropped into attention. He waited without saying a word, his eyes on the golden veil at the other end of the large room. It seemed that he was alone, but he didn't trust that perception.

Kearney counted the minutes as they ticked by.

Then movement shifted beyond the golden veil.

Kearney kept his eyes from the figure, knowing the baron could feel his gaze upon him and not wanting to offend the baron.

"Tell me of the situation in the Outlands that I've generously given you to deal with," the baron said. His tone was sibilant, barely above a whisper, yet it carried throughout the room.

Kearney hesitated, wondering what response he should give. "Everything is under control, Baron Cobalt."

"Of course," the baron said. Anger tinted the words, changing the music of the cadence. "If it had not been, you would have been terminated like your predecessor, Abrams."

"Yes, my lord," Kearney said.

"You were put in charge of that operation to prove yourself," the baron said. "And to protect the efficiency level at which this ville conducts its business." He paused. "*My* business."

"Yes, Lord Baron."

"Tell me of Chapman, the trader." The baron paced behind the golden veil, as deadly as a cobra weaving hypnotically before striking. His feet made no sound as they traversed the distance.

"He is still en route."

"You know this to be true?" the baron demanded.

"Yes, Lord Baron. I flew out to the communications grid we have west of Duchesne yesterday and talked to him myself. He's expecting no trouble."

"Then he's a fool," Baron Cobalt sneered.

Kearney felt the judgment hit him with the severity of a termination warrant. "Yes, Lord Baron."

"The raiders in those areas have taken down seven shipments in the last six months. Three of those have occurred in the last two months, during which time the security of that area was given over to you."

"Yes, Lord Baron." There was no denying the charges, and Kearney's throat dried out of fear. He hated feeling it.

"But I choose not to deem you inefficient at this juncture," Baron Cobalt said. "I believe you will find a way to defeat these raiders. Do not disappoint me."

"I won't, Lord Baron." And if he did, Kearney knew he wasn't coming back to Cobaltville ever again. It was frightening to think of life away from the only world he'd ever known, especially when the outlanders living in the broken lands might be able to recognize him as an ex-Magistrate. If they did, his death was certain at their hands.

"Chapman has the items we discussed?" the baron asked.

"The trader didn't tell me what they were," Kearney replied.

"Of course he didn't," the baron snapped. Despite his evident anger, his pacing remained as fluid and unhurried as ever on the other side of the golden veil. "That isn't for you to know."

"He did confirm that he had them," Kearney said. "He told me you were sure to be pleased, Lord Baron, that it was more than you'd expected."

"Good, because I've got very high expectations." A pleased note sounded in Baron Cobalt's voice. "Has there been any sign of the raiders?"

"No, Lord Baron. Despite the scouts I've had in the area, a raiding party the size of which we're looking for hasn't been found."

"They're there," Baron Cobalt said. "They're just not there all the time."

Kearney had no idea what the baron meant by his cryptic statement.

"Your scouts have also been searching that area for a redoubt?"

"Yes, Lord Baron. That territory was not overly populated even before skydark, and the earthquakes and flooding of the Great Salt Lake nearly decimated everyone there.''

"I'm well aware of the history of that place," the baron snapped. "I'm also well aware of how important that area has become of late. If we are to maintain our standard of living in this ville, worn-out machinery has to be replaced, buildings have to be replaced. If we are to continue to grow, we'll need even more of the ores that are mined in those areas, as well as the salt we import. Nearly all of the minerals we could easily get from the surrounding countryside have been mined. We need those ores, and we need the trader caravans able to operate in relative security to get them at a fair price. If they're constantly harried by raiders, they can escalate that price.''

"Yes, Lord Baron.''

"I will not allow those prices to escalate," Baron Cobalt stated. "Otherwise I will institute a mining community in Utah territory and place you as overseer. Such a community would draw the harshest wrath from the people who live there, I should expect.''

Kearney remained quiet, but he knew it was true. The posting would be only one short step from suicide.

"Tomorrow will be critical," the baron went on. "Tomorrow Chapman and his band will link up with one of the larger caravans headed east from Duchesne.''

"For protection, Lord Baron. When Chapman told me of his plans, I agreed with him. The protection afforded by a larger caravan will—''

"Then both of you are imbeciles," the baron accused. "Joining a larger caravan will only slow Chapman down, make an even bigger target for the raiders. He should have proceeded on his own.''

"Yes, Lord Baron.''

"I'm entrusting the fate of this mission to your hands,''

Baron Cobalt said. "Chapman couldn't be convinced of his error, so you and your team will remove all doubt."

"Perhaps we could do that better by actually joining the caravan ourselves," Kearney said.

The silhouette revealed through the gold veil stopped, its head turning slightly. The Mag felt the full weight of the baron's attention on him. It wasn't a calming influence.

"You would think that would prove detrimental to the raiders," the baron agreed.

Kearney felt proud.

"But I don't want these raiders simply scared off," the baron went on, stripping away Kearney's newfound pride with his quiet, sibilant voice. "I want a lesson made of them. The way we've been posting lessons in that area to discourage any further enlistment from the local ranks. My authority *will* be recognized. And feared."

"Yes, Lord Baron."

The silhouette began pacing again. "I want you there. Tonight."

Kearney hated the thought of returning to the Outlands. The Utah territory was so far away from the protection offered by Cobaltville's sec teams. But he struggled to make sure none of his apprehension sounded in his voice. He also tried to keep his mind clear of such thoughts. He'd been told at one time that barons could read minds, which was only one of the various powers that had been attributed to them.

"As you wish, Lord Baron."

"Spring the trap carefully," Baron Cobalt said. "I've given you men and resources. All of those things are precious to me at this time. I don't want to regret empowering you in this way."

"I won't fail you, Lord Baron." Kearney bowed his head.

"Not," Baron Cobalt promised in that cold, soft voice, "more than once in matters this weighty. Go."

Kearney spun an about-face with Mag precision, slipping the toe of one boot behind the other and twisting sharply until he was facing the other direction. He walked from the room with his head up, controlling the chill fear that filled him.

No one was going to be allowed to interfere with Chapman's delivery.

Chapter 5

Kane was drowning in a sea of loose, shifting sand. The mutie creature maintained its tentacled hold on his legs, dragging him deeper into its lair.

He remembered the vague legends told by Magistrate veterans of Outlands campaigns. One of these concerned the dread mutie monster of the sands, the grim Ourboros Obscura. Only a few weeks before in New Mexico, when he had glimpsed a tunneling machine rising from the desert, his first thought was of the giant burrowing monster. Later, he had laughed at his surge of irrational, superstitious fear.

Now, if he weren't struggling with a myth for his life, he would have laughed at the irony.

As soon as he'd known there was no way to escape the creature's grip and that he was going to be pulled down into the sand, Kane had closed his eyes and stopped breathing. In the next instant, the sand began to slide all around him, getting inside his clothing, abrading his skin, filling his ears. Out of the direct baleful glare of the sun, much of the sand was cool to the touch, but small pockets of heated sand swirled around him.

He kept hold of the double-barreled shotgun, kept his finger off the triggers till he could confirm a kill or was certain he'd come close to running out of time. He didn't hold out any hope for help either from Domi or Brigid and Grant. The latter two were too far away, and he doubted the albino had seen him go under.

His next breath depended on his will to survive and the skills he possessed.

As a Magistrate, Kane had been taught to kill with blasters and blades, with all manner of things he could pick up and with his bare hands. Mostly, he'd been trained to keep on killing as long as he lived, and continue killing till whatever was trying to kill him was dead. He focused on that now.

Abruptly, the tugging stopped, though the tentacles stayed wrapped around his legs.

Kane kept his eyes shut, struggling against the instinctive urge to open them and allow the alkaline sand to pour in. Concentrating on the motion he felt swirling around him, Kane tried to make it clear in his mind. The tentacles seemed more loosely wound around him. Rapidly, thoughts flashed through his mind. If the mutie creature lived in this kind of environment, it would have a high sensitivity to pressures. Maybe it sensed things in the sand the way a spider did about its web, depending on vibrations to let it know when it had live prey.

He remained still with effort, hoping his lack of fighting would confuse the Ourboros. He knew he couldn't hold still for long. He'd need to breathe soon, and when he did, all he'd be sucking up was the choking dust that would fill his lungs.

The thought of dying a slow death frightened him. As a Mag, he'd always expected a sudden death.

He waited, remembering the creature's huge mouth. The tentacles rearranged him, changing his position in the sand, but he kept his hands locked on the 12-gauge.

An empty space opened up on the left side, a vacancy that he couldn't see and didn't hear. He knew instinctively that it was caused by the mutie beast opening the gigantic jaws he'd seen when it had first crawled out of the sand.

His will to survive burning strongly inside him, Kane shoved the shotgun toward that empty spot. His forward hand grazed the scaled lip of the gigantic beast's mouth. He locked the shotgun's barrels inside, feeling a hard clink against teeth.

The Ourboros Obscura tried to gulp Kane down. He felt some kind of wet, rough membrane slide across the hand he had on the creature's mouth. He had no doubt that the shotgun's double barrels had filled with the loose sand when he'd been pulled under. If they were still packed when he touched the triggers, he knew the weapon would blow up in his hands, maybe doing as much injury to him as he planned on doing to the mutie creature.

He counted down, hoping that membrane wasn't blocking the shotgun's barrels so the sand could drain. Without warning, the mutie creature's mouth closed on his hand with enough strength that he knew he wasn't going to be able to pull it free. Almost out of time, Kane hoped the barrels were clear and pulled the triggers.

The double-blast of buckshot sounded muffled in the thick swamp of sand, but Kane felt the vibration of the detonation all around him.

In the next moment, the Ourboros went crazy. It flip-flopped its massive body, wriggling in the sand and releasing Kane.

Free, his lungs pounding with the need for air, Kane reached upward through the dust, then opened his splayed hand, finding enough purchase to pull himself up a few inches. Four more strokes as if he were swimming in the loose sand and he reached the solid bulk of an uneven wall that ran down into the depths where the mutie beast lived.

He hooked the fingers of his free hand into the cracks that he found in the wall. When he pulled himself close enough, he found purchase with his boots, as well, and shoved himself upward.

The creature was incapacitated by the damage that had been done to it, was maybe even in its death throes. The unaccustomed detonation of the shotgun had to have been excruciating.

Lungs burning, his field of vision filled with swirling black spots, Kane forced himself up the wall. A moment later his hand shot through the loose crust already re-formed by the desert heat over the mutie creature's subterranean home, even in the minute or so he'd been dragged under.

He reached around, finally finding the edge of hard ground that surrounded the sand pit. He pulled himself to the surface, pushing hard with his feet. As soon as his head cleared the sand, he took a deep breath, making sure he kept his mouth closed. If he was still too close to the sand, he knew his nostrils would close down if he sucked dust up into them. Breathing it into his lungs would have done irreparable damage.

"Nukeshit!"

Kane recognized Nell's voice at once. Sand still clung to his face when he forced his eyes open. Harsh sunlight stabbed into his eyes, making his vision uncertain and hazy. He saw the coldheart leader bringing up her Mini-14.

Pushing his feet hard against the wall, Kane shoved himself free of the sand. He tucked himself into a roll, throwing himself onto the hard ground.

Bullets speared into the sand, dimpling the surface.

Kane rolled to his knees, all fluid motion and survival instinct. Grit clouded his vision, causing pain that he was able to ignore only because of the adrenaline rushing through his system. His life was measured in heartbeats.

Ignoring the holstered pistol at his hip, knowing the sand might have gotten into it, as well, he swept the fourteen-inch combat blade from his boot. He flipped it end over end in his hand as Nell tried to back away and fire the rifle at the same time. His arm whipped back and forward, knowing the balance of the knife from years of familiarity. The blade left his fingers in a rush, the matte black finish standing out against the yellow alkaline sand and reddish clay of the crevice walls.

Then it was lodged in Nell's throat, piercing just below the jawline on the left side of her neck. Blood spurted in thick ropes, the jugular neatly severed.

The force of the knife sinking home knocked her backward.

Coughing and sneezing dust, Kane broke open the shotgun's breech, automatically blew down both barrels to clear them, then slammed two fresh shells home. He closed the shotgun and rolled the hammers back as he got to his feet and crossed the distance to her. He gripped the knife handle and pulled the blade free. Kneeling, he slipped the water canteen from Nell's corpse. After removing the cap, he smelled it to make sure the water wasn't too heavily laden with the chemicals used in the area to remove dangerous impurities. Satisfied, he upended the canteen over his face, keeping his eyes open so the lukewarm liquid would sluice them clean.

He kept pouring until the canteen was empty, blinking his eyes only a few times to shift whatever sand might have gotten trapped under the lids. He hated wasting the water because it was hard to come by, but being blinded during the next few minutes might mean the difference between life and death.

Feeling only moderate burning in his eyes, Kane slung the canteen over his shoulder. Even empty, the canteen was worth something. Containers that held water were hard to come by in the desert lands.

He took a moment to blow and brush the sand clear of the .45's action, then left the holster's flap open. He wasn't expecting Chapman to welcome him and Domi with open arms.

Reaching down, he stripped Nell's Mini-14 from her and reloaded it with one of the two spare magazines she had for the weapon. Then he pulled her corpse across his shoulder, leaving his hands free for his weapons.

Their plan hinged on being accepted by Chapman. But Kane was enough of a pragmatist that he knew that might not happen. He walked back the way he'd come.

"HE'S ALIVE." Brigid trained the binoculars on Kane as he walked through the crevice, the dead woman draped over one shoulder.

"He's a hard man to chill," Grant commented.

Someone who didn't know him, Brigid knew, wouldn't have heard the relief in his deep voice. But she was cautious about revealing her feelings, too.

Over the past few weeks Brigid had reflected on the reasons for her deep anger toward Kane. He had shot and killed a woman, a distant relative of Brigid's, whom he'd perceived as a threat to her life. Intellectually, she realized that under the confusing circumstances Kane had no choice but to make a snap judgment call. Making split-second, life-and-death decisions was part of his upbringing, his training, as deeply ingrained as breathing. He had assessed a threat and dealt with it.

Emotionally, she felt as if Kane was a murderer, cruelly snuffing out a link to her past without remorse, thought or twinge of conscience. What conflicted her was not so much finding the strength to forgive him but coming to terms with what he really was and accepting the reality rather than an illusion.

She watched him through the binoculars, judging by his gait that whatever he'd fought beneath the sand hadn't hurt him. The magnification power of the binoculars didn't allow her to discern his expression, but she wished she could. Kane's face always revealed his emotions to anyone familiar with him.

As it was, even if everything went according to the plan they'd worked out, it might be days before she could actually speak to him.

And when they did speak, she knew there was every chance that they'd argue the way they so frequently did.

She hadn't known she would miss the face-to-face this much.

Reluctantly, she turned the binoculars back to Domi to see how the albino was faring.

"THAT'S FAR ENOUGH," Domi called. She stayed under cover, watching as Chapman and the three scouts climbed the ridgeline.

Chapman waved his men to a stop. They obeyed instantly.

Domi was impressed. Most traders scrabbling a living from the harsh lands around them kept the people who followed them under reluctant control. The only way most leaders led was by being more intelligent and more vicious than the people they led.

Chapman, according to Lakesh's information, was all that and more.

Domi kept her eyes roving, moving across the men around her. She made sure she watched Chapman, knowing the other three men would take their lead from him.

"Who are you?" Chapman wore hand-stitched road leathers, jacket and pants. The brown rough-out material showed matted stains and accumulated road dust. The bandanna hung around his neck with his goggles. His gray hair was windblown and tangled, sticking up in spikes. A bushy mustache made a horseshoe around his mouth. But the huge purple birthmark that claimed his face was what attracted most people's attention.

"Be death you step any closer," Domi promised.

A wicked grin split Chapman's mottled face. "You a girl?"

"A good shot," Domi retorted.

Chapman shook his head. "Didn't get a good look at you. Thought mebbe you was a girl way you moved."

"Fuck you, scab-face. Try anything, I chill you where you stand."

"Don't see too many women out here," Chapman said. "At least, not one ain't built big enough to stand up and slap a mutie grizzly into a coma. This here's a harsh land."

Domi kept quiet, watching the men. She knew Chapman was talking to put her at ease, let it really sink in there were four men around her. He wasn't the kind of man to be dictated to.

"Got me wondering what you're doing here," Chapman went on.

"Chilling folks." Domi smiled, knowing all Chapman could see of her was an occasional glimpse of her white hair.

"By yourself?"

"Done my share." Domi knew Chapman wasn't sure how many people were still alive on the ridge.

"Figure you had. You think you can take all of us?"

"Take many as I can," Domi told him.

"I just want to talk to you."

"Talking now." Domi watched them, knowing that Grant was still on the ledge and would step in if things got too dicey. Chapman and his men were toying with death if it came down to it.

"What are you doing here?" Chapman asked.

"Traveling through."

"To where?"

"Duchesne, you dumb fuck. Only thing at end of trail this way, right?"

If Chapman took offense, he didn't show it. The cold smile stayed in place, causing his left eye to close up more than the right because of the purple birthmark. "You're not from around here."

"No."

"Where do you call home?"

"Anyplace I go sleep, wake up with head on shoulders next morning."

Chapman laughed. "You figure you're tough, don't you?"

"Double tough," Domi agreed. "Damn fine shot. Piss me off, I shoot you in good side of head. Mebbe even let you live so you can remember you once only half-ugly."

"You got a mean way about you," Chapman growled.

"Only talking now," Domi pointed out. "Steada shooting."

"I've been wondering about that." Chapman lifted a nickel-plated handblaster.

Domi dropped below the line of rock she was using for cover. The bullet chipped splinters from the stone surface. Her eyes cut around, watching the man behind her break from his position and try to run closer to hers. The other two men didn't move.

Shouldering the .30-30, Domi led the running man slightly as the rolling thunder of Chapman's shot rang out around her. She aimed low, not wanting to hit the man in the chest or stomach. She squeezed the trigger, riding out the painful recoil as best as she could.

The boom of the rifle cracked through the air. A split second later, the running man left his feet, thrown violently to the side. The man started screaming at once, rolling through the rock and sand until he reached cover. Blood trailed after him.

Domi ducked back to cover and levered another round under the firing pin. She supposed she could have seriously altered their plans by shooting the man, but she'd deliberately not chosen to kill him. The spent brass twinkled through the air and landed on the sand beside her.

"You stupe bitch!" the man roared in pain. "Gonna die slow now!"

Rolling over and over, Domi came to a stop on her stomach. She sighted down the barrel at the top of Chapman's head. "Didn't chill your man, scab-face. Could have just as easy."

"What do you want?" Chapman asked.

The wounded man still screamed and cursed.

"Go on my way," Domi answered.

"To Duchesne?"

"Only way go from here. Not going to walk desert again without supplies and water."

"Who're these people?"

"Coldhearts," Domi answered. "Laid ambush. Wanted jack to go through."

"You didn't want to pay it?"

"Not have much," Domi said. "'Cept blasters and motorcycle. Wasn't leaving here on foot."

"So you chilled them."

"Wasn't easy. Could have gone other way." Domi held her rifle steady. It felt better knowing Grant had her back, but she wondered what had become of Kane. The way Nell had taken off, the albino guessed the coldheart leader had had a plan in mind.

"But it didn't," Chapman said. "You do this by yourself?"

"What you think?"

"I think no," Chapman said. His head twisted as he glanced uneasily around.

"Mebbe I ask you surrender." Despite the tension of the moment, Domi's wicked sense of humor kicked in and she couldn't help smiling. She lifted her head up, attracting Chapman's attention thirty yards away. She let him see the .30-30's muzzle first, making him aware that she could have already put a round through his head. Her smile stayed in place.

And just as suddenly, a smile split Chapman's mismatched face, too. "Mebbe we got something to talk about after all," the trader caravan leader stated.

"Convince me," Domi challenged. She never took her sights off Chapman.

Without a word, Chapman stood, dropping his blaster down at his side.

"Drop the blaster," Domi instructed.

Chapman shook his head, his long gray hair swinging. "Ain't no way. You can pry it out of my cold, dead hand, but I ain't giving it up. I meet you on your terms, you meet me on mine."

"What terms?" Domi asked.

"We're going to Duchesne, too."

"Chill the bitch," the wounded man shouted. "She fucking shot me."

"Shut your hole, Frank," Chapman ordered. "It was you that screwed up and got your own self shot. She didn't chill you. It'd have been me, I'd have done it to show I meant biz."

Adrenaline thrilled through Domi's body. Being so close to certain death made her feel more alive than at any other time. And she guessed that Grant, lying up in the hills and watching through the Barrett's scope, was about to have a fit. It'd give them something to talk about later. She'd learned from experience that an angry man was also one short step from passion.

Chapman glanced back at Domi. "When I give my word that a hand won't be lifted against you, I give it for all of us. Any man or woman working with me, they'll obey. So what do you think, Ivory?"

"Think bedding down with rattlers safer," Domi answered.

"Be happy to fucking arrange it for you," Frank muttered loud enough for her to hear.

"How do you want to handle this?" Chapman asked Domi.

"Let you get your motorcycles, get the hell off ridge," Domi replied. "Give me five minutes head start."

"To where?" Chapman asked.

"My business."

"Girl alone out here," Chapman said, "ain't got much of a chance."

"Not alone," Domi said.

"Doesn't look like it to me," Chapman said.

Then Kane's voice cut across the distance. "She isn't alone."

Chapter 6

Kane stepped out of the crevice, silently cursing Domi. He'd emerged from the canyon just after Domi had shot one of the caravan scouts. He knew from experience that the albino's violent tendencies usually had lethal repercussions. The flip side was that she was good to have in a fight.

Chapman turned slowly to face Kane, his eyes widening when he saw Nell's body at Kane's feet. "Who're you?"

"Call me anything you like," Kane said. "I'll know when you're talking to me."

The grin on Chapman's face deepened. "You can call me Chapman."

Kane nodded, keeping up the hard-edged act. "If I feel a need to." He stayed aware of the wounded scout, wondering how much Chapman's word would bind the man. From what Lakesh had heard, Chapman ran a tight crew.

"Who's that?" Chapman indicated the dead woman at Kane's feet.

"I heard her called Nell," Kane answered. "I never saw her before today."

"Nell," Chapman repeated. "I've heard of her. Can I take a look?"

Kane kept the double-barrel resting easy across his left arm, his finger on the triggers. He stepped back from the corpse. "Sure. I'm done with her."

Chapman crossed to the dead woman and knelt down. He looked straight into her dead face. "It's Nell."

"Was she a friend of yours?" Kane asked.

Chapman remained in a kneeling position, his handblaster at his side. He smiled, squinting against the harsh sun. "You mean am I gonna want to chill you for chilling her?"

Kane nodded.

"No," Chapman answered. "I knew her some time ago. Back when we were both in the same line of work."

"Ambushing?" Kane asked.

"Some would have called it that," Chapman answered honestly. "We just called it surviving. Out here, a man can live by trading his back and hours of labor for a minimalist existence, or he can fetch up a blaster and take what he wants. I reckon you're a man that's mebbe done a little of both."

Kane let the comment slide.

"We took up separate paths a few years back," Chapman went on. "It was kind of easier not seeing each other after that. If you don't mind, I'll see her buried proper. Don't want to just leave her out here for the animals."

"It doesn't matter to me," Kane said. "As long as we get off this ridge in one piece. We're also claiming salvage rights to these bodies. Including that Browning machine gun."

"You came up on the motorcycle over there, right?" Chapman pointed to the motorcycle lying atop Joad's body.

"Yeah."

Chapman pushed himself to his feet and brushed his knees off. "Then how do you plan on hauling their salvage around?"

"I found a wag," Kane told him, "while I was coming back this way. They had it tucked off in a dead end in this canyon. It'll hold what I need it to."

"What kind of shape is it in?"

"It looked good enough," Kane said.

Chapman nodded. "Nell always did put store by a decent-running wag. Looks like you're in position to go into biz for yourself out here."

"It's the only business I've ever been in," Kane replied.

Chapman gazed at the Browning machine gun. "You know, I'm not sure if Nell knew I was coming up that trail or not, but with that machine gun and surprise on her side, she could have cost us a lot. Mebbe chilled us all before we could have gotten clear."

"I was wondering why she didn't just cut down on us," Kane said, though he'd known when he rode up on the coldhearts that they were waiting for a bigger prize. "I guess she was waiting for something that looked like better pickings than we were."

"Definitely weren't easier, though, were they?"

"No," Kane said.

"I've got a caravan out there a little ways back," Chapman said. "I'll have them join us here. They've got fresh water, mebbe something to eat to hold you till we reach Duchesne."

"How much are you charging for the food and water?" Kane asked.

"You're a cautious man, but you're not afraid to take chances. I like to see that. The meal's free. So's the water. We're both headed for Duchesne. Might as well go together and increase sec power all the way around."

"I'll think about it," Kane said.

Chapman glanced at the woman's corpse at their feet. "You have till I finish burying her. Then I'm pulling up stakes and heading out. You can stay or go as you please."

"DAMMIT," Grant grumbled quietly. "We didn't figure on Chapman wanting to stick around and bury somebody. This bastard rock is getting hot."

Brigid silently agreed. They'd spent more than an hour in position before Kane had approached the ridgeline, waiting until all the elements were in place. It was an hour and a half beyond that, the nuclear-white sun sinking with agonizing slowness in the west.

The rocky outcrop they'd chosen had a perfect view of the ridgeline. However, there was no shade from the direct glare of the sun. Brigid's clothes were drenched now, and perspiration ran in rivulets down her arms as she held the binoculars up.

"Keep thinking mebbe I could slip down to the Sandcat without being seen," Grant said. "Long enough to grab another canteen from our supplies. Feels like my tongue is already swelling up on me."

"If you're seen, it could mean Kane and Domi get chilled," Brigid replied.

"I know. That's why I haven't gone already." Grant mopped sweat from his eyebrows with the back of his hand. "I hope we don't have to stay here much longer. We do, and those guys might get confused and draw attention to us anyway."

Brigid pulled back from the binoculars. She followed the line of Grant's pointing finger.

Forty feet above them, on the tall, thin spire of stone that jabbed up from the outcrop, three vultures sat at different levels. Territorial by nature, they gave each other plenty of room. But their flat black gazes rested contentedly on Grant and Brigid.

As she watched, one of the vultures flew off in a lazy circle above the ridgeline, then dropped. For such an ungainly-looking creature, the vulture flew with quiet elegance.

It landed near one of the corpses on top of the ridgeline, away from Chapman's wags. It waited only a moment, making sure none of the nearby living humans posted any kind of objection, then hopped over to the corpse. It inspected its newfound treasure, then attacked the eyes first.

Brigid held on to the contents in her stomach with difficulty. Thirst had made her a little nauseated as well, and made the task even harder. She closed her eyes, seeking relief from the heat in the cool darkness of her mind.

"They'll have to be moving soon," Grant said. "If they want to reach Duchesne before nightfall."

Realizing that, Brigid knew in a way that she wasn't ready for Kane to go. Once he'd made the link with Chapman, she and Grant would stay farther back, trailing from a distance so they wouldn't be spotted. If something went wrong, they wouldn't be able to help so quickly.

KANE LOOKED DOWN at the fresh grave. The newly turned sand, wet under the top crust, had already started to dry, sapped by the thin wind. It looked lonely on the ridgeline, and he didn't think it would deter predators for long. Even the vultures had grown bolder.

Chapman stood to one side, drinking deeply from one of the canteens the caravan carried. Black sweat streaks still mottled the back and armpits of the gray T-shirt he wore. He'd dug the grave on his own while the other seven men and two women set up a perimeter guard to protect the convoy.

Kane was impressed with their tight organization and the absence of bickering that was common in an outlander caravan. And their provisions—fresh clean water and even a bushel of apples—suggested Chapman was in charge of no ordinary caravan.

Kane watched the man. It was hard to know what kind of emotion was at the forefront of Chapman's mind. The large purple birthmark lent him an alien appearance. Black

sunglasses took away his eyes, the lenses already covered
with a film of yellow alkaline dust.

"Here's to you, Nell," Chapman said after a time. "You
were a hell of a woman once. Good in bed, good to have
at your back, but a stubborn bitch all the same. Got you
chilled in the end, and I guess mebbe I'm sorry to see that."
He turned the canteen over and poured water into the center
of the grave. "I figure you'll need something cool to drink
where you're headed. Mebbe this'll be the last you get."
He capped the empty canteen. "So long."

Without another word, Chapman turned from the grave
and approached Kane.

Kane stood with the double-barreled 12-gauge cradled in
his left arm, his finger still on the triggers. He still wasn't
certain how things were going to shake out.

"You staying or going?" Chapman asked.

"Going," Kane replied.

Chapman nodded. "Let's go see if you got fuel enough
to make it."

THE FUEL GAUGE on the coldhearts' wag wasn't working.
Kane made certain it started by twisting the wires together
under the steering wheel. The engine stuttered for just an
instant, then fired right up.

Chapman grinned. "Told you Nell always set store by
her wag. May look like bastard hell on the outside, but she'll
be solid transport."

The wag had a long bed and increased suspension, and
sat high enough on the four-wheel-drive chassis that Kane
had to use the step-up rung to pull himself up into the cab.

"Suspension's going to be a bitch," Chapman said, "and
her top end is going to be low on speed."

The cab smelled as though something had died inside it.
Fringe hung down along the top of the cracked windshield

on the inside. Red fuzzy dice hung from the rearview mirror. A faded blue blanket covered the cracked vinyl of the bench seat.

Kane found a slender three-foot chunk of board under the seat that was marked Full, Half-Full, and Fukkin Dry, Stupe in bright orange paint. Guessing what it was for, he opened the gas cap beside the cab and shoved the stick in. When he pulled it back out, less than two inches at the end were wet.

"She was really getting desperate," Chapman commented as he looked at the stick. "Mebbe you got enough to get to Duchesne and mebbe you don't."

"Got saddle tanks," Domi called out, ducking under the sides of the truck bed. She slammed a hand against them. Only dulled bonging answered her effort. "Empty."

Chapman leaned back against the truck bed and hauled a homegrown cigarette from his pocket. He cupped his hands and lit the twisted paper end.

"Well," Chapman said, "you got two choices. You can try to make it with what you got."

Kane was aware that they both knew he wouldn't make it. Otherwise, with all the shovels and digging tools Nell had stockpiled in the back of the wag, she'd have headed to Duchesne.

"Or," Chapman said, "you can buy some fuel from me. You pick."

"I could always take the motorcycle I came in on," Kane pointed out.

Chapman nodded. "Sure. But you lose all the swag you captured by chilling Nell."

To play his part convincingly, Kane knew he'd have to take the wag and the supplies. "How much for the fuel?"

"I figure you're going to need four or five gallons to make it to Duchesne," Chapman said.

Kane waited.

"The Browning machine gun," Chapman told him.

"Fucking robbery," Domi said instantly. "No way fuel's worth price of big blaster like that."

A malicious twinkle lit Chapman's eye. "I disagree. Out here, right now, I figure that fuel's worth about any damn price I care to put on it. It's your lucky day it's only going for the cost of one machine gun." He shrugged, returning Kane's flat gaze full measure. "Besides, that Browning used to belong to Nell. I figure she'd want me to have it. Kind of a keepsake."

"The Browning for the fuel," Kane repeated.

Chapman nodded.

"Done," Kane said, ignoring the sour look Domi gave him.

Kane stepped to the back of the wag where they'd placed the Browning earlier. He cleared the action, stripping the ammo belt from it. Holding it by the long, ported muzzle, he handed the weapon across to Chapman.

"The ammo," the trader leader said.

"That," Kane said softly, "that's going to cost you extra. You struck a deal for the weapon, not the ammo." For a moment, he thought Chapman was going to challenge him over it.

The orange coal of Chapman's cigarette glowed sharply. Then he let out a tense breath. And smiled. "You're a hard man. Knew you were going to be a hard man. This is going to be interesting." He raised his voice. "Wylie."

One of the men stepped forward, a bearded giant in a fatigue shirt with the sleeves ripped off.

Chapman handed Wylie the Browning. "Put that in the truck," the trader leader said.

Wylie took off with the weapon.

"What do you want for the ammo?" Chapman asked.

"I need something," Kane said, "I'll let you know. But I'm going to let you know now, I don't plan on needing anything else between here and Duchesne."

Chapman nodded. "You never know, though. Shit happens."

"As long as it's just bad luck," Kane said evenly, "we're going to be just fine."

DOMI DROVE THE WAG they'd acquired while Kane took the motorcycle. He wore goggles and pulled his bandanna over his lower face. The sound of the motorcycle's engine filled his hearing, so he kept his gaze on the move, knowing any warning he got would come from what he could see.

The trail was wide enough for the wag, but it kept twisting through the earthquake-ravaged land. The sand varied from a light covering across treacherous rock to inches deep. Every time Kane felt the wheels churn into one of the deep pockets, he couldn't help looking down, wondering. He figured the mutie sand-fish he'd fought with wasn't the only one of its kind.

After a while, the upward grade leveled briefly, then descended. As they approached the desert's floor under the wide blue sky, he spotted figures on a distant hill near the bottom of the trail.

Two of Chapman's motorcycle scouts shot ahead of him, their machines chewing across the uneven terrain. They spread out automatically, keeping each other in overlapping fields of fire.

They showed a Mag's discipline, Kane thought, and realized how uneasy he was with that thought. They were a hell of a long way from Cerberus redoubt and any kind of help.

He sped up, shifting through the gears, reluctant to let the scouts get out of his view. He glanced over his shoulder and waved at Domi, who drove right behind him.

The albino looked small in the wag cab, but she drove confidently. She sped up, as well, pulling into the dust cloud Kane dragged after him. If the scouts' movements were an attempt to split them up, Kane wasn't going to allow it.

He drove on, watching warily for the endless potholes that dotted the wag trail. When he saw the vultures circling over the figures below, he knew he wasn't going to be surprised to see what he found.

Chapter 7

Blessed with an eidetic memory, Brigid Baptiste didn't have to look at the map they were using because she'd already seen it and filed it away in her photographic memory. She looked at it simply to give her hands something to do.

The half hour since Kane and Domi had departed with Chapman and the caravan was the longest stretch Kane had been out of her sight since they'd started the mission. That made her uncomfortable. That she was uncomfortable in the first place only compounded her anxiety.

She also felt angry at herself, and even though the Sandcat's interior was large enough for four people, it was too small to let the anger eat at her.

Grant sat in the pilot's seat beside her, both hands resting on the horseshoe-shaped steering wheel. His eyes roved restlessly across the ob slit in front of him. "Thought you already looked at that map."

"I did."

"Something you didn't see the first time?"

"No," Brigid answered after a moment. "Everything's exactly the way I remember it." Grant left her alone with her thoughts for the moment, for which she was grateful. He and Kane had received the same training, been taught to think along the same lines, yet she hardly ever got mad at Grant even when he disagreed with her. She wondered how it was that Kane seemed to understand less about her than Grant did.

She drank from one of their canteens, taking only a few sips to slake the residual thirst from the time they'd spent exposed to the sun. Her skin held a rosy glow, promising something of a sunburn in spite of her tan. The tan itself denoted a change from her old way of life. In the Cobaltville archives, she'd gone days without a glimpse of the sun, only the electric glow of the lights.

She and Grant had supplies for only a few days, and getting caught anywhere in the mining territories was perilous at the best of times. Brigid knew Grant and Kane could feed themselves off the land under most conditions, but the desert spreading out around them would have tasked their abilities to the limit. Domi would have managed—one way or another. The outlander albino girl had taken care of herself nearly from the day she'd been born.

But Brigid Baptiste knew she'd never fit in the harsh, barren world that spread out around her. Even as she thought about that, she remembered how much Kane hated being inside Cerberus redoubt.

She'd been feeling at home there for a while, enjoying the privacy of a room that was truly hers. And Lakesh made everything available to her. There were no restricted areas. Or, at least, the ones that Lakesh kept private weren't tantalizingly in the open.

She returned her attention to the map, trying to figure out what bothered her about it. Then she realized she had to admit it wasn't the map at all.

Compiled from old, predark maps they'd found, the map in her hands had been revised according to the stories Lakesh had gathered through his sources. Added to those revisions were actual surveys Baron Cobalt had ordered when the mining efforts began.

Carefully, she folded the map and put it back in the boot under her seat.

Grant looked at her, but thankfully didn't say anything. He returned his attention to his driving.

Brigid slipped free of the harness that held her in the copilot's seat. At the midpoint of the Sandcat, she climbed up inside the armored bubble of the gun turret. She sat in the abbreviated seat, keeping her hands away from the twin USMG-73 heavy machine guns.

She knew the Sandcat had started life based on a predark framework. The design was customized according to their needs and the resources available to the Cerberus engineers. Equipped with a 750-horsepower engine, built with a blunt-nosed prow, covered in ceramic-armaglass armor designed to go opaque if it was attacked with energy-based weapons, the Sandcat was a lethal dreadnought. The low-slung, blocky chassis was supported on twin treads capable of propelling it across all terrain.

It was a vehicle designed to meet every need, yet it wouldn't fit in a civilized ville without attracting a lot of attention. In fact, the Sandcat and Kane had a lot in common, which spoke volumes about the differences between Brigid and Kane.

Her world had always been quiet, focused on the pursuit of knowledge. Kane's was a world accustomed to daily violence and fueled by a belief system that insisted on loyalty and a ruthless campaign to enforce baronial authority.

They were different as night and day in so many ways.

What was the bond between them? Why was it so strong?

Anam-chara, or "soul friend."

That was the term Kane had given her, and the truth of the words was undeniable; beneath the physical attraction and beyond their constant arguments there was a bond. It was one thing to acknowledge that bond, but quite another to decide what to do about it. The one thing she was sure of was that she didn't want to see Kane die. They'd risked their lives for each other, struggling against the machinations of Baron Cobalt and the remnants of the Archon Directorate.

Yet now she didn't know for sure where he was or what he was facing. She and Grant would stay away from the main routes. By driving all night, taking turns in shifts, they would trail the convoy without being seen and be there to help Kane if things went badly.

She looked across the vast, dry wasteland. "Be safe, Kane."

DEAD MEN HUNG from steel crosses at the top of the hill. There were six in all, a silent testimony or threat to anyone who looked at them. They'd been hung ten feet up, high enough they could be seen a long way. One of them had a hand-lettered sign hanging around his neck from a frayed piece of rope. Fukkin Radurs Kild Ded By Tait's Minning Ko.

Kane straddled the motorcycle and looked up at them. Their deaths had been hard and a long time in coming, inscribed by knives and whips. Strips of flesh hung from the bodies, and broken bones showed through in several places. Vultures had been at them for a few days. The faces were almost gone, and the open body cavities writhed with islands of yellow-white maggots.

The steel crosses had been fashioned from discarded support struts taken from buildings or some other structure. Ropes bound them to the crosses. They'd been stripped naked, probably to save anything worthwhile, but also to make the posted warning more stark.

Domi pulled the wag beside him. She gave the bodies only a brief glance. She'd seen too much death to register much interest, much less surprise.

Chapman rolled his motorcycle up beside Kane. He

pulled his bandanna down but left his dark sunglasses in place. "Raiders," he said. "Nobody around Peabody's Roadhouse is willing to put up with them working so close to home. Bad for biz."

Kane left his own bandanna up, knowing it filtered out some of the coppery, rotten-egg stink of death. Every breath he took tasted like dust. "How much farther to the road-house?"

"Three, mebbe four miles," Chapman said. "Ain't no marker around here. See it soon enough." He glanced back up at the bloated corpses meaningfully. "Peabody pays his sec teams a bonus for every raider they chill and post. Gives them a pretty good incentive. Roadhouse makes a lot of jack handling supplies needed by crews making the long haul into Cobaltville."

"That's where you're headed?" Kane asked. Lakesh's information hadn't been clear whether Chapman's caravan was heading for Cobaltville or a meet with another caravan.

"Yeah." Chapman lit another homegrown cigarette. He kept his dust-covered sunglasses lenses focused on Kane. "We get to the roadhouse, mebbe we'll talk a little biz ourselves."

"Mebbe," Kane said noncommittally.

Chapman dropped his foot on the gearshift and let out the clutch. His motorcycle's rear tire spewed out a rooster tail of dust and he roared away.

Kane took a final look at the dead men, knowing if he and Domi were found out in the roadhouse, they couldn't expect any kinder fate. He slammed the motorcycle into gear, then sped after the trader leader. They were in too far for Grant and Brigid to be much help at this point, and they had no option except to play out the hand they'd been dealt.

Chapter 8

"Have you located all of them, Mr. Bry?" Mohandas Lakesh Singh stood with his arms folded over his thin, narrow chest as he surveyed the Mercator map that occupied one whole wall in the command center of the Cerberus redoubt.

The command center was a long room with high, vaulted ceilings. Comps and electronic devices filled every available inch of space along the walls, all of them possessing consoles with dials and switches. At one end of the room was a door to the nearby ready room where Lakesh usually held court. The mat-trans unit sat at the other end of the room, the brown armaglass walls as opaque as ever.

"They're all there," Bry replied. He sat at a console, eyes locked on the comp screen in front of him. His blunt fingers tapped a cadence on the keyboard. He was a small man with rounded shoulders and thick copper-colored hair.

Despite his small stature, Bry was healthy and robust compared to Lakesh. The old man looked as if he'd been annexed by death but hadn't quite given up the struggle. Disheveled ash-gray hair covered his head. His pale blue eyes were covered by thick-lensed glasses with a hearing aid attached to one earpiece. "And their health, Mr. Bry, what of it?" His voice was quiet, barely audible over the hum of comp drives and electronics in the command center.

"Domi's and Kane's signs are back to normal," Bry answered. "But they're all showing degrees of accumulated fatigue."

Lakesh nodded. Bry was able to track the movements and vital signs of the personnel from the Cerberus redoubt thanks to a transponder that was injected subcutaneously. The transponder was a nonharmful radioactive chemical that bound itself with the individual's glucose and one of the middle layers of the epidermis. It was one of the miracles of organic nanotechnology that had virtually disappeared after the nukecaust.

Lakesh had managed to resurrect the technology from the tangled webs of what-had-been-and-now-was. But he had an affinity for such things. He'd been born in 1952 himself.

As a young genius, he'd been drafted into the web of treachery the Totality Concept had spun in the last years of the twentieth century. As a physicist and cyberneticist, he was recruited for Project Cerberus, which dealt with matter transfer via hyperdimensional travel. Contrary to the public image presented by the ultrasecret organization within its own ranks, he'd learned that the basic technology of mattrans units wasn't the product of research and development by human minds. The Totality Concept was blessed with the technology bestowed by an alien race known as the Archons.

The Archons' nefarious schemes resulted in the nukecaust of 2001, part of their plan to cull the human population to a size they could conquer and control. The subsequent Program of Unification was their effort to take over what was left of the rest of the world, allowing the barons—who were human-Archon hybrids—to assume the role of god-kings.

After the nukecaust, Lakesh had volunteered to be placed in a cryogenic tank in the Anthill, the largest of the hidden Totality Concept facilities.

Fifty years ago, he'd been revived and brought back into the fold of the Archon Directorate's newly revised and aggressive agenda. It was only then that he discovered the magnitude of his error.

It had taken hard, bitter years of plotting as a senior archivist in Cobaltville, taking carefully calculated risks almost daily to achieve a game plan that would allow him to rebel against the monstrous evil the Archons represented. He'd been forced to flee to the Cerberus redoubt, where he oversaw the continued battle against the barons, who sought to discover the whereabouts of Lakesh and his fellow exiles.

Now, depending on the success of the operation in the Utah territory, he had a chance to perhaps find a new ally.

"The enemy of my enemy is my friend," he said to himself. And he smiled slightly as he studied the Mercator map. It was an opinion that he knew Kane would have approved of.

Still, there was a certain amount of caution to maintain. So many things had been done wrong, or for the wrong reasons.

And Lakesh did so love mysteries. As long as somewhere in there he got to solve them. This one, as yet, remained unsolvable, but he'd taken drastic steps to get to that solution.

"What did you say?" Bry asked.

"Simply musing aloud to myself, Mr. Bry," Lakesh said. "Nothing you need concern yourself over."

Lakesh turned as DeFore, the redoubt's medic, entered the command center from the outer hallway. "Ah, the good Dr. DeFore. What brings you to our sanctum sanctorum?"

Buxom and stocky, DeFore wore the one-piece white jumpsuit common among the redoubt's personnel. Her ash-blond hair was tied up in intricate braids, the color contrasting sharply with the bronze coloration of her skin.

She gestured to the comp screen in front of Bry. "What is all this about, Lakesh? Where are Kane and the others?"

"In what used to be known as Utah State," Lakesh answered. "Once the home of the Mormons, the Osmonds. The state whose motto was simply 'Industry.'"

"Why?"

"To gain information," Lakesh replied. "And quite possibly meet with someone who might be interested in joining our struggle against the forces of the united villes."

"Another recruit?" DeFore asked.

Lakesh favored her with a smile. "My dear doctor, quite possibly this could be one of the greatest coups I've ever arranged." He walked toward the Mercator map and placed his hand on Utah. "Are you aware of the mining going on in Utah?"

"The fact that mines have been reopening there over the past few years?" DeFore asked. "Sure, I knew about the search for raw materials to make steel and other metals."

Lakesh moved his hand to Colorado, where Cobaltville was located on the Kanab River. "Bridging the gap between those various industrious souls in Utah and the coffers of Cobaltville, however, is a veritable no-man's-land wherein dwell the coldhearts who raid the ore caravans. Of late, though, my contacts in the Outlands have been mentioning other far more interesting tales. I've been told of an army that has risen from the sands of the desert and swallowed whole shipments of ore."

DeFore's brow wrinkled. "Why?"

"I don't know," Lakesh admitted. "Why would anyone want ore?"

"To build. To construct," DeFore mused aloud. "But why intercept ore shipments when they could just take over a mine and produce it themselves?"

"The conundrum deepens," Lakesh went on. "From the reports I've heard, this group of ore snatchers numbers around sixty or seventy people. Possibly more. And they are exceedingly well equipped.''

"You can't pinpoint where they're hiding?'' DeFore walked to one of the nearby comps and seated herself.

Lakesh felt a warm glow as he watched the woman bring up comp files detailing the Utah territory. She was a prize pupil, had been since the day he'd won her over to his cause.

"That many people,'' DeFore said as she studied a map of the eastern Utah territories, "would be hard to hide. Not to mention the fact that they'd be even harder to feed and clothe. And getting water over there is hard. Usually they have to barter for it. Or drink stuff that's not really fit for man or beast.''

"Yes. It would be a logistical nightmare in those harsh lands. That's one of the reasons I sent our friends into the area to investigate. Even more interesting is the fact that Baron Cobalt appears to have developed an exceptional regard for an individual named Chapman.''

"I don't recognize the name,'' DeFore admitted.

"Nor should you. The man's nowhere near your caliber, my dear doctor. He's a scavenger purported to have great native cunning, and is remarked to be a bad man to cross.''

"Kane and Grant know this?''

Lakesh nodded. "I took great pains that they should understand such a thing about such a man.''

DeFore shook her head. "Knowing those two, they probably took it more as a challenge than a warning.''

Lakesh offered the ghost of a smile. To a degree, he could manipulate Grant and Kane by drawing on their training as Mags. Both men were physical and pursued forums that would allow them to exercise their training. "Chapman has evidently got another business going on.''

"Instead of mining?''

"Quite right. He was never a miner. My sources have

indicated that Chapman regularly undertakes long trips *through* the mining territories—not to them.''

''He's transporting something,'' DeFore stated.

''Exactly, my dear doctor. Not only do I wish to learn of these hostile forces and where they might be encamped, but I would like very much to know what Chapman is couriering and selling to Baron Cobalt.''

DeFore glanced at him for a moment. ''What have you heard?''

''Only that the baron regularly schedules support staff to aid Chapman and his people to make the delivery.''

''Sec teams?''

''Yes.''

''But you don't know what it is?''

Lakesh shook his head. ''Sadly, no. I hope friend Kane and the others will be able to better elucidate that answer.''

''But you have a clue?'' DeFore persisted.

''You've heard of Seattle?''

DeFore wrinkled her brow for a moment. ''The ville on the West Coast of the old United States?''

''Exactly,'' Lakesh said. ''And do you remember Silicon Valley?''

''Big comp tech design place.''

Lakesh nodded.

''Lost all that when the earthshaker bombs hit the West Coast and put most of California at the bottom of the Cific Ocean.''

''Quite right,'' Lakesh said. ''But in the 1990s, the comp design business migrated. Many of the corporations pulled up stakes and moved into Seattle, Washington.''

''The Cific Northwest is high in rad count.'' DeFore brought up a newer map that had been revised over the past few decades. ''It'd be pure suicide to go into that area. Like

Grant and Kane call it, a real hard-nosed one-percenter of a chance.''

"Perhaps, my dear doctor, things have changed there of late. Those maps you're perusing are decades old. As far as I know, neither Baron Cobalt nor any of the other barons has sent people into that region.''

"Except Chapman.''

"Provided my information is accurate.''

"You think he has to be bringing something back from there?''

Lakesh walked over to her and tapped the keyboard. A satellite picture swelled quickly to fill the comp screen. It clearly showed a pair of wags flanked by motorcycles speeding across the desert.

"There are between nine and eleven people in that caravan, but only the two wags,'' Lakesh explained. "How much do you think you could put in those two vehicles?''

DeFore nodded slowly, understanding lighting her features. "Not much.''

"But enough,'' Lakesh stated quietly, "that Baron Cobalt sees fit to send a team of sec men to meet Chapman when it's time.''

"So whatever it is,'' DeFore said, "it's small.''

"Exactly. And a rather largish army of raiders has set their sights on it.''

"If that's true, why didn't they simply seize the shipment before Chapman got this far?''

Lakesh smiled. "You understand my own curiosity in this matter completely.''

"Seventy people,'' DeFore repeated. "That's a lot to move around. Mebbe getting closer to Seattle or farther away from the eastern part of Utah was too hard.''

"Yet the reports indicate those raiders strike with impunity, arriving and disappearing like wraiths.''

"What else do you know about them?"

"Nothing. Hardly anyone lives when they strike. They're well trained and well armed."

"An army."

"For all intents and purposes," Lakesh said.

"And Kane and Grant, Brigid and Domi are supposed to go up against that?" DeFore's gaze was an accusation.

"No. They're merely to observe, then report back."

"They could get caught up in this."

Lakesh hesitated. "There is that possibility, yes, but the need to go and see outweighed the risk factor."

"In your opinion."

"And friend Kane's and friend Grant's." Lakesh's gaze locked on the map. "Someone in that area has chosen to make war against Baron Cobalt, to thwart him and seize things he would claim for himself. It might behoove us to seek this person out and learn if we can be of mutual aid."

"You'd trust an outsider with knowledge of the Cerberus redoubt?"

Lakesh frowned. "No, of course not."

DeFore chuckled. "But you might string them along and get what you can out of them."

"I'm hoping for something more beneficial than that. But I'll settle for that if that's all that can be managed."

"You've restored my faith in you."

Bry called out from his comp console. "Trouble," he said.

"What is it, Mr. Bry?" Lakesh asked.

"I just picked up a Deathbird winging west toward Utah from Cobaltville," the comp expert said, tapping the keyboard hurriedly.

Interested and irritated all at the same time, Lakesh limped over to Bry's comp station. The command center was uplinked into two satellites, and recent refinements allowed them to take fuller advantage of the satellite's potential. The Comsat allowed Bry to monitor the transponders and track the movements of Cerberus redoubt personnel.

The second satellite, the Vela, carried narrow-band multispectral scanners that detected the electromagnetic radiation reflected by every object on the planet, including subsurface geomagnetism. Those scanners were linked into a high-resolution photograph-relay system that at the moment were locked on Cobaltville.

Bry had highlighted the image of the Deathbird as it moved rapidly across the uneven terrain.

The air wag was based on the old Apache AH-64 gunships used at the close of the twentieth century. On-screen, they had a distinct waspish shape. All of the Magistrate wags were heavily armed and equipped.

"Do you know who's aboard it?" Lakesh urged.

Bry continued stroking the comp console. He pointed at another screen beside the first one. It showed the Magistrate helipad inside Cobaltville. "The one sec cam we've hacked into and have access to in the Magistrate heliport didn't have a view of that Deathbird at the time it was boarded."

"Can you pick up the comm signals?"

"I'm trying. I get flashes every now and then, but they're encrypted. If I get them decoded, you'll be the next man to hear about it."

Lakesh's mind raced, factoring in the ramifications of the Deathbird's jump toward Utah. It only added up to trouble. He watched the Deathbird streaking across the screen, wondering how duplicitous the whole operation in the Utah desert had suddenly become.

And he had to wonder whose deceits were going to prove the most dangerous.

Chapter 9

Peabody's Roadhouse swelled into view as Kane roared down the darkening road with Chapman's convoy. His headlamp was weak and flickering. He guessed he'd damaged it when he'd run into Joad earlier.

From the look of the abandoned buildings and broken-down structures surrounding the roadhouse, Kane knew that Duchesne had been a large ville before the nukecaust had brought the world tumbling down. Nearly everything had been destroyed during the ensuing 190 years or so, but here and there he spotted dull yellow light from candles or lanterns in windows of buildings that had been claimed or built out of the old ville's corpse. Heavily rutted roads meandered through the confusion of destruction and limited, halfhearted rebirth.

According to Lakesh's intel, most of the people who lived in the area were squatters, who lived off what they could fish in the river or hunt in the hard rock of the desert. If a man could get by on the taste of lizard every night, Kane had the opinion that man would eat whenever he wanted to. There were a lot of lizards living near the rivers.

Peabody had built his establishment where the Duchesne River butted into the Strawberry River. The water taken from the rivers had to be chem-pured, but not as much as other places. The last dying rays of the western sun kissed the uneven water bloodred, looking like a major artery had been sliced neatly in two behind the roadhouse.

When the roadhouse had been constructed, care had been given to clear away everything else for a hundred yards on the three sides that faced land. The back half of the two-story roadhouse hung out over the river on tall stilts that had been made out of tree trunks.

The roof was slanted against the seasonal snows that fell in the mountains, and sloped down on all sides over the verandah that encircled the building. Hammered-tin sheets covered the roof and walls, proof against the elements and protection from any attempts to set fire to the structure. Cross-shaped windows that doubled as gun ports were located next to real windows.

Kane was of the opinion that the roadhouse was as much a fort as it was a business. He pulled the motorcycle in beside the dozen wags parked to the left of the building in a ragged line, then took the time to turn the bike around so it faced the dirt road leading to the roadhouse.

Straddling the motorcycle, Kane watched as Chapman assigned three of his group to sec duty over the wags. Then he led the rest of them toward the roadhouse.

"Coming?" Chapman asked as he passed Kane.

"In a minute." Kane pushed himself up from the motorcycle, slipped the double-barreled shotgun from the boot mounted on the side and crossed over to Domi.

"Want me stay with wag?" the albino asked.

Kane shook his head. "There's safety in numbers. And I don't think we'll have anything taken here. Stealing's about the same as raiding. And there's nothing in this wag that I've gotten so that I can't live without."

Domi clambered out of the wag's tall cab and dropped lithely to the ground.

Kane didn't know how she did it. After being beaten by the rough road for hours, he felt worn-out. He missed his bed back in the Cerberus redoubt, then chided himself when he realized what he'd just thought. Too much comfort took the edge off the senses, the reflexes.

He left the flap on his pistol holster loose. He also kept the shotgun in his fist but didn't pull the hammers back. The wooden walkway thumped when his boot heels struck it, letting him know it was hollow underneath.

A huge, black metal door with Peabody's written on it in white over an old listing of Janitorial Supplies filled the door frame. It pushed open when Kane shoved, but from the smooth way it moved he knew it wouldn't be easily moved when it was locked down tight.

The roadhouse's interior glowed from lanterns hanging from ceiling mounts. Buckets of sand sat around the floor, against the walls between tables. If a fire broke out, they were to be used as fire extinguishers.

Despite the rough exterior, Peabody's claimed a quiet elegance on the inside. Pecan paneling covered the walls, and the tables and chairs looked to have been scavenged with care, then repaired with a woodworker's sure and loving touch.

The bar occupied the center of the floor, serving out on all four sides in an eight-foot square. Stools lined the bar, but only a handful of men and women sat there drinking by themselves.

Nearly thirty more, broken into groups, claimed tables across the floor. They all looked rough-hewn and burned red and brown from the sun on a daily basis. They all carried blasters, either on their persons or lying on the tables quick to hand.

Across the room, a woman dressed only in a pink bra and pink bikini panties danced on a small stage, twisting and grinding her body to the fast tune played on a guitar by an old blind black man sitting on a nearby chair. Paper jack hit the floor at her feet, and men and women sitting in chairs in front of her whistled shrilly and urged her on. While Kane stood there waiting for his eyes to acclimate, the woman reached behind and unsnapped her bra. She teased her audience, pulling the straps free, then finally letting it fall forward till she revealed her hard-nippled breasts.

To the right, a flight of stairs led up to the second floor. A pool table, one of only a handful Kane had ever seen intact, surrounded by a small group of players, sat next to the stairs.

Kane's pointman senses marked the layout in his mind as he approached the bar.

"Something I can do you for, mister?" the bartender asked. He was a small, thin, bald man with glasses.

"What do you have?" Kane asked.

"You got jack or trade?" the bartender countered.

Kane eyed him. "What's the difference?"

"Jack'll get you something to drink sooner," the bartender said, "but we aren't too keen on ville scrip around here."

"I got trade," Kane told him. "Out in the wag."

"What you got to trade?"

"Digging tools. Shovels, picks."

That caught the attention of a big man sitting on the stool to Kane's right. He was a behemoth, built up and torn down by hard labor. And he was drunk. "Fucking raider," he mumbled. "We don't allow no fucking raiders around here." He went for the handblaster tucked in the front of his belt.

Moving only slightly, Kane took a step toward the man and slammed the shotgun's buttstock into his forehead.

The man went over backward, falling from the stool into a loose sprawl. The handblaster tumbled from his nerveless fingers. A thick, angry bruise was already swelling on his forehead, but he was still alive.

"I'm not a raider," Kane growled loud enough that everyone in the room could hear him. "I'm just a man stopping in for a drink."

Not many of the bar crowd appeared convinced.

"Stand down, you bunch of hardasses. I'm vouching for him." Chapman joined Kane at the bar. "He chilled Nell earlier today and took what she'd taken. She set up an ambush, hadn't counted on him being pure hell on wheels. I put her in the ground myself."

Nell's name raced around the room as a number of people spoke up at the same time. A few seemed angry or saddened that she was gone, maybe remembering her from other times. But most appeared glad she was gone.

"Trust him for what he wants, Shorty," Chapman told the bartender. "I'll make sure he settles up." He turned to Kane. "You and her come on back here and let's talk."

Kane and Domi both got thick heady beer dipped from an oaken cask behind the bar. They followed Chapman to the verandah hanging out over the Strawberry River. The dancer was down to skin. She'd gotten a candle from somewhere or someone and sat on the stage, no longer dancing, simply working to excite her audience. Her passionate moans sounded real.

Chapman sat at one of the tables near the river's edge. With night coming on, the heat had left the desert in a rush, vanishing with the sunlight. Cool air blew in off the river.

Kane sat across from the trader leader and sipped his beer.

"What are you doing out here?" Chapman asked bluntly.

Kane noticed Chapman's people at two of the tables flanking them. The man hadn't casually chosen his table. "I'm minding my own business," Kane said quietly. "It's something I sometimes advise other people to do."

Dark anger stirred in Chapman's face, but only a smile surfaced. "Think you're a hard son of a bitch, don't you?"

Kane didn't say anything to that. He took another sip of his beer.

Chapman relaxed back in his chair. "You and Ivory took out Nell and her people like it was nothing."

"Wrong," Kane said. "We almost got chilled in the doing of it."

"Are you that good, or are you that lucky?" Chapman asked.

"It matter?" Domi asked. "Did what needed did." She was watching the woman on the stage, acting hypnotized by the sexual frenzy the woman was playing out.

"No," Chapman admitted, "it doesn't matter. What I meant by my question earlier was whether you were interested in a job."

"No," Kane answered without hesitation. "I've had enough of jobs."

"You got something against working?"

"Working doesn't bother me," Kane said. "It's having to put up with bosses I don't care for."

"That'd be me," Chapman said. "And I can be pretty easy to work with."

"I didn't come out here looking for a job," Kane said.

"Then what?"

Kane didn't answer.

"Are you running from something?" Chapman asked.

"A question like that," Kane warned, letting some of the Mag attitude show, knowing it would mirror the part he needed to play now, "might get a man chilled."

"Sorry." Chapman held up an apologetic hand. "I didn't mean that the way it came out. It's just that I'm going to need someone, and I thought you might fit the bill."

"You have a full crew," Kane said.

Chapman shook his head. "I don't think so. Not anymore, because I think you're going to have to chill Frank before we walk out of here tonight. He ain't got over Ivory shooting him earlier today.''

Kane cursed silently. He'd been so intent on Chapman and getting in with the man that he'd forgotten about the threat Frank posed.

"I got two choices about ol' Frank," Chapman went on. "I can back his play, mebbe help him chill you and Ivory, or I can let you chill him. Now, chilling you and Ivory, that's going to run a risk to the rest of my crew. So I figure if Ivory makes his play, it's his own ass."

Kane glanced at Domi's chair to make sure she'd heard.

But her chair was empty, the .30-30 sitting beside it.

DOMI WAS BORED. And even though she knew that was a dangerous thing to experience, especially when she should have sat still and done nothing, she got up and walked back into the roadhouse.

She ignored the woman on the stage, who was yelping now in feigned ecstasy.

As she moved toward the bar, she palmed a knife in each fist and stayed alert for any move from Frank. She knew it was only a matter of time before he'd seek revenge, and the roadhouse provided him with both an opportunity and an audience.

He came at her without warning, stepping from the bar where he'd sidled up to be closer to her, thinking he was going to get anywhere near her without her knowing. He held a machete in his hand, raising it over his head, the razor edge gleaming as it caught the light.

Domi moved, laughing as the machete sliced through the air over her head, missing her only by inches.

Blood stained the big man's wounded shoulder, but he was able to grab at her as he tried to bring the machete back into play. His face was florid, and his eyes held only tiny pinpricks of pupils from the beer he'd been drinking.

"Gonna fillet you, you mutie bitch," he promised.

Domi back-flipped without using her hands, gaining enough height to land on her feet on the table she'd spotted behind her. The stage show had stopped abruptly, and now every eye was on Domi.

Frank flung himself forward again, trying for another overhand blow.

Domi turned sideways, letting the machete blade pass her. She felt the vibration in her feet as the razored edge slammed into the tabletop, burying the blade deeply.

The two men seated around the table bailed away with scathing curses.

Before Frank could free his machete, Domi sprang forward. She put a clenched fist on top of his head and flipped forward. As she levered herself over his head, she swiped at Frank's right ear with the knife hidden in her other hand.

Frank's ear left his head in a rush, plopping down onto the hardwood floor at the same time Domi landed on her feet behind her opponent.

Bright crimson spurted out over Frank's shoulder. He screamed in pain. "You fucking bitch!" He freed the machete and put his forearm to the side of his head. It came away wet with blood.

"Gonna chill me double?" Domi taunted as she stayed in motion.

Frank rushed at her, swinging the machete from side to side, trying to cut her in half.

Domi dropped to the floor, dodging the heavy blade. She caught Frank's foot in the crook of her elbow as he shot past, then yanked it up to throw him off balance.

Unable to stop himself, Frank slammed into one of the

support posts running from floor to ceiling. His head hitting the post made a dull thump.

Domi rolled forward, coming to her feet easily. Her shoulder twinged, hurting some from the stiffness caused by the recoil of the .30-30 earlier, and from the demands she was making on it now.

Staggering slightly, Frank grew more cautious. But his cursing didn't improve at all.

Domi shut it out, watching the man. Blood matted the side of his head, causing his hair to stick together in clumps, and bright crimson streamed down the side of his neck to soak into his shirt. He pushed the machete ahead of him, poking it to test her reflexes.

Staying on the balls of her feet, pushing off on her toes, Domi reacted to every tentative stab, getting him used to the idea of her moving. She circled to the left, drawing him after her.

Shorty the bartender shouted at Frank from the safety offered behind the massive bar. "Stupe bastard! Put that big pig-sticker away or I'm going to cut you in half!" He held a chopped-down shotgun that was guaranteed to clear half the room.

People at the nearby tables scattered. A man beside the bar drew a handblaster and pressed the muzzle up against the bartender's head. "Shorty, put down that fuckin' blaster before you chill half the people in here dropping jack."

Shorty appeared reluctant.

"Do it, damn you," the man ordered. "You touch off any powder in that fuckin' piece, you're gonna chill a lot of damn people. Peabody won't like that at all, you cutting down on the number of his paying customers."

Gingerly, Shorty put the shotgun away.

"It's their disagreement. Let them work it out."

Oblivious to the exchange, Frank came at Domi, his

breath sounding like a bellows. The albino knew the big man thought he had her trapped, thought she hadn't seen the bar coming up behind her.

Instead of rushing at her this time, Frank pulled up, letting her see where she'd gotten to. He kept the machete moving slowly, under his control.

Domi glanced over her shoulder, seeing the bar's edge exactly where she'd known it would be. Dodging a machete blow would be difficult even with her speed. And she could tell by the piggish glow of triumph in Frank's eyes that the man knew it.

"Got you now, you little bitch," Frank crooned sadistically. "Gonna chop you up into kindling."

"Come do it, little prick," Domi taunted. She turned the knives over in her hands, like a cat flicking out its claws. Lantern light glinted from the needle points.

The threat didn't throw Frank off his stride. He feinted with the machete, as if he were going for another sweeping cut. As Domi started to move, he stabbed the blade forward, throwing all of his weight into the thrust.

Domi turned sideways, avoiding the machete. She let him crash into her, counting on her strength to keep him from breaking her back against the bar. She hit with bruising force, losing the breath from her lungs. Still, she smiled up at him as he realized he'd missed.

He threw out his free hand, trapping her in the circle of his arms. He pressed up against her hard, and she felt his arousal through the thick material of his pants. Killing really was a pleasure for Frank.

Too quick for the big man to follow, Domi whirled and brought the knife in her right fist crashing down toward his left hand where it lay flat on the bar. The thin knife slid easily through the bones in his hand and penetrated deep into the wood.

Instinctively, Frank tried to tear his hand back. It didn't come free, since it was securely nailed to the wood. He spit out a litany of pain-filled curses. With his other hand, he yanked the machete free and lifted it for an overhand strike.

Domi grabbed his shirt with her free hand and pulled him into her again. His swing slammed into the bar, missing her by inches and knocking over a nearby quart bottle. Twisting viciously, she grabbed the rolling bottle and swung it at Frank's machete hand before he could get his balance back.

The bottle broke across Frank's knuckles, drawing blood. He released the machete as his hand jerked. Before he could get it clear, Domi levered her free arm over it, trapping it briefly against the bar. Then she drove her second knife home through the back of his hand, impaling it against the bar.

Frank cried out in pain and fear.

Slipping from the embrace that the big man had believed would pin her, Domi grabbed the alcohol lantern from the hook overhead. Holding the lantern in both hands, she smashed it across Frank's face.

The thin, soot-encrusted glass broke at once, spilling the contents across the man's face. The alcohol caught fire at once with a liquid whoosh, burning blue and yellow. His scream was high-pitched.

Domi stepped back, her hands flaming from some of the alcohol that had spilled on her. She'd been expecting it. Before the flames had time to burn her, she rammed her hands into one of the buckets of sand.

The heat blackened Frank's features and consumed the oxygen from the air as it fed. He couldn't scream anymore, simply jerked against the knives nailing his hands to the bar.

Domi yanked the knives from his hands. "Bye, Frank," she said.

Released, Frank dropped to his knees, the flames burning almost two feet tall now, slowing as the alcohol burned away and the flesh beneath didn't ignite. The stench of charred flesh and burned hair filled the air, and the gray smoke coiled restlessly against the ceiling.

The big man holding the blaster on Shorty reached behind the bar for a pitcher of water the bartender used to make drinks with. He dumped it over Frank's head, extinguishing the flames and soaking the floor.

Frank wavered on his knees for a moment, then fell face forward onto the wet floor with a meaty smack. He didn't move.

Domi looked at the bartender challengingly. "Problem?" Her knives were still naked in her fists.

Shorty seemed a little stunned. He shook his head. "Not with me. But somebody's gonna clean up that damn mess."

The big man put his blaster away, then reached down and hauled Frank's corpse up by the belt. "Little lady, this one's on me." He carried the corpse out front, and Domi watched as he threw it into the back of a wag.

"FRANK WAS AN OKAY GUY, but he didn't listen well. Didn't know sometimes you just cut your losses and went on."

Kane glanced back at Chapman. Under the table, Kane's hand was on the .45, the barrel pointed at Chapman's groin. "You're not taking any of that personal?" His next targets were already marked in his mind, as well as an escape route if he lived so long.

Chapman leaned back in his chair. He took a homegrown cigarette from his pocket and lit it. "Coulda stopped Frank, I suppose."

"Yeah."

Chapman stroked his mustache idly and looked into Kane's eyes. "You gonna fault me for that?"

"Not as long as it worked out."

"Stupe bastard getting himself chilled leaves me a man short for this run. That's why I wanted to talk to you."

"There's plenty of other people in this bar," Kane observed.

Chapman nodded. "And I know most of them. All of them got big mouths. I show them what I'm doing, how I'm doing it, they're gonna come back to Peabody's, mebbe drink a little too much pop-skull one night and tell somebody else. Next thing I know, I got competition crawling out of my ass. Which I don't need. I got a sweet deal right now and I know it."

"You're not worried about me telling?" Kane asked.

"I ain't got that far with my thinking." Chapman took a hit off the cigarette and blew the smoke into the air. "Right now, I'm offering you a chance to ride shotgun for my caravan tomorrow. After that—well, we'll see."

"How much are you willing to pay for the sec duty?" Kane asked, trying to sound as if he cared. The hook was set. All he had to do was reel Chapman in. And the biggest part was getting an invitation to the caravan tomorrow.

And somehow stay alive.

"I'll be fair," Chapman said. "To you and me." He gazed up as Domi joined them. "And to your little pyromaniac."

Domi, her pale skin still flecked with blood, only smiled.

"I need a decision," Chapman said, "now. We're pulling out first thing in the morning."

Domi looked a question at Kane with her arched white brows, playing her part guilelessly. "Who we?"

Kane looked at her evenly. "We have a job. If we want."

Domi shifted her attention to Chapman. "How much?"

Chapter 10

Kearney waited while Carter, his second in command, switched on one of the battery-operated lanterns the Mag force had brought with them from Cobaltville. He stood at one of the folding tables in the makeshift command center they'd set up in one of the smaller desert caves. On the table was a map of the ambush site that had been chosen for the next day.

Carter joined him at the table.

"You've had scouts out?" Kearney asked.

"I've got them out now, sir," Carter replied.

Kearney glanced up at the man sharply. "I don't want them exposed."

"They won't be seen, sir," Carter said. "These are good men at ground cover. And I wouldn't have them out now if we knew where the enemy forces were."

"There's still been no sign of them?"

"No, sir."

Kearney gazed at the map again, harder, as if that gaze could rip the answers he needed from the paper. "During the last attack, how many were there?"

Carter answered without checking his notes. In the past weeks, Kearney had learned the Mag had a good memory for combat situations and action. "At least sixty people in all. The caravans they attacked had a hundred strong. The raiders went through the caravan like a grudge force serving termination warrants in the Tartarus Pits. What the raiders didn't take, they destroyed.''

''They had war wags, too.''

''Yes, sir. From the reports we got, there were anywhere from three to seven war wags. Heavily equipped bastards with guns capable of taking out a wag with a couple rounds.''

''But no air support?''

''No, sir.''

Kearney traced his finger along the path he knew Chapman's caravan would be taking. They'd leave Duchesne in the morning, travel east along the Strawberry River, then turn south along the river toward what had been the Colorado state line almost two hundred years ago. Cobaltville was only three or four days' journey for a slower-moving caravan.

The problem was figuring out where the raiders would attack the caravan.

''There's been no sign of the raiders?'' Kearney asked.

''No, sir.''

The answer made the back of Kearney's neck itch, something he'd learned was a sure sign of trouble. ''No scouts, no tracks?''

''No, sir. We've kept Deathbird traffic low, not wanting to scare them off since we've prepared for them this time. But ships' scans haven't picked up anything. Neither have the satellite scans.''

''So what do you think?'' Kearney asked. ''Mebbe they've got caves and tunnels under this bastard desert?''

''I don't know, sir,'' Carter replied.

Kearney checked the anger he felt. Carter didn't know and neither did he. Nor, he suspected, did Baron Cobalt. But where the hell could a small army of raiders be hidden that they couldn't be spotted by all the resources available to him?

HUNCHED OVER A TABLE, Lakesh studied the maps he'd prepared for the mission.

To the east of where the Strawberry River split into the White River, a washed-out canyon had been highlighted. Both Kane and Grant, based on their training, had selected the spot as an ideal ambush spot. The canyon, fittingly enough, was called Deadman's Waltz.

The caravan would be bunched up between the two rivers, limiting their choice of places to go. However, the raiders could come from the open desert to the north, or from the foothills of the East Tavaputs Plateau to the south. Maybe even from the rivers themselves, as Grant had pointed out.

However, there was no conclusive evidence the raiders possessed underwater equipment. All of their attacks in the past had been from land-based vehicles.

Lakesh sighed in frustration. As brilliant as he was, the answer to the present conundrum seemed annoyingly distant. War was more the sphere of Kane and Grant, which was why he'd engineered all the events that had birthed Kane as well as moved the man in his direction.

"How long before we have satellite contact again?" he asked.

Bry paused a moment before answering. "With the orbit the Vela is presently holding, three hours thirty-two minutes."

"Have you been able to lock on to the site the Mag forces have set up?"

"I'm working on it," Bry answered. "During the search we just conducted, I also picked up some radio burst transmissions. I'm trying to decrypt them and triangulate the sources."

"But they're close to the canyon?"

"Yes."

It was somehow reassuring to Lakesh that Baron Cobalt's military advisers had chosen the same ambush point as Kane and Grant. Yet, at the same time, he knew it meant Kane and Domi would be running even more danger to get out of the situation alive.

"Have you found out how many Mag units are involved?" Lakesh asked.

"I managed to ferret my way into the Mag Division's motor pool comp," Bry said. "I think I've found the authorization documents. I'm decrypting it now, so we'll know in a couple of minutes."

"Very good, Mr. Bry." Lakesh was impressed with Bry's progress, as their previous efforts at tapping into Cobaltville's Magistrate Division's comp system had met only with failure. "I hadn't considered the motor pool a resource we could use."

"It didn't occur to me, either," Bry said. "I didn't find it till I was checking recent promotions within the Mag Divisions. I turned up a man named Kearney, who I believe is in charge of the Mag force in Utah. While attaching all documents that bore his name, I found some recent ones regarding the motor pool."

"And you knew that the Deathbird we spotted earlier had to have been ordered. Impressive deduction, friend Bry." Lakesh joined the man at the console, listening as Bry's fingers clipped the keys in rapid syncopation.

Abruptly, the comp display cleared, revealing rows of names and numbers.

Lakesh read the sheer number of wags and Deathbirds Baron Cobalt had invested in the effort to bring the raiders to ground and realized the extent of the danger facing Kane and the others. It was staggering.

He moved away from the comp, his mind working rapidly. He paced restlessly, making his legs work. "Friend Bry, if those raiding forces do make an appearance on the morrow and we haven't been able to pick them up on the sat scans and the Mag force hasn't been able to seek them out, there's only one reasonable explanation for how they're capable to accomplish this amazing feat."

He went back to the Mercator relief map. Pinpoints of light spread across the continents and countries showed the location of the Cerberus network of mat-trans units. The known ones, he reminded himself. Over the decades, he'd realized even the Totality Concept hadn't been completely honest within its regime. One of the most frightening possibilities that had occurred to Lakesh was that no one had ever known everything about all of the projects, that they'd been protected by overlapping fields of secrecy.

"If they're popping into the area and out of it," Bry replied, "it only points to the existence of a gateway there."

At present, there were no pinpoints of light in Utah to indicate a mat-trans unit.

"When you remove all the possibles," Lakesh muttered, "then the impossible, no matter how improbable, has to be the answer." He grew more agitated when he had to admit to himself he simply didn't know if the gateway existed.

There were, however, no other answers. And what that meant for Kane and the others, he couldn't determine. He was even a little afraid to guess.

Chapter 11

"Tub big enough for two."

Kane looked in the corner of the rented room on the second floor of Peabody's Roadhouse where Domi was bathing in the large galvanized container that served as a bathtub. Since they'd come across to Chapman as a couple, Kane hadn't wanted to disrupt that line of thinking when the caravan leader offered to arrange for a room.

Rooms were at a premium in the roadhouse. Chapman had kicked out the man who'd been supposed to share the room with Frank and given it to Kane and Domi. If Chapman hadn't had the booking and gotten there in time, they'd have been sleeping in their wags or one of the wrecked buildings that sometimes served as campsites.

Domi squealed happily in the water, blowing wads of white, soapy bubbles into the air. She hadn't hesitated at all about stripping down and climbing into the tub.

Kane made an effort not to look at her as he stood vigil by the window. He peered down into the rutted street, watching a few wags crawl laboriously across the hard, uneven surface. A few more men and women walked, moving through the shadows effortlessly enough that he knew they spent a lot of time in the area.

"What about it, Kane?" Domi called.

"No."

"Water going get cold."

The bath had cost extra. Kane had struck a bargain with

the bartender, Shorty, trading the extraneous equipment they'd taken from Nell. The water had been kept heated out back, part of the purification system that Peabody's maintained with the river. Shorty had paid some of the regulars to haul the water up to the tub in buckets.

The bath was obviously an extravagance.

"Cold water never hurt me," Kane growled irritably. Getting stuck in a gaudy room with Domi hadn't been in the plans they'd made.

Domi blew more soap bubbles from her hand. "Cold cause shrinkage. Not good." She giggled. "Not flattering."

Kane ignored her. Domi had a way about her, an honesty and directness that he sometimes really enjoyed. However, those attributes could also wear on the nerves.

"Or mebbe you afraid you not stop with just sharing tub," Domi suggested.

In truth, Kane felt some stirrings of desire for the albino girl. He liked her well enough, and there was trust between them, both things he hadn't had in the past when he'd slept with whatever available woman who was impressed—or intimidated—by his status as a Mag in Cobaltville. Back then, she wouldn't have had to ask but once.

"You look fine," he told her.

Things had changed since that time. Including some of his own perceptions of self. Mainly, those changes had come about because he'd met Baptiste.

Again. He was certain of the fact that it was again. The visions he'd seen of past lives together weren't jump-inspired near nightmares.

"Mebbe more than fine," Domi suggested, and moved seductively.

Kane felt the anger building inside him. Domi was pressing the issue way the hell too far.

"Mebbe you like woman and candle better," Domi said.

She let her hand drift down to her sex, rubbing lightly at the soapy pubic triangle.

"No," Kane answered.

"Been long time since you got laid, Kane. Must be raging inside with need."

It was true to an extent. Although he was attracted to Brigid and felt that she was attracted to him, they hadn't gone beyond that. Except for a New Year's Eve kiss that had died a couple hundred years ago in a world that no longer existed.

Domi continued to touch herself, taunting him with her body. "Me and you," she said. "Tonight. Nobody needs know. I won't tell Brigid."

Without a word, Kane moved from the window and took Domi in his arms. She was warm and wet, smelling soapy and clean. She was as desirable as hell, and Kane felt the control inside him slipping as carnal need made itself known.

Domi smiled, snuggling in his arms, enjoying his attention. Her eyes were bright with triumph.

"Sounds good," Kane told her in a harsh whisper. "Mebbe we won't tell Grant, either. What do you say?"

Domi stiffened in his embrace. Her feelings for Grant were strong. Kane didn't know how deep they ran, but everyone knew Domi wanted Grant.

"When was the last time you got laid, Domi?" Kane asked. "Must be some kind of raging monster inside you, too."

She didn't say anything.

"So why don't you slide on over in that tub." Kane looked down into her ruby eyes.

Abruptly, she pushed against him, breaking the eye contact. "Go away."

"No games, Domi," Kane said, not releasing her. "Not

between me and you. Not between us and Baptiste and Grant. Mebbe you'd like to think about them going at it out there somewhere while we're in here.''

"Stop, dammit." The ruby eyes glittered with tears. "No fun anymore.''

Kane felt sorry for her then. For whatever reason, Grant was reluctant to return all of Domi's affections. He drew the line at physical intimacy.

Domi slumped out of Kane's embrace, settling back into the tub. She pulled her knees up to her chin and wrapped her arms around them.

"No fun at all," Kane agreed.

"Why you and Brigid not together?" Domi asked.

Kane considered the question and tried to find an answer. "Mebbe this is as together as we can be and still survive. Mebbe if we get too close, we're afraid there won't be anything left of ourselves.''

"Two become one," Domi said.

"Yeah, but mebbe on a level that'd be hard to deal with. We're good apart—each of us have our own strengths.''

"Hard being apart." Domi looked up at him, tears tracking her cheeks.

"Yeah.''

She was silent for a moment. "Why Grant not with me?"

Kane hesitated. "I don't know.''

"He say?"

"No.''

"Talk about it?"

"No. Grant keeps things to himself if they're his things. Even from me. It's always been that way.''

"He sleep with other women?" Domi asked.

"Yeah.''

"A lot?"

"Yeah.''

"Any since he met me?"

"No," Kane said. "None that I know of." He hadn't asked Grant what had happened when he'd traveled to alternate Earths, and he hadn't told Grant about his wild lovemaking with Brigid in an alternate world. He kept his things to himself, as well.

"Why not?"

"You'd have to ask him."

"Grant had a woman once," Domi said.

"Yeah."

"He loved her?"

"A lot," Kane agreed.

"Then why can't he love me? He was with other women since she left."

"Mebbe," Kane said quietly, "he cares too much to be with you like he was with those other women."

"You mean just to fuck?"

"Yeah."

"But fucking's okay. Find out if like."

"Evidently not for Grant. If he was there just to fuck you, he'd have done it by now. Hell, anybody would have."

"Had plenty offers," Domi agreed. "Downstairs, men said would pay big jack. Thinking about somebody wanting me made me even hornier. Miss Grant even more."

"Yeah."

They were quiet for a time, the sound of raucous voices in the bar below drifting up to them. Kane knew they were both hurting in their own way, and it made him feel less lonely.

THE FOLLOWING MORNING, the convoy assembled in front of the roadhouse. Kane would follow Chapman and the wags with the motorcycle.

After a brief discussion with the wag master, Chapman

placed his wags near the middle of the convoy. It was one of the safest spots in the line. Chapman's bribe was conducted in full view of anyone who wanted to watch. Jack called the shots, and no one objected. But there was still safety in numbers.

The wag master, as Kane discovered, took another cut of each caravan's profit. No one argued with him or with the amount.

Their wag master was called Macon, a wiry little rat of a man with a shadow of a beard grazing sunken, sallow cheeks. His gaze was always roving, and he never made eye contact with the people he talked to. It was hard to figure out his age, though Kane guessed somewhere between twenty and forty. Macon wore leather and carried blasters in shoulder rigs, on his hips and in his boots. Kane spotted at least one more blaster at the small of his back as Macon clambered into the prop plane moored out on the river.

Kane didn't recognize the plane, but it stood on pontoons near the back of Peabody's Roadhouse, rocking gently on the slow current. Fifty-caliber machine guns were mounted under the wings. It was painted olive green, the color mismatched in places where it had been patched over.

Once places were assigned, Macon fired up the prop plane and took off, the engine straining as it skimmed along the top of the Strawberry River and fought its way into the air.

Personally, Kane thought the plane made a hell of a target. But Macon had evidently been lucky with it.

Then, just shy of three hours after daybreak, the convoy got under way.

Kane followed Chapman's second wag, breathing in the dust and the strong scent of exhaust. His muscles creaked, still sore from the hard use over the past few days.

FRANK'S BODY HUNG from a steel cross at the top of the tallest hill on the way east out of Duchesne. Kane stopped the motorcycle for a moment and looked at the forest of bodies pinned there. He counted seventeen, but Frank's was the freshest, most favored by the cloak of scavenging ravens that had descended on the corpses.

The sign around Frank's neck read Raydir.

The blackened face showed red where the ravens' beaks had slashed at it, and the eye sockets were already empty.

Chapman came back and stopped by Kane.

"Raider?" Kane asked.

Chapman looked up at his ex-employee, then spit at one of the birds clinging to Frank's foot. Someone had stripped his boots and his pants. "Yeah," Chapman said, grinning. "I got paid a little jack for the body since he was one of mine. Don't tell Ivory because I got the feeling she'd want her cut. The other two guys that went up there last night, they weren't raiders, either. But Peabody pays for any bodies that go up on those posts."

"As a threat," Kane said.

"Fuck that," Chapman said. "As a promise. Also, seeing those corpses up there keeps the out-of-towners chill when they walk in."

"Yeah," Kane said grimly. "I can see where it would."

LUCKILY, EVEN THOUGH the headlight on the motorcycle was going out and the tripometer wasn't working, the odometer was. Coming out of Duchesne, Kane had marked the mileage in his mind. By late afternoon, they were three miles out of Deadman's Waltz, the canyon he and Grant had determined as the most likely spot for an ambush.

If it was coming.

Kane dropped his speed and slowly sailed back to join Domi, driving at her side.

She handled the wag easily, looking small in the cab as

it jostled and bucked across the uneven terrain. Her bandanna covered her lower face, and her goggles protected her eyes as the thick yellow dust swirled through the wag's interior. It was too damn hot to roll up the windows.

While Kane had been out checking the wags with Chapman, Domi had negotiated a deal with a caravan to haul the extra tires and parts they wanted to bring along but didn't have room for. She'd flashed the jack at Kane, grinning broadly.

Chapman had shaken his head, pleased by the enterprising manner Domi displayed.

Kane tried to peer ahead but couldn't see through the dust clouds stirred up by the long line of wags. Sweat drenched him, and the vibration of the motorcycle passing over the ruts and rocks went all through him, making his senses seem alive and numbed all at the same time.

As he watched the dust clouds spiraling up to touch the blue sky above, he knew they were clearly marking the convoy's location to anyone who might be watching. Not all of them, he knew, were friendly.

Above it all, Macon's prop plane sailed sedately.

BRIGID BAPTISTE TRAINED her binoculars on the line of advancing wags, anxious because the blowing dust made it almost impossible to identify the vehicles at this distance. She could identify the wag Domi and Kane had gotten into yesterday, but she wasn't able to confirm that it was with the convoy. There were too many motorcycle and ATV riders to spot Kane there, either.

Glancing overhead, careful of pulling the sun into her vision accidentally, she spotted the plane. Her eidetic memory identified it as a Cessna 180. Mil-spec wags and vehicles had been one of the first things any archivist had learned to recognize while working in Cobaltville. Information was the backbone of any operation, and misinformation was one of the chief weapons.

"Can you see them?" Grant asked.

Brigid shook her head. "No. How far out do you think they are?"

"Couple miles. They're not going to get any closer than this. We'll have to settle for watching them go by."

Brigid looked away from the binoculars, her eyes hurting. She wore a covering over her lower face so the dust wouldn't constantly be breathed in. She glanced up at the tarp covering them and the Sandcat.

The heavy tarp provided some protection from the hot sun. But it was desert-camou colored, too, blending in with the sand and brush around them. "Do you think the plane will spot us?"

"Not unless the pilot gets a lot closer," Grant answered. He peered through his own binoculars, as immobile as the stone around them.

Brigid glanced ahead of the convoy. From their position high up on the East Tavaputs Plateau, they peered down into Deadman's Waltz. The canyon twisted slowly through the harsh land, broad and gently tapered, flanked by rolling hills.

No one else appeared to be in the canyon. Lakesh had warned them of a grudge force dispatched from Cobaltville, but so far there was no sign of any imminent ambush.

Brigid sat in her grimy clothes and wished she could go bathe. She didn't like the unclean feeling and liked the sand in her clothes even less.

The lead convoy tipped down into the canyon, slowly stringing the rest of the wags through like beads on a string.

"There!" Grant pointed to the east.

Even without the binoculars, Brigid saw the sudden

plume of dust cresting the far hill. She lifted the field glasses to her eyes.

A line of mil-spec wags sped across the hilltop toward the convoy.

"They're not going to notice the wags," Grant growled. "Not with all the dust that convoy's raising."

"The plane, then," Brigid said. She glanced up into the sky and watched as the Cessna dipped a wing over and lost altitude rapidly.

"I'VE GOT CONFIRMATION, sir. The convoy is under attack."

Seated in the copilot's seat in one of the Sandcats, Kearney looked up at Carter. Then he looked at the comp display screen on the Sandcat. It was blank. He lifted the comm handset and was immediately patched through to the Mag Division in Cobaltville.

"Yes, Shieldmate," the dispatch officer said.

"It's begun," Kearney said, not bothering to introduce himself. They'd know.

"Okay, Shieldmate, we're patching the coordinates through now."

Kearney turned to Carter. "Give the signal. We're going to move in."

"Yes, sir." Carter sent the information over the comm band inside the protective helmets.

Kearney paid only small attention to the information going out over the comm systems. He kept his gaze focused on the comp display.

"The feed is through, Shieldmate," the dispatcher said. "You should be receiving now."

The display juiced, taking the data feed. The image immediately formed, showing the surrounding terrain and wags on the move. Kearney easily identified the convoy from Duchesne. His gaze swept up, taking in the advancing line of attacking raiders. He started counting the number of wags showing on the screen.

"Can you give me a count?" Kearney demanded.

"Roger." There was a pause.

Around him, Kearney heard Sandcat engines starting up. Then Carter green-lighted the six Deathbirds.

"Dispatch reports twenty enemy wags."

"Can you get a visual?"

Without warning, the comp display wavered and broke down for a moment. Nearly ten seconds later, it came back on-line.

"Neg on the visual, Shieldmate," Dispatch replied. "Something's jamming our access to the satlink. What you're seeing now is as close as we can get to observation."

Onscreen, the wags looked blurred and indistinct, moving from side to side and tilting back and forth as they raced across the uneven canyon floor.

"Dispatch now confirms twenty vehicles."

"All wags?" Kearney asked.

"Dispatch can't answer in the affirmative, Shieldmate. They all appear to be ground-based vehicles."

Carter gave the order for the Deathbirds to take to the air.

Kearney moved from the Sandcat's copilot's seat to the turret gunner's seat. He felt more comfortable behind the twin USMG-73 heavy machine guns and the special armaglass armor. He twisted his head, watching as the six Deathbirds rose in a flock and headed south toward Deadman's Waltz.

He waited till Carter slipped into the copilot's seat, then gave the order to roll. The Sandcat he was in took the lead, racing the five others and the three war wags. Even at twenty wags, Kearney felt the raiders were seriously understaffed for the engagement. The convoy would recognize the Mag wags and know help had arrived.

And the Deathbirds would make all the difference. Kearney smiled in anticipation, no longer worried at all. It was going to be a slaughter.

"THE MAG FORCE IS to the north."

Brigid followed Grant's pointing finger, spotting the other line of approaching dust instantly. Six Deathbirds shot into the sky, screaming toward the advancing line of raiders.

But the raiders' wags were faster, intercepting the front line of the convoy before the Deathbirds could reach them. Suddenly the convoy's lead wag jumped into the air and was wrapped in a wreath of fire.

Brigid watched the stricken vehicle spiral lazily in the air. The wag crashed to the ground upside down. Flames ran rampant over it for a moment, then it exploded into a giant fireball. Black smoke swept into the air.

The wags behind the flaming wreckage fanned out to avoid the overturned wag. Not all of them got clear; one wag, its sides looking filled to overflowing with ore chunks, collided with the burning wag. The driver hurled himself from the door as flames crawled up the nose of his vehicle. More men tried to scramble out the other side. By the time the driver slammed into the ground, the wag caught fire and exploded, as well. A series of detonations raced through the twisted frame. The driver made it to the ground, but the other men were caught in the series of blasts, dead before they landed.

"Carrying munitions," Grant stated. "Set them off."

The sound of the first of the explosions finally reached Brigid, booming over her like rumbling thunder. She watched as the ore blown out of the wag by the artillery piece rained down over the wags behind it. More wags went out of control, causing more of a tangle. She tried to find Kane and Domi but couldn't.

"They're turning them," Grant observed quietly as the cannonfire rolled over their position. "Trying to drive the wags back over each other, get them rammed up against the Strawberry and White rivers so they can pound the fuck out of them."

Brigid recognized the tactic as the one Kane and Grant had discussed during the briefing with Lakesh.

"The river will drown the wags out," Grant said. "Mire them down and create another blockade against wags that might have a chance escaping through the water. First thing the convoy people are going to try to do is get the wags in a circle, create some makeshift walls. But with the artillery these people are packing, they're going to blast the shit out of the convoy."

Brigid knew it was true. It was already starting to happen. And somewhere down in that rolling miasma of death and destruction, Kane and Domi were getting set to fight for their lives.

Chapter 12

Kane watched the wag master's plane as it dived toward the advancing line of raiders. He had to admire Macon's nerve. The plane was almost within a hundred feet of its target when a cannon round hammered it, knocking the wings off and sending the flaming fuselage screaming to the ground.

The ease the raiders' ground wags showed in hitting the flying target told Kane they were equipped with on-board electronic targeting systems. Nothing in the briefing Lakesh had given them mentioned that.

He glanced over his shoulder at Domi and saw her face behind the bug-spattered windshield. She had her eyes on him, waiting to follow his lead. He gazed ahead desperately, watching as the raiders' cannons shattered the front line of the convoy. The escape route was rapidly choked with disabled vehicles. Other wags ran up behind them, slamming into the stalled wags, running down drivers and sec crews trying to flee on foot.

According to Lakesh, the raiders had never gone in for wholesale destruction. They'd often killed every person involved in the convoys, but they'd carefully taken the loads. He didn't know why the raiders had chosen to make this attack different.

Chapman dashed out of the billowing dust churned up by the fat tires of the desert wags. He stopped short of Kane. "We're going to try to break through," Chapman yelled.

"It's our only chance. We get clear of here, head back for Duchesne. They won't follow."

Kane nodded. At best, he figured their chances amounted to a one-percenter. But it had been odds that had served him well occasionally.

"We may have to run a wag through it to get free," Chapman yelled over the sound of racing engines. Gunfire started along the convoy's front line. "We'll use your wag to run blocker, break a hole through. My payload can't get captured."

Kane nodded, listening to the sound of small-arms fire that broke out all around him. The convoy was still too far away from the raiders to do much even if they took careful aim. And careful aim was in scarce supply given the erosion of discipline in the convoy. The raiders worked with surgical precision while the convoy members fled for their lives, willing to offer up anyone else as long as they got away.

More explosions ripped through the convoy wags. Craters opened up in the sand and became new hazards.

"Get it done," Chapman ordered.

Kane dropped his foot on the gearshift and brought the motorcycle around in a tight circle. One of the other convoy wags nearly ran him down, causing him to lock tight on the motorcycle's brakes to avoid it. The motorcycle skidded like a protesting mount, then the ore wag passed him, hitting one of the cannon craters and overturning. Out of control, the ore wag slid across the sand and crashed into another wag, disabling it, as well.

Kane stopped by Domi's window, having to repeat himself to be heard over the pandemonium. "Break through the line! Back to Duchesne!"

She nodded. With a ragged grinding of gears, the big tires twisted through the sand, hurtling the wag forward.

Kane sped up in front of her, looking toward the south where the foothills lay across the river, wondering if Grant and Brigid had made it there.

Domi drove the wag hard, aiming to the north, following his lead as he sped toward the opposite end of Deadman's Waltz Canyon. She clipped fenders with a bigger wag loaded down with ore. Her wag shuddered and slipped sideways, unable to withstand the ore wag's much greater weight. Spare tires bounced crazily from the wag's bed.

Kane dodged hard right, barely avoiding a wag that had gotten turned over by one of the cannon rounds. Men crawled out of the overturned wag with blood flowing freely. One of them swung a rifle butt at Kane's face, making a play for capturing the motorcycle. Kane dodged again, yanking the motorcycle with him.

Domi hit a stalled fuel-support wag, battering it out of her way. The smaller wag rolled forward into a line of machine-gun fire an ore wag rattled off in the general direction of the raiders. The ammo had to have been equipped with tracer rounds because they stitched through the spare fuel cans in the back of the support wag, setting off the gasoline with a boom that scattered flaming fuel cans in all directions.

A cannon round landed in front of Kane and the concussion of the explosion almost tore him free of the motorcycle. He recovered and rode on, the falling dirt blown out of the crater raining down over his back and shoulders.

The convoy line had stalled completely and was almost turned in on itself. The wags at the rear of the convoy had started to turn away, but the raiders were already setting up an interception course that would reach them before they got around the bend of the river in Deadman's Waltz Canyon.

Machine-gun fire from the raiders chopped into the wags

leading the retreat. The .50-calibre rounds hammered through glass and sheet metal, shredding the flesh and bone beyond. Only corpses finished the journey living beings had started. The wags went out of control, ramming into one another and creating another jam.

Less than a minute into the attack, while threading his way through blasted and abandoned wags, Kane heard a familiar sound above him. He glanced up and spotted the phalanx of six Deathbirds bearing down on the raiders' positions.

The trap had sprung on the trappers. He smiled grimly, looking for a way out while Domi slammed through obstacles behind him.

KEARNEY WATCHED the Deathbirds close in for the attack. He manned the Sandcat's USMG-73 machine guns, pouring hot lead into the ranks of the raiders. Dust flurried up around them, making it hard to judge what effect his guns had.

Then the Deathbirds launched their rockets, unleashing hell on the raider wags. The raider wags raced through roiling flames, still on fire themselves. But they went on, delivering complete devastation to the convoy. The armaglass hulls of the lead war wags were proof against the flames, and only two of them appeared to have been disabled.

Kearney watched the convoy with some concern as the wags were blown to pieces. He'd planned on the convoy giving a better accounting of itself, of actually aiding in the Mag attack. Instead, very little effective fire was being returned. They were all running.

The Mag leader cursed, tracking a blistering line across the lead war wag in the approaching group. He listened to the Deathbird pilots talking to one another, delegating overlapping fields of fire the way they'd been trained.

One of the raiders' wags disgorged a small knot of men

while still moving. They ran immediately, taking long weapons cases with them that Kearney recognized.

Focusing his attention on them, Kearney pulled the machine-gun triggers. A double row of rounds stitched after the men, catching the last two and sending them spinning to the ground.

Then the rest of the team was gone, vanishing behind a sand dune.

"Vogt," Kearney yelled down to his driver.

"Sir," the Sandcat driver responded.

"Adjust your course. I want to get that ground team."

"Yes, sir." Vogt made the correction immediately, setting the track on the left side just long enough to bring the Sandcat around sharply.

Only the belts strapping him in place kept Kearney in the seat. They streaked in pursuit of the unit moving on foot. He called for the Deathbird's leader, wanting to get the choppers on line, as well, in case he didn't get the shot he needed.

Before the Deathbirds could respond, something flashed from the ground. It struck the lead Deathbird, shattering it into a million pieces that were claimed by a mushroom of twisting, greedy flame. Before any of those pieces had time to hit the ground, the second, then the third Deathbird also blew up.

From the telltale explosions, Kearney knew the raiders had come equipped with antiaircraft weapons. He cursed, the first real fear starting to flood through him. The course of the battle was changing rapidly. The raiders had come prepared for the Mag assault force. Somewhere in the Cobaltville ranks was a traitor.

The Sandcat hurtled over a sand dune where the men had run. The treads caught one of them, chewing him into bloody pulp as it rolled over.

Kearney spun the Sandcat's turret, turning to face the ground squad. He opened up with the machine guns at once. The heavy rounds bored into the sandstone side of the hill where the raiders had taken cover. Even as he struggled to bring his line of fire to bear, he saw one of the raiders shoulder a long tube. Then the rocket launcher belched smoke from the back, driving the raider backward.

The heat-seeker jumped from the rocket launcher, twisting only slightly in the air to lock on to its target.

The fourth Deathbird was a crumpled memory by the time Kearney found the range and blasted into the antiaircraft unit. His rounds hammered one of the men to the ground, but the rest went to cover. "Bring the Cat around!" Kearney ordered the driver.

Vogt hauled on the wheel hard, causing the Sandcat's treads to bite deeply into the loose sand. Chalky stone crushed in their wake, sounding like machine-gun fire from underneath.

Kearney moved the turret, tracking the antiaircraft unit. High overhead, the fifth Deathbird exploded, letting him know the raiders had fielded more than one antiaircraft group.

Abruptly, one of the raiders broke from cover behind a stand of sandstone and scrub brush that Kearney ripped to pieces with the withering machine-gun fire. The Mag commander yanked the guns around, trying to lock on the man.

Less than fifty yards out, the raider threw himself prone, then slid a tube over his shoulder. He took deliberate aim at the Sandcat.

"Incoming," Carter yelled from the copilot's seat.

"Shit!" Kearney screamed in fear and anger as he kept firing. The machine-gun rounds smashed through the ground toward the man, leaving fist-sized pockmarks to mark their passage.

A puff of smoke jetted from the rocket launcher.

Then the explosion erupted against the Sandcat's left rear tread, shaking the war wag. Kearney had a brief impression of the track coming loose, flapping like a multitoothed monster as it attacked the armaglass hull.

Although the rocket launcher warhead didn't actually penetrate the Sandcat's armaglass hull, the detonation combined with the shattered tread was enough to flip it twice. The impacts slammed Kearney violently against the armaglass, smashing his lip and flooding his mouth with the taste of his own blood. Only the seat harness kept him in place as the Sandcat came to a rest on its side.

"Shieldmate Leader to Shieldmate Squadron," Kearney called over the comm. "Leader is in need of assistance." He watched in helpless frustration as the raider troops hurried toward him. "I repeat, Leader is in need of assistance."

Only white noise sounded in his ears. For the first time he noticed that all of the comm channels had been jammed.

"Vogt, keep this vehicle locked down," Kearney ordered.

"Yes, sir." Vogt hit the sec switches, locking all the Sandcat's doors tight.

Kearney watched the raiders race toward him. The Sandcat was designed to handle a lot of damage. He told himself they could hole up there, wait out the attack until the raiders fled. But he couldn't think of what they might flee from. There'd be no other attack.

"Electrify the exterior," Kearney commanded. The Sandcat had the ability to channel all the voltage from its onboard batteries through the insulated armaglass. Anyone who touched it would get electrocuted. He waited, the small part of him that wasn't filled with fear relishing the moment the raiders touched the war wag. Chances were good that the electricity might be able to get a couple of them. Then they'd see about organizing an escape.

But the raiders pulled up short of touching the Sandcat. They trained their weapons on the armaglass ob slit facing the pilot's and copilot's seats. Normally the ob slit was proof against conventional rounds, but the raiders had come equipped with armor-piercing rounds. They chipped through the ob slit like a knife through cheese, blasting Vogt and Carter to death.

At least two or three of the bouncing rounds slammed into Kearney's legs. They felt as if they'd caught fire and gone numb at the same time. From the Sandcat's position, he couldn't bring the USMG-73 to bear. He flexed his wrist, popping his Sin Eater into his hand. He brought it up to the ob slit and fired rounds through the empty space, catching one of the raiders in the side and knocking him away.

Then a shadow filled the armaglass hull of the turret.

Kearney looked up and saw the raider holding an assault rifle pointed at him. The man stood on the ground, able to peer into the turret housing. The Mag knew the barrier wouldn't stop the armor-piercing rounds.

The raider checked his wrist, and Kearney caught a brief glimpse of the picture tucked into the plastic pocket lining the raider's flak vest.

"Throw down your weapon," the raider ordered. "You get to live, Kearney."

The man spoke with an accent Kearney didn't recognize, but he had no problem understanding the words. The assault rifle's barrel never wavered. The Mag commander hesitated for only a few seconds, then he disengaged the Sin Eater and tossed it away.

KANE WITNESSED the destruction of the remaining Deathbird as he raced for the only chance they had at an opening through the raider interception effort.

A heat-seeker slammed into the Deathbird as it tried to deliver its payload of antivehicle mines in front of the advancing line of raiders. The chopper fell to earth and bounced twice, the failing rotors shredding into shrapnel that chopped into the convoy wags.

Raider wags approached the fallen Deathbird and killed the gun crew as they staggered out. The only mercy given was a swift execution.

Kane's throat burned with the dust that had slipped in under his bandanna. He downshifted to avoid the flaming remains of an ore wag that had taken a direct hit from a raider cannon. The motorcycle's tires skidded briefly, then found traction again. He slid close enough to the burning ore wag to feel the heat from the fire. He roared past it just as the fuel tank blew and threw out a huge gout of flame. He glanced at the rearview mirrors to check on Domi.

Unable to cut the turn as sharply as Kane had, Domi slammed into the burning ore wag just as the roiling fireball exploded from the ruptured fuel tanks. The flames wreathed the front of the wag and splashed over its side as it passed. Then Domi was through, the clinging fire dying quickly as the splashed fuel was quickly consumed.

Chapman and his wags followed closely behind.

Kane scanned the line of destruction before him. Choices were limited. The raiders' attack had been devastating and thorough. A part of him acknowledged the expertise with which the attackers had arranged their assault. Burning and blasted wags blocked the path, and more raider vehicles were racing to completely block all egress from the canyon.

Kane spotted two wags almost still in line with each other. Dead men hung from the shattered windows, and black smoke licked up from the flames sending greedy fingers through the vehicles. Something more than four or five feet separated the two bumpers. Both of them were ore wags, nearly loaded. He wasn't sure if Domi's wag could smash through, but it was the only chance they had.

He waved at Domi, pointing.

She waved back, then accelerated, gaining on Kane's motorcycle.

Kane pulled off to the side, slowing to let her take the lead. If she didn't make it through, he could pick her up. If she survived the impact.

Chapman and his people stayed right behind her, dropping back only slightly.

Domi smashed into the gap between the two burned-out wags. Her wag shuddered and popped up.

For a moment Kane thought the wag wasn't going to go through. Then Domi downshifted and the tires grabbed purchase, bulling through the two ore wags.

Domi drove her failing wag through the widened gap, cutting the wheels sharply to head up the incline leading out of Deadman's Waltz Canyon.

Chapman and his two wags roared through after her, not hesitating at all as they sailed past her up the incline. Neither vehicle slowed at all to help Domi.

Kane popped the motorcycle's clutch and raced for Domi, his throat dry and tight as he watched the raider wags bearing down on their position.

Cannonfire erupted along the top of the ridge, blowing smoke and rock and dirt high into the air to create an artificial cloud over the area. Then the raider gunners found the range and blasted Chapman's wags from the incline. Neither of them took a direct hit, but the concussions threw both wags out of control. The jeeps had no real protection, though, and Kane guessed that the gun crews were dead almost instantly. The crates they'd been carrying spread over the terrain.

Kane thought Chapman got away over the top of the ridge, but the swirling dust made it impossible to tell. He glanced back at Domi, watching as the albino dived from the failed wag. She hit the ground running, nearly fifty feet from the wag when a cannon round smacked into it and blasted it to pieces.

Domi took a couple staggering steps, then fell.

Cursing, watching the advancing raider line, Kane hit the brake and barely managed to keep the motorcycle under control as he skidded to a stop beside Domi.

She glanced up at him, her beautiful white face covered in sand. "Fucking close," she said, obviously shaken by the detonation.

"C'mon." Kane reached down for her, wrapping his fingers around her wrist. When she wrapped her own fingers around his, he helped pull her to the back of the motorcycle. The smoke from the burning wag obscured them from the raiders for the moment, but he knew it was a temporary reprieve.

When Domi threw her arms around his midsection, Kane stomped the gearshift into low, then twisted the throttle just as the first of the raider wags whipped through the smoke blowing across the battlezone. A cannon round detonated thirty yards away.

Luckily it was a high-ex round and not an antipersonnel round.

Still, the concussive force almost knocked the motorcycle over. Kane threw out a foot and shoved them back upright as the tires found traction again. He went back the way they'd come, speeding between the two ore wags. Escape up the incline out of Deadman's Waltz was no longer an option.

Machine-gun rounds hammered the ground and ricocheted from the fire-blasted wags around them.

Kane drove, leaning over the handlebars so he and Domi would make smaller targets. He leaned out and kicked, forcing the motorcycle to stay upright, willing it to hold together as he raced for the White River.

Chapter 13

The raiders overran the convoy, blasting the few wags remaining in operation, executing everyone with extreme prejudice to send a message to whoever happened on the carnage that had once been a convoy.

As a raider wag slid in from Kane's left, Domi pulled the .45 pistol from the holster on Kane's hip and flicked the safety off with her thumb. Firing from the back of the racing motorcycle at a moving target wasn't easy, but Domi put rounds into the wag's side.

The raider driver moved away.

The smoke had dissipated as they approached the river. Kane spotted other wags from the convoy already in the water. The riverbed held a gradual slope, judging by the distance the wags had gone before they'd drowned out. And it was the low season, when the river was drying up from the summer months.

The river was the only possible escape. Even if the motorcycle could make it to the other side where Grant and Brigid hopefully were, the raiders would only track them down and kill them all.

Accelerating, Kane aimed the motorcycle at the river, choosing a section of the ridge that overhung the water.

"Go!" Domi screamed in his ear. She shoved the .45 into his hip holster and secured it, then wrapped her arms around him tightly.

One wag's machine gunner found the range, but he was

a moment too late. Even as the motorcycle left the ground, hurtling over the edge of the ridge toward the river below, Kane felt the machine shudder as at least two rounds cored through the rear wheel.

Kane grabbed Domi's shirt, managing only to get one fistful of material instead of two, taking her weight onto his back and shoulders, then kicked them free of the motorcycle. He had a brief moment to realize they were going to hit the water and to worry about how shallow it was.

They hit the water and went under at once. It seemed like only a few short feet till he hit the muddy river bottom, but he couldn't tell for sure. The mud helped cushion the impact, but it still drove the air from his lungs in a stream of big bubbles.

The water was brown, murky, hard to see through. Kane pulled Domi to him as he pushed up from the river bottom, seeing that her eyes were still open. She nodded at him, her bone-white hair eddying around her face.

Kane released her, then kicked downriver. She followed, swimming gracefully. A moment later, bullets ripped through the water where they'd been, inscribing white runnels through the murk.

Surfacing briefly to grab a breath of air, Kane discovered he was twenty yards down the White River, behind the raiders' line. Raider wags occupied positions along the river and machine gunners systematically fired at other convoy personnel who'd abandoned their vehicles.

Domi surfaced nearly five yards away.

"Stay under," Kane gasped. "Long as you can. Before coming back up. Get some distance. From here."

Domi nodded and disappeared.

Kane dived again, narrowly avoiding a line of bullets that slapped at the water around him. He stroked hard, taking advantage of the maximum depth of eight feet.

"THEY GOT AWAY," Brigid said, focusing her binoculars on the river's surface. She let out a deep breath.

Grant nodded, saying nothing at all. He hadn't spoken during Kane's and Domi's desperate run back to the river, either.

The sound of the cannon fire still thumped around them, echoing in the East Tavaputs Plateau foothills.

Brigid was unable to see either Kane or Domi anymore because they were underwater. The sun's reflection on the surface made focusing on the river almost impossible. She swung the binoculars back to the battle site.

The destruction was staggering. She'd been in pitched firefights before, battling beside Kane and Grant, but she'd never seen one on this scale that hadn't been part of an old vid she'd seen in the Cobaltville Archives.

"How long?" she asked Grant.

He knew exactly what she was referring to, just as she'd known he'd automatically mark the passage of time. "Less than three minutes."

All this destruction in less than three minutes, she reflected, keeping a distance from the mixed emotions running rampant through her. It was hard, even with her archivist training, to watch the brutality and finality dispassionately.

The raiders left no one alive. Almost no one, Brigid amended when she saw one of the wag groups unload and pull out a man dressed in Magistrate black.

She focused on the man, barely able to discern his features at the distance even with the high-power magnification available. "Do you know him?" she asked.

"Kearney," Grant answered. "I don't know him, but I do know of him. Bastard must have rated a promotion." He grinned evilly. "Course, promotions are probably coming faster these days with Baron Cobalt sending his little search-and-destroy teams after us the way he has."

"They kept him alive," Brigid said.

"Turn him into a messenger boy," Grant said. "To tell Baron Cobalt and the Trust how bad things were, what kind of opposition they're up against."

Two raiders dragged Kearney to a clearing within the burning wags. Brigid knew from the way he moved that the Magistrate had been wounded.

"They knew Kearney and his team were going to be here today," Brigid said.

"Oh, yeah," Grant agreed. "Looks like Lakesh isn't the only one who's got his hooks in Cobaltville's comm and Intel sections."

"How many wags do the raiders have?"

"I counted twenty. Mebbe a couple either way."

Brigid silently agreed. That was the number she'd come up with. Only three of the raiders' wags had been damaged. "If the raiders had gotten here last night or this morning, Cerberus redoubt's satellite systems would have picked them up."

"Guess that means Lakesh called it right," Grant said. "Somewhere out here there is a gateway we don't know about."

It wasn't surprising, Brigid knew. No one knew exactly how many of the mat-trans units had been built. Toward the end of the twentieth century, they'd been set up all around the globe. Even the Totality Concept itself had started to schism along faction lines. Groups had been hedging their bets, putting in gateways the other groups hadn't known about.

But the question then arose of where the raiders were ultimately from.

A war wag stopped in front of Kearney. His guards forced him into a kneeling position, their weapons trained on him.

The war wag's side door opened, and Brigid focused the

binoculars again as the raiders' leader stepped out. She wasn't prepared for what she saw.

The woman was tall, taller than some of the men around her, and striking. Her silver hair hung past her shoulders, flowing unrestrained, shining with a bluish cast that made it resemble a metallic casing. Her skin was warm bronze butter, and she revealed a lot of it in abbreviated Kevlar armor the color of blued steel. The armor had been deliberately chosen to showcase the woman's voluptuous figure, Brigid knew, not for protection. It left her arms and legs bare except for bracelets and knee-high boots of the same color. She wore a huge pistol on her right thigh. Brigid identified it as a .454 Casull, a five-shot revolver capable of taking down big game with a single round. A sword handle jutted up over her right shoulder. She looked surprisingly young.

"Fireblast," Grant swore. "Do you know who that fucking amazon is?"

Even without her photographic memory of all the faces she'd seen at Cobaltville and in files at the Archives, Brigid knew she'd never seen the woman before. She was someone that would be easy to remember.

"No." Silently she wished they were close enough to overhear the conversation.

PAIN FLARED through Kearney's legs. His guards had secured his hands behind his back with disposable mil-spec restraints. His fingers had already gone numb from the loss of circulation.

He stared at the woman before him, thinking she had to be the tallest woman he'd ever seen in his life. At least six feet, maybe a couple inches taller than that.

The Kevlar armor gleamed in the harsh sunlight, the deep rich color reflective. It scooped up her breasts, revealing a lot of cleavage. The bottom half of the armor was fashioned like a skirt that barely dropped low enough to cover her sex. But it wasn't just for show, he saw, noting the bullet scars on the abdomen and one breast. Surprisingly, there were no scars at all on her body.

"Commander Kearney," the woman said in a dulcet tone that was distinctly feminine.

He looked at her, more afraid than he'd ever been in his life. His throat was dry and it was all he could do to keep from crying out from the pain in his wounded legs. He'd taken four hits, but none of them appeared to have broken bone.

"I'm going to let you live to get a message back to Baron Cobalt," the woman said. "Do you understand?"

Kearney just gazed at her, trying to maintain his dignity. If she'd wanted him dead it would have already happened.

"You don't need fingers to take my message back," the woman said. "You'll speak when you're spoken to or I'll take a finger for each and every affront you offer me."

"I understand," Kearney croaked. She stepped closer, and for the first time he got a look at her eyes. Hard, cold aqua, the color of the Caribbean Sea he'd seen pictures of, gazed at him without any hint of weakness or sympathy.

"Good," she said. "My name is Ambika."

"Ambika," Kearney repeated, knowing her pause was designed to elicit response from him.

"Tell your precious Baron Cobalt that these territories in Utah are off-limits for him. There will be no trade from the mines carried east anymore. My men will inform the mining communities. Once they hear of the massacre that took place today, they won't trade with Cobaltville, either. Unless they want to die. And I will have them put to death."

Kearney breathed shallowly, trying not to pass out from the pain.

"Any Magistrate forces that attempt to infiltrate this territory in the future will be immediately eliminated," Ambika went on. "Tell those in the Magistrate Division when you get back to Cobaltville. Tell them that I've declared a special war against those who wear the black armor of the Magistrate and who seek to do Baron Cobalt's bidding."

"I will." For the first time, Kearney noted how disciplined her troops were. Their uniforms bore the colors of aqua and white in three vertical bands, two bands of aqua outside a band of white that covered chest to crotch. There were women, as well as men, their faces masked by polycarbonate helmets a deeper shade of aqua.

"Your wounds will be bound," Ambika went on, "then you'll be set free in a wag."

Kearney nodded. He didn't bother arguing that he wouldn't be fit to travel. If she was going to offer a wag and his life, he would go.

Another flurry of gunfire sounded. Kearney jerked in response, but the woman never batted an eye.

She turned and left him without another word, and the final killing stretched out around her.

The guards jerked Kearney onto his back and a med tech was called for. The man worked professionally, quickly and without anesthetic. In the middle of the med tech's ministrations, Kearney thankfully passed out.

SOMETHING LESS than an hour passed while Brigid and Grant remained in hiding under the camou tarp. They stayed still in the event that the raiders set out motion detectors to warn them of anyone who might try to approach.

"They're letting Kearney go," Grant said.

Brigid shifted her binoculars around and watched as Kearney staggered to a jeep that had been salvaged from the trader convoy. The Mag seemed barely able to move under his own power, but he got the wag going, heading east along the White River.

"So they are sending him back to Cobaltville," Brigid said.

"Yeah." He looked at Brigid and smiled. "The Cat's faster than that wag is. If we get out of here any time soon, it might be interesting to look ole Kearney up, see what the message is that he's supposed to deliver."

"I want to find Kane and Domi."

Grant nodded. "Lucky for us, the river's headed the same way. We'll find one, then we'll find the rest."

"SOMEBODY'S COMING."

Kane turned from the river, his eyes aching from watching the water for anything that might benefit them. He and Domi had floated downriver at least a klik or more, surfacing only to grab a deep gulp of air until they were out of sight of the raiders. A war wag had trailed along the north bank for a while but didn't wander out of sight of the others.

Evidently the raider commander was interested only in securing the canyon.

They'd been out of the water for twenty minutes. Along the way, Kane had pulled three corpses from the river, stripped their bodies of anything useful, then shoved them back in so they wouldn't mark the spot where he and Domi had left the river.

He knew Brigid and Grant would be along as soon as they could. Provided they hadn't been found out by the raiders. Provided something hadn't happened to them even earlier. He'd pushed the thoughts out of his mind time and time again, refusing to consider that anything could have happened to them. Grant was too well trained, and Kane believed his connection—whatever it was—would allow him to know if something really bad had happened to Brigid.

So far he'd added an M-14 to replace Domi's lost .30-30 rifle. They also had a .38 handblaster, a chopped-down shotgun with a pistol butt and extra rounds for the .45. They weren't armed well enough to withstand an attack, but they weren't helpless any longer, either.

Domi lay on her stomach atop one of the few hillocks that swelled up at the river's edge, a bare outcrop of sandstone blasted smooth by the wind over centuries. They'd chosen the place because it afforded a view of the river, as well as access to the tall stand of rock overlooking one of the trade routes.

Kane trotted up the grade, keeping low to the ground as he made his way. After staying out in the blistering heat and the dry wind, only his pant legs were wet from wading in after the last corpse. He held the shotgun at his side. It had five rounds in the magazine.

He lay beside Domi, close enough to the ground that his breath raised tiny plumes of dust.

The wag rolled over the desert erratically, as if the driver was struggling with the wheel. The driver was the only person in the wag, and he was dressed in the polycarbonate black of a Mag.

Kane considered the possibilities as the wag approached. He estimated the speed at around thirty or thirty-five miles per hour, pressing it, actually, for the terrain and adding to the driver's difficulty at controlling the vehicle.

If he had to, he figured he might be able to jump onto the front of the wag, maybe grab hold of the windscreen before he fell off. The other option was to shoot out a tire, but the sound of the shot might carry back to the battlezone. They'd heard shots themselves, widely spaced out now.

The wag kept coming, within a hundred yards.

Kane noticed the driver weaving uncertainly behind the wheel, a big man with a broad face he could almost recognize. Either way he figured it, he and Domi were better off with a wag than without.

"Do you see a spare tire?" he asked, pulling on the blood-spattered leather gloves he'd taken from another corpse. "I think I see one on the back."

Domi squinted. "It's there. Mebbe flat."

"Hope not," Kane said. "I'm going to try for the wag. If I miss it, shoot out a tire. One tire. Then cross your fingers we can change it quick in case the raiders hear."

"Shoot out tire now," Domi said.

"No." Kane handed her the shotgun and drew his combat knife. "Now I'm going to try to take the wag quietly."

"Jump on wag?" Domi shot him a look of pure disbelief.

"Not if you want to do it instead," Kane replied.

"Fuck no. That's stupe."

"I'll let you know." Kane waited until the wag was within thirty yards, maintaining the low profile. Then he pushed himself up, rushing at the wag from an oblique angle.

The Mag's unhelmeted head swung around, evidently catching Kane's motion out of the periphery of his vision.

As Kane rushed at the wag, the Mag's name suddenly dropped into his head. Kearney. Kane had pulled an assignment in the Pits a couple times with the man, but had never talked to him at any other time.

Kearney reacted slowly. Kane was almost on top of the wag before the Mag tried to pull it to the side and avoid him.

Kane pushed himself, summoning up his full speed, stretching his legs out as his feet pounded the ground. Less than ten feet from the wag, he flung himself forward.

Kane hit the front of the wag hard enough to drive the breath from his lungs. It almost stunned him for a moment. He grabbed the fold-down windscreen with his left hand, hoping the leather glove was strong enough to keep the metal from slicing into his hand.

He slid across the front of the wag, watching to see if Kearney tried to pull a blaster. His left boot dragged against the ground, striking rocks and creating enough of a drag to almost pull him off the wag.

Over Kearney's shoulder, Kane saw Domi stand and raise the M-14. He fought against the pull to yank him from the wag, knowing he had to either get on or get off before Kearney escaped the shot Domi needed to make.

Kane locked on and pulled, hauling himself up by strength alone. He got one knee up under him, staring into Kearney's fear-filled features.

Kearney tried jerking on the wheel, but it was too late. In the next moment Kane stepped over the windscreen, slapped away the man's arm and pressed the combat knife against his throat.

"Stop the wag," Kane ordered.

A trickle of scarlet blood started down Kearney's neck. He put his foot on the brake and brought the wag to a rocking stop.

Kane scanned the man carefully, noting the empty place on Kearney's arm where the Sin Eater would normally have been. He guessed the raiders had stripped him and set him free. Still, he was careful enough to search the Mag.

"Out of the wag," Kane ordered. He glanced at Domi. "If he moves when I don't give him permission, put a round between his eyes."

Domi nodded, holding the M-14 just out of Kearney's reach.

"Kane," Kearney said weakly. He stood on trembling legs. The white bandages around them were dark with blood. "I'd heard you were a traitor, then I heard you were dead, alive, and then dead again. Cobaltville doesn't seem to be able to know what to call you.''

Kane gave the man a wolf's grin. ''You had your head handed to you today, Kearney.''

''Guess there's more than one fucking traitor in Cobaltville these days,'' Kearney said.

''I don't remember you as being a right and proper flag waver,'' Kane said.

''Times change.''

''Not you. The baron must be getting desperate.'' Kane watched the anger sweep through the big man. ''No.'' He kept his voice soft and jerked his thumb over at Domi. ''You couldn't take me when you had two good legs under you, and you're sure as shit not going to outrun that bullet.''

Kearney relaxed. ''I've got to sit. They shot my legs to hell.''

Kane nodded.

Kearney did it right, moving slowly, keeping his hands in sight at all times, then lacing them on top of his head. Just the way, Kane knew, that he'd learned it in the Mag Division.

''Another wag's coming,'' Domi called.

Kane looked up sharply, spotting the Sandcat streaking along the desert on the other side of the river low enough to get a Sandcat through, but he didn't think any of them would have gotten away this late after the ambush. Still, he waited tensely while it stopped on the other side and the USMG-73 machine gun locked in on their position from less than thirty yards away.

Grant stepped out of the pilot's seat and waved.

Chapter 14

"Tell it," Kane instructed. "All of it." He and Grant and Domi stood over Kearney. Brigid stayed with the Sandcat to act as defense. In reality, Kane knew she didn't come over because she knew if Kane and Grant believed Kearney was lying to them, they wouldn't stop short of using whatever means they saw fit to get the truth.

As for Domi, she didn't mind torture at all. In fact, she could be quite creative.

Kane listened as Kearney told them of the ore caravans that had been raided. None of that was news.

"But then," Kearney continued, "the ore shipments started disappearing."

"How?" Kane asked.

Kearney shook his head. "Nobody fucking knows, Kane. That's why we were sent out here. To get the ore convoys going again."

Kane studied the man's eyes, noticing the way Kearney couldn't meet his gaze. "That's part of it. What's the rest?"

Kearney hesitated.

At Kane's signal, Domi flipped one of her knives into the sand less than an inch from his crotch.

Eyes widening, focused totally on the knife buried to the hilt, Kearney said, "There was a man named Chapman."

"What about him?" Grant asked.

"He's a scavenger," Kearney explained. "Up around Seattle. Place used to be some kind of comp design lab back before skydark. He's been bringing tech to Cobaltville, selling it straight to the baron's reps.''

"What kind of tech?" Kane asked.

"Comp progs. Hardware. I don't know, Kane. You remember how it is—they don't tell you everything, just enough to point your ass in a direction and tell you who to chill. Most of this I put together out of what little I was told or overheard.''

"Why'd they let you go?" Grant asked.

Kearney took another sip of water. His eyes were bright with fever, and Kane wondered if the man would survive the trip back to Cobaltville. "That fucking bitch wanted me to take a message to the baron.''

"What bitch?"

"Big silver-haired bitch running the raiders. Calls herself Ambika. Looks like no one I've ever seen before.''

Kane glanced at Grant.

"I saw her," Grant told him. "He's telling it true.''

Kane shifted back to their prisoner. "You've never heard of her before?"

"No.''

"What are you supposed to tell the baron?"

"That he's got to stay away from the Utah territories 'cause she's taking them over.''

"Ambika?"

Kearney nodded.

"She say where she was from?" Kane asked.

"No.''

"Do you have any idea where she's from?"

Kearney shook his head. "All I know is she's not from around here. Fuck, Kane, think about it. She's got goddamn mil-spec hardware. Uses bastard ammo like she shits rocket rounds after every meal. And a trained crew looks like they're getting three square meals a day and a good bed to sleep in. If I knew where they were taking enlistments, I might go sign up myself.''

KANE SAT in the Sandcat's copilot's seat and stared at the topographical maps they had of the area. Nowhere on the maps could he find a place where Ambika and her raider forces could have appeared from thin air.

He folded the maps as Brigid approached the Sandcat. ''Did Lakesh tell you anything he didn't tell the rest of us?''

Her jade gaze tightened and narrowed. ''You realize you just accused Lakesh *and* me of lying to you, don't you?''

Kane shook his head, trying to understand her logic. ''It wouldn't have been the first time Lakesh held something back from us.''

''But you also assumed that I'd held it back on you.'' Her words were hard, accusing.

Too late, Kane realized she was exactly right. It was a mental glitch, maybe just thinking out loud. But he hadn't survived this long by blindly following orders. His tone softened, though no apology was offered. ''How do *you* think Ambika moved her troops around in this area without being detected?''

''Through a gateway,'' Brigid answered. ''That's fairly obvious at this point, isn't it?'' Her sarcasm was biting.

Kane figured she had at least one shot coming after his own indiscretion. He let out a deep breath, trying to force the frustrated anger away. ''Has to be a gateway out there somewhere, Baptiste. The raiders didn't come from this direction.'' He and Grant had briefly explored both sides of the river and discovered no tracks that indicated the passage of all the rolling stock Ambika and her raiders had used. ''And I don't think they could have come from around Duchesne without being noticed.''

''We did,'' Brigid pointed out.

Kane squelched the immediate irritation he felt at her answer when it conflicted with the supposition he wanted to build on. "You and Grant were one wag, Baptiste. Ambika fielded twenty. The gateway has got to be located somewhere to the north. There's a mountain range up there."

"The Uinta Mountains," Brigid said. "I know. I looked at the maps, too."

Kane got out of the Sandcat. "Let's go back to the canyon and see what we can find out from there."

"I don't think that's a good idea," she replied.

"It probably isn't. Ambika could have positioned guards to cover her tracks. If there's a gateway up here that nobody knows about it, it's going to be protected." Kane gave her a hard look. "But it's the only way we're going to find out anything. It's a slim chance at best."

"A real one-percenter," Brigid told him.

He gave her a look, checking to see if she was still being sarcastic. But nothing in her green eyes or the set of her mouth gave her away. He thought she was the most desirable woman he'd ever seen, and the most damnably frustrating.

"Yeah," he told her, "a real one-percenter."

Brigid held his gaze for a moment as if challenging him. Then she looked at Kearney, still under guard from Domi. "What are you going to do with Kearney?"

"I'm going to give him some supplies," Kane said. "Give him a couple pills to keep his pain down to a manageable level and hope like hell he makes it to Cobaltville before he dies."

"Why?"

Kane gave her a crooked grin. "Don't worry, Baptiste, I'm not getting soft. He's got a message to deliver to the baron and I want to help see that it's delivered."

"Right," Brigid replied. "You wouldn't want to spoil

that ruthless-bastard image you've cultivated.'' She turned and walked away before Kane could respond.

LAKESH STOOD through force of will alone. He gazed over Bry's shoulder and waited for the satellite to come on-line and let them know what had happened in Deadman's Waltz Canyon.

"Have you slept?"

Glancing over his shoulder, Lakesh saw DeFore standing behind him. "Yesterday, my dear doctor. Thanks for your concern."

"Yesterday isn't good enough." DeFore came around beside him, automatically reaching to snare one of his skinny arms and start taking his pulse.

Lakesh politely and firmly retracted his arm from her grip. "Dear lady, there have been far too many things to do to consider sleep."

"He caught a couple twenty-minute naps in one of the chairs," Bry said.

"You haven't had any sleep, either?"

The little comp tech shook his head. "Too much to do."

"You can't keep pushing yourself, Lakesh." DeFore's voice carried real concern.

"Thank you for feeling protective," Lakesh said, "but I've been judging what I could and couldn't do for far too many years to be surprised, and I refuse to knuckle under to the ravages of time while I can still think."

"Have you heard of a simple principle of diminishing returns?" DeFore asked.

"Reaganomics," Lakesh replied. "Of course, he circumvented that by putting more money into the country, then devaluing the dollar."

DeFore hesitated, then spoke again in a softer tone. "You

push yourself too hard, and one day you're not going to be there when they do need you."

Lakesh nodded at the display screen. "They need me now. Even as we speak, a Deathbird contingent is streaking toward the region where they are. They're answering the plea for assistance that came from the Magistrate force already there. Kane and the others don't know that, though I am hoping they've taken that into consideration."

"Contact them," DeFore said. "Tell them to get out of there and get some sleep."

"We can't, my dear doctor," Lakesh said, watching as the display screen cleared as the sat uplink came on-line. "As yet, at least one of our unvanquished foes remains in the area. If we attempt to send a communication while they're possibly scanning the area, we could alert them to the presence of our people there." He paused, then spoke what was on his mind. "Provided any of them yet remain alive themselves."

DeFore eyed Lakesh calmly. "Even as good as I am, you realize that too much stress and lack of rest could cause rejection of those transplanted organs."

"Yes, I remember the warnings from the first set of organs I'd had transplanted. All I can say, my dear doctor, is that I yet remain." Lakesh remembered the fear he'd had when he'd first had to have some organ transplants after being revived from the cryogenic capsule. There'd been other transplants, just to keep him going. But though he could remember that initial fear, he didn't know for the life of him when that fear had disappeared. Or why it never returned.

"The raiders are still there," Bry said.

Lakesh leaned in closer, his eyes burning from looking at comp screens and the Mercator map all night. He spotted the wags highlighted on the screen. The satellite view was distant, pulled back to where each of the wags was reduced to half the size of one of his thumbnails. "Where are they?"

Bry turned to another display screen connected to his comp and console. "Past the Yampa Plateau. Farther west was a town called Vernal. Maybe there's a ville there now by the same name. North is the Dinosaur National Monument. Farther north is the Flaming Gorge Lake."

Excited, Lakesh asked, "What's the Dinosaur National Monument?"

Bry consulted the information open to him. "The Green River. And a quarry with a number of fossil remains of dinosaurs and other ancient animals." He scanned further. "It says that a monument and federal sanction was awarded to the site. Not all of the fossils were removed—many of them left visible in the different strata revealed by the erosion of the Green River as it dug deeper into the earth."

"Are there any reports among the Cobaltville Archives that mention the area?" Lakesh asked.

"I'll check."

While Bry was tapping out commands on the keyboard, Lakesh kept watch over the raider wags. They drove into one of the canyons. One by one, they began to disappear from the screen.

Chapter 15

Nearly three hours after the initial attack, a few of the convoy wags were still aflame. Black smoke twisted into the clear sky. A horde of vultures and other carrion birds warred with small rats and flies for the corpses that were already starting to stink from the heat.

Brigid controlled the nausea rolling in her stomach. Even the smell of smoke didn't totally mask the stench of death. In fact, some of the smoke contributed because it carried the taint of burned flesh.

Kane looked at the scene and seemed totally untouched by it.

His lack of reaction made Brigid feel resentful toward him. Kane was one of the most emotional people she'd ever met. Archivists were trained to suppress their emotions, to restrain their exuberances and their disappointments. Grant displayed some of the same reticence upon occasion, but not Kane. She knew from experience that Kane either felt something or he didn't.

And looking out over the battlefield where so many people had been killed in so ruthless a manner, he obviously felt nothing at all. It was only a further indication of the basic differences between them.

"How long were they here after the attack?" Kane asked.

Domi walked ahead of them, checking through the burned wags and dead bodies. Her enthusiasm for the scavenger hunt was apparent. She reached into an overturned wag and hauled out a body burned beyond recognition.

"An hour," Grant answered.

"They took the weapons," Kane said, looking at the empty supports on a jeep that had once held a machine gun. "Ammo." He glanced at a wag that had its hood up, revealing the place where the engine had been. "Parts."

"Like a bunch of fucking ants at a picnic," Grant said. "They had power tools, Kane, hooked up to gasoline-powered generators on three of the trucks, used gasoline they siphoned from the convoy wags. Then they stripped the wags fast as a mech crew back in Cobaltville with a grudge force breathing down their necks. They knew their stuff."

"They also took time to kill every person here," Brigid said.

Kane looked down at two of the bodies splayed in front of him, one male and one female. Despite the damage the vultures had done to their features, Brigid knew he could still plainly see the bullet holes between their eyes.

"Methodical," Kane noted. "They took their time, even though it was only an hour. Every person knew their assignment."

"Less than a dozen people escaped this, Kane," Brigid said. "Doesn't that mean anything to you?"

Kane looked at her. "It means they're good, but they're not good enough to do it all. That's a good sign."

"Did they lose any wags?" Kane asked.

"Three," Grant answered.

Kane scanned the battlefield. "I don't see them."

"And you won't," Grant agreed. "They fixed two of them up and got them running again. Chained up the third one and pulled it after them. They still had people working on the downed wags when we slipped off. We thought they might have been coming around to this side of the river, so we left. I don't know for sure how long they stayed, but it couldn't have been much longer."

"How're the fuel tanks in the Sandcat?" Kane asked.

"We could use some."

Kane nodded. "We'll check the wags here, see if there's any gasoline left. When word gets out about this massacre, anybody who isn't known in this area is probably going to get a faceful of lead and get asked questions later."

Brigid knew he was right. It was one more reason for them to get out of Utah, away from the mining villes. But she knew Kane wouldn't, not now that he was on the track of the raiders. And she had to admit she had her own curiosity about the woman named Ambika.

KANE FINISHED topping off the final spare jerricans they'd rummaged from the ruined wags. Despite the raiders' best efforts, they'd missed five of the cans. Enough gas still remained in a few of the wags and their spare tanks to fill them.

He and Grant stored them inside the Sandcat's cockpit. The wag had a rear storage area where they could carry six extra troops on two sets of three fold-down jump seats, which could also be used as beds.

Brigid had stayed away from him as they'd sorted through the battlefield. He'd been aware of it, but he didn't know the cause. To Grant, Domi and him, taking necessary equipment and gear from the dead was a matter of course. Mags were trained to salvage equipment, to know what was repairable and what was a waste of time and effort to cart back. Domi had lived the same kind of existence only on much meaner terms.

He stayed conscious of the passage of time. Chances were

no one would happen along and discover the battlefield, but the raiders were putting more distance between them.

"Kane."

He glanced up from a mini-Uzi he'd uncovered that had been buried in the sand when a war wag track rolled over it. If he had a machine shop, he figured he might be able to get it into shape again. At present, the weapon would only be deadweight on the Sandcat. He stood and tossed it to one side, turning to Brigid.

"It's Lakesh," she said. "He thinks he knows where the raiders went."

"DINOSAUR NATIONAL Monument?" Kane repeated. He had the comm on speaker function so everyone in the Sandcat could hear and talk. He and Grant occupied the pilot's and copilot's seats with Brigid behind them, and Domi manned the turret station so she could watch the skies. They also depended on the Sandcat's own scanners and the satellite view Lakesh had. "What's there?"

"I don't know, friend Kane," Lakesh admitted. "There were no files on it at the Cobaltville archives. Unless darling Brigid remembers some chance entry that I wasn't able to turn up."

Kane flicked his glance at Brigid.

"No," she replied. "I'd never heard of the place until you just mentioned it."

"What about military installations?" Grant asked. "Usually the gateways are placed around military installations. Or government offices."

"There were none that I know of, friend Grant. Nor have I been able to find mention of any such places there."

"But you're sure the gateway is there?" Kane asked.

"Friend Kane," Lakesh said, sounding patient, "I

watched the raiders' wags disappear myself. There can be no other explanation.''

Grant drove the Sandcat north, putting miles between them and the battlefield. When they'd left, the vultures had descended en masse again.

Kane relaxed in the thinly cushioned seat, grateful for the Sandcat's small attempt at luxury. Days of riding the motorcycle had left him worn and tired. ''Mebbe they just entered a cavern there.''

''And should they have done exactly as you suggest, wouldn't such behavior still warrant searching the area?''

''Yeah,'' Kane answered reluctantly.

''I think we should return to Cerberus,'' Brigid said. ''There's some information we need.''

Kane turned in his seat and faced her. ''What information? If Lakesh had any damn information, he'd give it to us. Or he'd lie to us and never admit it.''

''Dear Brigid,'' Lakesh went on smoothly, ignoring the gibe Kane tossed in his direction, ''time may very well be of the essence. Bry and I are going to be able to give you a satcom linkup that will allow you to tap into Cerberus's files over the comp links there in the Sandcat. I'll notify you as soon as Bry has everything in place here. Such a comm band will have to be heavily encrypted and concealed from the scanners Cobaltville has in place.''

When he'd first contacted them, Lakesh had also mentioned the Mag Deathbird squadron en route from Cobaltville. Kane had gotten everyone on board immediately and gotten them under way. Even if they showed up as the smallest blip on a Deathbird radar screen, he knew the Mags would pursue at once.

''You don't know who Ambika is, do you?'' Kane asked.

''No, friend Kane, I honestly do not.''

''She's a bloodthirsty bitch,'' Grant commented. ''If she

could have, she'd have killed everyone at the convoy. Damn near did it as it was. She's going to be dangerous to be around.''

"I understand, friend Grant. Based on your description of her and her behavior, I think she'd be the perfect person to consider for an annexation of sorts."

Grant snorted sarcastically. "Tell you something 'bout that woman, Lakesh. She's triple tough, and she doesn't give me the perception that she's looking for somebody to annex her."

"There is an old saying," Lakesh said patiently, "that goes somewhat like this—'The enemy of my enemy is my friend.' What I see before us is a singular opportunity to perhaps enlist a fellow compatriot in our battle against Baron Cobalt. It's an avenue I feel we must explore."

"Ambika got army," Domi said. "She got hiding place. Mebbe she not feel so friendly toward us."

"Darlingest Domi, I feel certain that with all the things I have at my disposal here at Cerberus I can find something that she'd find desirable."

Kane noticed that Lakesh didn't say "we." When it came to plans and objectives, Lakesh rarely used the plural pronoun. Unless he was trying to win them over to his side.

"Why should we be interested in her?" Brigid asked. "She's running a high profile, something we've worked against. Remember the Magistrates that Baron Cobalt sent against Cerberus?"

"We should be interested because Ambika goes out and kicks ass," Kane said. "Something we're rarely in the position to do. We keep a low profile because we have to. There's not enough of us."

"Friend Kane is correct in his observations," Lakesh said. "It will take years to put together an army and effect a successful campaign against the baronies. I don't know how many years I have left to me, in spite of DeFore's considerable skills and my own tenacity for self-preservation.''

''Old bastard will probably outlive us all,'' Grant said.

If Lakesh heard Grant's statement, he didn't remark on it. ''I strongly feel that this opportunity shouldn't be passed up.''

''Neither do I,'' Kane said. He looked back at Brigid and saw that she looked unhappy with the decision. He wasn't going to argue the point. ''What do you suggest, Lakesh? A face-to-face with Ambika?''

''Should the situation arise and such action be warranted,'' Lakesh answered. ''I leave that decision in your hands.''

Kane refrained from making the observation that there had been damn few decisions left in their hands about the whole matter. But for now, Lakesh's agenda met his. Ambika was a possibility that had to be investigated, weighed and judged.

Lakesh had Bry send the coordinates where Ambika's forces had disappeared, then signed off. Even with the comm band encrypted, they ran the risk of the arriving Mag force from Cobaltville tracing the communications.

''Lakesh said there were twenty-seven wags that disappeared up there,'' Grant said. ''Brigid and I only counted twenty.''

Kane grinned. ''Then she managed to salvage seven from the convoy.''

''Two of the Sandcats were missing,'' Brigid said. ''Grant and I counted six. Only four were there now.''

''I'm impressed,'' Kane admitted. ''She took out the Mag force and the convoy, and drove away with a thirty percent increase on her rolling stock.''

"Being destructive doesn't mean she would be a good investment for us," Brigid said.

"It's not just about being destructive," Kane said. "Ambika rolled into this hellzone knowing it was a trap. She pulled the Mag's teeth, quashed the convoy and netted an increase of ordnance and transportation. That's strategy, Baptiste, and a hell of a lot of courage. I do respect that. I respect the hell out of it."

"She performed executions at the end of it," Brigid argued. "Chilling all those people wasn't necessary."

"It was if you wanted to send a message no one could ignore," Kane told her.

Brigid was quiet for a moment. "That's right. I suppose you've got experience in that, don't you?" Before he could say anything, she went back to the storage compartment.

Kane let out a tense breath, curbing the impulse to say anything. The Sandcat was too damn small and they had too far to go to express the frustration and anger her words had stirred up in him. He glanced over at Grant.

Wisely, Grant said nothing.

KANE GAZED OUT at the rolling hills and plunging canyons. Trees covered the landscape, green and tall, filled with dank shadows. They'd entered the tree line less than an hour ago. The battlezone at Deadman's Waltz Canyon lay two and a half hours' hard travel behind them.

Night was starting to touch the eastern sky, stabbing shards of obsidian into the deepening plum color.

Consulting the night sight provided by the screen on the heads-up display over the Sandcat's ob slit, Kane confirmed what he was seeing against what the sensors scanned. He had it set for thermographic properties, with an alarm tagged for anything larger than a racoon. They'd spotted plenty of those. When they'd first entered the forest, it had been squirrels. Now it was racoons.

The trail he followed wasn't clearly marked. The Sandcat had to push over a lot of small trees and tear through underbrush. The 750-horsepower engine met the task easily, but the ride got rough.

"Ambika must have another way into and out of the forest," Grant said. "She wouldn't take a route that would lead someone to her. Anybody follows us, they're going to have an easy time of it."

"Can't be helped," Kane said.

They crested another hill, and Kane peered down into the darkness before him. The Sandcat stuttered, sliding for just a moment before coming to a stop.

"Shit, but that's a long way down," Grant said quietly.

Before them, a canyon split the ridge, the ground falling away steeply. Treetops showed beyond and below the rim, stretching down into a darkness Kane couldn't penetrate with his naked eye. Even the night sight couldn't reach the bottom.

"Might be falling same time next week," Domi commented from the turret.

Kane locked the right track and powered the Sandcat around, dropping below the ridgeline and following the edge of the canyon at what he hoped was a safe distance. Tension knotted his belly, but he didn't feel the Sandcat wallowing in any loose earth that might slide out from under them.

It took a half hour to find the end of the canyon and get back onto the bearing Lakesh had given them. The forest deepened and grew taller. Four times deer set off the nightsight alarm.

"A man could live in this forest with all this game around," Grant mused. "Kind of makes you wonder why no one does."

"Mebbe we get a chance on the way back, we'll stop and check it out," Kane answered dryly.

"I'm just saying some of the miners have got to know about this place," Grant told him. "Got me curious thinking about why they wouldn't live here."

The forest rolled on by them for another forty minutes as they navigated canyons that looked as if they'd been cut into the ground with a blunt ax. There was no rhyme or reason to them, and Kane didn't know if they'd existed before the nukecaust or had been created by it.

He was drenched with sweat as they pulled into one of the small clearings they'd found along the way. He noted the path cutting through the forest. Closer inspection revealed that it had been worn down to the stone foundation, and something wet gleamed on the path ahead of them.

Kane got out. The Sin Eater was on his arm and he popped it into his hand reflexively. His finger rested on the abbreviated firing stud by the time his boots touched the ground. He went forward, his pointman's senses alert to all the movement in the forest around them. So far, all they'd seen was animals.

Movement burst through the treetops, coming in from the left.

Kane raised his arm, tracking the motion with the Sin Eater automatically, knowing Grant had stepped over to cover his back. Domi held the USMG-73 on the Sandcat.

A large owl fanned its wings out suddenly, grabbing a tree branch overhead with its thick claws. Kane had his sights set in the center of its body.

"Clear," he told Grant, lapsing into Mag terminology out of habit.

"Clear," Grant answered.

Kane walked forward to the gleaming spot in the middle of the road. Now that he was looking for them, he saw some behind them, and others yet coming. He knelt in a crouch he could move out of at a moment's notice and dragged his fingers through the wet spot. It was slick between his fingers, and smelling it identified it at once.

"Oil," he told Grant. "One or more of the wags Ambika took is leaking."

The big man smiled. "At least we know we're on the right track."

They returned to the Sandcat and started forward again. With the coordinates Lakesh had given them, forward was the only way to go.

Chapter 16

The trail played out less than a mile farther on, dead-ending up against a stone wall that rose over a hundred feet nearly straight up.

Kane let the Sandcat idle while they surveyed the area.

The trail remained narrow up to the point it ended against the rock wall. Oil spots dotted the stone road, mute testimony that the wags had passed that way. But there was no indication where they'd gone.

"Mebbe a lift of some sort," Grant suggested. "There could be a cave higher up."

"A lift to move twenty-seven wags?" Kane shook his head. "Even if it was motorized and still in good shape, you're talking about a hell of a lot of time."

"Then mebbe they just vanished," Grant said irritably. "You figure it out."

"Perhaps," Brigid spoke up, "you could try looking at the night-sight display."

Kane did. The display was set up to read thermographic signatures, as well as offering the night-sight capability. It showed the wall exactly as Kane saw it—except with one difference.

On the screen, a low rectangular spot appeared on the face of the wall, darker than the rest of the stone around it.

"Heat shows up on the thermographic scan," Brigid said. "Notice how the rock around that rectangle is lighter than the rectangle itself."

"So?" Kane answered. "The rock absorbed the sun all day—that's why it's still holding residual heat."

"Exactly," Brigid said. "It presented a reflective surface to the sun. That rectangle you see obviously didn't. It's showing the chill that must be inside the cave."

"You think cave's in there?" Domi asked.

"Yes," Brigid replied. "That's the only explanation for the shape we're seeing, and for the difference in the temperatures."

"A door?" Kane asked.

"Look at the ground," Brigid said. "If there was a door, there'd be scuff marks."

"Only if it opened outward," Kane said.

"Then there'd be hinge joints."

"Mebbe they're concealed."

"Either way," Brigid replied, "there's your entrance to the cave where Ambika and her army vanished. But I'm betting it's something else."

"What?" Grant asked.

"A holo imager," Brigid answered. "The quickest door to get through if someone was in a hurry. Drive up to it. We'll know soon enough."

Kane shook his head. "Even if you're right, Baptiste, you're only half right." He could tell by the look in her eyes that he'd angered her, but she kept it in.

"Why?" she asked.

"Mebbe you're right about it being a holo imager, but you can't just drive up to it."

"Gonna be boobied," Domi said.

"Yeah." Kane opened his door.

"I'll give you a hand looking," Grant offered.

Kane stood and breathed in the fresh air. It was laden with the rich scent of pine sap, not carrying the taste of alkaline dust at all. "Before we go in, let's get hard."

BRIGID WATCHED in tense silence as Kane and Grant dressed in the black polycarbonate armor of the Magistrate Division. And as she watched, she felt the old fear of the Magistrate image fill her.

Both men conducted the procedure in silence, their movements advertising the years over which they'd become accustomed to the ritual.

The Kevlar one-piece undergarment went on first, covering both men from ankles to wrists to neck, followed by the molded chest and back pieces. The arm sheathing came next, locking into place magnetically. Then the leggings and the high, thick-soled boots. They pulled on the gauntlets, then fitted the Sin Eaters onto their right forearms, testing the connections by popping the blasters into their hands with a twist of their wrist tendons.

Even when she'd been part of Cobaltville's community and thought she was doing a legitimate job in the Historical Division, Brigid had hated the Magistrates. They were egotistical, testosterone-laden brutes lacking qualities of mercy and compassion. A tool in the hands of the barons to batter a recalcitrant population into submission.

The first time she'd seen Kane he'd been in Magistrate armor. The first time he'd talked to her, invading her home, he'd been dressed in the Mag overcoat with the stylized scales of justice superimposed over a nine-spoked wheel. The Magistrate's badge stood for the promise the wearer had made to keep the wheels of justice turning in the nine baronies. And they turned them relentlessly, grinding anyone who stood in their way.

If events hadn't forced Kane out of Cobaltville, Brigid thought, he might still be a Magistrate. Brigid didn't like thinking about that. But it had only been the threats against her and Grant that had galvanized Kane into leaving.

He hadn't left on his own, hadn't recognized how evil the baronies were.

Then she felt ashamed for thinking that way. She hadn't known it, either, though she had started involvement in the Preservationists, the myth Lakesh had perpetuated to explain some of the things he did behind the backs of the Cobaltville Trust.

The black polycarbonate helmet removed the last vestiges of Kane's humanity. The high-planed face disappeared behind the helmet, leaving only a small portion of the mouth and chin revealed. The visor masked his gaze.

Kane and Grant hammered each other on the shoulders, making sure the armor was fully sealed. Then they popped the Sin Eaters into their hands and walked toward the blank wall.

Brigid watched from the pilot's seat, aware of Domi above her in the gun turret.

Kane stretched a hand out, reaching for the wall. He brushed his fingers against it for a moment, then shoved his hand forward.

It disappeared so suddenly that Brigid at first believed it had been lopped off. She resisted the impulse to look at Kane's feet, telling herself it was just an effect of the holo imager.

Then Kane took two steps forward and disappeared through the wall.

MANACLED, his legs throbbing from pain because the painkillers had worn off over an hour ago, Kearney was led through the brightly lighted hallway to Baron Cobalt's receiving room.

His Baronial Guard escort didn't help him walk although he was in obvious distress, but their presence was enough to cause him to reach inside himself and walk though every move was filled with mind-shrieking agony.

After Kane had let him go, he'd thought about running, trying to lose himself somewhere in the Utah deserts. Only there was ultimately no place for him to go. Trying to lose himself in the mining populations would have been a termination warrant in itself.

Nearly two hours after Kane had left him, he'd been spotted by the arriving Deathbirds. After his identity had been confirmed, he'd been flown back to Cobaltville. The Mags who'd brought him back made no effort to conceal how they felt about his survival. According to them, he should have died with his team. Wounds notwithstanding, he was no longer going to be considered one of them.

Kearney fiercely hoped that the baron would see fit to elevate him to an administrative post even higher in the division where he could make all of them pay for the things they'd said about him.

While he'd been sailing under the influence of the painkillers, he'd almost convinced himself that was going to happen.

Then he'd been met at the helipad by the two grim-jawed legends that escorted him now. It was everything Kearney could do to keep from throwing up.

The Baronial Guards grinned in obvious relish when they saw him, enjoying the darkness of his prospects.

Inside the twilight room, Kearney felt his legs collapse under him. The two Guardsmen reached for him, impatient.

He choked pained cries back in his throat, then forced his legs to take his weight again. Whatever his immediate future held, he was going to meet it on his own two feet.

He took a dozen shuddering steps, then got the rhythm again and walked through the four rooms to reach the fifth. He stopped in front of the golden veil. Long minutes passed.

Then movement shifted on the other side of the veil. "Kearney," the sibilant voice said. "You have failed us in many ways. You did not get Chapman's shipment through even though I expressed to you how important it was. You did not destroy the resistance, or show the populace of the mining territories that Cobaltville and the wishes of its baron are to be given preferential treatment without hesitation. In fact, you've shown only that we can be beaten. This is totally unacceptable."

"She said her name was Ambika," Kearney said, staring hard through the veil to see if the name registered with the baron.

The pacing stopped. "Ambika?"

"Yes. She said it like it was something you would know."

The baron said nothing.

"And if you knew that name," Kearney went on, "if you knew what she was capable of, then it was you who failed." He knew his words were sacrilege, knew it even before the lightning-fast hand of the Guard to his left swung up and hammered him in the mouth.

Kearney went down to one knee, refusing to go down all the way. The taste of blood filled his mouth. He spoke, and crimson droplets spattered the golden veil from the force of his words. "You sent us into that engagement undermanned. It was you that chilled all of those men. And you'd have chilled me if she didn't want me to bring back a message."

The Guard on the left drew back a boot.

"Wait," Baron Cobalt said.

The Guard froze in place. "Of course, Lord Baron."

The dimly lit silhouette approached the blood-spattered veil. "What message did she give you, Kearney?"

"She told me to tell you to stay the fuck out of the Utah territories. She said if you tried to interfere with what she's doing over there, she's going to hand you your goddamn head. And you know what?'' Despite the fear that filled him, Kearney unfettered the rage that boiled in a knot in his stomach.

"What?'' Baron Cobalt asked.

"I think she's going to do it,'' Kearney said with conviction. "The way she came out of those hills, out of nowhere and your people here couldn't even tell us they were there, and the way she slapped those Deathbirds out of the sky, she knows what she's doing.''

"Of course she does,'' Baron Cobalt agreed. "She's made of much sturdier stock than just human genes. Ambika is a formidable opponent, but not formidable enough to stand against me.'' He paused. "Sandstrom.''

"Lord Baron,'' the Guard on the right said.

"I need a man to hunt down Ambika. A strong man who can face her and be intelligent enough to work through whatever countermeasures she offers. Find me that man.''

Desperate, Kearney said, "Let me do it.''

"You?'' The baron sounded genuinely amused. "You come back to this ville, to my private chambers, a disgrace, Kearney. And you speak sedition in my presence. *My* presence.'' The musical voice rolled thunder. "You've suffered to live better than many others in Cobaltville by my choosing. Not yours. *Never* yours.''

"Give me the chance, Lord Baron,'' Kearney pleaded. Now that he'd vented his anger, he regretted his actions. He was aware of how badly his legs hurt, of how weak he'd become.

"To embarrass me further? Possibly to betray me?''

"I won't do that, Lord Baron.''

"No,'' Baron Cobalt said coldly. "You won't.''

From the corner of his eye, Kearney saw Sandstrom move. The combat knife glinted in his hand. Kearney felt the impact on the underside of his chin, then a cold numbness spread rapidly up from his chin to his mouth, past his sinus cavities and up into his brain.

Blood washed away his vision. Even in dying, there was a part of him that wanted to laugh. He hadn't mentioned Kane to the baron, hadn't told him that Kane had been there, as well.

And if Kane and Ambika got together, there'd be no stopping the judgment that would descend on the baron. Kearney wished them both well, prayed that they would take his vengeance for him, then felt the waiting blackness take him into its cold embrace.

KANE GRABBED a fistful of dust from the road and threw it before him. The powderlike dust swirled through the air in front of him, then collided with the light beams that crisscrossed the open space on the other side of the holo wall.

Despite the gray-black dust, the electric-eye beams glowed with a pale indigo tint.

"Nice," Grant growled. "They've also got subsonic emitters just inside the doorway to keep out the animals and insects."

Kane nodded. He'd seen the sonic emitters himself, knowing they'd been designed to operate on a multiband pulse that would be heard by everything except a human.

"If we'd rolled through the doorway without checking," Grant said, playing a microlight over the explosives mounted on the walls, floor and ceiling on the other side of the electric-eye beams, "we'd have been buried under a ton of rock. It would have been an inconvenience to Ambika to dig it back out again if she wanted, but it would have shut down immediate pursuit and probably sent a signal to her."

"There's a sec cam." Kane pointed his own microlight

on the small unit mounted high on the craggy wall behind the beams.

On the other side of the wall of light beams, the cave stretched back and curved around to the left, disappearing into the darkness.

"If someone was watching," Grant said, "they'd have sent someone by now."

Kane nodded in agreement. Even though they hadn't found them, he was certain sec cameras were mounted along the road they'd come up on, as well. Ambika had seemed too good at her chosen vocation to have missed something like that. Since they hadn't run into opposition, it stood to reason that no one was inside the cave.

"Let's get the electric eyes disarmed," he told Grant. As Mags, they'd both been trained to set and disable devices similar to the ones in the cave. He activated the comm-link in the helmet. "Baptiste."

BRIGID LISTENED while Kane tersely told her what they faced inside the cave. When he finished, she turned her attention back to the comp unit in the back of the Sandcat. She wore the rectangular-lensed glasses that had been her badge of office as an archivist. However, her glasses hadn't been for appearances only. After years of searching through nearly illegible documents, books and comp progs, her vision had weakened, requiring the glasses.

The comm-link to Cerberus was being handled on encrypted burst transmission, making them even harder for any Deathbirds that might be in the area to find. And it would be damn near impossible to trace.

She established parameters for her searches, constructed the queries, sent them and waited twenty minutes for her results. The first few files she received had to do with cultural history and literary references to the name Ambika.

She spelled it a dozen different ways since they'd only heard it from Kearney, not seen it written—every permutation she could envision.

The references were interesting, but had nothing to do with the present situation. Ambika's name had obviously been chosen for a reason.

On her next round of searches, she met with some resistance. Error messages filled her comp screen, blocking her attempts.

Brigid reframed her searches and sent them off again. The error messages came back twenty minutes later, but this time they included file extensions where the errors had occurred. She read through them, and fear ran gossamer tendrils down her spine.

Error reading
@#$(f&%$*ile#()@ "Over:?<Pro<>":<)*ject:<
@$#excali/.';:"bur#*$&,#folder<:".AMB@#%#IKA.
Re:@#%$:<>Con>#@% cep@!@>tion
M><<>?>Be@@o@*&$wulf@#&%#

She culled through the problematic symbology, looking for the words buried within. *Over Project Excalibur. Folder Ambika. Re: Conception: Beowulf.*

The Totality Concept had created Overproject Excalibur before the nukecaust. In its mission statement, Overproject Excalibur was supposed to map human genomes to the specific chromosomal locations. In reality, Overproject Excalibur's research attempted to create life-forms that would survive in a world laid waste by nuclear war. They'd been responsible for the first rush of scalies, stickies and other muties that had ranged over the Deathlands.

Intrigue won out over Brigid's fear. Lakesh had forbidden communication from their present location except by emergency only. She detested the burst transmissions. Waiting twenty minutes between was intolerable.

Kane and Grant remained inside the cave. Brigid caught occasional flashes of light that chipped away some of the perfection of the holo image, revealing it for the artifice it was. Up in the turret, Domi lazed back, eating soy-chicken chunks with her fingers from a self-heat.

At the end of twenty minutes, an answer took shape on the comp's display screen.

Search returned no results. Try again? Y N Abort

Brigid stared at the answer, knowing at the very least she should have gotten the same confusion of symbols. Someone had tampered with the access she had to Cerberus's files. And she had a good idea who; she just didn't know why.

Chapter 17

Kane guided the Sandcat through the cavernous tunnel that cut through the heart of the mountain range. His thoughts were as dark as the shadows that clung to the route ahead of them. Ambika's whole operation smacked of something much bigger than a woman risen to queen of the raiders.

He also didn't expect to find an underground ville ahead. The answer lay in a gateway and he knew it. But he had no clue as to how Ambika could have come by the codes necessary to use the mat-trans units. Those were closely guarded secrets, and they were kept through blood and death.

And the fact that she was using a gateway that even Lakesh didn't know about was astounding. Provided, he reminded himself, that the old man really didn't know about it. Or about Ambika.

"Penny for your thoughts." Grant sat in the copilot's seat, a Copperhead assault rifle lying loosely in his lap.

"I don't think I have a single one that you haven't thought of," Kane said.

The grade of the pathway descended into the mountain. Cracks were visible in the walls. Usually the surface of the walls was uniformly smooth, but some places bore marks from digging tools.

"Tunnel looks old," Grant said. "Except for the places where the walls were dug into. The curve we went around last time—"

"Doesn't look like it was part of the original tunnel," Kane said. "I saw it. Evidently the original tunnel collapsed sometime after it was built."

"A couple hundred years ago, mebbe. Which brings to mind, if everybody else has lost this gateway off the maps, how did Ambika know about it?"

"I don't know." Kane glanced over his shoulder. "Turn up anything, Baptiste?"

"No."

Kane heard the frustration in her voice. When he and Grant had returned to the Cat, Brigid had been moody and quiet. He'd left it alone, figuring she would tell him what was on her mind when she felt like it.

"At least," Brigid said, "nothing concrete as to who Ambika is or how this place came to be here."

"Nothing concrete?"

"My search tagged a corrupt file," Brigid said. "The file itself was originally part of Overproject Excalibur."

"Did you talk to Lakesh?" Kane asked.

"I left a message. He hasn't returned it."

The Sandcat rounded another turn, and the corridor ended in front of a pair of massive vanadium alloy doors. Kane braked the wag a few feet from the entrance.

"Looks big enough to take the Cat into," Grant observed.

"Then we'll take it," Kane said. "But I'm walking point. In case we run into trouble inside, we won't have all our eggs in one basket."

"Or blasters," Grant added.

Kane nodded. He pulled on his helmet and refastened the chin guard. Then he keyed the door open and stepped out.

"Brigid," Grant called.

Brigid slid into the seat as Kane closed the door. "Careful, Kane."

He nodded, wishing she hadn't chosen that moment to be

conciliatory. Walking into the redoubt, he needed to be all Mag, no softness, no weakness. And thinking about Brigid Baptiste at the right moment sometimes brought about both feelings.

He flexed his wrist tendons and snapped the Sin Eater into his hand. Then he walked forward, his pointman's senses alive and alert. He paused by the keypad next to the vanadium doors, listening. There was no sound except for the Sandcat's engine.

Turning his left side to the doors, he punched in the 5-3-2 sequence that unlocked every redoubt door he'd been to. The doors separated and rolled back into housings inside the rock quickly and quietly. As if they'd just had maintenance, Kane couldn't help thinking.

Weak light spilled out of the room and threw a rectangle over the Sandcat's nose. The corridor stretched on beyond it like a colossal throat.

Left hand cupping his right, securing the Sin Eater in a Mag-taught shooter's hold, Kane went forward, knowing Grant would signal Brigid when to move after him.

The redoubt walls were crisp and clean. There were no graffiti and no signs of disuse. Only the weak illumination suggested that it might not be working up to standard. Some of the redoubts had been lost in the nukecaust. Others had been destroyed by the people who'd taken refuge inside them, gone crazy from being sealed up in the ground in the middle of a nuke zone, everyone they'd known dead or dying outside the prison they'd chosen. Still others hadn't been able to maintain their integrity, and time and bandits had taken care of gutting them.

A clear armaglass plaque on the wall drew Kane's attention. In disbelief, he saw that the redoubt's layout was delineated on the paper inside the plaque.

There were three main branches. One led to the med tech

lab, one to the armory and one to the gateway. All of them were clearly, unbelievably, marked. The designation above it read Redoubt Oscar. At some time in the past, someone had crossed out *Oscar* with two smears of black paint and replaced it with the word *Minerva*.

Brigid's voice whispered over his comm-link. "Minerva, the Roman goddess of wisdom. That may be significant."

"How so?"

"We'll probably find out sooner than later."

He turned away, choosing to go down the middle corridor, the one that had the familiar oil spots they'd tracked. According to the map, it led to the gateway. He kept walking, the Sandcat lumbering after him like some great beast.

"OKAY, SO NOBODY'S HERE. So what do we do now?" Grant asked.

Kane looked around the gateway's control room. Compared to some that he'd been in, this one was huge. Comp equipment, consoles, dials and switches filled all the walls around the room. The massive mat-trans unit dominated the whole center of the room, leaving little space to navigate among all the equipment and desks.

Judging from the oil spots on the concrete floor, Ambika had rolled her army into the gateway and sent them through. The mat-trans unit was only large enough to hold one of the wags at a time, but Kane knew they'd had plenty of time to be long gone.

They'd confirmed that no one else was in the redoubt. The med tech unit and the armory were bare, all supplies taken.

Kane looked at his three companions, knowing they were turning to him to lay it out for them. "Staying here isn't an option, so we're going. The real question is where."

"I pulled the transit files from the gateway comp," Brigid

said. She'd spent most of her time getting around the encryption codes built into the gateway comp. Thankfully, she'd had access to encryption-code buster progs she'd designed that she'd downloaded from the Sandcat's comp. Still, it had taken her more than an hour to get the information.

Kane looked the question at her.

"Only one gateway code has been used," Brigid said.

"Can you tell where it is?" Grant asked.

Brigid shook her head. "The numbering doesn't have anything to do with the codes I know from the other gateways we've been to. It could literally be anywhere."

"We've found someone's own private back door," Kane said.

"Having that code," Brigid said, "we could make the jump to wherever it is they've gone."

"That's one option," Kane said. "The second option is to jump from here to Cerberus. Personally, I'd like to squeeze Lakesh until we get some more answers. He sold me on the idea of finding out what Chapman was hauling, and we did. We might not know where exactly he's getting it, but we know where to start looking if we need to. And there's the possibility that Chapman is still alive. There were a few who escaped today."

"Very few," Brigid said bitterly.

"There's a problem with making the jump to Cerberus," Kane went on. "If Ambika is as good as she seems to be, she might be able to get the Cerberus code from the gateway comp here after we go. We'd be letting her into our back door."

"We could try to get back to the Darks overland in the Cat," Grant said, "but I really wouldn't want to now. Baron Cobalt and his Mags will be trying to make their bones over the massacre that took place today."

"Hole up here few days," Domi suggested. "Then go to Darks."

"That makes sense," Brigid said. "It would be the safest course open to us."

"Unless Ambika decides to drag her army back through here for another run at Cobalt's forces," Kane stated. "If I'm going to be a target, Baptiste, I'd rather be one in motion."

"Moving targets aren't safe from lightning, either," Brigid said.

Kane glared at her. It wasn't her fault, he knew, but the anger at Lakesh's machinations demanded an outlet. "What we should do is jump back to Cerberus, let Lakesh deal with some of this shit he's brought down on us."

"As I recall," Brigid said hotly, "it didn't take much pushing on Lakesh's part to get you to accept this mission. If you want to blame someone for this mess, try looking a little closer to home."

"If he'd given us all the information—" Kane started.

"You'd have done what?" Brigid demanded. "Assumed you could handle it anyway?"

Kane curbed his anger, but he felt it straining at the leash. He let out a breath. "You're right, Baptiste. I'm as much to blame as Lakesh for us being here."

His change of view caught Brigid by surprise. "Maybe for us being here," she said, "but not for keeping us in the dark. I tried to get files on Ambika, but I was blocked at that end. Lakesh is responsible for keeping that from us."

Kane locked his gaze on the gateway. He couldn't keep up with the mercurial mood swings Brigid sometimes showed. What he needed most of all was a good night's sleep somewhere that he didn't have to keep a blaster in his hand.

The gateway's armaglass walls were translucent, as they

always were, but these were the color of fried egg-white mixed with swirls of pale blue. The door opened wide enough to accommodate even a full-sized war wag.

"If we jump," Grant said, "we can make our way back to Cerberus from wherever it is."

"Be interesting see where Ambika bitch ended up," Domi said.

Kane thought so, too. "Okay," he said. "We go. Anybody feels any differently had better speak up now."

No one did, so he drove the Sandcat into the mat-trans unit, parking it in the center of the six-sided chamber. Hexagonal plates studded the floor and ceiling.

There was no trace of any oil leak, even though the wag they'd trailed from the convoy must have sat on the hexagonal disks while waiting to be sent through the gateway.

Kane knew that whatever was in the gateway at the time of activation was broken down into its molecular components, then shot through the ether to the destination gateway, where it was reassembled.

Despite the fact that Brigid was certain they'd be able to jump safely inside the Sandcat, Kane ordered them all out. If the mat-trans unit chose that jump to get overtaxed regarding patterns in transit, he figured they stood a better chance on their own.

They made themselves comfortable, then Kane pulled the door shut, activating the jump sequence. The panels on the floor and ceiling started to glow, seeming to trigger the subsonic hum that filled the chamber.

Then white vapor curled down from the ceiling plates and rose from the floor. Fuzzy electric sparkles seemed to spread throughout the mist.

Heaviness settled over Kane, then the world spun away from him in a cataclysmic rush.

"LAKESH."

Wearily, Lakesh lifted his chin from his thin chest. For a panicked moment he wasn't sure where he was. He was so used to playing at a number of schemes, balancing them one against the other, that he couldn't remember when he'd last gone to sleep or what he'd been dealing with.

One wrong word at the wrong time, and the whole house of cards he'd built would come tumbling down around his ears. And the cost for his mistakes could be counted in lives.

"Lakesh."

He gripped the armrests on either side of him, realizing then that he'd gone to sleep in a chair. He turned slowly, removing his glasses and wiping them on his shirt to buy himself time to think, to remember. When he put the glasses back on, he focused on Bry across the room. He was safe, in the command center at Cerberus.

"Yes, Mr. Bry?" Lakesh inquired.

"You asked me to tell you when Kane and the others jumped from the gateway in the Utah territories," Bry said.

Carefully, the blood in his veins feeling sluggish from age and accumulated fatigue, Lakesh pushed himself to his feet and crossed the room to Bry's console. His head swam with the required effort. "You're sure they're gone?"

Bry nodded. "Just now. Only moments ago." He pointed at the comp display.

Lakesh studied the angular planes of the mountain that hid the redoubt. With the satellite feed scanning for the team's subcutaneous transponders, they had been able to pick up the signs even through the solid rock. The old man checked the latitude and longitude out of habit, confirming Bry's information.

Before there had been four glowing orange dots that had marked Kane and the others in the hidden redoubt. Now there was nothing.

"Where have they gone, friend Bry?" Lakesh asked.

Bry shook his head. "I haven't got a clue. I've widened the scope on the camera, taking in nearly the whole northeastern corner now, but I'm still not picking them up."

"They're much farther away than that," Lakesh assured the other man.

"You know where they went?"

"Quite possibly," Lakesh answered. He glanced up at the Mercator world map. "Try searching the Western Isles."

Bry turned slowly to face him, his eyes retreating from the comp screen. "The Western Isles?"

"Yes, friend Bry, the Western Isles." Lakesh ignored the other man's look, intent on the map.

Back during the nukecaust, when the bombs had flown, the Russians had also triggered "earthshaker" bombs planted by their submarines along the fault and fracture lines in what was then called the Pacific Ocean. ICBM missiles had pounded the Cascades, from western Canada down to California at the same time. The concentrated destruction initiated a series of active volcanoes, as well as earthquakes, that had ripped that part of the earth to pieces.

Inside the Anthill, a Continuity of Government installation constructed inside Mount Rushmore, Lakesh had listened to reports of incoming tidal waves from the Pacific Ocean that reached as much as a mile high. Pummeled by the volcanic activity, the earthquakes and the invasion of the sea, California had sunk. When it was over, the Cific Ocean lapped at the Rocky Mountains.

After a time, the sea had receded somewhat, leaving islands in its wake where most of the continent had once been. Some of the islands were the high points of what had been California, or regions that became more elevated with the destruction caused by the shifting tectonic plates. Still other islands had been created by the volcanic activity.

For more than a hundred years, the area had been rendered inhospitable by volcanic toxicity and rad fallout. There'd been reports from traders and scavengers of encounters with mutie beasts, stickies and scalies.

Baron Cobalt had never seen fit to explore what might be out there at present. The Western Isles remained a mystery, one that had never overly interested Lakesh because he knew how severely the cataclysm had struck there.

He had all but forgotten about the rogue agenda Wil Longley had begun while working at Overproject Excalibur. But Grant's description of Ambika had triggered Lakesh's memory.

He remembered Longley's reputation if not the man himself. He had been attached to Mission Invictus, a subdivision of Excalibur, working under Dr. Connaught O'Brien. He recollected rumors that Longley had been eliminated as a security risk.

The one occasion he had spent any real time with O'Brien, when they attended a Broadway revival of *Guys and Dolls* on New Year's Eve 2000, she had provided him with the true story.

Longley's nickname of "Wild Wil" derived from his tendency to make semicrazed leaps of reasoning regarding the Invictus project. Using O'Brien's researches as springboards, he made several aborted attempts to improve her mutagneic process and in the process jeopardized the entire undertaking.

Despite a number of reprimands, Wild Wil could not be repressed and he was dismissed from his post. He disappeared and a lot of classified data vanished with him. A few months later, the tale of Longley's assassination began circulating, but inasmuch as the missing data was never recovered, O'Brien suspected he had not been apprehended at all. She believed Longley to be in hiding, working on his own project, which dovetailed with the Invictus project.

Lakesh remembered how bitter O'Brien had been, but also regretful. She admired and envied Longley's genius at the same time she despised his erratic behavior.

Longley's research in the field of genetics had allowed Lakesh to influence Kane's own birth.

Bry's fingers tapped the keyboard in rapid syncopation. "I've got them."

Turning from the Mercator wall map, Lakesh consulted Bry's comp display. The four glowing orange dots had resurfaced. He glanced at the longitude and latitude. "Where are they, friend Bry?"

"As near as I can figure," Bry said, "they're on an island ten or twenty miles north of what used to be known as Los Angeles."

Even seeing it for himself, Lakesh thought, it was incredible. Will Longley had disappeared only a couple years short of the nukecaust. Most of the people who knew him had thought him dead, killed by the enforcement arm division of the Totality Concept. Human life had not meant much to a program whose ideal was the preservation of the world. Of course, looking back on it, Lakesh realized that the value of human life had *never* entered the equation.

"I can try to open up a comm channel," Bry suggested.

"What are their vital signs like?"

Bry accessed a pull-down menu and consulted it briefly. "They're all within acceptable ranges."

"Then don't try to open a comm channel, friend Bry," Lakesh said. "If someone in that area has access to a comm scanner, we might well set the hounds loose on them. Friend Kane will know that."

Chapter 18

Kane opened his eyes, feeling cold and limp, completely washed out. He took a deep, shuddering breath that felt as if it were the first one in a long time. His chest ached.

Brigid lay against his shoulder, still unconscious from the jump. She was warm against him, smelling of the road and the hardship they'd faced, and somehow smelling womanly even over that. A trace of herbal shampoo scent lingered in her hair.

Gazing around the mat-trans chamber, Kane spotted Grant still out of it, his massive arms dwarfing Domi as he held her. The albino had curled into a fetal ball against Grant's broad chest.

The Sandcat, though, looked to have weathered the jump just fine.

A dull headache throbbed in the back of Kane's head. He considered himself fortunate to be suffering only a slight headache.

Nothing moved in the shadows beyond the pale chartreuse armaglass walls. Even if it did, he wasn't sure he was in any kind of shape to handle it, so he didn't go hunting it. The only way into the mat-trans chamber was by the door.

The door was now on the other side of the room. Besides the different colored armaglass around them, the relocation of the door was a definite indicator that they'd made the jump. As a matter of precaution, he snapped the Sin Eater into his hand with a whisper of movement.

He knew Grant was awake by the slight change in the big man's breathing. They'd known each other so long that little things that others might miss spoke volumes to them.

"Anything?" Grant whispered hoarsely.

"Not yet." Having to use his voice made Kane realize how dry his throat was. He felt parched, as if he'd been without water for days. Concerned, he rolled his wrist over and checked his chron. Barely four minutes had elapsed since they'd initiated the jump sequence. He couldn't help wondering how far they'd traveled in that small amount of time.

Domi woke next, tensing for a moment, then uncurling like a cat, stretching unconcernedly over Grant's broad frame. Her movements became a little more pronounced, then bordered on the erotic as she pressed herself across Grant's groin, totally unembarrassed by her own behavior.

Grant wasn't amused. Or if he was, he didn't show it. He scooped Domi off of him, irritation showing on his face.

Kane watched his friend dealing with Domi. Grant had bedded women as a matter of course while he'd been a Mag. It was one of the perks and privileges of the rank. And during that time of wild carousing, sometimes shared with Kane, he'd never been hesitant about his own appetites.

That had changed when Grant had met Olivia. The woman had claimed Grant, heart and soul and mind, in ways that Kane hadn't understood until he'd gotten to know Brigid Baptiste. But Grant had seemed to understand Olivia, where Kane grew frustrated sometimes even simply trying to communicate with Brigid.

He didn't understand why Grant didn't respond to Domi's obvious interest. Then he remembered how Grant had been when his marriage contract to Olivia had been rejected by

the Mag administration. Those had been hard times, harder
even than losing a few of the friends he'd made along the
way.

Even as friendly as Kane and Grant were with each other,
Kane knew there was a distance between them, too. Enough
of a distance that if one or the other were lost, the survivor
could go on. Grant had had a hard time with that after Olivia's loss.

Maybe, Kane told himself, that was what the big man
was afraid of when he looked at Domi. It wasn't about what
he would be giving up in terms of personal freedom; it was
about embracing the potential for loss.

Kane glanced down at Brigid. If it was true that they had
lived other lives, that their bond stretched across centuries,
then he and Brigid had lost each other before. Or had they
never had the chance to have each other? Maybe whatever
tied them together also conspired to keep them apart. Sub-
consciously, he supposed, it was possible they both knew
that. To embrace those feelings meant losing each other.

He touched her red-gold hair, stroking it softly.

Then she opened her eyes and looked up at him. Realizing where she was, she pushed herself away. The movement was too quick after recovery and her stomach rebelled.
She retched, covering the gag reflex with a hand.

Kane pushed himself up and crossed to the Sandcat long
enough to get one of the wipes from the med-kit under the
front seat. He handed it to Brigid.

The nausea subsided after a moment. "Thanks," she said
weakly.

He nodded. "You going to be okay?"

"Give me a minute."

"Sure," Kane said. "Grant and I are going to recce the
redoubt, make sure we're as alone as it looks like we are."

"Do you know where we are?"

"Not yet," Kane admitted.

"If you'll wait a few minutes, I'll be able to go with you."

Kane shook his head. "I'd rather you and Domi stay here with the Cat. That way you can cover our backs in case things go wrong."

He saw the bright lights in her jade-colored eyes that told him she wanted to argue. But she didn't. "Fine," she said.

Kane took one of the Copperheads from the Sandcat and slipped his helmet back on. The built-in night-vision capability stripped away some of the shadows on the other side of the armaglass. Comps and consoles covered the walls of the other room.

He glanced at Grant, fully clad behind him. When Grant nodded, he opened the mat-trans chamber door and stepped out into the redoubt's abbreviated command center.

THE RECCE ONLY TOOK seventeen minutes to discover the redoubt they'd arrived in was laid out exactly like the one in the Utah territories. As with the other one, this redoubt had also been stripped of weapons and medical supplies. And no one was inside. The telltale oil spots gleamed on the floor.

Kane and Grant rejoined Domi and Brigid in the command center. He found a series of switches on the wall and flipped them. In response, soft light gilded the walls and removed most of the darkness. "It's empty."

"Know where we are?" Domi asked.

"Not yet," Grant said. "We could go outside and take a reading with the minisextant, but we were thinking mebbe we could get some information from the comps first."

"I'll see what I can do," Brigid said.

"We're going to move the Cat out toward the main corridor," Kane said. "In case somebody decides to come back."

Brigid seated herself at the console and tapped the keyboard experimentally.

Kane moved the Sandcat forward, effectively blocking the corridor's entry into the command center. If needed, the USMG-73 heavy machine guns could easily cover their hasty retreat while backing into the mat-trans unit.

"What about bath?" Domi asked. "Saw showers in other redoubt. Must be same here. I can use, so can Grant." She smiled impishly.

Kane considered it only briefly. They were in hostile territory, but they'd all been run to death over the past few days. The showers were close enough that they could return in a hurry, and there was the added benefit of mentally feeling better about the situation. Cleanliness had been beaten into the Magistrate Division, not because of any hygienic necessity, but because a soldier who was able to control his own environment, his own sense of self, felt more confident.

"There are sec vids on the main doors," he told Brigid. "I'll bring them up."

Immediately two display screens in a group of sixteen on the wall opened up to the left of Brigid's keyboard. They both showed overlapping fields of view inside the main corridor.

"This is the inside view." Brigid tapped more keys. "And this is the outside."

The displays were in color, but the night sky washed out most of the hues, leaving only grays and blacks. The exterior of the vanadium doors had been ravaged. They sat against a rugged hill, inset slightly. Old scars in the rock around the doors showed the effects of explosives being used in an obvious attempt to blow them open.

From the snug fit Kane had noticed when he'd inspected

the main doors from the inside, they'd held. "Can you rotate the cams, scan the territory around the doors?"

Brigid consulted a pull-down menu on the comp screen. "I can do better than that. There are cams mounted farther out that should give us a better perspective." She entered the keystrokes.

Almost immediately, four of the cam displays came up with Unit Unavailable written across the screens.

"They've been taken off-line," Brigid said.

Kane nodded. "Mebbe whoever couldn't get in through the front doors decided to take out their frustration on the cams they found." He turned to Domi and Grant. "As long as we've got visuals in here, we should be safe enough."

Domi gave a yelp of delight. "C'mon, Grant, you scrub my back, I scrub yours."

"No," Grant said firmly. "I'll stand guard, then you'll stand guard."

Domi was still wheedling as they exited through the door by the Sandcat.

"At least it's still dark here," Brigid said.

Kane was glad she'd broken the uncomfortable silence that had stretched between them. "That means we're still in approximately the same time zone," he said.

"We could try contacting Lakesh," Brigid said.

"Not until we know where we are," Kane said. "We're exposed here already. There's no reason to call attention to it. Can I get you something to eat?"

Brigid shook her head. "I want to wait until I've had a shower. Mebbe I'll be hungrier then."

"Okay."

"Go ahead."

"I'd rather wait," Kane told her. "A shower sounds good to me, too." He smothered a yawn.

Brigid looked up at him. "Didn't you get any sleep last night?"

"Not much," he admitted. "There was too much noise coming up from Peabody's. I couldn't believe Domi slept through it."

Brigid lifted an eyebrow. "You slept with Domi?"

"Leather it, Baptiste," Kane growled. "We shared a room. We were supposed to be together, remember? It would have looked suspicious if we'd slept apart. You're out on the road like that, you keep in mind there's safety in numbers."

"Oh." Brigid didn't sound convinced.

"She took the bed," Kane said. "I slept on the floor. Mebbe that's why the damn bar noise sounded so loud to me. You don't have anything to be concerned about."

"The only thing I was concerned about," Brigid stated coolly as she turned her attention back to the comp screen, "is the tension your involvement with Domi would create between you and Grant at the moment."

"Baptiste, do you realize you're insulting Domi, as well as me? Kind of like when I asked you if Lakesh had told you anything he hadn't told us."

"Domi has fewer moral compunctions than you do." Brigid's fingers hesitated on the keyboard a moment. "But you're right. I had no business saying that, and even less asking."

Kane struggled to try to think of something to say and couldn't.

"Go ahead and eat," Brigid said.

"I'd rather wait."

"Why?"

"I thought," Kane said cautiously, "that if Domi and Grant were willing to wait, we might all eat together."

"It'd be easier just eating as you want."

"Mebbe," Kane said. "There's a reason Mags were fed in mess halls."

"That's where the food was?" Brigid inquired with sarcastic innocence.

"It reminded you that you weren't alone," Kane said defensively. "I thought mebbe given the situation and the opportunity we have here, we might consider that."

Brigid didn't say anything.

Kane felt foolish, but his answer had been true. Over the past few days since they'd left the Cerberus redoubt, they'd all been stressed.

"We're going to try to find Ambika?" Brigid asked.

"Yeah. She's got an army out there, Baptiste, and she's been hitting Baron Cobalt where he hurts. Lakesh could very well be right in thinking that an alliance would be mutually beneficial."

"To what?" Brigid asked. "Even if Baron Cobalt could somehow be removed from office, then what? Someone would take his place."

"But they wouldn't be able to marshal the same commitment from the people living in Cobaltville," Kane said. He and Grant had considered the implications of such an opportunity. "Baron Cobalt rules because everyone in the ville believes he's some kind of deified creature. Not everyone knows he's a hybrid created from Archon and human genes."

"Chilling Baron Cobalt would only create a vacuum. Someone would rise to the top. Probably someone from the Magistrate Division."

"You could be right, Baptiste," Kane said. "But you've seen what's happened to Ragnarville after Tara chilled Baron Ragnar. Nobody there has the same power as the baron did. They're staging minor insurrections over there, and their Mag Division's more interested in consolidating the power base than in expanding their boundaries the way Cobalt is.''

''Yes.'' Brigid kept tapping the keyboard, her attention divided between him and the comp.

''Cobalt's gotten aggressive about getting the ore from the Utah territories,'' Kane pointed out. ''Do the math. What does he need that ore for? What's he planning on building?''

Brigid was silent for a moment. ''I know where we are.''

Kane came closer. ''Where?''

''The Western Isles,'' she replied. ''Near the area that used to be known as Los Angeles.''

KANE SHOWERED, letting the hot water sluice the dirt and fatigue from his body. He turned his face up to the water and closed his eyes. He used the bar of soap from the kit on the Sandcat that they kept on hand for small patchwork that might become necessary if the radiator or gas tanks cracked. Filling his hands with soap, he washed his hair, then used the straight razor Grant loaned him to scrape the days' accumulation of whiskers from his face.

The razor wasn't a personal grooming tool; it was a weapon Grant carried, a hide-out blade for cutting out of one-percenter situations, a tool for getting out of close shaves rather than giving them. Kane figured it had probably cut more throats than whiskers.

Grant kept the blade extremely sharp. Though Kane knew how to properly use it, the blade's sharpness still caused him to cut himself twice. When he was finished, he dressed in the clothes he'd taken off. The grime would wear back in quickly by doing that, but for the moment he felt clean. And despite being in the unknown redoubt, he even felt safe.

He returned to the command center, picking up Grant who'd stood guard outside the door. When he got there, he found a meal of self-heats had been laid out across one of the small desks.

Domi grinned at him. "Brigid's idea," she said. "She asked us if mind waiting to eat till you done with shower. Great, huh?"

"Yeah," Kane said. He glanced at Brigid. "Thanks, Baptiste." He sat and they ate, and they pretended they weren't about to step out into an unknown world first thing in the morning.

THE MORNING SUNLIGHT bathed the crest of the hill almost seventy feet above Kane as he stepped out of the redoubt's open doors.

Grant flanked him. Both of them were covered head to toe in Mag black, and carried Copperheads.

The trail wound down and away from the vanadium doors, leading to the forest floor almost two hundred feet below. Lush vegetation grew on the hillside in all directions, with tall trees bearing leaves of all sizes and shapes. Birds called from the treetops.

From his vantage point, Kane could see the Cific Ocean little more than two miles away. Looking to the left and right with the binoculars, he occasionally caught glimpses of the curving coastline hooking out toward the sea. Wisps of fog still rolled in from the ocean, obscuring the distance much of the time.

The trail was well-worn, speaking of the number of times Ambika had put her shock troops through the area, but stubborn grass tufts poked through the uneven rock revealed by the missing topsoil. There was no sign of a ville or outpost anywhere in the vicinity.

Kane took the lead, staying to the right of the trail. Grant walked nearly twenty paces behind and on the left side. The Sandcat brought up the slack, with Brigid at the wheel and

Domi manning the guns. The grinding of the transmission and steady hum of the Sandcat's diesel engine seemed to roar over the quietness of the forest. Birds flew from their perches, retreating with angry calls.

Following the grade of the hill, the trail snaked back and forth.

Kane felt the chill of the wind blowing in from the sea against his exposed chin. The climbing sun promised a lot of warmth in the near future, but he knew it wasn't going to be anything like the fetid hell of the Utah territories.

"We'd make better time if we just rode in the Sandcat," Grant groused over the helmet comm-link.

"We'd make better targets, too," Kane told him.

"Who the hell's going to take on a Sandcat?"

"Mebbe a couple bigger Sandcats," Kane replied.

Grant chuckled. "And wouldn't we be in a hell of a position to take them on?"

"We can always outflank them," Kane said. "Not to mention that we're a little more mobile on foot than we are in the Cat."

"Mobile for what?"

Before Kane could reply, the motion-detector band around his left wrist suddenly buzzed for attention. "I've got a reading."

Grant's voice lost its jocularity at once. "Where?"

"My side," Kane said, watching the motion detector as a third green dot joined the first two. He didn't know if that was all of them or not. The motion detector had a definite radius of operation. "About twenty yards in."

"Got 'em now," Grant said. "This close in, you know they can eyeball us just fine. Cat ought to scare them off."

Kane thought so, too, but he also knew they couldn't afford to let anyone get away who might report them. Leaving the Sandcat back in the redoubt hadn't been an option.

He'd been hoping to find a place to stash it before they were found. "I'm going to knock on the door," he said.

"I got your six," Grant said confidently.

Without a wasted move, Kane turned and sprinted into the brush. Branches whipped at his helmet but he'd been trusting it so long to protect him he didn't even blink.

The three men scattered in the forest, bursting into an all-out run. Other pockets of movement flared up, as well, letting him know the motion detector hadn't picked up all of the group that had been watching them.

He ran, leaping up onto a lightning-blasted tree that hung three feet above the leaf-covered forest floor. In the next instant, a heavy round crashed into his chest, knocking him backward and leaving no doubts at all about the intentions of the people who'd been watching them.

Chapter 19

The molded polycarbonate armor covering Kane's chest had a rounded surface designed to turn even heavy bullets. Still, the impact knocked him on his ass and promised a hell of a bruise from the blunt trauma. His chest burned, and he struggled to draw in a breath.

He forced himself to move, reflexes taking over. Whoever had shot him was good, or was damn lucky, snap-firing like that. Shoving the vicious snout of the Copperhead under the fallen tree he'd tried to leap over, he aimed at the man's legs as the guy ran, then squeezed the trigger.

The 4.85 mm steel-jacketed bullets chopped a short line through the ground, throwing up clods of dirt. The 15-round clip emptied rapidly but not before the running man's legs were cut out from beneath him. He screamed shrilly, calling out in a language Kane didn't understand.

Kane shoved himself to his feet, breathing steadily in spite of the pain that held his chest in a vise. He removed the empty magazine from the Copperhead, shoved it into a sheath on his leg, then pushed a fresh one into place. He used the tree for cover.

Hostile gunfire raked a flurry of splinters from the fallen tree, tearing white patches in the bark. Kane heard Grant's Copperhead roar, then the gunfire ended abruptly.

"Target's down," Grant called. "Clear?"

"Clear," Kane agreed. That was two down. His mind raced, trying to remember where he'd seen the others. He glanced at the motion detector on his wrist, noting four other targets now. He wasn't sure if that was all of them.

He levered himself over the tree, going lower. When he'd first leaped over it, he'd expected the suddenness of his movement and the black armor to surprise the men. The fact that it hadn't told him they were seasoned to gunplay, and maybe even used to seeing Mag black. It was something to think about.

He ran through the forest, keeping the snout of the Copperhead pointed down ahead of him. Even with the weapon's slight recoil, it had a tendency to rise, so starting low on a target and allowing it to naturally track up was the best way to handle the weapon.

The man he'd shot in the legs tried painfully to get back up. His pained screeches filled the forest. His outflung hand grabbed his weapon, a Dragunov sniper rifle that Kane knew held impressive stats for distance and knockdown ability.

Kane triggered a 3-round burst that smashed through the man's forearm.

The man released the sniper rifle and whirled, leaning heavily against the tree behind him. He was not much above five and a half feet tall, and was built slight. Oriental features held a mixture of hate and fear. A wispy mustache and beard covered his lower face. Gold earrings dangled from both ears, and tattoos marred his skin, including his face and neck. He wore loose-fitting homespun clothing.

Kane kept the Copperhead trained on the man. "Do you speak English?" he demanded.

A stream of invective flew from the man's mouth, not one word of it understandable. At the end, he spit at Kane.

Reflexively, the Mag ego asserting itself while in the battlefield, Kane squeezed the Copperhead's trigger. A triburst broke the man's head, splashing brain matter on the tree behind him. Kane was in motion before the corpse hit the ground.

The Sandcat burst through the forest to his right, knocking down all trees less than a hand's breadth in thickness. The treads cleaved through the dark earth, turning up roots and stones in their wake. The Cat was slowed by the need to find a way through the thicker trees, but it came on relentlessly, nearly at the pace of the running men.

"Dammit, Baptiste," Kane snarled over the comm-link joining them through the Sandcat. "What the hell do you think you're doing?"

"Backing you up," Baptiste replied angrily.

"Grant and I can handle this." Kane sprinted, checking the motion detector to track his quarry. Keeping his directions in mind, he knew they were headed toward the coastline. He guessed they were now less than half a mile away from the ocean. "If we couldn't, we'd have dropped back to the Cat."

"No one mentioned it to us." Baptiste powered the Sandcat on, knocking down more trees and tearing underbrush out of the way with the FAV's armored hull.

Kane cursed when he glanced back at the path of destruction left by the Sandcat. "The trail you're leaving, Baptiste, it's going to be hard not to notice."

"We can always go back to the redoubt and leave," Baptiste said. "I thought you would appreciate the help. The Sandcat's onboard sensors indicated at least a dozen men in the forest."

Kane gave up the argument. Baptiste wasn't trained as a Mag and didn't know that a low profile came in handy at times. A covert op at this point was out of the picture. He concentrated on running. As the land fell more toward the ocean, the grade grew more treacherous. He kept his arms folded across his chest, right arm over the Copperhead, and used his armored elbows and shoulders to knock through trees.

The forest thinned toward the coastline, finally ending at a rock-and-black-sand beach that stretched inland twenty or thirty yards. The black sand, Kane knew, came from the volcanic activity that had been unleashed by the earthshaker bombs.

The pale green of the Cific Ocean splashed against the beach in two-foot-high breakers. Farther out, the sea seemed more calm, and the sea green held darker patches.

Two ships sat at anchor off the coastline. One of them was an ancient mast-rigged cargo freighter that looked to have been around before the nukecaust. The sails were struck, folded and tied to the three masts. A bowsprit pointed at the beach while it rocked sedately on the waves.

The other ship drew Kane's eye instantly. During his days at Cobaltville, he'd had a little experience with ships and shipping from the trade along the Colorado River and the Kanab River that helped supply the ville. When he'd journeyed to New London and Ireland with Brigid and the others, he'd gotten even more familiar with sailing craft.

He couldn't identify the other craft, but the architecture stood out. It seemed all arches and angles, and the three sails weren't furled so much as they were let down like window blinds. And the wood was finished in a deep cherry red, cut with narrow black lines. It gleamed in the morning sun, looking like a bird that had settled into the water and waited to take wing again.

A puff of smoke rose from the red ship's side facing him. A moment later a cannon round hammered the beach less than thirty feet from where he'd emerged from the tree line. A tall tree cracked and folded like a jackknife, the branches slapping into the beach, sending rock and sand flying.

"Damn!" Grant growled.

The sound of the cannon shot washed over Kane at the same time some of the sand and the smaller rocks peppered his armor. The pain in his chest from the bullet earlier had turned into a dull ache and his breathing came easier.

"Bastards must have had radios on them," Grant said.

Kane silently agreed, then cursed himself for not checking the body. Movement from one of the big rocks shoving up from the beach drew his attention. He brought the Copperhead into line just as the Oriental man's head appeared above his rifle less than ten feet away. Only his shadow on the ground had attracted Kane's attention.

The man fired rapidly, squeezing off four shots before Kane's triburst tore his face away. The body staggered back, fighting the inevitable, then slumped onto the wet beach. The next foaming curler that came in rolled over the corpse and moved it a few inches seaward as it retreated, beginning the eventual reclamation.

Gazing behind the stand of a dozen rocks that ranged from a yard high to over a man's height, Kane spotted the small motorboat wedged onto the beach. Four men, fighting the tide and one another, struggled to push the boat back out into the water.

The ship's cannon put two more rounds onto the beach, closer to Kane's position. Luckily they didn't appear to carry any explosive charges in them, but the polycarbonate armor wouldn't offer much proof against the cannonballs.

Kane ran for the rocks, angling toward the men pushing the motorboat. He spotted Grant moving in from the other side, striding over a body sprawled out in front of him.

Another armed man leaned out from one of the rocks. Kane snap-fired a pair of rounds that left white scars against the rock but succeeded only in chasing the gunner behind cover. Still on the move, Kane closed on the man's position. When the man started to poke his head out again, Kane put a round through his eye, ripping away half his face in an explosion of red mist. The dead man spun and dropped.

Moving among the rocks, Kane took the Copperhead in his left hand then snapped the Sin Eater out, opting for its shorter length among the crowded rocks. Rounds drummed a deadly tattoo against the polycarbonate armor over his left side but didn't penetrate. Kane spun, bringing the Sin Eater up automatically. His eyes were gun sights, targeting the man hardly more than an arm's reach away. He put three 9 mm rounds through the man's chest, blowing him back.

In the next instant, the world dissolved into a maelstrom of whirling sand that temporarily took away his vision. The hum of a giant bumblebee sounded immediately after, letting him know another cannon shot had landed nearby.

When he could see again, the air still hazy with the dry dust of the beach, he spotted the crater between the stand of rocks and the motorboat.

"Kane!" Brigid called.

"Here," Kane replied. He moved through the rocks, finding another man and shooting him down before the guy could raise his weapon. Kane didn't know who the men were, but he reacted with a Mag's reflexes, killing anyone who dared try to kill him.

Farther down the beach, the Sandcat roared through the forest line, pushing down trees. The left tread locked and the FAV wheeled around, slewing wide as Brigid fought the controls. Sand and rock spewed out from behind it.

"Lock on to that damn red ship," Kane called. "Those machine guns will reach that far. Aim at the waterline. Stop, Baptiste. That armaglass hull will take a direct hit from those cannon if it needs to."

The turret on top of the Sandcat turned to face the sea. Brigid stopped the FAV. Almost immediately, the USMG-73 started its death song.

Kane regretted the use of ammo. He'd made sure the Sandcat was heavily stocked before they'd left the Cerberus redoubt, but they didn't have the resources here that they did back in the Darks.

He and Grant moved in tandem, covering each other as they took on the four men who'd been pushing the motorboat. "Keep the boat in one piece," Kane said.

"You going into the sailing business?" Grant asked dryly.

"That cargo ship out there looks big enough to take the Sandcat onto it," Kane said, taking a brief respite to recharge his weapons. "We get mobile again, mebbe we can leave the Sandcat somewhere else. Hell, we might need it somewhere else for that matter."

"Agreed. Give me a chance to load up. We'll clean them out together."

"Do it." Kane turned his back to the rock, taking the Copperhead in his left hand and the Sin Eater in his right.

The USMG-73's distinctive yammer filled the air. Glancing over his shoulder, Kane saw the flurry of activity aboard the red ship. The sails ran up the three masts, unfolding like accordions. Red material with black ribbing caught the wind, belling out.

"Ready," Grant advised.

"Let's go." Kane spun and pushed both weapons before him. He swept first with the Copperhead, knocking down the two men on the right of the motorboat. Only one of them survived, and he chopped the man down with a single round from the Sin Eater. Grant finished both of his targets at the same time.

Out at sea, the red ship was in full flight. The rectangular sails curved with the wind's breath, pushing away from shore. Domi's skills with the heavy machine guns kept the decks clear, and the crew only returned with small-arms fire that was relatively ineffectual against the Sandcat's arma-glass hull and the Mag armor.

The crew of the other ship struggled to get their sails up, as well, but weren't as crisp or clean in their efforts.

"Baptiste, keep us covered. We're going to try to take the cargo ship." Kane loaded the Copperhead and stowed the empty magazine.

"Why?" Brigid asked.

"To give us more options. The Cat gives us more armor and firepower if we need it, and it has a comm-link we can use to contact Lakesh. If the old bastard will come clean with us." Kane nodded at Grant and they took hold of the motorboat.

Even with both of them, pushing the boat out into the water was hard. It left a deep gouge in the wet sand as they shoved it backward.

"Get in and fire it up," Kane said as he kept pushing. With the water taking some of the boat's weight, it was easier going.

Grant heaved himself over the side, cursed when he slipped over the hardwood seats and made his way to the back.

Kane kept shoving, feeling his heavy boots smash deeply into the wet sandy bottom. Luckily and dangerously, the ocean floor fell away quickly. The Mag armor wasn't de-signed for water maneuvers. Thankfully, most of the seals were watertight, and not much of the brine seeped into the armor. Still, the water that did seep in collected in his boots.

Grant pushed the motor's starter button a few times. After a moment, the engine fired up, blatting triumphantly.

Kane hauled himself over the boat's side with effort. He checked his weapons automatically, making sure the actions on both were clear.

Powering the boat, Grant brought it around with a little

hesitation. Though both of them had extensive training with the Deathbirds and Sandcats, neither had spent very much time in the river patrol boats the Mag Division maintained. Usually if any Roamers or outlanders threatened Cobaltville on the Kanab River, they were summarily blown out of the water by the armored gun emplacements.

"Handles kind of like a Deathbird," Grant said, making adjustments to the outboard engine's steering and throttle arm. "A really slow, ungainly fucking Deathbird."

Kane said nothing as he sat in the prow. Whitecaps burst against the outboard's pointed nose, and some of the over-spill splashed onboard.

Only one of the cargo ship's sails was in place. The ship rocked dangerously from side to side. The sail twisted in the wrong direction as it fought the anchor. In the distance, the red ship was fast disappearing over the horizon.

"You think he's going to get friends?" Grant asked. "Or just gone for good?"

"I don't know," Kane admitted. "But I'm not planning on us being around long enough to find out."

As they neared the cargo ship, small-arms fire rumbled from the side. Bullets hammered the outboard's wooden hull, but the construction was solid enough that they didn't penetrate, though cracks in the finish did appear.

"They're not as heavily armed," Kane said, scanning the deck through the Copperhead's optical image-intensifier scope. "And they're not all Oriental."

He spotted only a half dozen men aboard who showed Oriental heritage. The others appeared to be a mix of whites, blacks and Hispanics, men and women. They were unarmed, and the Orientals kept them at a distance.

Even as Kane watched, members of the crew rebelled against the Orientals. Two of the armed men were dragged down to the deck. Blades flashed, then others were armed.

"Grant," Kane said.

"I see."

The mutiny aboard the ship continued, but the crew wasn't strong enough to stand against the Orientals. Mercilessly, the Orientals banded together near the bow and started killing the crew. It was turning into a bloody massacre. Reluctantly, no longer able to take refuge in their apparent desire to kill the Orientals, the crew gave ground. The insurrection was on the verge of being contained through sheer attrition.

"Get us over there," Kane directed. He held the Copperhead at the ready. "To the anchor."

Grant swooped in with the outboard, easily reaching the stranded ship dancing at the end of its anchor line.

Kane peered up at the side of the ship, and hung the Copperhead by its shoulder strap. Grant fought the outboard, trying to get it close enough to the anchor line that Kane could seize it.

Taking a deep breath, Kane threw himself at the line. With the armor on he wouldn't exactly sink like a stone, but he knew swimming wasn't an entertaining prospect. He caught the thick hawser, then started pulling himself up. He heard the chatter of automatic weapons overhead.

"Right behind you," Grant said.

Kane concentrated on pulling himself up, his arms straining with the effort, as well as managing the wet rope. In long seconds, his breath rasping inside his helmet, he reached up and grabbed the edge of the bow. He pulled himself up, peering over the edge.

Seven Orientals took cover in the bow, yelling out threats in broken English. Kane found it hopeful. At least he'd be able to understand someone on board.

He caught the railing and pulled himself up. Two of the

Orientals spotted him, positioned for a cross fire across the deck. They turned their weapons toward him.

Kane threw himself over the railing, rolling and coming up on one knee as he reached for the Copperhead hanging at his side.

Chapter 20

Kane fired from midcrouch, chewing through the two men with the 4.85 mm rounds. The two Oriental gunners stutter-stepped back as the bullets smashed through their chests. One of them went over the bow railing behind him without a word.

Dropping the Copperhead to hang by its shoulder sling, Kane flexed his wrist muscles. The Sin Eater popped out, slamming into his palm. His finger curled around the firing stud as the other Orientals turned to face him. He depended on his armor, and the surprise of the unexpected attack.

Grant was at his side, his own Copperhead roaring sudden death. Brass littered the deck at their boots, rolling away as the struggling cargo ship fought against the restraining anchor line.

Bullets struck Kane as he fired the Sin Eater dry. He stood his ground the way he'd been trained, and started to reload his weapon.

One of the Orientals broke ranks unexpectedly, charging at Kane. The man's weapon blazed in his hands, and the line of bullets hammered at Kane's chest, rising toward his unprotected throat and chin.

Cursing, Kane threw himself to one side. The impacts were painful punches through the armor. The extra magazine he'd been about to load into the Sin Eater skittered from his hands.

The man's weapon emptied, but he still raced at Kane.

"I'm out," Grant said, trying to reload his own weapons as two surviving gunners fired at him.

Kane retracted the Sin Eater with a flexing twist of his wrist. Even as the weapon holstered itself back along his forearm, he reached down for the combat knife in his boot. He fisted it, keeping the blade's edge pointing forward, laying it along his forearm.

The man raised his empty assault rifle in front of his chest like a club, evidently intending to drive Kane over the side of the ship.

Kane stepped forward to meet the man's rush, slamming his gloved right hand into the man's chin, knocking his head up and back in a martial arts blow. He followed the blow with his knife, twisting with the backhand strike to get more of his weight into the blade attack.

The razor-edged steel bit into the man's neck, slicing through his windpipe and jugular. He stumbled, his rush abruptly broken by the sight of his own crimson blood gushing over his hands and weapon.

Recovering his balance, Kane spun in the other direction, ramming his armored elbow into the middle of the dying man's back. The man left his feet from the force of the blow and went over the bow railing in front of him.

Kane crossed the deck and wiped the blood from the knife on a dead man's clothes. He sheathed the knife and reloaded his weapons.

Only one man remained alive, and he'd given up the fight. He ran pell-mell toward the stairs leading down from the bow to the main deck. Dispassionately, Grant locked the Sin Eater on to the man and pumped two rounds between his shoulder blades. The corpse flew from the top of the stairs and landed on the deck in a loose heap. The handblaster tumbled from his nerveless fingers, sliding across the scarred deck.

A man stepped from hiding behind the mainmast and plucked the handblaster from the deck. He was something less than six feet in height, thin and reddened from the sun. His bleached-blond hair was pulled back in a leather thong, and his fierce goatee carried more red than blond. Small seashells hung from his ears. He wore a sleeveless shirt and patched jeans. He handled the blaster as if it were a long lost friend.

Kane stepped to the bow railing overhanging the main deck. The cargo ship still pitched viciously, but the crew came out of hiding and started tending to the sails.

"Who's in charge of this ship?" Kane asked.

"I am," the blond man answered. "I'm Jeremiah Christensen, and this is my ship. Called *Sloop John B.* She's a free trader in these waters, and I mean to keep her that way." He waved the gun meaningfully.

Grant took his place beside Kane and gestured at the dead Orientals. "You people didn't look too goddamn free before we got here."

"A setback," Christensen said. "Free trading isn't without its risks. That's how a crew keeps its profits at a respectable level."

The ship pulled at the anchor restlessly, the sails billowing and cracking like it was ready to fly.

"Who were these people?" Kane asked.

Christensen looked at him for a moment, obviously puzzled. "You don't know?"

"I wouldn't ask if I did."

"Tong. They were members of Wei Qiang's organization."

Kane lowered his voice so it carried only over the helmet's comm-link. "Baptiste, help me out here."

"A tong was originally a meeting hall or place," Brigid

answered, "and the term was first used in the 1880s to describe illegal Chinese activities in San Francisco—"

"Cut the history lesson, Baptiste," Kane growled low enough that only the comm-link picked up his words. "Tell me what a damn Tong is."

"A criminal organization," Brigid said.

"Pirates by any other name," Grant said softly.

"You don't know that they're any worse than those people on that ship," Brigid put in.

"Yeah," Kane said dryly. "Free trader does have that ring about it, doesn't it?" He raised his voice. More of the crew had come forward to support their leader. "What are you doing here?"

"Trading." Christensen kept his answer short, and Kane knew it was because the man was watching the amount of information he was giving out. Plus he was obviously watching to see how much Kane knew.

Suddenly, the idea of traveling aboard ship didn't sound quite as entertaining. "Who do you trade with on this island?" Kane asked.

"Small villes," Christensen answered. He tucked the handblaster inside his waistband. The crew behind him only relaxed a little. "They make handicrafts and foodstuffs I trade for. Some scavenged goods I know buyers will pick up."

Kane nodded toward the ocean's western horizon where the red ship had disappeared. "Raiders?"

Christensen shrugged. "Competitors. Wei Qiang is a greedy bastard, and he's got enough ships behind him to back his play. He's probably locked up sixty percent or more of the free trade available in the Western Isles. Man's nearly eighty years old and still wants it all. His son is just as greedy and probably going to be worse to deal with. He's a flaming psychopath and a faggot."

Kane walked the deck and eyed the crew. They weren't well armed by any standards, and the ship only had three cannon on rolling wheels.

"*Sloop John B*'s strength is in her speed," Christensen said defensively. "Those assholes hadn't caught us cutting into shore, they wouldn't have caught us."

"Any chance they'll be back?"

"Yeah, there's a chance. And if they are, you can bet there'll be more than one ship. There's two things Qiang don't put up with. One's letting anybody get the better of him in a deal or a fight. Two's losing any of his ships. Despite the way the land around here's come back after the nukecaust, timber's a precious commodity."

"How long are you going to be here?" Kane asked.

"On Columbine?" Christensen shook his head. "Got a couple deals set up on the south side of the island I need to tend to, then we're out of here."

"We're going with you," Kane said.

"Going to have to dicker over the passage fare," Christensen said.

Kane kicked the dead man at his feet. "We're paid in full. And if you don't see it that way, I'll put you ashore and take any men who don't want to be here when those Tong get back."

The ship's captain made a face, but he didn't argue.

KANE STOOD beside Christensen at the big wheel as the ship made her way around the southern end of Columbine Island. Domi and Brigid followed along the shoreline in the Sandcat. Kane didn't want to leave the FAV behind, and Christensen said the next village on his route had a pier they could use to load the Sandcat aboard the ship. He hadn't appeared happy about the thought of bringing the vehicle along, but Kane hadn't given him any choice.

Kane surveyed the thick growth of forest that started just on the other side of the beach. "I thought this place was nuked to hell during skydark," he told the captain.

Christensen nodded. "You haven't seen the Blight Belt."

"Blight Belt?"

"There's a bunch of islands out here that carry hot rad. They stick up out of the water like stone-boiled blisters. Nothing grows on them, and sea creatures getting too close to them for too long wash up on the shores. They're part of the old land masses that were here."

Kane looked at Columbine Island. "What about this?"

"It's the miracle of tectonics, they tell me. Same as the islands that were made from volcanoes erupting along the bottom of the ocean thousands and thousands of years ago.

"What caused most of California to fall off into the Cific Ocean was two tectonic plates that overlapped right here. The earthshaker bombs opened those plates right up and let the sea in. Some time after the nukecaust, those plates opened again, and volcanoes spewed new islands out into the sea. The soil was scraped up from the ocean bed, so it's fertile."

"Where'd the people come from?" Kane asked.

Christensen bellowed out orders for the sails to be trimmed, telling the ship's mate that he could hear the sailcloth luffing in the wind. Within a minute, the ship's crew had tightened up the rigging, and even Kane could tell the difference.

"Hell," Christensen said, "the people came from everywhere. A lot of them were from villes scattered up and down the coast. Some of them were mariner families who survived on trading and scavenging. Wei Qiang and the Tong came over with his father, and a meaner or bloodier bastard there ain't been yet."

"Came over from where?" Kane asked.

"China." Christensen turned the wheel another couple notches, then tapped the glass over the compass mounted within his reach. "His father had set up a trading op in China that stretched up to Russia. His family and the families of anybody who worked with him were pretty much living on boats like the one you saw. Some of them have been around hundreds of years, even before the nukecaust."

"What brought them over here if things were going so well over there?"

"Greed must naturally run in Qiang's family," Christensen said. "The way I hear it, the old man damn near got himself whacked for trying to take over somebody else's action. He had more balls than bullets. So he ended up over here. If it hadn't been for Ambika, that old bastard would have already owned the Western Isles." He adjusted the wheel again, then nodded forward. "There's our port."

THE SLOOP JOHN B put into port at the end of the short dock and dropped anchor. The rough-hewn dock was assembled of split trees turned mostly flat side up. The logs themselves were of irregular lengths and diameters and fit together with large gaps.

Still, Kane figured the structure would be strong enough to hold the Sandcat.

Someone rang a bell out in front of the group of thatched huts along the shoreline. Immediately afterward, the area filled up with people. All of them were naked.

"Let me guess," Kane said, looking at the collection of naked men, women and children clustered around the dock, "you don't trade many clothes with these people."

Christensen smiled. "They're from an old faith. Call themselves Nude Hists. If you talk to them, you'll find most of them don't know where their religion came from, but they all worship the sun. They believe that a man putting on clothing separates himself from the life-giving rays.''

''And what do you think?'' Kane asked.

''I think there's still too many of these poor stupes getting cancer tumors from overexposure to the sun to suit me.'' Christensen walked toward the middle of his ship where his crew was putting out gangways under Grant's supervision. ''Not everybody died out in this area when the nukecaust hit. I mean, at least not in California. The Western Isles are full of a lot of people like this.''

Kane surveyed the line of naked people forming along the side of the cargo ship. The *Sloop John B*'s sails fluttered loosely in the breeze as the crew tied them down. A few of the ville dwellers carried old blasters, but none of them seemed overly cautious of the ship putting into port.

''Like this?'' he asked Christensen.

''Like everything you can imagine,'' the ship's captain replied. ''On some of the islands you'll find clans that make some of the harshest pop-skull you could ever imagine. Others have religious zealots that aren't anywhere near as friendly as these people. Military tribes. Fishermen. Boatbuilders. The Tong groups. Jolt growers and makers. Little empires that thrive on sexual slavery and have got gaudy houses the like of which you've probably never seen before since you haven't been out here. Other islands where they're trying to protect animals and give them the same rights as people. Stupe shit. But they all live to trade.''

Kane digested that. ''Where does Ambika fit into this?''

''How do you know her?'' Christensen asked.

Kane studied the man's face, not knowing for sure which way he should answer the question. Finally he replied, ''I don't know her. But I've heard of her.''

''What have you heard?''

Kane put steel in his voice. ''I'm asking the questions.''

Christensen held the eye contact for a moment in open defiance, then looked away. "They call her the Lioness of the Isles. And I don't know her. Very few people do. She's got an island fortress southwest of here that's more heavily armored and armed than anything the Tong masters have put together."

"Do you do any trading with her?"

"Not there. Nobody goes there. Except by invitation. Or if she's got a grudge she wants to work off."

The ship's crewmen brought crates and packs up from the hold and carried them down the dock to the shore. A makeshift marketplace set up quickly, and spirited bargaining began on both sides.

"I've got to go tend to my trading," Christensen said. "Otherwise I'm going to lose my ass on the things I brought to barter with."

"That's fine," Kane said. "But if you try to slip off, Grant or I will put a bullet through your head."

"You're a testy son of a bitch," Christensen said.

Kane smiled. "Hell, you're on my good side right now."

Chapter 21

Kane stood in the stern with Jeremiah Christensen as the breeze pushed the *Sloop John B* westward. The Sandcat sat in the middle of the main deck, tied down with thick hawsers and with its tracks locked. It wasn't going anywhere, wasn't even shifting with the roll and pitch of the cargo ship.

Christensen had taken on fresh water—a valuable commodity—and fresh fruit and vegetables, as well as preserved meat the islanders had traded. As Kane, Grant and Brigid sampled the food, Kane returned to the subject of Ambika.

"Where do you think she came from?" he asked Christensen.

"I figure she came through the redoubt on Columbine Island," Christensen said, "but some think she comes from heaven—or the pits of hell."

"You deal with her?" Kane prodded.

"Yeah. Deal with Qiang on occasion, too. I'm going to give him an earful over his people trying to pick off my ship this morning, but it won't do any good."

"Why?" Grant asked.

"Fucker'll tell me it was SOG did it."

"SOG?"

Christensen smiled. "Some Other Guy. It's one of his typical defenses. When Ambika established herself on her island about ten years ago, he tried raiding some of her war parties. Got a couple of them, too. She didn't put up with that shit.''

"What did she do?" Brigid asked.

"The Lioness walked into Dai Jia Lou, the biggest gaudy in Autarkic—"

"What's Autarkic?" Brigid interrupted. "I know one of the literal translations of the word means free."

"Basically, that's it," Christensen said. "With all the commerce and conflicting trade groups in the islands, some place had to be set up where trading could be done without interference."

"And Autarkic's the place?" Kane asked.

"Yeah. It's an island by itself located in the middle of the main island groups in the area. All the trading that takes place there goes on without any of the trading groups horning in." Christensen smiled.

"There has to be somebody who makes sure the place stays free," Grant said.

"It's a sec committee put together by all the islands," Christensen said. "But generally it's just a collection of some of the fightingest men in the islands."

"Nobody can buy them off?" Kane asked.

"Nobody can pay that high. The reason they took that post? Graft. They get a cut of every deal that goes through Autarkic."

"Doesn't sound so free that way," Grant rumbled.

"The deal's a hell of a lot better than working for somebody," Christensen said. "Of course, if you're shorting somebody else, you run that risk. And if you're shipping solo, like me, you run the risk of what nearly happened today. Still, I like calling my own shots."

"Ambika," Kane reminded. "Her wars with Qiang."

"Like I said, the Lioness walked into the Dai Jia Lou and braced Qiang in front of his own men. Told him one of his ship's captains had busted one of her ships, took the goods off it and sunk the ship. It's one thing to steal somebody's goods, but it's another to put a ship down. Ships are too goddamn hard to come by. She walked into the Dai Jia Lou, pulled out that fucking hand cannon she carries and chilled one of the Tong captains at Qiang's own table.''

"Woman's brassy," Grant said. "What did Qiang do?"

Christensen smiled. "Hell, he sat there. Mebbe he'd have tried something, or one of his lieutenants would have, but she put that on ice straightaway. Before the son of a bitch she shot could fall out of his chair, she tossed an explo-pak onto the table already wired for the big boom. Then she took out a remote detonator with two switches on it. She flicked one of them. Out in the harbor, you could hear the series of explosions. One right after another like autofire.

"When it stopped, she looked at Qiang and told him that was two of his ships sinking out in the harbor. And it was. She told him anytime he attacked one of her ships, she'd take two of his. And two ship's captains. Then she put that big pistol on Qiang and told him to pick a captain. He did, and she chilled that guy too without even blinking an eye. Then she turned and walked away.''

"And they fucking let her, with that explo-pak on the table?'' Grant asked in disbelief.

"Wei Qiang is triple greedy, but he's not stupe," Christensen explained. "His son, like I said, is a psychotic fuck who likes guy's asses. The only thing he fears is his father. When Ambika was standing there, Wei Qiang reached out and took that explo-pak in one hand, rolled it over his fingers as easy as you please and talked with her the whole time.''

"Letting her know she didn't dare chill him, either," Kane said.

Christensen nodded. "Yeah, and that's the way it's been ever since."

"Qiang never tried anything?"

Christensen grinned and raked the hair out of his eyes as he rolled the wheel. "Of course he did. He organized a couple runs against Ambika's ships. For every ship Qiang's Tong sailors put down, Ambika delivered on her promise to put down two of his. No more. No less."

"But no open confrontations?"

"No. The people on these islands are afraid if anything does stir up between Ambika and Qiang that they can't put down, it'll spill over onto all of the islands and chill a lot of people."

A small group of flying fish broke the surface of the ocean of the starboard bow. Kane watched them sail through the air, then disappear back into the water. The motion attracted his attention to the spire jutting from the ocean leading toward the horizon.

"What's up ahead?" he asked.

"Sunken buildings that'll rip the bottom out of *Sloop John B* if I'm not careful," Christensen said.

Kane took his binoculars out and focused on the distortion in the water. With the magnification available, he spotted the white gulls sitting on the broken rock shoved above the ocean's surface.

"That's a section of old Los Angeles," Christensen said. "I don't know what the buildings were."

The sun's glare on the sea kept Kane from gazing too deeply into the water, but he had the impression the building went down a long way. "How deep are we here?"

"Ninety, a hundred feet, mebbe even as much as one-twenty." Christensen glanced at the nearby compass and made an adjustment to his course. "Some of those predark buildings were huge. I'd seen them in books, but you don't really know how big they were till you're standing inside one."

Kane silently agreed, remembering his own trip to the twentieth century. The landscape of the large metropolitan area had been staggering, alien.

"You've been inside them?" Brigid asked.

"Sure," Christensen said. "You run a ship out here, you learn to scavenge whenever you get the opportunity to. I haven't ever been lucky enough to find much. The nuke-caust and flooding destroyed most things, and nearly every place you find scavengers have already been at. Still, it's worth the trip down every now and again."

"You have diving equipment?" Brigid asked.

Christensen looked at her with interest. "Some. You people do any diving where you're from?"

"I haven't," Brigid said.

"They do it there?"

"Mebbe."

Christensen shook his head. "You people sure are close-mouthed."

"How many people know about the redoubt back on Columbine Island?" Kane asked.

"Nearly everybody. Most folks knew about it before Ambika showed up. But after she did, everybody knew. She keeps a small navy on hand just for transporting those assault vehicles of hers. That's another reason Qiang doesn't want to mess with her. He's got a few wags, but nothing like what Ambika's got."

"Where does she get them?"

"Don't know. As far as anybody can remember, she's always had them. Just like that place she has in the Isles of the Lioness."

"The Isles of the Lioness? That's what she calls it?"

"She doesn't call it anything. That's what everybody else

calls it. Ambika doesn't tell anybody her business. But the place on the Isles of the Lioness is another redoubt. Until she came along, that place was locked up tighter than a constipated virgin."

"You've got a map of these islands?" Kane asked.

"Sure."

"I want to see it."

KANE STUDIED THE MAP of the Western Isles down in the captain's quarters.

The hand-drawn map was meticulously rendered and colored with pastel pencils that allowed the ink to show through. From looking at the number of islands scattered around on it, Kane doubted every one of the islands was shown. But it showed a lot of them.

"Do you think we have a chance of recruiting Ambika?" Brigid asked from the cabin's doorway. "From what we've heard this morning, she seems to be very independent-minded."

"She also has a reason to go up against Baron Cobalt."

"She *is* taking the ore from the mines."

"I'm sure that figures into whatever she's planning," Kane agreed. "There's no way we're going to recruit her."

"Why? Lakesh might want to."

"If he's thinking that way," Kane said, "he's fooling himself. Ambika's not going to play second banana on anybody's team. She's a first-stringer all the way."

Brigid was silent for a time.

Kane traced the route Christensen had told him they were taking, noting the distance to Autarkic from Columbine Island. The ship's captain expected to arrive there in two days' time.

"You like that about her, don't you?" Brigid asked.

Kane looked up at her, irritated at the accusation in Brigid's tone. "Hell, Baptiste, I don't even know her."

"Perhaps not yet," Brigid said, "but you like how she handles herself. I saw your eyes when Christensen was telling us the story about Ambika's confrontation with Qiang."

"It was a ballsy move. I respect it. 'Like' has nothing to do with it."

Her jade gaze explored his own eyes. "She's a warrior, Kane. Like you."

"I understand why she's doing what she's doing, Baptiste," Kane said. "That doesn't mean we're anything alike."

"In the Mags, you were taught to terminate as an example. The same way Ambika did those people in Utah."

Kane felt his irritation growing. "Is this about her or about me, Baptiste?"

She looked at him for a long moment. "I don't know." Then she turned and left him standing there.

"THE ISLE OF THE Lioness?" Grant repeated.

"Yeah." Kane spread the map out on the Sandcat's console, letting Grant see. "There's the main island here—" he touched the map "—surrounded by three smaller islands." He touched the map rapidly to indicate the remaining islands. "And these even smaller islands are basically support islands for the inner four."

"Somebody chose the spot well."

Kane nodded. "According to Christensen, the redoubt was already in place there."

"Waiting for somebody."

"Yeah. It's on the main island. The three outer islands have defense systems, including a standing navy ready. They've got heavy mil-spec weapons in place there."

"From the redoubt?"

"Best guess," Kane agreed.

"Anybody ever try attacking her there?"

"Christensen said a small pirate raiding party, probably paid off by Wei Qiang, attempted only a few months after she put up the fortress."

"They last long?"

A wolfish smile covered Kane's face. "No."

"Anybody try since then?"

"No."

Grant leaned back in the seat and scratched his chin thoughtfully. "That's something to keep in mind."

Kane glanced through the ob slit and looked to the stern where Domi kept an eye on Christensen. Brigid was only a short distance away, keeping her own counsel. He wished she understood more of his thinking, and the importance of a liaison between Ambika and Cerberus. The Lioness's resources could add a lot to any force rebelling against the baronies.

However, there still remained the question of where Ambika came from and what her intentions were.

"Christensen says we'll make Autarkic sometime late tomorrow morning," Grant said. "Have you figured out where we're going from there?"

"If Ambika's as good as I think she is," Kane said, "she'll have spies on Autarkic. All we'll have to do is let it be known that we're looking for her. She'll come to us. Or have someone come to us. For now, I think it's time we talked with Lakesh again. And got the truth."

KANE HATED trying to dig the truth out of Lakesh over the comm-link. The old man knew how to deflect and divert questions that were aimed at him from only an arm's length away. Over the comm-link, Kane found the experience even more frustrating.

He and Grant sat in the pilot's and copilot's chairs while Brigid manned the console in front of the electronic equipment on the Sandcat. Domi remained with Christensen, monitoring the ship captain's movements.

"Friend Kane," Lakesh said over the comm-link, his voice filling the FAV's pilot's module, "I must remonstrate with you for your accusations."

"Remonstrate all you want to, old man," Kane growled. "The fact of the matter is that you've been holding back information from us."

"Ask me whatever you wish, friend Kane, and I shall endeavor to free you from your doubts."

"What about Ambika, Lakesh?" Brigid's voice was harsh and unrelenting. "You said you didn't know she was involved when you sent us in, but you know about her, don't you?"

Lakesh hesitated. "I'm afraid, dearest Brigid, that I must reiterate the presentation I made in my defense earlier—I don't know this Ambika person."

Brigid shifted in her seat and squared her shoulders. Kane watched her, knowing she was about to unload. "Then tell me about Project Excalibur's Ambika Folder. Conception: Beowulf."

Only silence came from the other end of the connection. Kane started to think Lakesh had broken the comm-link.

"The truth, Lakesh," Brigid ordered. "I tapped into those files myself and only got a partial download. You blocked me from the rest of them."

"As you know," Lakesh answered, "Overproject Excalibur dealt almost exclusively with genetic manipulation. A geneticist named Wil Longley intended to create a more perfect human. He intended to eradicate illness and genetic imperfections, and improve upon the original template."

"Ambika?" Kane pressed.

"I didn't know about Ambika, friend Kane. It was just a name Longley assigned to his project."

"Ambika is the name of a mythological Hindu battle goddess," Brigid stated. "In her pantheon, she was one of the most powerful entities. She guided warriors in battle, delivered victories and rewarded bravery. She was also a warrior herself. The legends I read suggested that she declared she'd never take any man to bed that hadn't beaten her in battle."

"Now, there's a strong case of performance anxiety," Grant commented lightly.

Brigid ignored him and continued. "The references I pulled up on the comp also stated that Ambika could turn herself into Kali, one of the most feared goddesses in the Hindu religion. A group of coldheart chillers, even before skydark, called Thuggees selected her as their chosen goddess and committed atrocious crimes in her name."

"She isn't a goddess, Baptiste," Kane said.

"No," Lakesh said, "she isn't. She's just a woman."

"Is Ambika human?" Brigid pressed.

"Human?" Lakesh repeated. "Your definition of human, dearest Brigid, or mine? What yardstick will you prop her against to determine that?"

"She's cold, Lakesh. Life doesn't appear to mean much to her."

"That's your judgment, Baptiste," Kane interrupted. "Just because she can chill someone in cold blood doesn't mean she's not human. Grant, Domi and I can take a life the same way."

Brigid turned her bright green gaze on him. "Can you, Kane? I've seen you kill when you deemed it necessary but could you order the execution of helpless people the way Ambika did?"

Kane's voice thickened, remembering all the raids the Mags had orchestrated in Cobaltville's Tartarus Pits. Those had entailed mass executions, as well. And some of it had been under his direction if not under his orders. "You don't know everything I've done, Brigid."

His words hammered closed any rebuttal she might have thought about making.

"Friend Kane," Lakesh said hopefully, "you yet maintain an open mind about Ambika?"

Kane shook his head. "You mean, do I still think it's possible we could use her for our own purposes?"

"If you prefer to be so coarse, yes. Though I view the opportunity as mutually beneficial. She will, I trust, use us as much as we are able to use her."

"Yeah," Kane answered. "I want to see what she's all about."

"And she does have an army," Grant said. "We've seen it. Having her on our side would give us the chance to be proactive rather than reactive. I'm tired of being crowded into corners by Baron Cobalt."

"Right, then," Lakesh said. "So we shall proceed..."

Chapter 22

The next morning, Kane stuck close to Christensen as the
Sloop John B dropped anchor in the shallow port outside
Autarkic. Nearly five dozen other ships were also in the
anchorage. A third of them were the red lacquered ships of
the Tong. Armed men remained visible on their decks.

The anchorage was built around a natural spit of land that
stabbed out into the ocean over shallow waters. All the
docks, which were of no uniform size or shape or color
scheme, appeared busy.

On the hills leading up from the docks, a variety of buildings stood against a backdrop of young trees. Most of them
were single-level structures, but there were some two-story
structures, as well. One of the buildings, poised nearly in
the heart of the ville, even stood four stories tall. Nearly all
of the structures were made from secondhand materials. The
tallest building, like a few of the others, was crafted of mor-
tised stone.

The port bustled with activity. Skiffs and barges hustled
freight to and from the docks, two of which obviously belonged to the Tong.

"Where do the labor groups come from?" Grant asked.

"Other villes on the island," Christensen answered.
"Some of them even come in from outlying islands. In the
past, other islands tried to set themselves up as trading ports,
but they couldn't field the sec forces Autarkic had to offer."
The ship's captain frowned. "Also, Allen Spelling orga-

nized the local labor groups enough to guarantee the competition wasn't going to stay.''

"How?" Kane asked.

"Though it couldn't be proved, or mebbe nobody wanted to prove it, Spelling and his people burned out the docks on other islands. Once they were burned out and knew they weren't going to get the support they thought they would, they didn't try again."

At Kane's urging, Christensen turned the shipping details over to his first mate, then had the small outboard lowered over the side.

"I don't want to leave the Cat unguarded," Kane said, "even though we've got Christensen with us." He swept his companions with his gaze. "Grant and I will go into Autarkic. We should be back in a few hours."

"I don't like that," Brigid said. "You and Grant have the same view of Ambika. I'd rather go."

"We don't even know if she's here," Kane said.

"Yes, we do," Brigid said. "Those are her ships." She pointed at a cluster of transport ships much larger than the *Sloop John B.* The flags on the ships bore the profile of a big, snarling lioness with its ears flattened against its yellow-gold head on a field of light blue and white split diagonally. Kane studied them for a moment, easily spotting the tarp-covered wags on their decks. The ships he saw didn't number enough to account for all the vehicles that had been reported in the Utah territories, so he assumed Ambika had sent some of them on.

"Good," Kane said. "It'll save time looking for her." Provided she proved still worth finding. He didn't mention that to Brigid. He stepped into the outboard, hanging only a couple feet below the cargo ship's railing.

"You don't represent the combined interests of Cerberus," Brigid said coldly.

"No," Kane agreed. "And neither do you. But for now I agree with Lakesh about finding Ambika." He paused as she gazed at him hotly. "I can't make you stay here, Baptiste. If you want to go, go. But you're going to be leaving Domi on her own with this crew."

"Grant could stay," Brigid said. "Or you, for that matter."

Kane shook his head. "No. I'm going. And if I'm going to walk into that ville, Grant's going to cover my back. He's the only one who's had the experience in ville surroundings to do the job right." He paused, hardening his voice. "If it comes down to it, I know he won't hesitate to chill somebody needs chilling, or deciding if it needs to be done."

Brigid watched him silently.

"You decide what you want to do, Baptiste," Kane said. He signaled the deckhands to finish lowering the outboard after Christensen and Grant joined him. Before the outboard lowered out of sight of the deck, he watched Brigid turn and walk away. Anger swirled within him, directed at himself because he hadn't wanted to speak to her so harshly, and directed at her because she failed to see things the way he did.

He pushed the emotion from his mind as best as he was able, and sat in the prow. Christensen started the outboard's engine and powered them into the sea-lanes between the ships at anchor.

WHEN THEY DOCKED the outboard, minutes later, Christensen hopped out of the craft and tossed the mooring line to one of the several young boys that had run over with offers to help. Most of them called Christensen by name.

Christensen grinned at the boys and playfully cuffed their arms and heads as he talked with them. With quick questions amid the clutter of talking voices, Kane heard Christensen get the news of the island. It seemed the Tong leader Wei Qiang himself was in the ville, as was Ambika.

Christensen flipped a few coins among the boys, and they gleefully scrambled for them. The ship's captain led the way up the rise to the ville. The incline was steep enough at times that the earth had been cut into, then laced with heavy timbers that made steps.

Kane followed to Christensen's left and back while Grant covered the same position on the captain's right, a couple steps farther back. They'd left the black Mag armor in the Sandcat and opted for traveling wear that allowed them to blend into the crowd. But they'd worn the heavy Mag trench coats that covered most of their bodies.

Autarkic's trade moved briskly. Hardly anyone gave them a second glance. At least, that was what Kane thought until he spotted a group of six Asians standing in the shade of a tarp thrown over the eastern-facing wooden walkway in front of a salvage and repair shop. A handwritten sign in the multipaned window advertised Bait and Dive gear.

The Asians conferred among themselves for a moment, obviously deep into decision making, then one of the men split off from the others. The five remaining kept their eyes on Christensen, Kane and Grant.

"They've been looking for us," Christensen said. "Evidently the ship you blasted made it back here just fine."

"It's hard to sink a wooden ship," Kane replied. He wasn't sure how he knew that so surely with the inexperience he'd had in Cobaltville, but he was aware of some kind of misplaced memory in the back of his head surging restlessly. However he knew it, he also knew it as truth.

"The side trip we took trading put them even farther ahead of us," Grant said.

As they passed the repair shop, the five Asians drifted onto their back trail.

Kane and Grant kept silent. It wouldn't do any good to brace any of the men then. They knew the territory, and they definitely had more help they could call on.

The streets remained narrow and rutted from wag wheels and horses' hooves. Crowds of hawkers flocked out to greet the newly arrived ships. Males and females of all ages offered everything from goods to sexual services, accosting the sailors shamelessly.

Kane and Grant both immediately attracted women and men currying sexual favors, undercutting each other in their bidding. Kane had no desire to get close to any of them. They were ill-dressed, and cleanliness wasn't even an afterthought.

"C'mon," a young woman with Indian heritage pleaded, grinding her thinly disguised mound against his leg as she darted her quick hands through his pockets. He had to give it to her; her touch was damn light.

"I can be very good to you," she promised in a breathy voice.

Kane noticed his Asian followers had increased the distance separating them. He bored his gaze into the young woman, looking at the thin scar over her right eyebrow under a shelf of waxed hair that fit her head like an abbreviated helmet.

"Make you forget your name after a little while," she went on. Her free hand cupped his buttocks as if she were pulling him in to her crotch, but actually she was getting him closer to check out his back pockets.

"I can make you forget yours," Kane told her.

She smiled as if it were a joke.

Then Kane flexed his wrist muscles and the Sin Eater leaped into his hand. He pressed the muzzle against her forehead. She'd been so close to death at different times in her life that the suddenness of his move didn't immediately send her into a panic. "And I can make you forget it permanently."

The girl froze, but the cocky smile remained in place. "You're making a mistake."

"By letting you live?" Kane asked. "Probably. But I won't make that mistake twice. Step away from me." He pushed her back, the Sin Eater's muzzle nearly eating into her flesh.

She backed away slowly, keeping her eyes locked with his. A half smile flickered on her lips, but her eyes held some of the crystalline fear she felt.

"Kane," Grant warned in a low voice.

The warning wasn't necessary. It came a moment after Kane heard the scuff of leather against the hard-packed earth of the street. He watched the woman as she continued to back away. Her features never revealed any of what was going on behind him.

"Chill them only if you have to," Kane told Grant quietly. He popped the Sin Eater back into the forearm holster. Some of the nearby hawkers were making a point to seek out other targets and get clear of the immediate area.

"Shit," Christensen swore, stepping away from Kane.

"Don't go far," Kane growled. He ducked and listened to the whoosh of the knotted chain as its length whizzed over his head. Before coming up, he planted a hard-thrown fist into his attacker's groin.

The man gurgled in pain, and vomit sprayed as he violently emptied his stomach. Kane shoved him back with his other hand, taking in the four men following the first. Beyond them, the Asians stood watching in silence.

The second man came at Kane with a camp ax, lifting it high. Kane reached for him, reflexes trained by hard years as a Mag. Grabbing a double fistful of the man's shirt, Kane butted him in the face with his head.

His attacker's nose broke with an audible crack, and blood spurted as from a swatted mosquito. He still tried to stay on his feet and use the ax again. Kane set himself, then backhanded the man in the throat, slapping him from his feet.

Grant wheeled faster than the man attacking him had thought possible. Before the man could get away, Grant clotheslined him in the throat, lifting him up and driving him backward nearly ten feet. Grant kept moving, pulling his hands up close to his face, fists half closed.

The next man Kane faced took all his attention, causing him to lose sight of Grant, but he kept the big man at his back, neither of them stepping away far enough to leave the other open to attack. The attacker came at Kane with knives in both fists, steel shimmering before him. Kane lifted an arm, depending on the Kevlar weave of the Mag jacket to turn the blades. Even as the razored edges sawed uselessly in a double-lick against the coat, he spun on his left heel, set himself and kicked the man in the left knee.

Bone broke with a sharp crack that was followed immediately by howls of pain. Kane kicked the man in the face as he fell. The blow twisted the man's head to the side and knocked him unconscious, sprawling him in the street. Turning, Kane watched Grant drive two blows into his opponent's face, putting him down.

Christensen hadn't moved. There hadn't been time, and he was secure between Grant and Kane.

In front of her, the gaudy slut held a knife that was long enough to be considered a short sword. She'd taken two steps forward, stopping just out of Kane's reach.

"Think about it," Kane advised.

Without another word, she turned and fled back to the docks.

The two men who were still conscious after the attack hobbled after her, leaving their three accomplices behind.

"I thought you said security was tight on this island," Kane told Christensen.

"It is," Christensen said. "You won't find anyone stealing from those ships out in the harbor, and the pilferage from the warehouses is almost nonexistent."

"But a man walking the streets isn't safe," Grant said.

"Not if he can't take care of himself," Christensen agreed. "For that they charge extra. That's why most of the trading's conducted out on the ships."

"What about the trading that takes place at the Dai Jia Lou?" Kane asked.

"A man only goes in there if he's got balls made of brass."

"You ever been in there before?" Grant asked sarcastically.

Christensen smiled, not taking offense. "I told you about the time I saw Ambika confront Wei Qiang. Over the years, I've been inside mebbe three, four other times. Seats inside Dai Jia Lou cost a lot of jack, too."

"Tell me again why we're going in there," Grant said.

"Wei Qiang will be in there," Christensen said.

"We're looking for Ambika," Kane stated.

"And he's the one person on this island I can guarantee will know where she is at all times," Christensen replied. "That's only one of the things he makes his business."

"He's going to generously share this information with us?" Grant asked.

Christensen didn't hesitate as he approached the long flight of steps leading up to the Dai Jia Lou's main entrance. The double doors occupied a corner rather than one of the sides. They stood under a tall wooden canopy that sported carved wooden ducks on the frontispiece, as well as on the support columns. Stained bottle-green glass filled the small latticework over the generous windows. More scrollwork covered the window ledges and the shutters around them. Bullet scars marred the exterior, but none of them looked fresh.

"Wei Qiang does things that amuse him," Christensen explained. "Mebbe I'll tell him you're looking for Ambika and that'll raise his curiosity or spur on his lust for amusement. You two guys definitely don't come across as a fun time. Qiang's no stupe—he'll figure that out straightaway. Mebbe he'll put you with her just to see what happens."

Kane stayed to Christensen's right and a half step behind as he pushed through the double doors and went inside. Grant stayed to the left and a little farther back.

Even after seeing the commanding presence the Dai Jia Lou had in the ville, Kane still wasn't quite prepared for the elegance that existed inside the place. Craftsmen who cared about their work had put the interior together, using a combination of dark, hand-rubbed woods, four-inch tiles of white rock and the bottle-green glass.

Small round tables filled the middle of the immense room's floor, flanked on three sides by high booths that permitted privacy. White curtains with bottle-green glass beads and dark wood ribs hung from rods strung across the ceiling that could be pulled to further enhance that privacy.

The fourth wall held a stage with a piano and a large harp. A woman sat at the harp, gently but quickly plucking the strings. She sang, but not in a language that Kane knew. She wore a long, flowing gown that still managed to show off a lot of cleavage.

Only a few of the tables and booths were filled. Wait staff dressed in dark red uniforms worked the tables, refreshing drinks and bringing out platters of food. The sweet smell of burning incense hung in the air.

Sec men wore black uniforms, and they were just as easy to pick out. They didn't wear their blasters openly, but Kane could tell from the cut of their clothes that they had them. They were a mix of all races; all of them hard men who'd grown up looking over the sights of one blaster or another.

"Eight," Grant said quietly.

"Eight," Kane agreed, knowing Grant had caught the two sec men stationed on the second floor looking down on the first. A long and winding staircase curled up to the left, allowing a partial view of the second floor. Judging from the way it was laid out, Kane assumed only rooms for rent were up there.

Christensen paused only to glance around, then headed for the corner booth, which was three times the size of the other booths. The rods on the ceiling allowed curtains to be drawn to cover the large area, as well, but they were open at the moment.

Seventeen Asian men sat at the table, all of them gazing at Kane and Grant. All were young to middle-aged except for the man who sat in the back against the wall.

He was without a doubt one of the oldest men Kane had ever seen. Lit by the candles floating in a large glass vase in front of him, the old man looked leathery and reptilian. His coloration was buttery-rum, and despite the fact that he was rail-thin, his skin hung on him as if it were three sizes too large. He was bald, but his gray, ropy eyebrows jutted ferociously over gnarled pits of gristle that contained eyes the color and texture of ball bearings. He wore a handmade dark blue suit that gleamed from the candles' glow.

Four of the men seated at the table stood immediately and formed a flesh-and-blood wall in front of the old man. They kept their hands folded in front of them, but their stances told Kane they were ready to move in an eye blink.

Christensen didn't hesitate in his approach, but he stopped

just out of arm's reach from the sec men. "Qiang, I want to talk to you."

Kane and Grant stopped farther back and stepped apart. They kept their eyes on the men in front of them. Their only edge was the Kevlar weave of their long coats, and that would last only the moment or two the sec men needed to recognize the coats for the armor they actually were.

One of the sec men started forward in an obvious approach to move him back.

Qiang spoke, his raspy voice so dry and brittle that it almost didn't carry. He spoke rapidly in Chinese.

The sec man turned to his lord and bowed, then moved away to give Christensen room. Qiang spoke to one of the men next to him.

"You may," the other man said, "speak from there. What is it you wish to speak to Lord Qiang about?"

"Yesterday at Columbine Island," Christensen said, "one of his ships attacked me. Damn near took my ship."

The man spoke to Qiang, who answered back briefly. The ball-bearing eyes swept over Kane and Grant, barely resting on Christensen.

"Lord Qiang wishes you to know that he's sorry to hear of your troubles," the interpreter said. "But he also says you tread on dangerous ground by inferring that he is in any way to blame for your ill fortune."

"I'm not inferring," Christensen stated. "I'm telling him flat out that I know that ship was his."

"Perhaps you mistake that ship for one of another Tong," the interpreter suggested.

"The hell I did," Christensen said.

Kane bit back his anger. What was Christensen doing baiting the Tong warlord? It didn't make sense.

The sec guard who'd stepped out of the way for Christensen spoke to the interpreter. Kane didn't understand the words, but he understood the intent and the body language just fine.

The old man nodded.

Smooth as oil rolling off water, the man drew a hand-blaster from under his jacket.

Kane moved even faster, stepping forward. He flexed his wrist and popped the Sin Eater against his palm. As his fingers closed around it, his forefinger settling against the firing stud, he grabbed the sec man's wrist and yanked it to the ceiling.

The sec man's blaster went off, gouging splinters from overhead.

Before anyone could move, Kane put the Sin Eater's sights on Wei Qiang and stepped behind the sec man, using him as a shield. To his credit, the Chinese warlord stared down the length of the barrel without batting an eye. As if they'd planned the whole thing, Grant backed his play.

One of the sec men moved slightly, getting ready to throw himself in front of Qiang.

Kane shifted his aim only slightly and squeezed the trigger. The boom of the detonation filled the room, followed immediately by dead silence. The round caught the Tong sec man in the shoulder, spinning him around away from his master.

"No!" Kane said harshly. He kept his gaze locked on Qiang. "It stops now. Next man up or moving and I put a round between your eyes, old man."

Chapter 23

Qiang didn't move, just regarded Kane openly. "You are that good?" he asked in perfect English.

Kane didn't hesitate. "Yes."

"But you didn't kill this man." Qiang pointed to the wounded sec man lying on the floor.

"I didn't try," Kane said. "So far I haven't cost you any lives. Other than the ones of your men on the ship that tried to take Christensen's."

"You're not from this place," Qiang said.

Kane didn't bother to deny it. With his age and the way the man obviously took care of his business, Qiang would know him.

"So, then," the old man said, "I must ask myself how you came to be in this place. And why."

"Does it matter?" Kane asked.

"No," Qiang replied, "because you will not leave this building alive." He pressed his palms flat against the table and levered himself out of his seat. Despite the infirmities foisted on him by his age, he moved smoothly.

"Then neither of us will," Kane said.

"Should you succeed in killing me, I have men who will make it their life's work to track you to the ends of the earth and claim your head. And they will be quite handsomely paid for their efforts." Qiang smiled. "My insurance policy. In the unlikely event that something untoward should happen to me."

"If I was here to chill you," Kane said easily, "it would have already been done. You wouldn't have seen me coming. But that's not what I'm here for."

Qiang folded his hands at his waist. "Then why are you here?"

"Business. Same as everybody who comes into this place."

"You intrigue me," the old man said. "I have your word that you won't try to harm me?"

"You're that trusting?" Kane asked.

"With you," Qiang said, "perhaps. We'll see. While you're with me, you shall be even more of a target than I am."

Kane flexed his wrist tendons, putting the Sin Eater away with a sudden rasp of leather.

Qiang waved to three of the chairs on the other side of his massive table. Sec men vacated them immediately.

Christensen sat, no longer quite as belligerent. Kane sat to the right of him, both hands resting comfortably on the table. The leather holster containing the Sin Eater reminded everyone how quickly the weapon could come into his hand if he needed it.

"Please release my man," Qiang said as he also sat.

Grant released the sec man with a small push that created immediate distance between them.

The interpreter spoke in rapid Chinese. The sec man bowed and moved away, chastised.

Reaching into a red lacquered box, Qiang took out an unfiltered cigarette. He made a production of smelling it, then licked one end and stuck it into his mouth. "Do you smoke?"

Kane reached into his pocket with his left hand and took out a cigar. "Yeah."

"You may smoke if you wish." Qiang took one of the

floating candles from the vase in front of him and lit his cigarette, then handed the candle over to Kane.

Taking the candle, Kane noticed that it had been carved in the shape of a rose, delicate and many petaled. He lit his cigar, then passed the candle to Grant. He smoked contentedly, but his pointman senses searched the room constantly.

"Mr. Christensen?" the interpreter offered, pushing the lacquered box over to the ship's captain.

Christensen took a cigarette, then got a light from Grant. He sat meekly in his chair, his fingers trembling slightly. For all his posturing, Kane knew the man was putting up a braver front than he honestly felt. He also noticed the way Qiang's interpreter knew Christensen's name.

"You say you were attacked, Captain Christensen," Qiang said.

Christensen nodded. "The way the ship looked, it had to have been one of yours." His tone indicated decision laced with doubt.

"But it wasn't," Qiang said. "I hope you understand that."

Christensen took his time getting a hit from the cigarette. Kane remained silent, waiting for the man's attention to return to him. Qiang was watching him, reading his face.

"What I understand," Christensen said deliberately, "is that if anyone makes another move on the *Sloop John B,* someone's going to pay."

Qiang's voice grew quieter and harder. "If I'm not mistaken, Christensen, I was just insulted and threatened. In my business, I can't allow that. Once word got around that I had been treated so disrespectfully, others would get the impression that anyone could treat me that way."

Kane got the feeling that things were not going to go their way. But he and Grant didn't move, didn't let any body language show. Christensen, however, wasn't so schooled. Sweat beads popped out on his forehead.

"You might rethink this," Kane said.

Qiang shifted his gaze to Kane. "I don't see any way around it."

"I do." Kane rounded the end of his cigar in a large ashtray in the center of the table. "There's no mistaking the ship that attacked the *Sloop John B*. It was one of those red jobs that fill up the harbor right now. The only way you're going to hush up the story is to chill everyone on Christensen's ship."

"I assure you that wouldn't be a problem," the Tong master replied.

"I didn't think that it would. I've seen people in this situation react that way. But you do have an option."

Qiang watched Kane, remaining silent.

"You can explain to Christensen how that ship that attacked him was one taken from you by another Tong, or that some of your navy has gone rogue."

"Why should I do that?"

"Because," Kane said, "it would be easier than chilling all of us. I assure *you* that I'm not getting up from this table while I feel in any way threatened."

Qiang's eyes narrowed. "Exactly what is your position in this matter?"

"I don't have a position in this matter," Kane said. "I was there and gave Christensen a hand. And I'm here now working on keeping my skin together."

Qiang's gaze remained stony. Then his bright ball-bearing eyes crinkled up in the wrinkled pits of gristle surrounding the sockets. "You're right, of course." He flicked his gaze to Christensen. "If you say you were attacked by one of my ships, it must have been one that has been taken from me. I can see how such a mistake can arise."

Christensen maintained the eye contact for a moment, then glanced at Kane. "If I back his story, word's going to get around. Other independent ships will get targeted, and he'll have the ready-made excuse that it was some *rogue* ship of his that did it."

"Mebbe," Kane said. "You walked in here with this. Have you got another card to play?"

Christensen shook his head in disgust.

Qiang smiled.

"However," Kane went on, "if more of this starts happening, other ships are going to get trigger-happy any time they see red ships around. In fact, the braver captains might be ones who take over red ships caught by themselves, certain they're *rogue,* as well."

"A sword that cuts both ways," Qiang said. "That amuses me. Well, Christensen, how are you going to handle this?"

"It was a rogue ship," Christensen said dully.

"Good. An unfortunate and regrettable circumstance in any business venture, but part of the whole experience of free trading." Qiang looked at Kane. "What is your business here?"

"My own," Kane said.

Qiang puffed on his cigarette. "Perhaps I could help you. I have an interest in many things that go on throughout these islands."

"I'm looking for Ambika," Kane answered softly. A moment of silence stretched between them at the table. He let it play.

"Why?"

"To discuss business."

"Might I suggest that I could be as helpful to you as she is," Qiang said.

"You could," Kane said, "but I'm going to talk with her."

Qiang crushed out his cigarette and released the final lungful of smoke through his nostrils. "Why, then, did you come to me?"

"Christensen said you'd know where she was."

The smile on the Tong warlord's lips never touched his eyes. "I always know where she is," he stated. "But I'm not in the habit of performing menial services."

"After your ship had gone *rogue*," Kane said, "I knew there was a chance that you might have heard which ship it had attacked. You might have heard that Christensen picked up someone from Columbine Island. I figured I'd stop in and clear up some of the curiosity you might have. Before you got too interested in what we're doing here."

"A careful man who yet moves boldly," Qiang said. "You don't see that combination often."

Kane said nothing.

"In answer to your question, Ambika has taken rooms upstairs for the day," Qiang said. "On the fourth floor. It's where she conducts her business. It's an arrangement we worked out. You'll find her there now."

Kane nodded. "Then we'll take our leave and go see her."

"Of course." Qiang held up an open palm, and Kane knew it was a gesture meant to command the men around him.

Kane got out of his chair carefully.

Grant remained sitting. "I'll be along in just a minute. Catch up with you."

Kane knew Grant was going to stay there to cover his back. It saved them both the trouble of growing eyes in the backs of their heads. He nodded at Qiang.

"In the future, perhaps we might yet get the chance to

do business together,'' the Tong warlord said. ''You're a most interesting man. And I don't even have your name.''

''It's Kane.''

''I'll remember you, Kane.''

Guiding Christensen, Kane pushed the other man ahead of him to the broad, sweeping stairs curling up to the second floor. Another flight of stairs led upward to the third floor, though not nearly as impressive as the first. And a final set led to the fourth floor.

At the stairs, Kane went up, watching the posted sec men there move back. He paused at the top at the railing and covered Grant. Qiang lit up another cigarette, and the conversations around the table began again.

Together, Kane and Grant went up the flights of stairs, followed by Christensen. No one tried to stop them until they reached the fourth floor.

The rooms there were opulent by any standards Kane had ever seen. The floor space alone in each unit had to have been hundreds of square feet, like small houses.

There was no mistaking which unit was Ambika's. It was the largest unit, taking up one full side of the building. Guards stood in front of all three doors leading to the suite of rooms. They were dressed in the blue-and-white colors of her flag, like an honor guard. Their movements when Kane and Grant approached erased any thoughts that they were purely ornamental.

''State your business,'' a burly man said.

Kane glanced at the short line of men and women seated in chairs out in the hallway. Evidently they were all waiting to have an audience with Ambika. All of them had the look of ships' captains about them, their faces leathery and worn.

''We're here to see Ambika,'' Kane said.

''So are all these people. What's the nature of your business?''

Kane felt irritated. He hadn't imagined taking place in a line of people waiting to see Ambika. "Tell her we're from Utah territories." It was the best trump card he had.

A look of surprise flashed across the man's face, but he quickly squelched it. Up close, Kane couldn't immediately identify the man's race. He had the Asian eye folds, but his skin held a dusky color hedging more toward black than olive.

As he looked at the other guards and the people waiting in line, Kane noticed that they were of more mixed blood than he'd seen before. From what little Brigid had told him of California before the nukecaust, he knew a broad range of people had lived there.

"Wait here," the man said. A quick hand signal drew the attention of the rest of his crew, and they immediately focused on Kane and Grant.

"Nuke-shit," Christensen said. "I didn't think we were going to live through the confrontation with Qiang."

"You walked us into that one," Kane growled.

"Yeah, well, it wasn't like he wasn't going to notice us," Christensen said. "Those men who picked us up at the docks weren't there by accident. He knew we were coming."

Kane knew that. After the confrontation at Columbine Island, it would have been hard to maintain a low profile.

The man stepped through the double doors, giving Kane a brief glimpse of the expansiveness of the room inside. Voices conversed within, but he couldn't understand any of the exchange. The man returned bare moments later.

"This way," he said.

Kane and Grant fell in behind him, moving easily, aware of the other men flanking them. Surprisingly, no one demanded their weapons. It meant Ambika, or whoever they were going to meet, was fully confident of their ability to take care of themselves.

The man opened the second set of double doors and pushed them inward. He led the way inside.

Kane trailed him, taking in the sitting room at a glance. Doors across the room opened onto a balcony with a small brass telescope on a tripod. A trio of sofas filled the center of the room. A small kitchenette was off to the left along with a bar, complete with two women who waited within. The right side held a fireplace, though Kane couldn't see how it would be needed in the gentle climate of the Western Isles. Beside the fireplace were double doors leading to the room everyone outside was waiting to get into.

The room impressed Kane. It would have been perfectly at home in the upper levels at Cobaltville.

"Sit," the sec leader said, gesturing to the sofas.

Kane and Grant did, sitting at two of them so they faced in different directions that gave them a view of the whole room. Christensen sat in the third sofa.

"Can I get you something to drink?" the sec leader asked.

Kane and Grant both answered no, not wanting to give anyone the chance to put something in their drinks. Christensen asked for a beer, and the sec leader had one of the women in the kitchenette pull a draft from a tap mounted on the wall. She brought it to the ship's captain, gleaming bright amber with a foamy head.

The sight of it made Kane thirsty, but he ignored the feeling. He gazed through the window, noting that it afforded a view of the gentle sloping beach leading down to the Cific Ocean and the harbor beyond. With the telescope, a person would have no problem identifying ships out in the harbor. Or people who'd come in on them.

After a few minutes, the doors opened and Ambika strode through.

Kane gazed at the woman, feeling the reaction to her femaleness hit him like a forty-pound sledge. He'd talked with Grant, away from Brigid, and listened to his friend's description of the woman, but it hadn't come close to the beauty that she held.

Her tight blue leather pants hugged every luscious curve, and a white shirt with belled sleeves and a drawstring front revealed the lack of a bra underneath. Her breasts were rounded and heavy, the same dusky complexion as the rest of her. Large nipples pressed against the fabric, taut and firm. A pearl band held her long blue-black hair in a tail, and strands of silver crisscrossed through the tail, further binding it. Her huge Casull .454 blaster was nestled in a cross-draw holster on the front of her left side. A trio of stilettos on her right thigh almost escaped Kane's trained eye. She wore knee-high black boots that put her an inch or two taller than Kane.

She swept into the room, drawing the eye of every man there. She gazed at Kane and Grant, disregarding Christensen almost immediately. "Tell me who you are and why I shouldn't have you chilled this very minute."

Chapter 24

Kane looked at Ambika, knowing she meant every word she'd just spoken. "My name is Kane. That's Grant. We came here thinking mebbe we could talk."

"About what?" she demanded, eyes flashing.

"Cobaltville," Kane replied.

With an impressive economy of motion, Ambika turned and gestured at the women in the kitchenette. One of them brought her a drink in a glass. "Wine," the warrior woman said. "Would you care for any?"

"No," Kane replied.

She sipped the bloodred liquid and regarded them with bright interest. "It took years after the nukecaust for the grapevines to take hold again. And they had to be carefully imported from France where the nuclear fallout hadn't quite destroyed everything. It took even more years to produce vines that took to the soil and conditions here. We're still not producing enough to export at more than marginal profit. But it will come."

Kane waited, watching the way the woman moved, the way her mouth moved when she spoke. Her presence had an immediate effect on him, and he could tell from the way Grant was shifting that the other man was experiencing the same feeling. Ambika was incredible, oozing sexuality and more than a hint of danger.

She remained standing. "I've heard of you before. Both

of you used to be Cobaltville Magistrates.'' She turned to speak over her shoulder. ''McIlwain.''

''Yes, lady.''

''Take your men and go.''

Kane watched the sec chief's face, noting the displeasure the man displayed. Obviously he wasn't used to being dismissed so cavalierly. Still, he signaled to his men and they left without a word, closing the double doors behind them.

''Do you think me foolish or overly confident for asking them to leave?'' Ambika asked.

''Not less confident or foolish than for us to have walked into this room to speak with you.''

Ambika smiled back at him then, and Kane felt the effects in the pit of his groin. Part of him couldn't help wondering what she would be like in bed. Her strength was apparent, as well as her dexterity. He had no doubt that she'd be a demanding and challenging partner.

''I knew you'd probably come,'' she said, ''after I was told about the Sandcat that had attacked one of Qiang's ships off the coast of Columbine Island.''

''Who told you?'' Kane asked.

''Would it surprise you,'' she asked, ''to learn that I have spies within Qiang's organization?''

''I'd be disappointed if you didn't,'' Kane answered.

''Just as I have spies within Cobaltville. Baron Cobalt is much more suspicious these days. Over the past year, three of my spies who sometimes worked within the Administrative Monolith were chilled. The baron made sure I knew, and sent a message out to everyone else who might consider accepting bribes.'' She gazed at him. ''But I don't have spies within wherever it is you're from.''

''No,'' Kane agreed.

''Where are you from?''

Kane shook his head.

"I could make it worth your while," Ambika said.

"Tempting," Kane said, "but we have an agenda here."

"We?" Ambika glanced at Grant. "I'm guessing you're talking about more than just the two of you."

Kane nodded.

"How many?" she asked.

Kane shook his head.

She smiled, obviously enjoying the puzzle his presence presented. "It has to be a small group," she mused. "Otherwise you'd have taken a more aggressive posture with the barons yourselves. Though I did hear that you were responsible for chilling Baron Ragnar."

Kane didn't bother correcting that misconception.

"However," Ambika went on, "you've obviously got resources I hadn't considered. You found the gateway and got through while Baron Cobalt couldn't."

Kane let that one pass. Christensen was watching and listening, taking everything in.

"What are you wanting from this meeting?" Ambika asked.

Kane shrugged. "To find out if we can work together."

"What kind of information can you get?" she asked.

"Intel about movement, supplies, personnel. We've been able to get pretty much whatever we wanted." Kane knew Lakesh had more information about Cobaltville than he'd ever willingly share.

"You believe I need this?" she asked.

"If you don't," Kane answered, "then I'm wasting both our times." He gazed into her electric aqua eyes, noting gleaming lights deep within them.

She sipped her wine, taking a moment as she raked him with her eyes, as bold and imperious as any man gawking at a woman. "You're not wasting your time. Meet me at the dock before sunset tonight. We'll be leaving then."

"At night?" Grant asked.

Ambika flicked her glance over him. "My captains know these waters well and the tide is favourable. Tonight there'll be less traffic, and it's easier to avoid spying eyes. Qiang has his own watchers. I'll see you then." She turned and left the room.

Kane watched her go, noting the smooth roll of hips beneath the tight leather pants.

"Man," Grant said in a tight voice.

"Yeah," Kane said, "I know what you mean."

"WE SHOULD GO BACK to Cerberus," Brigid said, trying to control the frustration she felt. She stood on the *Sloop John B*'s deck with Kane, Grant and Domi, listening as Kane made plans to accompany Ambika. Christensen stood at the wheel only a few yards away.

The Cific Ocean drank the scarlet sun down to the west. Vermilion-red fingers spilled across the greenish cast of the sea, interrupted by curling white waves. Some of them slapped rhythmically against the cargo ship's hull, while others ran to crash against Autarkic only a little farther north.

"We don't know enough yet, Baptiste," Kane argued.

Brigid crossed her arms in frustration. "When is it going to be enough, Kane? When she's holding a knife to your throat? Or maybe when you're bleeding down the front of your shirt?"

She was angry for a few reasons, not the least of which was Kane's decision to go with Ambika, and also for staying in Autarkic for so long. She'd been worried about that, but not overly so because whatever trouble found Kane would have spilled over onto her and Domi on the *Sloop John B*.

Kane's own anger showed in the way he held his head and made an effort to breathe deeply and evenly. He rubbed the back of his neck and turned away from her. "Do you want to leave this half done?"

"No," she said in a softer voice. "I don't want to leave it half done. But getting chilled before we get back to Cerberus is the same as leaving it half done."

Turning to her, Kane gave her that half smirk of full-wattage confidence that she hated about him and found appealing all at the same time. "I'm not planning on getting chilled, Baptiste, but I would like to look at her setup here. Lakesh agrees."

Brigid knew that, too. They'd finished the conversation with Lakesh only a few minutes before. The professional, detached part of her that had made such a good archivist agreed with Kane's assessment. They wouldn't be in any more danger from Ambika as part of her flotilla than they would staying in Autarkic. "Tell me how she's different than any of the barons. You saw those people she chilled in the ambush in Utah."

Kane nodded. "Yeah, I did. It's a terrible thing to look at, Baptiste. An even more terrible thing to order it to be done. But it was necessary."

"You saying that doesn't convince me."

"I know," he said in a softer voice. "And I'm glad it doesn't. But I recognize that sometimes things like that have to happen in order to cause change. When it comes to changes like this, you need a sinner, not a saint, to get the job done. Lakesh recognizes that. It's why he recruited Grant and me."

Brigid turned away from him, unable to continue the argument. Her feelings of dread had grown with the coming of the night. She couldn't make up her mind if it was from the lateness of the hour or knowing they were on the verge of departing.

"There she comes," Domi said, angling her chin toward the beach.

Brigid went back to the railing and watched as Ambika and her entourage reached the beach. With so many men around her dressed in their blue-and-white uniforms, she would have been hard to miss even under harsher circumstances.

Ambika was met at the pier by a cabin cruiser. Once the woman was aboard, the cabin cruiser heeled around and powered toward the *Sloop John B,* avoiding the barges and small boats still off-loading trade goods in both directions.

The cabin cruiser's pilot pulled alongside the cargo ship with expert skill. Ambika stood on the deck, dressed in the Kevlar armor, the sword sheathed down her back. Close up and even in the dark, she was an impressive woman. Brigid experienced an instant pang when she saw Kane watching her so intently. Part of her wondered if she'd have objected less to the meeting if Ambika had been a man—or ugly. She didn't like considering that.

"Kane," Ambika called.

"I'm here," Kane responded.

"Take passage on my flagship," the warrior woman urged. "It'll offer a better ride and it's better protected. The waters between Autarkic and my home are often treacherous with free traders and scavengers."

Kane gazed at her. "What about my companions and our vehicle?"

"Your companions are as welcome as you are." Ambika turned her attention to Christensen. "You can bring their vehicle. I've no time to spare to arrange loading it onto one of my craft, and I don't think they'll be too willing to leave without it."

Kane shook his head, and Brigid felt one of the knots in her stomach loosen. Kane out in the field was as alien to her as an Archon. There were things he'd do, risks he'd take, that she clearly didn't agree with. But the percentages bore out his tactics. Even the one-percenters he and Grant chose to play out rather than let pass. Still, it was impossible to sit by on the sidelines.

"I've got other places to be," Christensen said.

Ambika smiled up at him coldly. "I can make the trip worth your time or I can have your ship sunk after we take the time to transfer the vehicle. Profit or loss, Captain Christensen?"

"You don't give a man much choice."

"I'm forcing you to make money. Besides, you've never been to my islands. You could find whole new worlds open to you."

Christensen said nothing.

"Kane," Ambika called out, "will you join me now?"

"Yeah," Kane called down. "Give me a minute." He turned to Brigid. "I don't want to leave the Cat unprotected."

"So you want me to stay here with it?" Brigid asked sarcastically.

Kane shook his head. "Actually, Baptiste, I was going to ask Grant and Domi to stay here with the Cat. Unless you don't want to go."

Brigid bit back an angry retort. Kane was dependable for being undependable. "Why do you want me to go?" she asked.

Kane scowled at her, obviously feeling she should have figured out the answer by herself. "She's a woman."

"As you're no doubt very aware."

"Yeah, I've noticed," Kane admitted easily. "That's why I want you along. Mebbe you'll get a better read on her than I do."

"Meaning I won't be as prone to be distracted and forget why I'm there as you will be."

Kane frowned. "Dammit, Baptiste, this isn't some kind of competition. If you don't want the job, I'll ask Domi to go."

"No," Brigid said. "I want to go. I want to see her for myself. Let me get my gear."

Chapter 25

"Is she your woman?"

Kane looked at Ambika in surprise. They stood on the prow of the warrior queen's flagship, a three-masted motor sailer that cleaved the Cific Ocean and rode like silk on glass. "Baptiste?" He glanced over to where Brigid stood on the main deck. "No. She's her own woman. She'll be the first to tell you that."

Ambika looked at him, the aqua eyes intent and glinting in the moonlight, deeper blue now in the shadows the ending day had drawn. "Have you had a relationship in the past? I thought perhaps I sensed something between you."

That was a harder question to answer. Nothing had happened between him and Brigid in this time and place, but there were those memories of past lives to consider. He still remained unclear about those. He chose his answer. "No."

The aqua gaze remained fixed on him. "It's unusual for me to be wrong about such things."

Kane listened to the sails pop occasionally overhead, the sound of the ropes being drawn tight to take up any slack. The surge of the flagship knifing through the water was heady, almost feeling like he was falling at times. He glanced behind them and saw the other ships sailing along in their wake.

"Have you got a woman back where you come from?" Ambika asked.

Kane was overly aware of how close they stood together.

In the chill of the night air rushing by them, he could feel the woman's body heat, could smell the musk of her over the delicate vanilla scent she wore. "No."

"But you've known women?" Ambika pressed.

"Yes." Kane grew uncomfortable with the conversation. The aqua gaze grew hot and challenging. "Have you known many of them?"

"Why?"

She raised an arched brow, obviously irritated that he'd interrupt her flow of questions. "Because I like to get to know people I do business with. It helps me understand where they're coming from and what they're willing to risk to accomplish the things they set out to do. I think that you're a driven man, Kane. I can see it in your eyes, in the way you hold your head. You let few things stand between you and what you desire."

"That's not always a good way to be," Kane said.

"It's the only way to get everything in life that you want," Ambika said. "Thinking is good to accomplish things when events grow cold, but when things are hot, ready to be taken by force, passion is the tool best used."

"You give me the impression of someone who thinks things through," Kane said.

"I do," Ambika said. "I'm very ambitious. I won't settle for second best or anything less than I feel I deserve. I believe you're the same way. The woman, Baptiste, doesn't understand that. She doesn't like me."

Kane started to object, but Ambika cut him off.

"I can see it in her eyes," the woman said. "It's nothing that's going to stand in the way of us working together. I do business every day with people I don't like."

"Like Wei Qiang?" Kane asked, hoping to change the subject.

Ambika laughed, and it was full-throated and rich.

Kane found himself laughing with her, carried away by the genuine exuberance she displayed.

"Actually, no," she answered. "I like Wei Qiang very much. More than that, I respect him. If we weren't in conflict over some of the same territories, maybe we could even enjoy a friendship. Believe it or not, we even exchange gifts every now and then."

Kane was intrigued, but maybe it was her voice. It held a certain hypnotic sway over him. "What kind of gifts?"

"Wei Qiang collects objets d'art," Ambika answered. "Especially things from the San Francisco area known as Chinatown. Paintings, sculpture, jewelry."

"San Francisco?" Kane repeated. "Wasn't that a ville in California?"

Ambika nodded. "Actually, it was one of the biggest."

"But it was a coastal ville. It should have been lost to sea during skydark."

"It was," Ambika agreed. "For a long time it lay at the bottom of the Cific Ocean, nearly two hundred feet down. When the Western Isles were re-formed almost a hundred years ago, the area came closer to the surface. Now it lies only fifty or sixty feet down. Scavengers discovered it nearly thirty years ago and began harvesting salvageable items from it. Now I supply crews that work that area."

"And in the meantime you're working on taking over the mining operations in the Utah territories," Kane said.

"Ambitious," Ambika reminded.

"You've got the manpower to do that?"

"I'm doing it."

"Baron Cobalt isn't going to sit back and let it happen."

"No, and I'm not going to walk away, either."

Kane heard the resolution ring true in her melodic voice and he felt himself drawn to it. She had vision and she had fire. She was so many things that Brigid wasn't. The realization that he'd compared the two women shocked him, and triggered a spark of anger deep within him. Brigid didn't deserve that, and the fact that he'd compared them said a lot about how he felt about Brigid.

"I was born to conquer, Kane," Ambika said. "Have you heard of the Totality Concept?"

"Yeah."

"My spies in Cobaltville had heard rumors that your discovery of some hidden information the barons had held led to the issuing of a termination warrant on you."

Kane nodded, not willing to give her any more than he absolutely had to.

"You've also heard of Overproject Excalibur in the Totality Concept?"

"They were interested in gene manipulation."

"I, too, am a product of gene manipulation," Ambika said. "My father was a man named Wil Longley. He was part of Mission Invictus, and believed that the best way to effect a lasting change was to adjust the basic human genes, building toward a more perfect product," she continued.

"He believed he was close to perfect himself?" Kane asked.

The aqua eyes searched his, glints of suppressed anger in them. "My father was a great man, but he didn't have an ego like that. He used the sperm and eggs of the most perfect physical and mental specimens he could find. Rhodes scholars. Olympic champions. That was how the administrative staff of Excalibur found out what he was doing. They had more people under their control than my father expected. He was forced into hiding, fleeing for his life, ostracized from every person he'd once counted as a friend."

Kane listened to the woman's words, wondering why she was being so open with him. He already knew enough about her to know that it wasn't without reason.

"Fortunately, my father had prepared," Ambika said. "He had a vault set up with a hibernation chamber high in the Rocky Mountains, chancing that he'd survive the coming nukecaust. He'd kept his files duplicated there. He worked up until the end of the world, perfecting all his experiments. When the world died, he climbed into the hibernation chamber."

Below, one of the sailors drifted close to Brigid and started talking. The sight of the man talking to her irritated Kane. He forced himself to look away and concentrate on Ambika's words.

"Fifty-two years ago, the hibernation chamber opened. The vault he'd set up suffered some damage and disrepair, but he picked up where he'd left off with his research." Pride swelled in Ambika's voice. "Twenty-six years ago, after a considerable number of failures, I was born."

Kane looked at her in the moonlight, amazed at her age. Not so much by the way she looked, but because she was able to achieve what she'd achieved at that age.

"Why are you so surprised?" she asked.

"You've raised an army and an empire in that amount of time?"

"I started when I was fourteen," Ambika said.

"At fourteen?"

She glanced at him sharply. "When did you start serving with the Magistrates?"

"I was sixteen."

"I was only two years your junior," she said.

Kane shook his head. "But I was joining a unit, being a follower, not a leader."

"I was bred to lead. And by fourteen, I had attained my full growth. I looked then as you see me now."

"It takes more than leadership ability and a willingness to do that to lead people," Kane said.

"You're wondering what I did with those who thought they could lead instead of me?"

Kane nodded. "I don't figure a group would let a fourteen-year-old girl step in and start telling them what to do."

"They didn't," Ambika said. "I chilled the ones who tried that. Immediately. After the first few, they fell in line."

Kane looked at her in wonderment, trying to understand how a fourteen-year-old girl—even grown to amazonian proportions—could have stepped into such a life-style. He couldn't fathom it. Yet he knew of Roamer kids in the Outlands who'd risen to prominence, and who'd marshaled ragtag bands that had ambushed and killed Mags.

"My father trained me to kill," she said. "And when he'd taught me all he knew, he brought warriors in from outlying villes. They trained me further. The rest, I've taught myself or learned from men I've fought."

Kane examined her more closely. Her skin tone was flawless, stirred warm cinnamon butter. The absence of scars suddenly struck him. "You've never been wounded?" he asked.

She laughed at him, her blued-silver mane blowing in the breeze. "I've been wounded several times, Kane. Nearly chilled a half dozen others. The closest I ever got to death was when a portion of my skull was blown away." She touched her head above her left eye. "That was three years ago, part of an assassination attempt by a group of organized free traders who objected to my taking over their area. When I recovered, I tracked each of them down and chilled them with my own hands."

Kane peered at her head. Only unblemished skin met his gaze.

"You don't believe me?" she asked.

"I don't see how I can," Kane responded. "I've never

seen anyone survive the kind of injury you're talking about. And there's no scar, no sign of such a wound existing."

"There never is," she said. "As I told you, my father's plans for me were perfection. I was designed to be the ultimate survivor."

"Then why didn't he make more of you?" A cold breeze gusted over the ship's railing. Ambika didn't seem to notice at all, but the chill thrilled through Kane, tightening his skin.

"Because only one queen bee can exist in a hive," Ambika replied. "If there had been another, we would have fought and one of us chilled the other. He birthed me to bring some order to what was left in this world."

Listening to her speak, Kane figured that Wil Longley and Lakesh shared a lot of the same elitism. Both had evidently worked to bring about the end of the old world so a bright new one could begin. And both believed they were working to salvage what was left of civilization. "Do you think that you can do that?"

"It's not a matter of thinking," she told him. "It's a matter of doing." Her gaze turned hard and cold. "I will accomplish those objectives. Baron Cobalt will be the first to go down. Then I'll systematically seize and control the rest of the Outlands until I've hunted them all down."

The fierceness in her voice kept Kane from saying anything. He realized she believed every word she said.

"What about the people who live in the villes?" Kane asked.

"When the time comes, they'll be given their choice whether to serve me or serve the barons."

Kane was getting increasingly uncomfortable with the conversation. Even Lakesh in all his grandiose plans and counterplans had never talked of becoming a ruler. Lakesh had only talked of freeing the people from the yokes of the barons. Without resorting to civil war. To Kane, it seemed that Ambika would stop short of nothing less than civil war. "You want everyone to follow you?"

"Leadership ultimately falls into the hands of one," Ambika said. "Power always resides with one. To believe anything less is stupe. One can provide one decision, one set of rules, one proper view. There can be only one."

"That's you?"

"Do you see anyone else better equipped for the job?"

"No," Kane said.

"Look around you," Ambika said. "One leader is the natural order of things. Villes are ultimately run by one person. A person who is strong, who is both loved and feared. Coldheart gangs have one leader. Pack animals. Bees and ants."

The logic was flawed, Kane knew, but he wasn't going to debate it. The thinking was as true as it was false. Mags went into an area of chaos and confusion, then beat and killed it back into a semblance of order. Even that order, as destructive as it had been, was better for everyone who lived there. He'd seen it. Violence was a tool to create fear in those who would rebel against the wishes of the majority. Violence was also used, as in the case of the barons, against those who rebelled against the wishes of the strong minority.

"Do you understand what I'm saying?" she asked after a moment.

"Yes."

"Do you agree?"

"I can see your point, but there are some who do just fine when left to their own devices."

She shook her head. "You haven't seen enough, Kane."

Anger surged up in him then as she talked to him like a child. "What haven't I seen?"

"You grew up in Cobaltville," she said, not responding to the heat in his voice. "You didn't see much of what goes on in the Outlands. Cobaltville is established. They make enough food for themselves, but not enough for any others. Or did you think they were being selective about who they let into the ville?''

Kane had always been taught that. There were those who deserved and who would contribute to a ville, and there were those who were only leeches. It had been the Magistrate Division's job to keep things running smoothly and keep the parasites out of the villes.

''They kept only those they could feed and care for,'' Ambika said. ''Even then, there are the privileged few among them. You were one of the lesser privileged in Cobaltville, but can you imagine living down in the Tartarus Pits?''

''No,'' Kane answered honestly.

''What set those people apart from you? Or anyone else in the Enclaves? Birthright?'' Ambika shook her head. ''They were controlling the numbers. The first ville I ran didn't have enough game and harvestable foods around to supply all of the people who had nowhere else to go. The ville broke up, torn by the lack of things I needed to help provide them.''

''It wasn't your fault,'' Kane said softly.

She whirled on him, her face tight with anger. ''It was! I made those people believe in me! I should have taken better care of them!''

''You were young,'' Kane said. ''You didn't know any better.''

''I trained to take care of those people,'' she objected. ''I just didn't learn my lessons well. After the ville fragmented, some of them dead by each other's hands, I made myself a promise that it would never happen again. And it hasn't. My father told me there was a possibility we'd find something

out here. When we came, we found the redoubt near where
Los Angeles used to be and we started building there."

"And ten years later, they call it the Isles of the Lioness,"
Kane said.

She looked at him, studying him as if to make sure of his
emotion. Satisfied, she said, "Yes. We continue to grow
there."

"Wei Qiang doesn't know about the redoubt with the
functioning gateway?"

"He knows about them," she replied. "But he can't get
into them."

"If your next move is to consolidate a power base in the
Utah territories," Kane asked, trying to puzzle through all
the information he'd gotten, "why not begin here?"

"It's the iron ore, Kane," Ambika said. "It's important
to what I have to do." She sighed, looking southward.
"You'll see tomorrow."

Kane nodded, curbing his impatient curiosity. The woman
interested him more than ever now, and he was all too aware
of the proximity between them. Brigid, he noted, was standing by herself at the railing. Twice he caught her looking
up to see him. Both times she'd glanced away hurriedly.

"How many women have you had, Kane?" Ambika
asked softly.

"I don't know," Kane said. "A long time ago, I stopped
counting."

Her aqua eyes searched his face. "And how long has it
been since the last one?"

He shook his head.

"But it has been a long time," she told him. "I can tell."

A little embarrassed, Kane glanced away from her.

"I can see your passion burning within you," she said.
"I arouse you. You can tell me that's not true, but we'll
both know you're lying."

Kane chose not to say anything. Her words coiled around in the pit of his loins, having a strong and immediate effect on him. His erection surprised him.

"Kane," she said, her voice barely above a whisper, "in my whole life, I've never had a man. Never suffered a man's touch or his demands."

Kane couldn't believe it. How could anyone so aggressive deny the needs that burned through her body? He knew it wasn't just men who had those needs.

"I saw you today," she went on, "when you faced the men out in the street, and when you walked into my suite to face me, and I saw something in you that I've never seen in a man before."

Struggling, noticing how dry and tight his throat had gotten, Kane tried to think of something to say. He failed. His pulse beat at his temples.

She left him without another word. She never even looked back.

Kane hung on to the railing for a long time, reaching out into the night to bring him the calm he needed. He felt as if he were dancing on a strand of razor wire.

Chapter 26

Kane rose late the next morning. The past few days of hard travel still wore on him. He and Brigid had slept in hammocks in the crew's quarters. The crew aboard the flagship had about a third as many women as men, and the quarters had been subdivided by sheets. Kane had looked for Brigid after he'd come down from talking with Ambika but he'd never found her.

He found the mess by following his nose and the steady line that filtered into the galley. The area was clean and crisp, filled with stainless-steel surfaces. The cooks worked briskly, getting the crew through the line.

Breakfast was white-pepper gravy over thick biscuits served with homemade butter, small pork chops and two different kinds of melon. He piled it all onto a plate and headed back out onto the deck after looking around and finding Brigid wasn't there, either. He ate with his fingers, discovering the gravy was extremely hot to the touch. But it was welcome warmth, serving to burn off the chill created by the patchy fog hanging over the ocean.

Brigid was in the prow by herself. She scanned the sea with her binoculars.

Kane joined her, sopping up gravy with one of the half dozen biscuits he'd piled on his plate. "Where the hell were you last night, Baptiste?" he asked.

"I could ask you the same question," she countered.

"I was in crew's quarters."

"So was I." She regarded him with her jade eyes. "You looked like you were going to be getting in late from the looks of things last night."

Kane gnawed fried pork from the bone, enjoying the taste of the grease. "Nothing happened."

"That's not the impression I got," she said coolly.

"The hell with your impressions."

"I thought those impressions were what I was here for," Brigid told him shortly.

"You're jumping to conclusions, Baptiste. I was talking to her."

"I saw that. I saw more than that. Getting interested in that woman, Kane, you're playing with fire."

"I'm not interested," Kane grumbled, and he felt good because that was only half a lie. Maybe even less than half. As he ate, he quickly relayed the information he'd gotten last night. He left out the parts about her sexual proclivities.

"She told you she'd been wounded?" Brigid asked.

"Yeah. Several times."

"I showered with her this morning," Brigid said.

Kane almost choked on a mouthful of biscuit.

Brigid ignored his reaction. "Community bathrooms, Kane. If you'd gotten up early enough, you'd have found out about them. Maybe even gotten a chance to use one."

"I'll ask around," Kane said sarcastically. "Mebbe I still can."

"I watched her," Brigid admitted. "Someone who looks like that, you can't help but watch and be kind of awed."

"You might remember that in the future and quit busting my balls about it," Kane said.

"I'm not a man. She's not going to have the same effect on me."

"Mebbe not the same one, but she had one."

"She's a handsome woman," Brigid admitted. "But what

I'm getting at is there were no scars. Her body was perfectly unmarred.''

"She also told me she had part of her skull blown away at one time," Kane told her. "I couldn't see that, either."

"Do you think she's lying?"

Kane finished chewing and swallowed. "Hell, Baptiste, I don't know what to think about her. But she seems very driven. I've never met anyone like her."

Brigid peered at him, her eyes narrowed slightly. He couldn't read her expression, but he had the immediate feeling that he'd said something wrong. "No," she said, "you probably haven't."

"Being on this ship like this," Kane said, "it might be an idea if we stayed in contact."

"We're on a ship. How many places can you go?"

Kane finished his last biscuit, then peered through the sails at the ships that followed them. He spotted Christensen's craft easily. "That's not the point," he told her irritably. "The point is we're supposed to cover each other."

"That's hard to do when you're working on covering someone else."

"Leather it, Baptiste," Kane ordered. He could tell by the set of her jaw that he'd overstepped his bounds.

Before she could make the heated reply he knew was coming, a drone filled the air above them.

Kane craned his neck and looked up, spotting a bright red wasp shape above him. Brigid trained her field glasses upward. "It's an air wag," she said incredulously.

"Let me see." Kane placed his empty plate at his feet and took the field glasses when she offered them. He stared up through the wisps of fog and spotted the air wag. It was long and slender, its delicate fuselage sandwiched between long, wide wings and equally large stabilizers. When it banked, he saw it was prop-driven and carried only one man in an open cockpit. It wasn't big enough to carry passengers.

Two other air wags flanked it.

Looking at them, he realized they were the same scarlet color as Wei Qiang's ships. The banking aircraft lost altitude deliberately, dropping toward the ship. The air wag fell behind for a time, barely skimming above the surface of the Cific.

The sailors crowded the decks, squeezing in against the railing. The air wag's sputtering engine squealed more loudly as it closed the distance and drew closer to the ship. The other two air wags maintained their positions overhead.

Kane flicked his wrist, popping the Sin Eater into his hand before he thought about it.

"It's all right."

Kane glanced over his shoulder and saw Ambika standing there. He hadn't heard her come up, which was unusual with his pointman's awareness. "Do you know who it is?"

"The air wag has to belong to Qiang," Ambika said, gazing at the approaching craft. "He's the only one who has them."

When the air wag drew close, Kane saw that it was actually a pitiful thing, nothing at all like the Deathbirds he'd flown as a Magistrate. It flew incredibly slowly, seeming to struggle to catch up with the ship blown by the wind. The fuselage was made of lightweight wood and canvas, heavily coated with the red lacquer to keep it together. The prop didn't have the gleam of metal and he guessed that it was wood, but it was taller than a man, batting at the air. The engine didn't sound very powerful at all. A well-thrown rock could probably knock it out of the air.

"All it takes is a high-ex package set to explode on contact and they can put this ship down," Kane pointed out.

Ambika disagreed. "Qiang wouldn't do that."

"You seem awfully sure of yourself," Brigid said.

Ambika smiled, but humor never touched her eyes. "We've been enemies for a long time. It's the new ones you have to watch out for. You don't know what they'll be capable of."

Kane figured that was a message meant for both of them. He ignored it and glanced back at the air wag.

The spluttering engine droned on, and the air wag caught up with them. When it drew abreast, less than ten feet out, the pilot threw a cylinder shape toward the deck.

Kane stayed locked on his target, nervously waiting. Dynamite sticks held that kind of shape.

The cylinder bounced against the deck twice, then started rolling in a half arc back and forth. One of the crewmen ran over to it, then brought it to Ambika.

The air wag began its slow ascent into the heavens, the motor straining.

"It's a message," Ambika said, unfurling the paper. She scanned it briefly. "Raiders are attacking one of my fuel shipments only a few miles to the west." She handed the note over to Kane.

He read through it quickly. The writing was succinct, shaky from the pilot writing it while flying. He gave it to Brigid. "Qiang keeps scouts in the air?"

"Not just for scouting," Ambika said. "But also to remind people that he has the air wags. As you said, it only takes a high-ex package set to explode on contact to take out a ship and her crew. He's ordered it done in the past."

"Why not do it now if he's interested in protecting your fuel shipment?"

"The free traders and raiders have learned that trick. As soon as one of Qiang's air wags get close, they blast them from the skies. It doesn't take much firepower to knock one of the air wags down, and they're time-consuming to construct.'' Ambika turned and shouted orders to her helmsman, correcting their course to follow the air wag, and to the first mate to alert the other ships.

"Why would Qiang be interested in protecting your shipment?" Brigid asked.

"Because it's going to him," Ambika said. She ran her hands across her weapons, mentally taking inventory. Kane knew because he'd done the same thing before. It was a habit that came from long training. "I've got a processing station set up down in Mexico. They had an abundance of petroleum products the United States wouldn't buy before skydark. My father had maps that detailed some of the storage spaces. Many of them survived. We found personnel and equipment, and set it up as we started enlarging. I sell the overflow to Qiang and some of the other villes. It keeps me in their good graces because getting a navy together to make the hauls would be expensive. And those fuel runs can be very dangerous."

"It also makes them somewhat dependent on you," Kane said.

"Yes." Ambika grinned. "That's why I knew Qiang wouldn't do anything to me. He's protecting his investment."

"How soon before we reach the fuel shipment?" Kane asked.

"Fifteen, twenty minutes."

He nodded and took his empty plate up from the deck. "I'll be ready."

KANE PULLED the polycarbonate armor on down in the crew's quarters. He had his helmet in place, listening to Grant's conversation over the comm-link and trying to keep up with Brigid's protests.

"Participating in this isn't what we agreed to do," Brigid said.

"How do you want to handle it?" Grant asked.

"Fill in where you can," Kane said. "Don't use the Cat's machine guns unless you have to. I want to keep the ammo we have there." He locked his chest plate into place, then reached for the leggings. He looked at Brigid, letting her know he was talking to her. "What do you propose to do, Baptiste? Watch?"

"It's not our fight," Brigid said.

"I'm sure the raiders' bullets will know that and understand."

She scowled at him. "We're not in control of this thing, Kane. Don't you see that? We've gone well past what we'd agreed to accomplish."

"You want to make a decision on what we've seen so far?" Kane asked.

"My vote is yes," Grant replied. "The lady impresses the hell out of me. She's definitely going to give Baron Cobalt a run for his jack. And I'd say she could be the odds-on favorite."

"Yes," Brigid answered. "I do."

"And what would that decision be?" Kane snapped the leggings into place.

"We don't need her."

"Hell, Baptiste, she's got an army, a navy, an armored division and supplies to keep it all moving. Cerberus is years away from that."

"But it's in the direction of her agenda," Brigid said. "Not ours."

"And what the fuck is ours?" Kane asked explosively. "Do you think for a minute that Lakesh had opened up his whole treasure trove of secrets and plans? He's a bigger manipulator than Ambika. At least she comes at you straight on. You get a chance to see what you're dealing with.''

''That's only one of the things I like about her,'' Grant said over the helmet radio.

Brigid shook her head. When she spoke, her voice was surprisingly calm. ''You're not seeing it all, Kane. You're seeing what you want to, what she wants you to and what you understand.''

''That goes for most people, don't you think?''

''You brought me along to give you feedback on what I thought of her,'' Brigid said. ''Or don't you remember that?''

''I remember.'' Kane pulled his gloves on last, and as he'd donned the armor, he'd felt the old Mag certainty settle in on him. He was right in what he was doing. No other course was the one they needed to choose. ''I listened and I disagreed.''

''Big surprise.''

''I don't have time for this, Baptiste,'' he growled.

''When do you think you will?''

''You're operating out of your own feelings,'' Kane admonished. ''You don't like her, you don't like the way she does things. Well, sometimes, Baptiste, they're the only way to get things done.''

''According to you.''

''According to history, according to the kind of world we're in now. The barons, no matter how outnumbered they may be, aren't going to give up their villes. They'll dig in, sacrifice every life they can to prevent anyone from throwing them out of power.''

''And you'll take every life they offer up?''

''To make it better for everyone else?'' Kane shook his head. ''Yeah, Baptiste, I will. Because I believe it has to be done. In order for a garden to grow, you have to pull the weeds. You can't talk them into going away.''

"You've got a narrow view of life," Brigid accused.

"It's a narrow life." The sound of gunfire topside drew Kane's attention. Without another word, he brushed by Brigid and clambered up the ladder.

SEVEN RAIDER SHIPS engaged three refurbished small tanker ships less than three hundred yards out from the flagship. Kane took in the scene at a glance, then raced forward to join Ambika on the prow deck.

The tankers moved much more slowly than the raiders. They were short and wide bodied, and sailing north as they were, they pushed against the wind. The seven raiders worked with the wind, moving rapidly around as they fired their cannon.

Ambika stood tall on the prow deck. She wore a helmet now that covered her head but left her face exposed. A slant of edged metal ran down her nosepiece, and Kane recognized it as yet another weapon the woman could use in close-in fighting. She held the huge .454 Casull in her hand. "Ready starboard cannon!" she yelled.

The cry was taken up the length of the deck. The crew members hastened to their posts like a well-oiled machine.

"Helmsman, take us straight in toward Connister's ship," Ambika ordered. The order was repeated until it reached the man at the wheel. "One volley with the cannon, then stand by to board. Grapples ready!"

Kane watched in fascination as the flagship bore down on the raider. He picked what had to be Connister's ship out from the others by the black flag with the skull and crossbones on it stacked over a red flag with a shark.

The men on the decks of the raider vessel hurried to meet the new challenge, wheeling the big cannon over to port side. Gunfire cracked, and bullets sang through the rigging and the sails around Kane. The gunners didn't have the range yet, but they would. The raiders' cannon opened up, but most of the balls went well over the approaching flagship.

Kane drew the Copperhead from his shoulder and held it at the ready. He glanced down to the main decks and saw men running forward with planks. Others stood at the railing with grappling hooks attached to lines.

Less than fifty yards out, Ambika yelled, "Fire!"

Immediately, the nine cannons lining the starboard side of the flagship thundered, filling the air with giant puffs of gray-black smoke from the powder burn.

Chapter 27

The vibration of the cannon recoil fighting the flagship's forward momentum ran through Kane. Almost immediately, the machine guns on the flagship's stern and prow decks opened up. The machine gunners' aim raked the other ship, chewing through wood, ropes, sails and flesh. Men spun like puppets with their strings suddenly cut. Sail billowed and flapped as rigging was torn free and great holes opened up in the cloth.

"Grapples!" Ambika shouted.

The grapples sailed across the ten-yard distance that was only growing slightly smaller now. Kane knew they were still going to hit the other ship, but the helmsman had timed the impact well. The slung grapples locked on to the other ship's railing and trapped men unlucky enough to be standing too close. Some of the grappling lines pulled railing sections free and dragged men into the sea, but the other lines held.

The flagship's greater bulk manhandled the raider's ship, heeling it over in the water. Then the helmsmen, aided by the men running the sail, brought the flagship into the raider's side. The grappling-hook teams tied the ships fast, holding on to their catch.

Gunfire from both sides sent men flailing to the decks and to the water. Blood ran rich against the grain of the wood, creating hazards for footing. Then the boarding planks were thrown across.

Ambika leaped from the prow, landing on the deck below. She ripped the sword free of her back sheath with her left hand and fired the Casull with her right. "Board!" she ordered. "Booooaaaarrrrdddd!" She led the charge onto the nearest boarding plank.

Kane ran at her heels, surprised by the woman's aggressiveness. He leaped onto the plank after her, the Copperhead in both hands. He fired short bursts, running the limited ammo magazine dry quickly because there were a lot of targets and reloaded.

Ambika fired the Casull in the face of the man who met her charge on the other side of the boarding plank with a pitchfork. The huge .454 round caught him and flipped him backward, throwing him into two men behind him.

The warrior woman turned to her right and fired into the knot of men trying to shove the second boarding plank from their vessel. The four remaining shots in the cylinder cycled through between heartbeats. She showed no sign at all of struggling with the immense recoil.

The two men under the first man she'd shot pushed the corpse from them and brought their weapons up. Kane shot one of them through the chest but couldn't get a clear shot at the other because Ambika moved into his line of fire.

She moved mercilessly, swinging the big sword in a glistening arc. The heavy blade cleaved the man's skull to his chin in an explosion of blood and brain matter. She kicked the dead man in the chest and freed her sword.

Kane smiled in appreciation of the move, then he was kept busy with his own part of the battle. The raiders put up a desperate fight. The captain, a tall man with a hooked nose and close-set dark eyes, roared in the midst of them. His black beard was neatly trimmed, and his clothes chosen for looks rather than service. A black Kevlar vest wrapped around his chest.

The Copperhead blasted empty in the opening moments of the battle. Kane slung it automatically and popped the Sin Eater free of its holster, then kept firing. He wasn't sure where to go, so he stayed with Ambika, protecting her flank.

Ambika didn't need much protection. She was a whirlwind of death and destruction with the sword. Men dodged out of her way when they could, and the slower ones died where they stood.

Traveling behind her, blasting anyone not wearing the familiar blue and white of Ambika's crew, Kane stepped over slashed bodies of the dead and dying. The warrior woman was ruthless in her attack, gutting men, cleaving their skulls. It was raw carnage the like of which even Kane had seldom seen.

And the whole time, a blood-spattered smile stayed on Ambika's face.

Kane relished her in that moment, felt the fires of passion stirring in his groin. He'd never met a woman like her, as fierce and bloodthirsty as anyone he'd ever met.

The captain moved out of the crowd suddenly, using Ambika to throw off Kane's field of fire.

"Look out!" Kane yelled. He thrust the Sin Eater into a man's mouth and pulled the trigger, emptying his skull in a pink-and-gray rush. He grabbed the falling corpse and used it like a battering ram to clear the other men in front of him. He tried desperately to bring the shot he needed into line. Bullets hammered against the polycarbonate armor, bouncing off his head once when a woman shot him almost point-blank between the eyes. Tears filled his vision for a moment from the blunt trauma the bulletproof helmet couldn't protect him from. He lifted the Sin Eater.

The captain dodged under Ambika's sword, and the heavy blade cut deeply into the chest of the man behind him. Unable to retrieve her weapon quickly enough, the captain attacked her, plunging a knife into her ribs under the Kevlar bustier.

Crimson spurted suddenly, and Kane saw the white gleam of bone within the wound. Kane brought the Sin Eater up, but Ambika freed her sword then and stepped into his way. Before the captain could jump back or strike again, she swept the sword around in a horizontal arc. The blade sliced through the man's neck just below his jaw, sending the head tumbling.

Kane fired twice more, killing the raiders around them. He reloaded the Sin Eater as he moved to Ambika. The battle raged around them, but it was in its last moments. The few raiders that still survived were trying to give up, but Ambika's crew slaughtered them where they stood. Some of the raiders threw themselves over the railing and to the bleak mercy of the sea, but gunners shot them when they surfaced.

The same events were being played out on all the other raider ships. There weren't going to be any survivors. Not intentionally.

Kane glanced at Ambika and saw the knife sticking out from her ribs. It had buried to the hilt, and he guessed that the blade was at least seven or eight inches long. Without proper medical care, he judged she was going to die maybe in minutes.

"Hang on," he told her. "Baptiste knows some first aid." He put his hand under her arm, thinking maybe she was in shock and didn't know how badly she'd been injured. He silently cursed her foolhardiness in wearing the abbreviated armor. She should have been wearing a full bodysuit if she was going to fight like that.

"I've got my own doctors," Ambika said. "If I need one."

"You need one," Kane said.

She pushed him away and shook her head. "I told you I'm not like others, Kane. My father designed me to be a survivor. He improved on the original design of the human body." She grasped the hilt of the knife and gave a small groan of pain. Her knuckles whitened as she started to pull it out.

"Don't," Kane said. "That blade could be the only thing keeping you from bleeding to death."

"I won't bleed to death." Ambika kept pulling, bringing the razor-edged blade from between her ribs. Blood spread down her side, running over her armor. "I told you, I've been hurt much worse than this. And lived."

Incredibly, the blade came free. Kane expected a rush of blood and was prepared to try to put pressure on it, knowing full well that wasn't going to stop any internal bleeding. He watched her standing there, certain that she was about to fall over or pass out at any moment.

She smiled at him, crimson staining her lips. "This didn't even go through, Kane. It's nothing." She threw the blade down on the deck and calmly reloaded the Casull. Then she reached over and grabbed the back of his helmet, pulling his face to hers. She kissed him, hard and deep, her tongue sliding between his lips, salty with her own blood.

Instinctively, his passion soaring, Kane kissed back. When she finally let him go, he was breathless.

"Let's go," she said, turning from him.

Kane followed her, amazed. Even as he watched, the blood flow was shutting down.

"No survivors!" Ambika ordered in a strong voice. "None! Chill every one of these stupe bastards and throw them overboard for the sharks!" And she joined her men, using the sword to kill any of the raiders that remained alive.

Kane stayed out of it. A battle was one thing, but he

didn't feel like joining in the scorched-earth policy Ambika insisted on.

"Why aren't you over there helping?"

Kane glanced over at Brigid. Her face was smeared with blood, too, telling him she'd also joined in the fight, but none of it was her own. "I don't think what she's doing is right," he told her. "But it's not my fight. These aren't my enemies."

"They should be," Brigid said, "if you're so intent on joining up with her." Her words carried a double meaning, and he knew she'd seen the kiss Ambika had given him. Her eyes showed hurt and anger, and she was moving away from him before he had a chance to think of anything to say.

There was no excuse. He'd willingly returned the kiss, and only now regretted it—a little. Brigid was right about one thing, though. If they did join up with Ambika, her enemies would be his enemies. But he didn't join in the bloodletting.

AFTER THE LAST RAIDER had been executed, Ambika salvaged six of the seven raider ships. She split her crews so they had enough to man each ship. According to her, the main islands were only a few hours away. One of the raider ships had been too badly damaged in the steering section to make hauling it back to her island worthwhile. They'd left it behind, but not without marking the territory and the battle that had been fought there.

Kane watched the abandoned ship for a time as they sailed away. Corpses from all the ships had been positioned in the vessel's rigging, hanging there by broken and twisted limbs. Still others dangled from nooses slung around the yardarms of the masts.

With the trade in the area, Ambika said she knew some

ships would see it, and the story would be told. Even Wei Qiang's air wags stayed around for the final display. They'd had to land on their pontoons and take fuel from Ambika to make the return flight.

"Woman leaves a hell of a calling card, doesn't she?" Grant asked. He stood beside Kane in the flagship's stern. After the battle, Brigid had decided to join Domi, and there was no confusion about why.

"Yeah." Kane rubbed his jaw, feeling the whisker growth there. He'd shaved two days ago in the Western Isles redoubt, he remembered, but that seemed like a week or more ago now. "It's meant to carry a message."

"She seemed to take a lot of pleasure in it," Grant said. "Reminds me of some of the Mag commanders we both knew."

Kane scowled at the mention of those men. In the Magistrate Division, some of the commanders specialized in shooting people in the back. They got their promotions, but they didn't get much respect. They were also the ones who often demonstrated sadistic tendencies.

"Mebbe she was just glad to be alive," Kane said.

Grant looked at him without expression. "Mebbe so."

"Do you have something else you want to say?" Kane asked irritably.

Grant shook his head. "Nope."

"You look like you do."

"I will say this," Grant told him. "There are times when you have to work through things for yourself. But you'll get there."

"What the hell is that supposed to mean?"

"It means that I'm wondering about Ambika's pleasure in chilling those raiders and setting that twisted hell afloat. I saw your face when she was ordering it done. It didn't look like you enjoyed it much."

Kane turned away from his friend. "We'll be at the Isles of the Lioness by nightfall. We'll see more of what Ambika's about then."

"I'll be waiting for that," Grant said, "but not nearly as faint of heart as I was before."

AFTER THE FLAGSHIP was under way and making good time, Ambika went to the stern castle to her private quarters. Kane had watched her go and didn't say anything. Christensen's ship had remained within visual range of the flagship and he'd noticed Brigid on deck. He knew part of the reason she was out there was to watch him.

He thought about the kiss Ambika had given him. Her lips had seared his, reminded him of all the things that were different about men and women. And it had made him remember how long it was since he'd had a woman.

But he remembered Brigid's kiss, too. It had been on a New Year's Eve that never existed in the world he knew. He thought about the memories he shared with Brigid, of other times and other places, and he wondered again what all that meant.

Anam-chara. The term echoed in his head, but the heat of Ambika's kiss felt nearer.

Cursing himself because he was more confused than he felt any reason for, he turned from the railing and approached Ambika's quarters. He knocked on the door. He hadn't bothered to remove the polycarbonate armor, and he was sweltering underneath. But at the moment he didn't feel much like taking it off. It would leave him too open, too vulnerable.

"Come in," Ambika called.

He twisted the knob and followed the door inside. The room was dim, lit only by a swaying lantern that hung from a rafter over the ceiling. The room was also spacious, not at all like Christensen's quarters aboard the *Sloop John B*.

A large bed occupied the back wall. In the center of the wall was a window that looked over the white churning foam following the flagship. Glass panes and latticework covered the window, but there were also heavy wooden shutters with metal plates that could be closed over it. A freestanding armoire was bolted to the floor to the right of the bed. Ambika's armor lay strewed at the bottom of it. A vanity sat to the left, the large oval mirror catching the light from the lantern.

Ambika sat in a claw-footed wooden bath in the middle of the room. The water was warm enough that it still steamed, and it did little to cover her nakedness. Her hair tumbled down around her shoulders, glinting with the lantern light. Her breasts stood out proud and firm, the nipples pointed and turgid.

She slid forward unhurriedly as he stood there, then wrapped her arms around her knees, pulling herself close to them. It only partially covered her nudity, allowing the full globes of her breasts to hang out on either side of her legs.

"Sorry," Kane muttered. "I'll come back later." He turned to go.

"Kane, there's no reason to leave," she said. "Unless you're embarrassed."

He looked back at her, taking in the expanse of gorgeous flesh. "No," he told her. "I'm not embarrassed at all." She didn't act coy and she didn't act overbearing about her lack of clothing.

"I didn't think you would be. Shut the door. I don't really want the crew to see me like this."

Off balance by the situation, Kane reached for the door and closed it. He looked into her aqua gaze and tried to keep his eyes on hers. It was damn near impossible to do.

"Was there something you wanted?" Ambika asked.

"I just wanted to make sure you were okay. I never saw a doctor come in after you." Actually, it had crossed Kane's mind that she'd walked into the room and passed out, maybe even died from the wound. He glanced at the water, then realized it wasn't blood smeared as he'd thought it would be. Her wound should have still been bleeding, and the water should have been pulling it out.

"I'm fine."

"I wanted to make sure," he repeated. She had her feet crossed and he couldn't help noticing that they just managed to cover her sex. His pulse thundered at his temples, and he remembered that she said she'd never been touched by a man before.

"That's thoughtful of you, but there was no need."

Kane raised his eyes with difficulty. "That was a bad wound."

"It's already gone." Effortlessly, she stood, and the water sluiced down her body, tracing every generous curve. Standing in the tub, she was taller than Kane, a work of feminine flesh done in amazonian proportions. Her breasts hung heavily and were firm. Water droplets clung to the fleece of her pubic triangle, which was just as silver as the hair on her head.

It took Kane a moment to remember he was looking for the wound in her side. Amazingly, the wound had already closed and appeared to have been healing a week or more. The flesh was pink, supple and pulled together neatly.

"That can't be," Kane said.

"But it is." Ambika smiled at him. "I told you I was different." She ran her fingertips over her side, touching the place where the wound had been. "Feel." She took his hand in hers, then ran it over the flesh.

Kane felt the heat of her, the taut muscles that had reknitted under the soft layer of woman flesh. He stood, hypnotized by the touch, by the miracle of the wound's healing. Then he noticed that she'd kept pulling his hand, dropping it down to the silver fringe between her thighs. He felt the moisture there, and it wasn't all from the bath.

"I've been thinking about you, Kane," she said in a low, throaty voice. She kept his fingers trapped there, just on the edge of penetration.

Kane felt the power of her grip, the sleekness of the soft flesh just beyond his touch. His pulse throbbed at his temples and in his groin as waves of lust pounded at him.

"I was lying here in my bath," she went on, "remembering the way you covered my back when we took that ship. It was like you'd been doing it for years. And I can't believe how comfortable it felt for you to be there. No man has ever made me feel this way before."

Kane tried to take a deep breath and regain control, but the room seemed to lack air.

"You've been thinking about me, too," she said. "I can tell." She pulled his hand closer, allowing his fingertips to touch the molten heat of her inner sex.

It was all Kane could do to keep from grabbing her and forcing her to the bed.

"Take me, Kane," she said, looking into his eyes. "You know it's meant to be. You must feel it as strongly as I do." She pulled him in close to her and kissed him with bruising force.

The image of Brigid came into Kane's mind even though his senses were swimming. He tasted Ambika's breath, fresh with the flavor of mint or another spice, but it was Brigid he thought of.

Anam-chara. Kane heard the words again in his mind. He turned his head away from Ambika, then took back his hand, as well.

"What's wrong?" she asked. "Did I do something wrong?"

The insecurity sounded alien to her, and Kane felt sorry about that, knowing he'd caused it. She probably hadn't had too many moments like that. "No," he said. "It's not you."

"Then what?"

He shook his head. "It's me."

"You don't want me?"

He looked at her. "Hell, Ambika, you can look at me and know that isn't true."

She glanced at the front of his crotch, and he knew the material was straining to hold him back. "It's the woman, isn't it? Brigid Baptiste?"

"No," he told her, shaking his head. "Brigid doesn't have anything to do with this."

She looked at him, pushing the uncertainty away and standing there naked to face him. "We could be good together, Kane. I've never had the experience of a man. But I know it would be good for me, and for you."

"It would be," he said. "But I'm not ready for something like this. I'm sorry. I only came in here to make sure you were okay."

Her face turned to stone. "We could be more than partners. You came here to find me and get me to join with your group, but we could be more than that."

Kane looked at her, torn between the want and the memory that haunted him. *Anam-chara.* "Not right now," he told her.

"Then there's hope?"

"I don't know."

She sank back into the bathwater, wrapping her arms around her knees again. "You've seen I'm all right," she told him.

Dismissed, Kane walked back through the door, closing

it behind him. He took a deep breath outside, finding some measure of solace in the chill, brine wind that wrapped around him. He cursed himself for not knowing what to do. As a Mag, he'd never been pulled in two directions before. Even when he found out about the Archon Directorate and the fact that Brigid and Grant had had termination warrants issued on them. He'd changed sides in a heartbeat. Yet now, there was no way to handle the situation with either of the women that had stepped into his life.

"Something on your mind?"

Kane looked up at Grant, who lounged at the nearby railing smoking a cigar. He knew Grant had seen him enter Ambika's quarters. "Don't even ask," he told the man.

Chapter 28

Sunset dappled the western sky when Ambika's flotilla reached the outer islands of her empire. Kane stood in the prow with Grant, studying the towering rock that jutted up from the sea. He saw the gun emplacements on the island they sailed by and watched as the first mate waved a blue-and-white flag in quick movements. They had the radio hookup, as well, but Kane guessed the flags were the secondary system and would be hard for imitators to duplicate.

Besides the rough, craggy surface of the standing rock, some remains of buildings could also be seen. But some of the ruined brick and mortar had been used to construct the garrison. Uneven walls ran around the perimeter, and were topped with gleaming bits of glass and metal that would hold off most attackers who'd try to simply climb over.

Even as they passed the outer island, the main island came into view. The flagship sailors ignored the sight of the fortressed area, but Kane and Grant pressed forward.

"Damn," Grant swore.

Kane agreed with the sentiment. The view of the main island was staggering. It wasn't just one island as he'd seen on Christensen's map. The cartographer had been lazy, or had never been to the island. Even staring at it from out at sea, Kane saw that it was a series of promontories that broke the Cific Ocean's surface. He couldn't tell how far across it was, but it gave the impression of being huge.

In many places bare rock showed through the green haze

of the sea, given relief only by the white-capped curlers that slammed at the barren beaches. In the heart of the islands, verdant growth covered the high, irregular hills, broken only by the buildings and walls of the keep.

Some of the buildings were new. Kane could tell them from the others by the way they stood. The newer buildings stood straight, while the older ones leaned in different directions. A surprising number of them remained whole, showing signs of repair rather than decay.

"We tried to salvage as many of the old buildings as we could."

Kane glanced over his shoulder at Ambika as she came to a halt behind him.

She wore the blue Kevlar armor again, and her face was impassive, revealing nothing that had gone on between them earlier. "When I first moved my people here, my father was still alive. We stayed on the ships we'd built and taken by force. Once we made sure the vault protecting the mat-trans gateway existed intact, we set about building more permanent dwellings. All of the old buildings you see there were above the waterline then. We stayed in the ones we were able to clean, then set about repairing the ones that we could."

Looking at all the work that had been done, Kane knew it had taken considerable manpower. He tried to estimate how many people might live there but couldn't. He guessed the buildings could accommodate at least a couple thousand people, and probably more lived there. Evidently they all contributed to the fortress's construction. "That's a big achievement," he said.

"It had to be done," Ambika stated. "The vault was below the waterline. We had to have a permanent place to work from, and we had to be able to defend it. During the first couple years, raiders succeeded in driving us from the islands three times. Twice, they stayed until they made certain there wasn't anything worthwhile for them to take.''

"And the third time?" Grant asked.

"We waited till they settled in for the night, till almost morning, then we attacked. We chilled raiders until there weren't any raiders left to chill. I ordered all the bodies placed in a common grave near this edge of the island, knowing it was going to be the one most often approached. We left the corpses to the animals and the sea. The waves created tidal pools in the bottom of the grave. A number of hungry bottom feeders were trapped there. They didn't go hungry. Nothing on that island that could fly, walk or swim did.''

Kane felt a chill pass through him. Not from the story because he'd heard worse, and arguably done worse in his time. But the callous smile that twisted her lips was devoid of any warmth. For her, it was a pleasant memory.

"A month after the feeding frenzy took place, I took my people back down to the grave. We harvested the skeletons of every man, woman and child that had been with the raiders. Then we built the Bridge of Bones. We never had to worry too much about the raiders coming onto the island again.''

Raking the shoreline, Kane saw the bridge she had to be referring to, but it was too far away to make out the details. The flagship raced with the wind, cutting through the chop and cutting the distance.

"NUKE-SHIT!" Grant exclaimed quietly. The flagship was within twenty feet of the shore and the Bridge of Bones was clearly visible.

Kane raked the bridge on the shoreline before them with his gaze. It was six feet wide and forty feet long, created entirely of interlaced yellowing bones wired together. The floor was eight inches thick. Posts, created from bundles of leg bones and arm bones wrapped with barbed wire, stood at least eight feet tall every ten feet on both sides. Skulls sat on top of the poles and on top of the fence line. All of them faced toward the front of the bridge.

"How many people did you have to chill to make this?" Grant asked.

"All of them," Ambika answered flatly. "We took their ships and left them nowhere to run. Then we tracked them down in groups and finally one at a time. It took most of a week." Ambika looked at the bridge. "For a while, there was a rumor that we were cannibals."

The skin across the back of Kane's neck tightened at the thought. He'd seen it among muties and outlanders, and sometimes among the most desperate of the Dregs, but he'd never gotten used to the thought.

Under Ambika's direction, the flagship led the way toward what looked like a solid wall. Then Kane remembered the holo-projected entrance to the Utah redoubt. They passed through the wall effortlessly.

Electric lighting illuminated the huge cavern on the other side of the fake wall. They sailed past it, still picking up some wind coming through the cavern. Bats fluttered along the ceiling forty feet above them.

"No one knows this way," Ambika said. "I don't allow anyone to leave the islands unless I'm sure of their loyalty. We've had children born into the community now, and our population still continues to grow."

A little farther on, Kane spotted Sandcats and other wags sitting on flat places on either side of the water that cut through the cavern. Motor pools had been set up, and work was already being done on several of the vehicles.

The other ships carrying wags and Sandcats dropped anchor at the vehicle bays. The flagship and four others continued on, trailed by Christensen's ship. The cavern took a bend, then another cave mouth opened up before the flagship. It plunged through, racing the setting sun, which no longer reached orange fingers into the bowl-shaped area inside the conglomeration of islands and buildings.

Kane glanced over the side, peering through the water.

"The water here is relatively shallow," Ambika said. "No more than thirty or forty feet. We were able to go below with some of the diving equipment we found and load nets with rock and other building supplies. We dragged it to the surface, then began building what we needed. But we also used what we had."

Kane looked around the towering buildings surrounding them. They were tall and crooked, but all of them showed evidence of habitation. Clothing hung out windows on lines. Children played at the foot of the buildings that were above the waterline. Other children played on stairways that had been added to the outside of the buildings mired in the water. Docks fronted the buildings on all sides, and small craft were tied up at them.

Well above the flagship, above the masts and sails, catwalks made of rope and wooden slats crisscrossed the area. People walked along them, going about their daily business in the ville. Even small children ran lithely along the catwalks.

"We've made do with what we could," Ambika said. "It was easier to create housing out of the existing buildings, and easier to get people to move into them. Then we built the other buildings we needed."

The buildings on the center island weren't connected to the other buildings. The only way into them was through a well-guarded main entrance, followed by other guard posts leading into each structure. No buildings had windows lower than thirty feet from the ground.

The buildings looked rounded on the top, like tall mushrooms.

"We built the administrative buildings taller than the surrounding hills," Ambika explained. "Occasionally over the past several decades, the Cific Ocean has been known to rise for unknown reasons. It hasn't in almost thirty years now, but I wanted to make sure our command posts weren't lost. No rooms or offices exist in the bottom floors, in case we are flooded. Protected by the rocks as we are here, I don't think there'll ever be enough of a current to rip them free of the sea floor."

Despite the uneasiness between Ambika and himself, Kane was curious. "What do the people do?"

"My people," Ambika said, "help shape their own destiny by following the edicts I lay down. They fish to help provide meals, and they salvage so that we can continue to grow and have goods to trade with other islands that have things we need or want."

"The gasoline you're getting out of Mexico," Grant said, "must really give you a leg up on the local competition."

Ambika smiled. "In the end, it's my control over that gasoline plant that scares even Wei Qiang. He knows I'd see it burned and destroyed before I'd allow him to take it from me."

"What about the ore you're taking out of the Utah territories?" Kane asked. "What are you doing with that?"

"Building," Ambika answered. "I've started a munitions factory in that tower." She pointed to the second tallest one. "In there is the machinery to make simple single-shot rifles. Granted, they're not very useful against an assault rifle, but they beat the hell out of a bow and allow me to field more troops. If three people are shooting at a man carrying an assault rifle, there's a chance that one or two of them will survive long enough to chill that man."

Kane looked at the building. Lakesh would appreciate the effort Ambika was putting into her plans, but he knew Brigid would stand against them. Ambika was talking of starting a blood tide with her simple weapons, an overpowering surge that would change the face of any territory she involved herself with. She'd already changed the Western Isles.

"Most people are desperate, Kane," she said, gazing deep into his eyes. "There are people, like the ones I've found, who are waiting for a leader strong enough and brave enough to lead them out of the pitiful existences they have into a brighter day."

Kane didn't say anything. He knew that wasn't true of all the outlanders and Dregs. Some of those preferred to live their own lives.

She continued looking at him. "They would follow you, Kane."

He looked at her, trying to play the statement off a little. "Where would I take them?"

"Anywhere you wanted to," she answered.

That answer scared the hell out of Kane.

Chapter 29

Brigid clambered over the side of the *Sloop John B* and dropped to the dock at the bottom of the main island. Grant and Kane waited there, gazing around in a mixture of fascination and unease. Brigid knew the feeling. It was one thing to be on Ambika's ships, but another to be surrounded by the empire she ruled.

And Brigid had no doubts that the warrior woman ruled the Isles of the Lioness with an iron fist.

Brigid kept the Uzi subgun she carried on a sling at her side. She also kept her distance from Kane. Anger still burned within her because he'd made noise about bringing her along to get her opinion, then totally disregarded her advice. The kiss she'd seen Ambika give him hadn't helped, either. She tried to keep it out of her mind by using the concentration techniques she'd learned as a Cobaltville archivist.

Ambika directed her crew. The flagship was securely anchored along the wooden ramp that stretched out into the lagoon water. Peering down through the emerald sea trapped in the enclosed area, Brigid doubted they were in water much deeper than thirty feet. The flagship's draw put it within a yard of the sea bottom.

Domi leaped from Christensen's ship and landed lithely at Brigid's side. "Big place, huh?" the albino asked.

"Yes." Brigid kept her voice neutral with effort.

"Something wrong?"

"No. Why should anything be wrong?" she asked sarcastically. "We've just walked into the queen spider's web."

"You not like her much?" Domi asked.

"No."

Domi made a face. "Me neither."

Brigid glanced at her, surprised. Domi hadn't said anything about how she felt about the situation while they'd been on the *Sloop John B.* "Why?"

"Dead raiders," Domi said. "No reason do that. Chill, mebbe. Not that. Too much like baron."

Brigid glanced around, noting how close Ambika stayed to Kane. "Too much like baron," she agreed. As she watched Kane and the warrior woman, she noticed the way they reacted to each other, maintaining space between them. She couldn't help wondering what had caused that. She also grew frustrated with herself when she couldn't get it out of her mind.

Once Ambika had her personal entourage together, packed down with crates and boxes she'd evidently bartered for in Autarkic, she continued along the floating dock. Guards stood at regular intervals. The dock wound into the stone hillside, then to a chamber that had been carved out.

The air inside the cave was cooler, letting Brigid know air vents had been tapped in, as well. At the end of the cave tunnel, Ambika pressed her palm against a metal plate. A door opened in the stone, so seamlessly put together that Brigid hadn't expected it there. The interior held a makeshift elevator cage that swayed a little when Ambika stepped on it.

Only ten people fit onto it. Brigid hung back enough that she didn't go in the cage that took Kane and Ambika up first. Grant also hung back, but Brigid got the feeling it was to stay with her and Domi, to make sure they were okay.

She got mad at Kane because he hadn't thought to do the same thing.

The cage returned, creaking along the wooden cables, a few minutes later. Brigid entered, followed by Grant and Domi, packing in close to one corner. The sec men who joined them laughed and joked among themselves. They carried kits containing goods they'd robbed from the raiders, and maybe from other excursions.

The elevator creaked along its way as two of the men automatically pulled on the rope in the center of the cage. Weights counterbalanced it, making it easy to pull upward even with the extra weight.

At the top, the elevator opened at a small alcove lighted by torches that promised some aspects of elegance. Brigid followed the sec men out of the alcove into the hallway proper beyond.

There was no sign of Kane or Ambika. She continued following the sec men down the corridor but she kept the Uzi subgun close at hand.

The hallway ran long and clean, totally devoid of features except for the coded doors on either side. None of them was open. At the end of the hallway was a final checkpoint consisting of two secure cages built into either side of the wall. Sec men stood behind light blue-tinted armaglass running from floor to ceiling that had cross-shaped gun ports cut into them. Heavily armored double doors blocked the way. No announcement hung on it, no sign of office—just a big impenetrable-looking set of doors.

One of the sec men operated a camera with a toggle box on the wall. The camera swung around, locking on to Brigid and the others. A moment later, the doors opened with a pneumatic hiss that let Brigid know the place was airtight, as well.

Where the opulence and grandeur the archivist had ex-

pected in the building hadn't been apparent in the hallway,
the room they next entered more than made up for it. The
room sprawled gigantically, bigger even than the caverns in
the Cerberus redoubt. A hydroponics garden grew in the
center of the room, filled with flowering bushes, trees and
plants that obscured the other side of the room. It also led
the eye naturally to the raised dais with an immense high-
backed chair that could be considered nothing less than a
throne.

The chair was thick and sculpted of silver-gray stone,
inlaid with bright gold thread. Silver satin cushions softened
the seat and the high sides. Six steps led up to the chair,
putting whoever sat there higher than anyone else in the
room, guaranteeing the center of attention.

"Takes herself serious, doesn't she?" Grant asked in a
quiet voice. He glanced upward.

Brigid followed his line of sight, spotting the armaglass
sections near the top of all four walls. Through the subtle
blue tint she saw shadows moving on the other side.

"Takes sec serious, too," Domi said. "Mebbe has to."

"Yeah. And that kind of troubles me," Grant admitted.

Spotting Kane and Ambika talking at the foot of the chair,
Brigid said, "That's the kind of sec defenses you and Kane
should appreciate."

Grant looked at her. "Don't make any mistakes here. This
shit isn't getting by Kane. He's not as enamored of that
woman as you might think he is."

"And how would you know that?" Brigid asked, even
though she wanted to just keep her mouth shut and not let
Grant know she'd even been thinking along those lines.

"Because she's made some moves on him, and he's
turned her away," Grant growled. "So keep your mind on
the reason we're here and don't confuse the issue."

An angry retort died at Brigid's lips as she regained control at the last second. She turned away from Grant without saying a word, then fell into step with him as they walked toward Kane. She spotted more sec men around the hydroponics garden and the outer walls of the room. As her anger died away, wariness settled in when she realized how vulnerable they were inside the fortress.

Ambika acted relaxed and totally at home, but Brigid noted that Kane looked edgy. Most people would have missed it because of the arrogance of the Mag demeanor he displayed. That awareness threw more of the resentment she'd felt about him into the back of her mind.

"Few people have ever seen the rooms you're going to be seeing, Kane," Ambika said. "This is my inner sanctum. No one comes here unless I've invited them."

Glancing back, Brigid noted that Christensen and his crew hadn't followed them up in the elevator. "Where's Christensen?"

Ambika regarded her coolly. "Down in the lower quarters. There are guest rooms there, as well, though not nearly of the caliber you'll be seeing." She turned her attention back to Kane. "I had this structure built to my father's specifications. This doesn't mean much to me, but I do enjoy the comfort it provides."

"It's large," Kane commented.

"There are smaller rooms," Ambika said, "that provide more privacy if you want."

Kane remained noncommittal, but Brigid felt the comment was directed more at her anyway. The archivist kept her face free of emotion, returning the cool azure stare of the taller woman.

"Let me get you settled in," Ambika said. "Then perhaps we can talk more."

THE ROOM KANE WAS shown to was actually a suite of three interconnecting rooms that contained a large bedroom, a small kitchen and a spacious living room. He assumed that Grant, Domi and Brigid had been shown to similar quarters, but he didn't know for sure. Ambika had shown him his quarters personally while sec men guided the others.

"Are these quarters going to be suitable?" Ambika asked. As before, she kept her distance from him, never letting her personal space overlap his.

Kane had noted the difference, and women scorned weren't to be ignored.

"I've never been in anything like this before," Kane admitted. "I've seen some ornate rooms in the barons' quarters, but never had rooms like this for myself."

Some of the tension left her face, and she smiled at him warmly. "Good. I'm glad I'm able to give you something you've never had before."

Kane stepped to the window and pulled the drape aside. He noted that armaglass filled the pane, thick enough to offer proof against bullets and probably low-gain incendiaries. Dusk straddled the Cific Ocean, drenching the western skies in nuclear oranges and deep, jet-laced ochers and royal plums. He gazed at the other buildings, noting that most of them appeared to be lit by oil-burning lanterns and candles.

"The other people here don't live as well," he commented.

"Space is at a premium," Ambika said.

"How many people live in this building?"

"My support staff and personal sec crews," she replied. "Essential personnel."

"Not a lot."

Ambika's gaze sharpened and grew cold. "You sound as though you're finding fault with me."

"Not exactly," Kane said. "I know as well as the next that true equality is never going to exist. There are always those who are more equal than others. Otherwise you never have those who can and will lead."

"Yes. You do understand. So why do you bring this up?"

"Because," Kane said, thinking of Lakesh, "the guy I'm thinking of would never accept any bargain that didn't offer equality."

"All the way around?"

Realizing Ambika's remark had carried a tone of levity in it, Kane smiled. "Definitely. And he'd want more equality than the next guy."

"He sounds like a hard man to deal with."

"Make no mistake," Kane said, "when he has all the cards, he is a hard man to deal with."

"You work for him?"

"Only as far as I want to."

"But you're subordinate to him?" she asked.

"He has an operation," Kane conceded, "that listens to him."

"You're part of that operation."

"When I want to be."

"Yet he wants you to be."

Kane nodded. "Mebbe more than I do at most times. Which gives me an edge over him on occasion."

"Join me, Kane, and you'd have a position of respect and authority. You're not the kind of man who should walk in another's shadow."

Kane shook his head. "That'd be trading his shadow for yours."

"Perhaps," she replied. "But I can promise you that you'd be walking much bigger in my shadow than you sound like you are in his."

Intrigued by her offer and the confidence that accompanied it, Kane looked into her eyes. "What are you after, Ambika?"

She gave him a coy smile and rested one hand on her hip. "With you, Kane? I thought that was obvious." Though her words sounded brave, there was still a trace of resentment in them.

"Not with me. With this whole operation."

"Do you really want to know?" she challenged.

Kane stared back at her, suddenly feeling he was standing on the edge of a precipice.

"I'll tell you if you want to know, Kane. And because I want you to see what I'm capable of. But that may frighten you more than what you're ready to accept."

Kane couldn't ignore the feeling that swirled within him, but he couldn't ignore the challenge in her eyes, either. "Let's do it."

Chapter 30

Kane accompanied Ambika down another elevator, this one hidden in her own opulent suite of rooms. He'd only gotten a brief glimpse of the rooms as they'd passed through. They'd been filled with weapons and treasures, vases and scavenged predark items, and hundreds of books filled the walls. All of it was neatly placed as if it had been filed away. He'd gotten the impression that not all of it was hers, that some of it had belonged to her father.

The elevator was small and powered, letting Kane know she'd purposefully left some areas of the more accessible buildings without power. It made the building harder to take, he realized, in case of an insurrection.

The elevator dropped quickly, humming the whole time. Three of Ambika's sec men accompanied them, keeping a careful distance between Kane and their warrior queen as if he might offer some danger. That order, Kane was aware, came from Ambika. In spite of that, he retained his weapons. He was also aware that Ambika had deliberately split him off from the rest of his group.

At the bottom of the drop, the elevator doors opened. The sound of the sea slapping rock and the brine stink of it filled a dark cavern. With the limited light available, he didn't know how big the cavern actually was.

Ambika led the way outside, her boots ringing on the metal platform. She turned and flipped a series of switches. Mercury-vapor lights exploded into harsh brightness, running quickly from the front of the cavern to the back. The incandescent light slammed down at the water, creating illuminating pools that overlapped in seconds.

Hypnotized by the display of the flashing lights, Kane watched the huge object being revealed in the water. Maybe the cavern had started out as a natural structure, but it had been enlarged with machines. Now, it was a harbor, except that there appeared to be no way out.

The object in the water was a submarine but the flotation equipment around it suggested immediately that it wasn't seaworthy anymore. Farther back on the port side, a gaping hole offered mute testimony that it hadn't even gotten to the port under its own power. Pockets of dark red rust showed like metallic age spots on the hull.

"Do you know what this is?" Ambika walked down the narrow metal stairway to the stone floor surrounding the mooring area.

"A predark submarine," Kane growled.

"You've seen one before?" Ambika's hips swayed suggestively as she walked toward the wooden plank that led from the stone floor to the conning tower.

"No."

"This one's Chinese," Ambika mused. She walked onto the conning tower and placed her hands on the rust-pitted railing. "Old by far even when the nukecaust of 2001 occurred. It was first made in the early 1960s, part of the Cold War buildup that was going on then. You're aware of that war?"

"It wasn't actually a war," Kane answered. He couldn't remember if he'd learned that in Cobaltville or Cerberus redoubt. "It was more of an escalating defense."

"True," Ambika said, "but it also neared all-out war on a number of occasions. Do you remember the Missile Crisis of October 1962?"

"President Kennedy ordered Fidel Castro to get Russian missiles out of Cuba that year or he'd invade Cuba," Kane answered.

"Close enough. As you're no doubt aware, several tactical maneuvers were made on both sides. This submersible, a Chinese sub called *Octopus Lotus,* was part of that action. At that time, the sub was loaded down with deadly nerve gas and biological agents. It was on its way across the Cific Ocean to join the action breaking out in Cuba."

"The Russians and the Chinese were both Communist countries," Kane said, "but they didn't work together. Not on something like that."

"Ah, Kane, but they weren't going to work together." Ambika smiled. "*Octopus Lotus*'s mission was to surface off the southern coast of Florida and release the deadly weapons it carried. They were going to let the Russians and Cubans take the blame."

"They wanted to start a war?" Kane couldn't believe it. The whole concept of nerve gas and biological weapons smacked too much of the macabre practices of the Archons. Maybe it had been an early attempt to destroy the civilized world.

"Think forward a little more in time, Kane, to see the beauty of it. Both the U.S. and Russia were gaining dominance militarily, as well as economically. The Chinese would have stood to gain years on their competitors if a war broke out. And they would have been sought after as an ally, allowing them a much better position than they'd have had."

"And they could have waited long enough to figure out who the victor was going to be." Kane understood the reasoning, and quite frankly approved of it. The scenario was pure Archon strategy.

"Yes. Most of the work they'd been doing in the field of

nerve gas and other biological agents had closely paralleled the research done by the Russians. It would have taken days or weeks for competent researchers to find out the agents had actually been Chinese in origin. By then it would have been too late."

"But the sub didn't make it?"

"No. The American military found out and sent destroyers out to intercept it. They did."

"They took the chance on spreading that shit in the ocean?"

Ambika shook her head. "According to the reports my father found and read in the Totality Concept files, the American ships depth-charged the *Octopus Lotus* and got it nearly up to the surface. But help arrived too soon to remove the biological weapons from the submarine. They had to settle for sending a team of frogmen down to intercept it and sink it. That, they were successful at."

Kane thought about the implications involved in the story. First, about the lever that the weapons gave Ambika. And second, about how the submarine had come here to the Western Isles, and to the Isles of the Lioness in particular. "How did you get the sub?"

"While my father and I were setting up the gasoline plants down in Mexico, we discovered the *Octopus Lotus,* washed ashore after a seaquake. We spent months getting it afloat, then pulling it back here."

"What about the weapons?" Kane asked. "After all those years at sea, they shouldn't have survived."

"Several of the sub's compartments survived intact," she answered. "They're built to be airtight, remember? The aft compartments holding the biological weapons remained that way. But we didn't try to open them there. My father knew that some of the containers might have ruptured. So we worked with the submersible's seals. We drilled through the plates here, under very strict conditions, then we extracted the gases and liquids, sealing them up in other containers. We left the submersible here.''

''Why?''

''We couldn't get into some of the compartments safely enough. And some of the compartments maintain a biological residue that's quite deadly by itself.'' Ambika shrugged and smiled. ''It's a bomb, Kane, one which I can transport as I see fit. Should the day come, I could float the *Octopus Lotus* into Qiang's holdings and explode it, releasing all the toxins into his communities.''

A cold chill rocketed along the base of Kane's skull, exploding when it touched his mind. The woman talked of massive sudden, horrifying death as if it were nothing.

''So when you talk to your friend, you might tell him I'm planning on being real equal,'' Ambika pointed out. She walked back down the gangplank, stopping near Kane, close enough that he could feel her heat in the chill of the cavern. ''I'm telling you this, Kane, to show you what I'm capable of. To prove to you that it is possible to sit beside me and have more power than you've ever known before.''

Kane restrained himself with effort. Biological weapons weren't something he'd ever want to see used. The technology involved reminded him of his father and how he'd been used to service the barons.

''That's why I'm building up my army here,'' Ambika went on. ''The Utah territories are going to allow me to establish a beachhead that I can use to launch attacks on Cobaltville. The Baron can hide behind his steel walls from blasters and knives, but microscopic germs?'' She shook her head.

''If you use those things against him,'' Kane said, ''you're going to render that area uninhabitable.''

''For a time, perhaps.''

"Mebbe for a long time."

She drew a sharp fingernail along his jawline. "I can afford to wait, Kane. You've seen how my body reacts to wounds. It builds new cells where diseased or injured ones were." Her azure eyes held his with baleful fire. "My father designed me to be better than human." She licked her lips. "I know my life span is easily longer than a normal person's. How much longer, I'm just going to have to wait and see."

Kane breathed shallowly, trying to maintain his calm. "Where're the biological weapons you've taken from the sub?"

"In safekeeping. I'm not going to allow anyone to stop me, Kane. I'll have you know that. I was bred and born to rule, and I will."

"Then why haven't you broken Qiang before now?"

"Haven't you ever studied Sun Tzu?"

Kane shook his head.

"He was Chinese," Ambika said, "so Qiang would probably appreciate this. He wrote a treatise on war, how to wage it and how to win it. One of the cardinal rules is to never take on a war you couldn't win. Fighting Qiang would definitely require using the germs I've rescued. Using those weapons would endanger my own holdings here, mebbe destroy the whole infrastructure of the ecological and economic systems that I'm depending on. Using them against Cobaltville makes better sense."

Kane understood. "Because you have the bolt-hole in the hidden redoubt. It makes a more controllable test area."

"Yes." The azure eyes sparkled. "And the effects will be restricted to an area that won't touch the Western Isles. You see how easy it is for you to understand what I'm planning, Kane? We could be good together. And you—you could be a king."

"After Cobaltville knuckles under," Kane said, "you're free to build another army there."

She nodded. "Exactly. And it'll be an army hidden from Qiang's prying eyes. Then, when the time is right, I'll move that army through the gateway and add Qiang's empire to my own with less bloodshed than it would take now. Qiang respects superiority in numbers. By that time, many people will have joined me. Qiang will give up. If he's not already dead by then."

"Ambitious," Kane complimented, forcing a smile.

"Totally ruthless," Ambika agreed. "I can do this."

"If anybody could," Kane observed, "I think it would be you."

She faced him squarely, arms folded across her breasts, less than an inch between them. Her blue Kevlar armor reflected the lights. "So what do you say to my offer now, Kane? You see that I'm going to rule."

He grinned at her, then reached for her, ignoring the way his stomach tried to roll when he thought of what she was planning to do. He kissed her long and deep, letting the raw passion and lust he felt for her build on the subterfuge he laid down bit by bit with every heartbeat.

The guards overreacted, shoving blasters in his face as they hauled him back. One of them smashed a barrel into Kane's cheek, splitting the flesh and nearly knocking him out. He went back and down on purpose, allowing the sec men to control his fall.

With a shriek of rage, Ambika drew her long sword and cleaved the head from the man's shoulders as he drew back his weapon to hit Kane again. "Don't touch him!" she ordered.

The headless corpse took a moment to realize it was dead. Blood spurted from the neck, and wheezing noises sucked through the windpipe as the lungs struggled to take their next breath. Then it crumpled.

The other sec men sprang back, obviously confused about what they were supposed to do.

Kane sat with his back against the cavern wall. He wiped the blood from his cheek, glancing at the redness staining his fingertips.

Ambika stood towering above him, the sword tight in her fist. Her eyes blazed volcanic blue. "What's your answer, Kane?"

"I thought that said it best," Kane said. "Mebbe I was wrong."

She stared at him a moment longer, then the full lips formed an uncertain smile. "I wish I knew you better, Kane. I wish I knew when you were telling the truth and when you were lying." Her voice sounded wistful.

"Why would I be lying?" Kane asked. "What would I have to gain?"

She shook her head. "I don't know. You remain alive on this island only by my command. That can change at any time."

"You made the offer," Kane said.

Her eyes searched his. "Yes. But you turned me down."

"Then," Kane agreed. "Not now."

"Why?"

"You asked me why I stayed with the guy I work for," Kane said, embellishing his half truths. "He promised me a barony of my own. Years ago. I could shit in one hand, hold his promise in the other. Guess which one would get full?"

"So that's the only reason you'd want me."

"Hell, Ambika, you knew back at the ship that I wanted you," Kane said. "I told you that."

"Then why didn't you come to me?"

"Because I don't like to be conflicted," Kane said honestly. "I can be one way or I can be another, but I can't be both. That game's too dangerous." He knew just how dangerous right then. If he hadn't tried to win Ambika's confidence, they'd have been free to play out the hand they'd drawn with her. But she'd have maintained all the biological weapons, and the possibility of using them against Cobaltville.

Kane had some problems with the innocents, even though there were damn few of them at Cobaltville, getting hurt. But there was a chance the unleashed germs could spread into the Outlands, and that couldn't be tolerated. Gaining her confidence and seizing whatever edge that gave was their only chance.

"Show me," she said hoarsely.

He pushed himself up and went to her, taking her in his arms. The guards stood nervously by. For a moment, he considered flicking his Sin Eater out and dealing with the two surviving guards. He knew he could take them, but putting Ambika down without killing her in the heat of it might have proved impossible. And for the moment, until he could clue Brigid, Grant and Domi into what was going on, he needed her alive.

His lips sought hers, and he gave himself over to the intoxication she presented. Her body was enough to set his senses on fire. Beth-Li had never held this kind of threat over him, or this much attraction. Ambika was strong-willed and capable, a force to be reckoned with, the kind that would come at a man head-on.

He kissed her openmouthed, his tongue pushing against hers. Blood beat at his temples, pushing his senses into overdrive. Her hand drifted down between them, finding him hard and ready.

She broke the kiss, her hand still clutching him with

fierceness. Her eyes raked his challengingly. Her breath was ragged. But her grip on her sword didn't loosen, and her stance remained ready. "Enough," she said. She trembled.

Kane was surprised at the reaction. Even under the best of conditions, he'd never had that kind of effect on a woman. That was compelling, as well, daring his male ego to take advantage of it. He drew in a hoarse breath, aware of how his heart exploded convulsively. He'd never felt the physical pressure like that himself. He guessed it had something to do with the gene-splicing that had been done to her.

"I've never felt like this," she said.

"Me, neither," Kane admitted, and tried not to think of Brigid so the guilt wouldn't eat at him.

"Meet me in my rooms," Ambika said. "I want to be ready, and I'm still unclean from the journey here."

"When?"

"An hour," Ambika replied. She turned from him and headed for the elevator. "Go back to your room. I'll send for you when I'm ready." In the elevator, she looked at him. "And, Kane, if you're not ready, I'll chill you."

Kane eyed her levelly. "I'll be ready."

"GRANT." Kane sat in the bathroom of his suite with the Mag helmet pulled on, hoping the comm-link worked. If it didn't, he was going to have to find Grant. It was a lot to think Grant would be sitting in his room waiting for him to call.

"Yeah," Grant answered.

Kane stripped off his clothing and prepared for the shower. He'd spotted the cams and aud-links in the other rooms, letting him know no privacy existed in the suite. He'd turned the bathroom dark to circumvent the cams there, and turned the water in the shower scalding to fog up the lenses as well as muffle the aud-links. "Didn't know if you'd be there."

"Nothing else to do in this place," Grant said, "now we're at the bitch queen's disposal."

"You don't like her," Kane said.

"No. Woman that would go to the trouble of building a bridge out of people's bones kind of hits me funny. It's one thing to be thorough, but it's another to glory in it."

"I know," Kane replied. "But it gets worse." Quickly, he filled Grant in concerning the biological weapons.

"Shit," Grant said. "If she's got something like that stockpiled here and intends to use it on Cobaltville, that's going to be more trouble than even Lakesh is counting on. How close is she to being ready to use it?"

"Weeks, months, a year or two," Kane answered. "She didn't say and I didn't ask. The fact that it's there at all is what we have to deal with. Plus, I get the feeling that we're not going to be allowed to leave these islands anyway."

"I got the same impression. So what are we going to do?"

"What we have to," Kane said. "Just like always."

"And what is that?"

"I'm going to take Ambika." Kane filled Grant in about Ambika's offer, and his acceptance of it. "I get her inside her rooms, mebbe she'll let her guard down and I can take her."

"You think you can do that?" Grant asked.

"Have to try. I need you to back my play." Kane swiftly gave directions on where Ambika's rooms were. "Get Domi and Brigid together. I don't want us spread out when we push this."

"A one-percenter," Grant said.

"It's the only play that will work."

"I know, but that woman isn't like any other you've ever

met, Kane. She's hard and vicious, and she'll chill you in a heartbeat if she thinks she needs to. In a lot of ways, she reminds me of you. Especially when you're convinced that what you're doing is right. And I don't think this bitch has experienced a minute in her life when she didn't think what she was doing was exactly right.''

''Well, mebbe we'll find out how good we really are.'' Kane glanced at his chron, marked off the time. ''Meet me outside her doors in forty minutes.''

''I'll be there.''

''And if it turns out bad,'' Kane said, ''you and the others get the hell out of here. Ambika's not going to cut you any slack once I turn on her.''

''Understood. But don't think negative.''

''Just preparing,'' Kane said. ''I don't make it, escape won't be an option for me.''

''See you on the other side,'' Grant said.

''Yeah.'' Kane took the helmet off, breaking the radio communication. Then he breathed deeply and tried to relax. He stepped into the shower to bathe, feeling the minutes slip away.

GRANT GOT DOMI FIRST. The room she'd been assigned was closest to his own. Sec men were posted in the halls, so he knew getting out of the rooms was going to be dicey. He knocked on the door and waited.

Domi answered the door totally nude. A smile lighted her face when she saw him. ''Come inside and play?''

''No,'' Grant growled. ''Get dressed. This is about to turn ugly.''

Domi ran her fingertips between her small breasts as if scratching an itch. ''Can't wait few minutes?''

''No.'' Grant turned from her door and walked down to Brigid's. He knocked and waited. There was no answer. He checked his chron, watching the time wind inexorably down. It wouldn't do to have them all spread out when Kane came up against Ambika. The wry side of his mind chuckled at the choice of his words.

He knocked again as Domi joined him, already dressed and ready in seconds. It was one of the things Grant truly appreciated about the young albino.

The door remained unanswered.

A bad feeling twisted through Grant's stomach. He opened the door and stepped inside. His eyes swept the small room, taking in the overturned furniture and obvious signs of struggle. He went to the bathroom, half expecting to find the archivist's body draining there.

It was empty.

But he had no doubts that Brigid had been taken. It didn't require much of a creative jump in logic to figure out who had done it. Kane was walking into Ambika's rooms thinking he had a handle on the situation, but he was about to get the pointy end himself.

"Fucking fireblast," Grant snarled. If there was anything less than a one-percenter, this was going to be it. And it was going to play out in minutes. He grabbed Brigid's Uzi and spare magazines, then hustled out of the room, moving toward the elevator, hoping no one stopped him from going to Kane's rooms. He knew he wouldn't catch Kane there, but he had to get the Mag armor Kane was going to need.

If any of them lived.

Chapter 31

Kane stood outside the main door to Ambika's rooms. Nervous energy roiled in his stomach, worse than anything he'd ever felt before. Or, at least, it was worse than anything he could remember at the moment. He took a deep breath, then knocked on the door. He'd dressed in the clothes Ambika had sent down for him: tight-fitting black leather pants, a loose red silk shirt with a ruffled collar and belled sleeves and red leather boots that reached to his knees. He looked worse than a male slut in an upscale gaudy.

Despite the danger, or maybe because of it, the excitement thrilling through him was intensified. However, he knew it wasn't only the danger. While he bathed, his mind had kept returning to the view he'd had of Ambika's body when he'd interrupted her in her bath. His hunger for her was real, spurred on by the conviction that they were so equally matched in physical prowess and sheer chilling ability and by his own lack of a woman for so long.

The speaker next to the door carried Ambika's voice from inside. "Come," she entreated.

The single syllable sent an excited tingle from the base of Kane's skull, down his spine, to gather in his groin. The door slid soundlessly aside, and he walked into the huge suite. He remembered where the bedroom was from his earlier visit.

The bedroom was dark when he arrived, and he fully

expected to find Ambika there. The covers were turned back, all azure lace and satin, but the bed was empty.

"Here, Kane."

He turned, spotting her out on the balcony that over-looked her empire. Beyond her, the night sky was dark as sin and cluttered with dozens of stars. The moonlight spread fire across her silvery mane as it ran free, blowing slightly in the wind. The balcony was small and rounded, everything curving to the woman standing there.

"Join me," she said in a low voice.

Kane strode over to her, feeling the pulse beat at his temples, then echo throughout his body. He felt hypnotized, sailing along on autopilot.

She wore a wispy black gossamer nightdress that was translucent, revealing the smooth, curving flesh beneath. It ended just below the sheen of her silver pubic triangle at the juncture of her thighs. "Do you like it?" she asked.

"Yeah," Kane said hoarsely.

The only thing that looked out of place was the huge Casull pistol in her right hand. She gestured with the hand-blaster, not quite ever pointing it at him. "We're alone," she explained. "No guards. And I don't quite trust you."

"It's okay," he told her.

Behind her, he could see the scattered few lights of the residences in the other buildings. The water looked dark below, with only a few whitecaps from the waves that made it in from the open sea. A few lights from sec men on patrol tracked the ground.

"You're a man of strong convictions," Ambika said. "I knew that about you from the moment I saw you, Kane. It was one of the things that most attracted me to you. But you knew that, didn't you?"

"No," he replied honestly. "I didn't know what attracted you to me."

"What about your attraction to me?" she asked.

He smiled. "You want it defined?"

"And if I did?"

Kane shrugged. "I'm a man of simple words. If you're looking for something flowery, I won't be able to do it."

Her eyes searched his face. "I could teach you elegant words, Kane. My education was quite complete under my father's tutelage."

"Would you want them from me?" Kane asked.

She hesitated. "I don't know."

When he took a step closer to her right side, she moved reflexively, keeping the Casull a safe distance from him. "I don't know why you're attracted to me," he told her, "but if you start changing too much of me, is what you have left going to be enough to keep you satisfied?"

"Are you thinking about a lasting relationship, Kane, or the power I've offered?"

"With you, I don't think I'm going to get one without the other."

She laughed, and the effort sounded almost normal. "You're probably right. You say what you think, and that's another thing I find appealing about you. Tell me, do you like what you see?"

"Yes," Kane answered without hesitation. Her body was flawless, a Molotov cocktail of desire and danger.

"You're telling the truth," she said. "I'd know if you were lying, you know."

"Yeah."

"Come to me, Kane."

"The blaster's going to make things complicated."

"Let me worry about the blaster," she told him. "I want you to worship my body, to show this newfound love you say you have for me."

Kane looked at her. "I didn't say love," he told her brutally. "I've just got a lust we're working on here, and I don't think you can tell me it's anything more for you."

The azure eyes fired in delight. "Lust is a good place to start, Kane, don't you think?"

"From what I've seen, that's where most relationships start. Problem is, that's where most of them end." Kane crossed to her and started to reach for her.

"Stop."

He froze at her command, his breath shuddering through him as the desire to take her warred with his planned escape. The smell of her musk was on the slow-moving air.

She kept the Casull out of his reach, then used her other hand to run over his body, searching for weapons. She didn't find any because he hadn't carried any into the room. He was depending on his own hand-to-hand combat abilities.

"No weapons," she said.

He smiled. "Just the one blunt instrument."

She reached for his hard length, stroking it playfully. "Worship me, Kane, show me your desire."

He took her into his arms, pulling her close and ignoring the Casull's cold barrel as it pressed into his rib cage on a level with his heart. He thought there was a chance he could knock the blaster away before she could shoot him, but the chance was too damn small to take. Her reflexes might be even faster than his. He also considered pushing her over the balcony behind her, but figured she stood too much of a chance of dragging him after her.

Instead, he concentrated on her body, letting his savage impulses follow their own design. He ran his hands over her body, slipping them from her thighs and up her buttocks under the satin nightdress. He kneaded her flesh, letting her feel the power in his hands. Her breath blew faster and warmer against his neck as her own desire filled her, shoving against the dam of control she maintained.

All he needed was one moment of distraction.

"Feel me, Kane," she whispered hoarsely.

But even as he heard the desire in her voice, he felt his own throat tighten in response, and his own breathing grew steadily more shallow. Her control wasn't the only one slipping. His hands rose to her breasts, pulling at the fleshy globes, tweaking her nipples and eliciting small growls of pain and pleasure from her.

Still, the Casull remained steadily pressed against his chest.

He trailed his fingers over the flat planes of her stomach, letting them fall to the silvery thatch between her legs. He felt the moisture there, already soaking her pubic area. She moaned in his ear as he penetrated her with his fingers. A pretremor raced through her body.

Caught in his own twisted web of desire, Kane missed his opportunity. She recovered before he could act on the weakness. He massaged her until she grew even more wet, soaking his fingers and his hand.

She trembled again, and he tried to keep himself ready. Even now, her body was betraying her, rocking back and forth as she glided her sex across his fingers. Kane shifted his weight, waiting for the moment when he could strip the handblaster away.

She kissed him as he was getting ready to move, then sank her teeth into his bottom lip with enough force to barely break the skin. He tasted the salt of his own blood and knew that if he moved then he'd lose his lip. She moaned as the tremors shook her again, but it still wasn't the release her body demanded.

Then she shoved him away. "Enough."

"Enough?" Kane croaked. "Hell, we're only getting started."

She smiled at him, continuing to push him away with her hand. "Enough for now, Kane. You're very good at pleasing someone, as I knew you would be. But how are you at taking pleasure?"

"I take pleasure just fine," Kane told her, his breath rasping at his own needs.

"We'll see." Ambika pushed him farther away. "Let's go back inside." She led the way to the bed, moving unerringly through the thick darkness that nearly filled the room. The moonlight splintering in from the balcony area lit the features of only a few reflective surfaces in the room. She halted at the end of the bed, turning to face him. "I'll only have your complete loyalty, Kane. You know I'll settle for nothing less."

"Yeah." Trepidation tiptoed through his mind, sending out waves of quiet unease. Something was wrong, but he didn't know what.

"If you try to lie to me, I'll know," she said. She pointed the Casull at him. "And you'll have to tell the truth now."

Something clicked, and the darkness pervading the room went away.

Kane blinked against the harsh light, then spotted the metal cage barely three feet high against the wall to the right. Inside the cage, bound and gagged, her jade-green eyes burning at Kane, Brigid Baptiste sat on her knees with her hands behind her.

Kane experienced a moment of disorientation, and his Mag reflexes were the only things keeping him from taking a step forward. He kept his face immobile as he turned back to Ambika. "She has nothing to do with this."

"That's not how I felt," Ambika replied. "From what I've seen of you, she's the one thing, the one person, that I felt would threaten your feelings for me. I couldn't have that, Kane, and I won't.'' She gazed at him over the Casull's sights. "So how do you feel about me now?"

A PAIR OF SEC MEN guarded the elevator up to Ambika's quarters. Grant walked toward them, his senses alert, Domi at his back. He carried the canvas bag containing Kane's armor, boots and weapons in his left hand.

"No one is permitted past this point," the sec man on the left said.

"Ambika sent for us," Grant said, though there was only a small chance either guard would buy it.

The sec men looked at each other, then tried to bring their weapons up.

Quick as a cat, feeling Domi glide effortlessly by him, Grant lifted his arm and twisted his wrist, snapping the Sin Eater into his palm. His finger depressed the firing stud, and the 9 mm bullet pushed through the man's face and emptied his braincase into the back of his helmet. He was already dead when Domi's knife raked against his partner's throat.

"Pull the bodies in after us," Grant ordered, snapping the Sin Eater back into its holster. He fisted the jacket of the man he'd killed and pulled him into the elevator cage while Domi struggled to do the same.

Using his combat knife, he cut loose one of the sec men's shirts, then used it to mop up the spilled blood. Hopefully the guard shift wouldn't change anytime soon, and the sec chief wouldn't be checking up for a time.

He thumbed the keypad and the elevator rose. He was restless, wondering how Kane was making out, knowing his friend couldn't have guessed how Ambika would have twisted his own subterfuge against him.

KANE IGNORED Brigid's eyes, not knowing what emotion was flashing through them. He couldn't afford to wonder.

couldn't afford to get caught up in her plight. He gazed at Ambika. He forced a smile. "You're a hard woman, Ambika. I guess I shouldn't have expected anything less. I should have known that you'd be this thorough."

"Meaning you'd have gotten her to safety if you could have?" Ambika asked.

"I wouldn't want to see her hurt."

Ambika shook her head. "That's not an answer I wanted to hear."

"Mebbe not," Kane agreed. "But you knew you were going to hear it when you involved her in this."

"She was already involved."

"Not this involved. I wasn't planning on a spectator."

"A spectator?"

"Is it more exciting for you to have someone watching?" Kane asked. He struggled to keep the belligerence from his voice.

"It's more exciting," Ambika admitted, "if she watches."

"Then let her watch."

"It doesn't bother you?"

Kane shrugged. "It doesn't do anything for me. I've never been one for an audience at times like these." He silently hoped the warrior queen would get Brigid out of the room. At least she wouldn't possibly be in the line of fire when he made his move. But he doubted Ambika would remove the archivist. Control was too much of an issue for her.

"It does something for me," Ambika said.

"Okay. But if you keep talking, you're going to spoil the mood." Only the intense desire the woman had created inside him kept him from losing his erection at the sight of Brigid in the cage. Somehow, he managed to keep the two events unrelated in his mind, relying on the Mag techniques he'd been taught to repress his own emotions. His sexual interest in Ambika didn't come out of anything emotional; it was pure lust, and that was no emotion at all.

"You're either speaking truthfully," Ambika said, "or you're the coldest man I've ever met."

Kane grinned at her frostily. "Your call, Ambika. You're the one who pushed these stakes onto the table."

The amazon woman stood there for a long moment, then she walked to Kane. "Strip," she ordered.

Without hesitation, Kane removed the shirt and the boots, then dropped the pants and stepped out of them. There was no hiding his erection.

Anam-chara. The term echoed through his mind, and it brought thoughts of betrayal to him. Quickly, he forced them away before they affected the physical response he presented to Ambika.

"Let's see," Ambika said, "if you're truly as good at receiving pleasure as you are at giving it. You'll find that my interest in sexual matters is quite thorough." She dropped to her knees before him and placed the blaster's barrel up to his scrotum.

"That's going to be distracting," Kane said.

"Not for long," she promised. She kept her eyes on him as she slowly moved forward, her mouth opening.

Kane considered his options, thinking about the possibility of ramming a knee into her face before she could get a shot off. Wounded, he would be no match for her, and he and Brigid would both die as a result. With her reflexes, with her deliberately in control of the situation, he didn't think there was time. So he stood there as she wrapped her lips over his hard length.

She suckled him, and the skill she displayed almost took

the strength from Kane's legs. She pulled back, then sank on him again, taking his full length deep into her throat.

Kane breathed hoarsely, finding it easier not to think about Brigid at the moment, letting the lizard mind at the back of his brain control all his autonomic responses. He almost had to remember to breathe. Despite his control, a quiver danced in his loins.

Then Ambika pulled away, smiling up at him. "You've got more control than I'd expected, Kane."

"Not much," he rasped.

"Get on the bed."

Without hesitation, Kane did as she ordered. He deliberately didn't look at Brigid in the metal cage. But he knew the archivist hadn't moved. He couldn't even guess at the thoughts running through her mind.

Lying on the bed, he watched as Ambika joined him. Her muscles moved fluidly, her desire burning crimson beneath the skin of her breasts, making them hard. Moving carefully, the Casull centered on his face, she straddled him. Then she lowered her sex onto his.

She began rising and falling on him, pressing against him fully, then rising till only the tip remained inside her. It was a roller coaster, Kane knew, and whichever one of them lost control first was doomed. He arched his pelvis, meeting her stroke for stroke, hammering his body against hers, willing her own pent-up frustrations to lose before his iron determination faltered.

Then he saw the explosion of bliss inside the azure eyes, the pupils expanding at her release. He felt her sex tighten against his, trapping him within her as she shuddered and rode him hard.

Both of her hands rested on his chest, pushing his upper body down as she forced his pelvis up into a more accessible position. She screamed, half out of her mind.

Then Kane made his move.

Chapter 32

Trapped in the metal cage against the wall of Ambika's bedroom, Brigid Baptiste could only watch the actions on the bed in frustrated agony. The sec men Ambika had sent for her hadn't been gentle; they'd left huge bruises over much of her body before they'd knocked her out and brought her here.

She tried to distance herself from Kane and Ambika, desperately wanted to close her eyes. Only she couldn't. Tears sprang into her eyes, but she couldn't be sure why they were there. She knew Kane had had other women before he met her, and maybe even since. For a time she'd had to deal with the possibility of a liaison between Kane and Beth-Li Rouch. Even Lakesh had confronted her with that.

Only it hadn't happened. And when Domi had killed the traitorous bitch, Brigid had been glad.

Watching Ambika buck on top of Kane, knowing he was giving her satisfaction, made a deep hurt well up inside the archivist. She pulled at the handcuffs that bound her, feeling the metal bite into her wrists and knowing it didn't hurt her as much as what she was forced to witness. She didn't know if the hurt came from what she and Kane had possibly been to each other in the past, or if it was some clandestine thing she clung to in their uncertain future.

Then, even as she heard Ambika's shrieks of release fill the bedroom, she saw Kane go into motion. She was of mixed emotions at the time as to whether he should live or die. And it didn't matter that she'd probably die with him.

KANE SLAPPED at Ambika's blaster wrist with enough force to send the heavy Casull flying. He'd hoped to grab it before she could, but the blaster skidded across the tangled sheets and dropped to the floor with a clatter.

Ambika, despite her stimulation, rode high on him, holding on to him with her vaginal muscles to the point of pain, and slammed a palm thrust back at his face. The blow caught Kane on the side of his face with enough force to send his overtaxed senses swimming.

Growling with anger and hatred, the woman grabbed him around the neck and started choking him. "You dare spurn me, Kane? After I've given you everything?" Her fingers locked around his windpipe with bruising force. "I'll chill you for that, you stupe bastard! And I'll keep your seed, raise your child and chill it, too!"

Almost on the point of blacking out, Kane drove his hands up between Ambika's, splitting them apart and breaking her choke hold on him. She struck at him again, holding him in place with her weight straddling his hips. A fist slammed against his jaw, splitting his lip and flooding his mouth with blood.

Reeling, barely hanging on to consciousness, Kane heaved up from the bed, lifting her weight with effort because it only drove them more deeply into the constricting mattress. Still, he managed to dump her off balance for a moment. He deflected her next blow, pushing it aside with an open hand and feeling her weight come down across him. Her breasts landed on either side of his face.

Incredibly, she wrapped her arms around the back of his head, pulling his face into the buoyant flesh between her breasts. He tried to draw another breath and found he couldn't. Her flesh blocked his nose and mouth, suffocating him.

Kane tried to push her away and couldn't. He balled up a fist and hit her, but the rigid slabs of muscle easily absorbed the punishment he was able to hand out from such a restricted blow. Her grip didn't loosen at all. Opening his mouth wider, he sucked in her flesh, then bit down, piercing her with his teeth. Her blood flowed into his mouth, mixing with his own.

Screeching in pain, she pushed away from him. "You bastard!" she screamed. Even as she pushed up, she thrust an open palm at his face again.

Kane thought for a moment that she'd broken his nose. He reached for her hair from behind, knotting his fingers in the silvery strands just as she cracked an elbow against his cheekbone. He groaned in pain, knowing flesh had split from that blow, as well. Then he pulled at her hair, yanking her backward.

She lifted a foot, releasing his hips, intending to drive her sole into his face. He shifted and she missed, and the force pushed her into a split position above him.

He shoved her to the side, trying to get out from under her. Scrambling through the twisted sheets, he clawed for the bed's edge. He spotted the Casull lying on the stone floor even as the front door to the bedroom exploded open.

Four sec men rushed into the room from an adjoining room, all of them armed with assault rifles.

Lying prone on the floor, aware that Ambika was throwing herself off the bed in the opposite direction, Kane plucked up the Casull from the floor. He snapped off two shots, cursing when he couldn't put any more into the air because the handblaster's recoil was too damn hard to control. And he cursed his own forgetfulness that the big blaster didn't have the magazine capacity of the Sin Eater. Two shots gone, both of them ripping through the chest of the lead sec man, left only three unexpended rounds—if Ambika kept a full cylinder under the hammer.

Kane rolled, throwing himself forward and coming up on one foot and a knee. He braced his gun hand in the other, targeting the three sec men. He squeezed off the shots as quickly as he could, working with the recoil instead of against it.

His first round spilled the guts from the next sec man in an explosion of blood, shoving him back from the man Kane had already killed. His second shot, tracking higher, caught the next sec man in the chest, coring through his heart and killing him instantly, flinging him back into the surviving sec man, who raked the room with autofire that tracked disastrously close to Brigid in the metal cage.

Letting out half a breath, Kane squeezed the trigger a final time, hoping a round was there. The big .454 round slapped into the sec man's head and threw it backward, almost decapitating him.

Motion to Kane's right drew his attention as he got to his feet.

Ambika came at him, bounding across the bed, naked and brandishing the long sword in her right hand. The edged steel glittered in the light. Her face wore only hatred. "Now you're going to die, Kane!"

He leveled the Casull at her, but she never broke stride. He shifted the aim to her leg, hoping to take her alive if he could, hoping she'd back down.

She didn't.

He squeezed the trigger and listened to the dry snap as the hammer fell on a round that had already been spent. He dodged backward, escaping the lethal length of the sword as she sought to cleave him in two. The blow missed by inches.

Still in motion, Kane picked up a chair in front of an ornate vanity. He swung it by the back at Ambika's head. She slashed at it with the sword, shattering it to kindling.

"More sec men are going to be here in seconds, Kane," she snarled. "What are you going to do then?"

"Give them reservations on the last train headed west," Kane told her, holding his hands out to his sides, his bare feet gripping the stone floor.

She grinned at him mirthlessly, twisting the sword in her grip. "Maybe I won't chill you, Kane. Maybe I'll just gift you with the life of an amputee." She gazed down in disgust. "And maybe that of a eunuch, as well." She circled, moving to his left. "Maybe I'll keep you around just to hear the pitiful mewling you'll make."

Kane hardened his voice. "It would never happen."

"We'll see." She came at him, sweeping the sword.

Kane fell backward, going prone as he slid forward. Then his feet tangled in hers, tripping her.

He'd expected her to smack flat against the floor. Instead, she rolled and got to her feet even as he was getting to his. She swung the sword again, forcing him to move. The blade sliced along his thigh before he could clear completely, and blood wept from the long wound in scarlet rivulets.

The sword clanged against the stone floor, scattering sparks in all directions and scarring the rock. She recovered immediately and turned to attack again.

Kane grabbed the leather pants he'd worn from the floor, ducking under the sword only by dropping to his knees. As Ambika drew the sword back to slash again, he pushed himself up and whipped the belt free of the pants. He responded to her feint, then whipped back in the other direction when she reversed the thrust. The blade scored along his ribs, leaving a trail of burning fire.

She drew back again, falling into a martial-arts stance that

Kane didn't recognize but fully understood. Gripping the belt by the end, he popped the heavy ornate buckle at her face. As he'd figured, she didn't try to block it with the sword for fear of tangling the weapon.

She slashed again, using both hands on the sword's hilt as she tried to cut his feet out from under him. He leaped and dived, knowing the sword whistled under him and would cut his legs or feet off if it touched him.

Kane rolled again, the belt strung out behind him as he rolled one more time. Then he cracked the belt forward, the heavy buckle skimming across the stone floor and striking sparks. It coiled around Ambika's right ankle even as she pulled her blade back into position.

She tried to get away, but the wrapped leather drew taut as the buckle held.

Standing, getting his weight into the move, Kane yanked. Her foot came up and her head went down. Her shoulders smacked into the stone with a meaty whack.

She came up from the floor a spitting, snarling hellcat. Before she made it, he doubled his fist and punched her in the face, putting all of his weight behind it. The blow knocked her backward in a shuffling stumble. Her sword left nerveless fingers, clattering against the floor. She landed against the bed, spitting out blood where her lips had gotten cut. She pushed herself to her feet.

Kane scooped up the sword and turned to face her with it, figuring she'd back down.

Instead, she came straight at him, ignoring the sword.

Still wanting her alive, thinking maybe she'd realized that or maybe she just didn't care, Kane pulled the sword away, then he slammed the sword hilt into her temple, dazing her.

Not as fast now, she reached for him, aiming for his throat.

Kane slammed the sword hilt into her head again, remembering the incredible constitution the gene-splicing had given her. The muffled thud echoed across the room, then Ambika folded back on her knees.

Cautiously, watching the woman for any signs of movement, Kane stood on his trembling legs, having to use the sword as support. He stared across the room at Brigid, noticing the tears that streaked her face.

Guilt stung him, but his instinct for survival got him in motion. He'd only done what he'd had to do, to ensure survival for all of them. Getting out of the Isles of the Lioness would have been impossible without taking her down first, and there was no way he was going to leave the nerve gas and other biological agents with her if he could help it.

He walked to the dead sec men and grabbed one of the assault rifles. He inserted a fresh clip, then approached Brigid in the metal cage.

Her jade gaze fixed him, but when he looked directly at her, she turned away from him, unwilling to meet his eyes. He dropped to his knees and reached through the bars to remove the tape over her mouth. He pulled it free tenderly, feeling her recoil at his touch.

"Dammit, Baptiste," he growled irritably, "be still so I can get this tape off."

She froze.

Part of Kane's attention remained on Ambika as he stripped the tape from Brigid's face with a quick jerk.

Brigid cried out with the pain, then flexed her mouth.

"Where're the keys to get you out of there?" Kane asked.

"The vanity," Brigid answered in a tight voice. "She put the keys to the cage and the handcuffs in there."

Kane retreated to the vanity and opened drawers till he found the large key ring.

"That's it," Brigid said.

He returned to the cage and worked through the keys till

he found the one to unlock the door. The cage door opened with a squeak and he helped Baptiste out.

"You might want to think about getting dressed," she admonished him.

"I will," Kane said, "as soon as there's time." He unsnapped the cuffs and took them over to Ambika. Working quickly, he fastened them around her wrists, trapping her hands behind her back. Hurriedly, he reached for the black leather pants he'd worn while Brigid grabbed an assault rifle.

"You know how to operate that?" he asked as he fastened the pants.

"I've read about it," she said in that cold tone. She worked the action slowly, but she got it right. Then she took up a bandolier of extra magazines and draped it over one shoulder.

"You okay, Baptiste?" he asked, listening for any sound from the other rooms that might signal the arrival of more sec men.

"Sure," she replied, glaring at him. "Why wouldn't I be?"

"I just thought mebbe Ambika would have done something to you."

"Why?"

"Dammit, Baptiste," Kane said, turning from his prisoner, "this woman's psychotic—"

"That's why the pair of you seem to get along so well," Brigid said icily.

Kane throttled his rage. "She's got nerve gas and other biological weapons on this island somewhere, Baptiste. She was intending to use them against Cobaltville. No matter how Lakesh feels about it, we're not allowing that."

Brigid glanced down at the unconscious woman. "She's even worse than I thought she was."

"Yeah," Kane agreed. He looked at Brigid. "What I did—" He hesitated, watching as Brigid refused to look at him. "It was the only way, Baptiste."

"I don't want to talk about it, Kane." Her voice sounded distant, hollow. "Let's get out of here."

Kane didn't bother dressing Ambika. He used the leather belt and bound her ankles together, as well, then looped a twist of cloth between her teeth and tied it at the back of her head. Even then he wasn't certain she couldn't cause him problems during their escape.

Footsteps sounded in the other room.

Kane lifted his assault rifle, waving Brigid to the other side of the door.

"Kane."

Recognizing Grant's voice at once, Kane called back. "We're clear in here."

Grant came through the door and glanced down at Ambika, then at the rest of the room. "Who kicked who out of bed?"

"Don't," Kane warned.

Grant looked contrite, but not much. He glanced at Brigid but didn't say anything, then back at Kane. "Got your stuff here." He handed the bag over.

Kane took it and began suiting up at once. With the armor starting to go back in place, he felt more in control than he had since they'd arrived in the Isles of the Lioness. "Anybody know you're here?"

"Mebbe seven sec men," Grant said, "but the next person they're going to tell isn't of this life."

"Where's Domi?" Kane asked.

"Watching the door. You know how you want to handle this?"

"She's got a private elevator in here," Kane said, locking the Sin Eater on his right arm. "Down below is an old

Chinese sub we need to send to the bottom. Then we need to scout out the nerve-gas depot she's got and see what we can do about that, too.''

"Incendiaries," Brigid said.

They looked at her.

"If you can get a fire hot enough around the biologicals when you blow them," she explained, "the heat can cause chemical changes that might render them inert.''

Kane nodded. "Sounds like the best chance we've got.''

"She's not going to leave the way unguarded," Grant pointed out.

"That's fine. But we're going to need one or two of the sec men we find intact. When we put the torch to this place, I want to give everybody living here the chance to get out.'' Kane fastened his helmet, grateful for the way it seemed to lock him away from his feelings as well as from harm. "Let's do it.''

Chapter 33

Kane rode down in the elevator with Ambika over his shoulder. The warrior woman remained deadweight, her breathing deep and even despite her being stretched across the armor.

When the door opened, Grant led the way out, using the helmet's passive night-sight capabilities, as well as the motion sensor strapped to his wrist. His Sin Eater was in his hand at the ready. Kane went next, flanked by Brigid and Domi.

"Guards," Grant whispered over the helmet comm-link.

"I see them," Kane answered. He put the unconscious woman down and went forward, depending on the black polycarbonate armor to keep him unseen in the darkness.

The sec men stood on either side of the cavern, guarding the submarine. Tunnels led back in both directions. He hadn't seen the guards earlier when he'd toured with Ambika, and he guessed that she'd ordered them into hiding. Maybe the tunnels had also been disguised behind false walls, because he definitely didn't remember them, either. But he'd been mesmerized by the woman and the sub, and the story she'd told.

He and Grant set up next to each other. "The close ones first," Kane whispered.

"Done," Grant agreed.

They stretched their silenced blaster hands out, using their other hands to support their arms. The subsonic bullets chopped into the two closest sec men there and sent them to the ground without much noise. The waves lapping at the sub covered the other sounds.

"Remember," Kane said, "we need at least one of these guys alive."

"Yours," Grant said. "I'm through being peaceable."

"Give me a minute." Kane moved forward, listening to the rumble of the sec men's voices as they talked, making sure he gave Grant shooting room. He paused at the corner, the Sin Eater raised as he took a breath. "Now." He stepped around the corner, dropping the Sin Eater into target acquisition.

Grant's rounds took the sec man on the right full in the face, destroying his features in crimson ruin and spinning him around.

The other sec man tried to bring his weapon up.

Kane showed him the business end of the Sin Eater. "Don't," he ordered in a cold voice.

The man hesitated, his face showing he was torn between acting and not acting.

"Listen," Kane advised in a friendly tone, "and you get to live."

The man put his weapon down.

Kane closed on him, the Sin Eater never wavering. "I'm looking for the weapons Ambika took from the sub. And you're going to show me where they are."

"Sure," the man said. He pointed to a set of double doors down the hall.

Kane used the key ring he'd taken from Ambika's room to open the doors, then carried Ambika inside over his shoulder as Grant took over their newly acquired prisoner.

Brigid found a light switch and turned it on, and they stared at the dozens of canisters stacked on wooden pallets around the large room. In no way did they look as threatening as they actually were. The room was also a conventional weapons dump. Racks of rifles and handblasters lined one of the walls.

"Got plenty of plas-ex here," Grant commented after checking. "And timers. We're good to go."

"Then let's get it done," Kane said.

Minutes later, covered with sweat from the humidity trapped in the caverns and from the nervous energy expended in setting the explosives, they finished setting the last of the detonation devices. Then Kane used a portable backpack acetylene torch to burn through the metal chains holding the sub to the flotation devices.

He started at the back end, watching as the flukes disappeared beneath the dark water. Within minutes, walking along the remaining flotation devices was no longer possible because the sub's weight dragged them under. Only the cables anchoring it to the wall remained. He burned through them in short order.

The yawning abyss below the sub slowly drank it down. Remembering what Ambika had said about being able to take the sub out to use against Qiang, he knew there had to be an underwater tunnel. Maybe the flotation devices would give it enough buoyancy to keep it moving for a time, but Kane didn't think it would ever really make it out of the cavern. He and Grant had used every bit of the plas-ex they'd found. When the caverns blew, the detonation was going to be something short of hell on earth. But only just.

Kane turned to the sec man they'd taken prisoner. "We're heading to the docks now," he told the man. "You show us the fastest way there, then you'll get the chance to get everybody out of here. You have one hour, then we blow everything you've seen here. Do you understand?"

The man nodded fearfully.

"Also, my friend and I are good at this sort of thing. Those explosives are boobied. Even if you've got somebody clever enough to undo what we've done, it's going to take more time than we're giving you. And if we hear one tiny boom, the whole thing goes up. No hour—just *boom*."

The man nodded again.

"WHAT THE HELL'S going on?"

Kane glanced over the side of the *Sloop John B* and spotted Christensen standing on the dock. Domi had been sent back into the main building and told to find the ship's captain and crew. Most of them, as it turned out, had remained on the ship at Christensen's orders.

"We're pulling out," Kane said. He glanced at his chron. "You've got forty-two minutes to get your crew shipshape and get us outside this island before one of the biggest explosions you've ever seen takes place." He finished bolting a 20 mm cannon to the railing. It was a makeshift job, but he knew it would handle being used at least for a time.

Grant was strapping another one on the opposite side of the ship. They'd raided weapons from the other ships, killing guards as they'd needed in order to acquire supplies. The Sandcat's twin machine guns would add further firepower to the munitions they'd taken. Kane had also put some of the crew to work, under threats, stripping other guns from the nearby ships. The *Sloop John B* was a hell of a lot better equipped than it had been when it had put into port in the Isles of the Lioness.

"I thought you liked it here," Christensen said as he pulled himself aboard.

"Changed my mind," Kane said.

"Looks like everybody did." Christensen pointed at the line of small boats already heading out to sea through the channel cut through the rock.

Kane nodded. "Move it. Time's going to work against us pretty soon. Take whoever you need to get us under way, but I want the rest of the crew you can spare to help out with the weapon refits.''

BRIGID STEPPED inside the captain's quarters where Kane had left Ambika. The woman, still naked, was handcuffed to the main support beam on the wall, the handcuff links draped over the beam. She'd been unconscious before, lying on the bed when Brigid had last looked in on her.

Ambika was awake now, sitting on the edge of the bed, her arms slightly above and to her side, trapped by the handcuffs. "We're on your ship, aren't we?" she demanded.

Brigid surveyed the woman and ignored the swirl of feelings that collided within her when she thought of Ambika and Kane together. "Yes," she replied. "How are you feeling?"

"Do you care?" Ambika challenged.

"Not much," Brigid told her.

"You're jealous of me, aren't you?"

Brigid knew that part of her was—the part that was irrational enough to care about Kane, or maybe it was the part of her that was somehow bound to Kane. "No. I just don't like you. You're a killer, only a step removed from a coldheart or a baron."

Ambika smiled. Her unnatural metabolism had already cured the wounds Kane had given her. "Yes, you are. You've never had him the way I had him."

"I've never wanted him that way."

"Liar," Ambika taunted. "You forget, I saw your face when I took him to my bed. I watched you as I climbed on top of him, and I saw you turn away when I started to fuck him."

"You're disgusting," Brigid said. "And watching people couple isn't something I'd care to do."

"Even so, memory of what Kane and I shared is going to haunt your dreams forever more."

"You didn't share anything," Brigid said. "Kane took advantage of the only weakness you had—your arrogance."

"Can you forgive him for that? Make your peace with what happened?"

"There's nothing to forgive," Brigid answered. "Nothing to make peace with. Kane beat you with the only weapon he had."

"And you admire him for that?"

Surprisingly, Brigid realized that perhaps part of her did respect Kane's bravery and cunning. "Not many men would have been capable of doing what he did. Nor would they have been able to remain as focused."

"I had all of his attention for those few minutes," Ambika said. "That's something you'll always be too timid to give him. I can see it in your face."

Brigid's features burned in embarrassment. The woman saw through her too clearly. It made her angry at herself that Ambika could get through her defenses so easily. "You didn't have his attention," she said roughly. "You were just another enemy he had in his gun sights."

"He didn't chill me."

"Yet," Brigid responded. "He needed you alive to get off the island."

"That was his mistake," Ambika assured her. "Attack. Don't hesitate. I want them all dead."

Understanding dawned with cold dread inside Brigid that the warrior queen wasn't talking to her or imagining things.

"Subcutaneous radio transponder," Ambika said. "I've found my body is surprisingly adept at handling all kinds of bio-friendly techware."

Brigid whirled out of the room, locking it behind her, and ran toward the prow deck to warn Kane. She gazed out on either side of the *Sloop John B,* spotting a few other ships in the distance. Then one of the big warships fleeing the island turned toward the cargo ship, its sails blossoming with the night air.

"WE WON'T BE ABLE to outrun it," Kane said when they finished listening to Brigid. They watched as the warship closed the distance between them. It was less than four hundred yards now. Luckily, none of the other ships seemed to be responding.

"Then we fight," Grant said.

Lights lit up the warship's decks. Kane used his field glasses to see the crew scurrying around to carry out their captain's orders. "If we have to," Kane agreed. "But if we try to field a protracted engagement, we're going to get the shit kicked out of us."

"Yeah, but even with the extra weapons we've moved onto this ship, we're not going to last long."

Kane smiled grimly. "Then we're going to have to double down on a one-percenter."

"What have you got in mind?" Grant asked suspiciously.

"You're not going to like it."

"THAT'S GOT TO BE the craziest thing I've ever heard of," Grant said when Kane finished laying it out.

"You come up with anything better," Kane assured him, "I'm willing to listen." He walked along the ship's railing as they approached Christensen. The pursuing warship had already cut the distance to less than two hundred yards. His chron showed that less than six minutes remained till the plas-ex back at the munitions dump on the island went off.

"That's the problem," Grant said, "I also think it might be our only chance to get this over quick. And quick's the only way we're going to be able to handle it."

Kane ran up the steps to join Christensen at the wheel. "They're going to overtake us."

"No shit," Christensen said bitterly. "I was just getting used to the idea that we might actually make it."

"If you can handle this ship," Kane said, "we just might."

Domi ran up and handed Kane a package. "Got all we got. No more."

Kane looked at the white-gray mass wrapped in oily papers.

"What the fuck is that?" Christensen asked.

"Plas-ex," Kane said. "When that warship comes alongside, we're going to keep our own blasters quiet for a time. Not fire till we see the fucking whites of their eyes. I'm guessing they'll try to grapple on to us, pull us in and board us. When they do, we'll open up. Then Grant and I will force our way across and drop this package down the hold."

"If you blow the bottom of that ship out," Christensen said, "she's going to go down like a hemorrhoidal duck."

"That's when your boarding crews will start cutting the lines and get us free again," Kane said.

"What if you and Grant don't make it back before we cut loose?"

"That's our problem," Kane said. "It's the only chance we've got. And we're out of time for a miracle."

Chapter 34

The warship drew closer.

Kane hunkered down beside the *Sloop John B*'s railing, sweating inside the polycarbonate armor. Less than four minutes remained before the munitions dump exploded on the island. The rigging creaked above his head, and the sailcloth popped in stretched agony.

Then the warship butted into the *Sloop John B* hard enough to heel her over in the water. Kane hung on grimly, retaining his balance with effort. He carried a pump shotgun in one hand, an assault rifle slung over one shoulder and the Sin Eater holstered on his forearm. Ambika's sword ran down his back in the scabbard she'd carried it in.

He glanced at Grant beside him, similarly outfitted except for the sword. He carried a double-bitted ax instead, for the time when they ran out of bullets. The polycarbonate armor would protect them against most weapons, but they still had to reach their goal.

"Domi," he called over the helmet comm-link. They were patched into the Sandcat's frequency.

"Here," the albino replied.

"You keep it calm till we give the word, no matter what."

"I will."

The warship butted the *Sloop John B* again, heeling her over harder. Men slid out of position across the deck, and small-arms fire from the warship pursued them. Some small-arms fire from the cargo ship's crew erupted in response. Kane knew he wouldn't have been able to prevent it all, but Brigid was there to make sure none of the transferred weapons were unleashed. That way their full potential wouldn't be revealed.

The first of the grappling hooks flipped over the side, and Kane could tell the difference in the *Sloop John B*'s performance at once. He peered over the railing, watching as the warship neared to within feet. Some of the sec men threw a gangplank across the distance. It had hooks that held it securely to the cargo ship while a crew held the other end.

"Now!" Kane growled to Grant.

They sprang up together, knowing the few feet spanning the open sea between the ships was going to be the most treacherous. If they slipped and fell, there'd be no saving them.

Kane took the lead, leveling the shotgun at the small cluster of sec men getting ready to board. He fired, and the burst of double-aught buckshot cleared the gangplank. Even the crew abandoned it, letting it slide sideways. Kane drove his feet hard against it, feeling Grant thundering along in his wake.

"Jump!" he yelled as he saw the end going over the edge of the warship's railing. He threw himself forward, landing just over the railing on his knees. Men rushed at him with their weapons upraised. He triggered the shotgun again, knocking down the men in front of him and clearing the deck for a moment. Then small-arms fire opened up and slammed into the Mag armor in a thundering staccato roar.

He glanced over his shoulder when he realized Grant hadn't landed beside him, fearful that the big man had fallen into the ocean. Then he saw Grant's gloved hands clinging to the warship's railing. But the two ships were closing on each other again, threatening to smash Grant between them.

Grant cursed when he realized his own plight, then hauled himself up, pushing at the ship's side with his feet. He rolled over the ship's railing just before the two ships slammed together again.

A brief lull in the gunfire followed the collision. Kane remained on his feet with difficulty. He pulled the shotgun up again as a machine gunner on top of the aft deck opened up on the *Sloop John B*. The heavy slugs ripped long splinters from the cargo ship's deck and punched new holes in the walls and trim and sailcloth.

Kane pulled the shotgun's trigger, riding out the recoil as the double-aught blast ripped the machine gunner from his post. The Browning machine gun spun crazily. Then Grant was at Kane's side, blasting away at the warship's crew.

Once the shotgun blew back empty, Kane dropped it and took up the assault rifle. Heavy slugs smashed into him, knocking him from his feet as the deck pitched because of the waves and because of the grappling lines connecting it to the *Sloop John B*.

The warship crew surged forward, intending to take advantage of Kane's fall. He rolled and brought the assault rifle up, holding the trigger down and emptying the clip in a long burst. As close as they were to him, he knew there was no way he wouldn't hit something.

The bullets shredded flesh and blew the attackers back. Survivors ran for cover, squalling in fear over the shriek of the timbers protesting as the two ships fought against each other on top of the water.

Kane forced himself to his feet, listening to Grant's assault rifle cut loose even as his own locked back empty. He let the assault rifle hang from the shoulder sling and popped the Sin Eater into his hand with a twist of his wrist.

"Stop him!" a man cried from the prow deck.

Kane spun instantly, tracking the voice. If the captain or

commander succeeded in whipping his troops into readiness, getting back to the *Sloop John B* could prove impossible. He lined up the shot, then squeezed off three rounds.

At least one of them hit the man in the face, shutting him up in midorder and snapping his head back. Even as his corpse fell to the deck, Kane turned and sprinted across the blood-slick deck to the open hold. He finished off the Sin Eater's magazine, then started in with the sword, hacking into anyone who got in his way. The sword jumped in his grip as it struck bone, but his opponents fell before him.

Kane pulled the plas-ex package from its pouch, armed the timer, set for fifteen seconds, and dropped it into the hold. Before he could get moving, the munitions dump in the main island blew, drawing every eye. Even Kane watched as a huge fireball of orange and black spewed high into the air.

Then he was conscious of the time passing. He ran for the gangplank stretching between the two ships, slapping into Grant as he went and moving the other man into action as well. He keyed up the radio in his helmet. "Domi!"

"Ready," the albino responded.

"Keep them off our asses! Baptiste, get ready to lock and load!" Kane watched the gangplank suddenly twist away and fall into the water between the two ships.

"Fucking fireblast!" Grant snarled, letting Kane know he'd seen it, too.

"Jump!" Kane yelled. "It's the only chance we've got!" He'd already lost count of how many seconds had elapsed on the plas-ex timer. Bullets hammered his back, turned aside by the polycarbonate armor. Then he had a foot on the railing and was leaping for the *Sloop John B*.

In the air, spanning the distance with not much to spare, not even sure he was going to make it, he heard the Sandcat's machine guns open up and watched as the door to the captain's quarters burst open. Ambika staggered out, still naked and blood smeared, her silver hair in wild disarray.

Without hesitation, she headed for Brigid.

Kane landed on the *Sloop John B*'s deck as the cargo ship's sailors surged to the railing under Brigid's direction. None of them noticed Ambika's approach. Moving quickly, Kane placed himself in front of Brigid.

Ambika's speed and strength drove him from his feet, knocking him to the deck. She stomped on the sword blade and kicked it from his grasp. The sound of small-arms fire, heavy machine guns, cannon and rocket launchers echoed around him.

Reflexively, he popped the Sin Eater into his hand and aimed it as he scrambled to his feet. He pressed the firing stud twice, then realized he'd emptied it on the warship.

"Brigid!" Kane yelled, pushing toward her as Ambika slashed with the sword.

Brigid turned, spotting the danger too late to avoid it. The sword whistled for her neck.

Almost on top of Brigid but not quite there, Kane knew there was only one thing he could do, and he knew the risk. He shoved his left arm up between the sword and Brigid, holding it at an angle, aware that if he got that angle too direct the sword's keen edge would probably sheer his arm off because the polycarbonate wasn't built to withstand such treatment.

The sword struck his arm only a glancing blow, skidding sparks from the armor as it arced up and over Brigid's head, cutting a lock of the blowing red-gold hair. Kane's arm went numb instantly, but thankfully the armor turned the sword's edge.

Kane stepped in front of Brigid, drawing the combat knife from his boot as Ambika prepared to strike again. The woman's face was a mask of dried blood.

Before she could swing, though, Brigid stepped around Kane and fired her Uzi from the hip. The plas-ex explosion aboard the warship cut through all the other battle noises, letting Kane know the time had elapsed.

The stream of bullets from the Uzi chopped into Ambika's body, driving her back to the railing. Her azure eyes burned fires of hate. Then Brigid fired again, knocking her over the railing.

Kane watched the woman fall, then realized the *Sloop John B* was heeling over toward the warship. He watched the other ship wallowing in the sea, taking on water in seconds, starting the final plunge to the bottom of the Cific Ocean.

"Get the damn grappling ropes cut or we're going down with those sons of bitches!" Kane ordered. He moved forward and hacked at the nearest rope.

Grant fell in at his side, bringing the double-bitted ax down with a headsman's skill. The ropes fell away rapidly as the rest of the crew pitched in.

Seconds later, the *Sloop John B* was free and surging forward under her own wind again. A great cheer rose from the cargo ship sailors.

Kane watched as the warship foundered and swiftly sank beneath the waves, realizing how close it had all been. He turned to Brigid. "Are you okay?"

"Yes," she said, moving toward him. "What about your arm?"

"The armor held," Kane said.

"It might not have."

"I knew it would."

The look in her jade eyes clearly indicated that she didn't believe him, that she had known the risk he'd taken even if she wasn't sure why.

Kane stripped his helmet off. "Did Ambika get you to take those cuffs off while you were in there, Baptiste?"

Hostility filled her voice when she answered. "No, Kane. I was already a believer in how dangerous she was before you tried to tell me. We got a lot closer to her than I ever would have."

While Kane tried to figure out exactly how she meant that, Grant called for his attention.

Grant held up a bloody piece of meat with the bone showing. "Bitch gnawed her own thumb off," he said. "Once it was gone, she slipped her hand through the cuff like it was nothing."

The callous act ignited a cold spot in Kane's stomach. He turned back to the ocean, studying the waves to see if he could spot Ambika's body. Though he looked for a long time, till even the Isles of the Lioness were out of sight, he never did spot her body.

Seeing it, he felt certain, would have helped ease some of the cold anxiety that threaded down his spine. Or maybe putting a stake through her heart before she'd gone over the side.

KANE WAS STILL AWAKE on the deck, smoking one of the cigars he and Grant had packed in the Sandcat, when dawn broke to the east and painted orange lines across the Cific Ocean's whitecapped green surface. Brigid and Domi slept in the Sandcat, both of them totally exhausted.

Grant had offered to split the watch with him, neither of them quite trusting Christensen or his crew. Kane hadn't been able to sleep because there'd been too many troubling thoughts. He'd talked with Grant in the morning hours, but neither of them had brought up the thing that bothered him most of all. There was only one person he could talk to, and he wasn't sure if that was going to happen.

Grant had finally wandered away when the cooking smells from the galley spilled out onto the deck and men began going to their breakfast in shifts.

Kane continued smoking the cigar as he watched gulls soar into the sky, then dive down to pick up whatever refuse in the water caught their eye. Lakesh hadn't been happy when they'd told him what happened last night, but he knew he was in no position to be argumentative. Kane was sure they hadn't heard the end of it.

Taking a final puff on the cigar, he pushed himself to his feet and walked to the railing, wishing he could find some way to relax, wishing he knew for sure what was bothering him. But he really knew what it was; he just didn't want to put a name to it.

He flipped the butt out into the water, watching it spin away. Maybe things were over with, just like the cigar. The end couldn't really be seen until it was reached.

Then he noticed the shadow on the deck at his feet as the ship bore slightly to the southwest to take advantage of the wind for a while. He looked up and saw Brigid standing there. Instantly he grew uncomfortable. "Morning, Baptiste."

"Good morning," she replied in a soft voice.

"Sleep well?" he asked, just trying to make conversation because he knew he couldn't have handled a silence that stretched out between them.

"Not as good as I'd have liked. You didn't get any sleep, did you?"

"I will," he said.

"It's a long trip back to the redoubt," Brigid said. "We should be able to make the jump back to Cerberus from there."

"I'll be rested by then." Kane wanted to leave it alone,

didn't want to mention it at all, but it kept troubling him. "Baptiste—"

"Kane—"

They looked at each other.

"Let me go first," he requested gently.

"Okay."

He lifted his head and made himself look her in the eye. "I'm sorry you had to see what you did back there. That wasn't what I wanted. Not for you, and not for me. I just wanted you to know that."

"I do know that, Kane," she told him. "You did what you did so we'd all survive. It hurt watching. Maybe more than you could ever know, even though I understood. Maybe I didn't understand then, but I did later."

His voice felt thick and hard to get out of his throat. "I just didn't want it to change things."

She smiled, but the effort was sad and kind of empty. "Things changing around us, Kane, I think that's the only constant we've ever had in this life or any other we might have shared. Maybe that's all we can hope for. Because as long as things keep on changing, we go on living. And that's better than the alternative."

"Yeah, I guess you're right." He turned away from her, feeling somehow strangely ashamed.

Then her soft hand covered his calloused one. When he turned to face her, her eyes locked with his. "In spite of all those changes and the fear of the unknown that goes along with them, despite the fact that we seem to argue over everything, I want you to know that you're the one constant outside myself that I rely on, Kane. And that's not easy for me to admit."

Kane didn't know what to say.

"So you may have lost something last night," she told

him, "*we* may have lost something, but I wanted you to know that because I realized it for myself, as well."

Kane didn't say anything. He didn't dare for fear of saying the wrong thing and spoiling the moment. So he stood there in the quiet of the morning, on a ship in a sea far from anything he was calling home these days, and he enjoyed the warmth of her hand on his.

It would change, he knew, but the memory of that quietly shared moment would be his to keep forever.

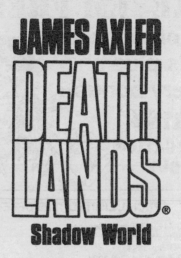

JAMES AXLER

DEATH LANDS®

Shadow World

Ryan Cawdor must face the threat of invaders that arrive from a parallel earth where the nukecaust never happened. And when he is abducted through a time corridor, he discovers a nightmare that makes Deathlands look tame by comparison!

GDL49

Gold Eagle brings you high-tech action and mystic adventure!

#119 Fade to Black

Created by

MURPHY
and SAPIR

Art begins to imitate life in Tinsel Town as real-life events are mirrored in small independent films...and the U.S. President's life is placed in jeopardy.

Available in April 2000 at your favorite retail outlet.